THE SINGULARITY TRANSFER

Singularity Series - Book 2

Copyright © 2020 by Dan Grant, all rights reserved.
First Edition

Cover art by MindScape Press, Inc.

Identifiers: ISBN: 978-1-953-76490-4 (hardcover)
ISBN: 978-1-953-76491-1 (trade paperback)
ISBN: 978-1-953-76492-8 (e-book)
ISBN: 978-1-953-76493-5 (audio book)

Subjects: fiction | mystery | thriller | suspense fiction | medical thriller | technothriller | FBI thrillers | illegal human research-fiction | mind-mapping fiction | mind-control fiction | conspiracy thriller | science fiction | hard science fiction

To learn more, see author notes, and read background material, go to www.DanGrantBooks.com

Publisher: MindScape Press, Inc.
www.MindScapePress.com

ALSO BY DAN GRANT

The Singularity Witness
Thirteen Across
The Singularity Transfer

THE SINGULARITY TRANSFER

A Thriller

Dan Grant

Mindscape Press

MONDAY, NOVEMBER 16th

There is nothing evil save that which perverts the mind and
shackles the conscience.
St. Ambrose, Bishop of Milan

PROLOGUE
SLEEPING BEAUTY AWAITS

NeuroSteps Labs, Glen Garner, New Jersey

Dr. Rikona Tanaka considered raising a man from near death an intriguing concept, but the man before her was the last person on earth who deserved such a chance.

Standing at the foot of a hospital bed, she loathed the unconscious man in it.

Stewart Richards didn't deserve a second life.

A month earlier, she'd fled the executions: friends, colleagues, scientists, brilliant minds with the potential to change the world. The mass house-cleaning eliminated those who knew the dark secrets about the Advanced Neurological and Cybernetic Research Institute (ANCRI).

The urban landscape of New York City had been the perfect escape, or so she'd hoped. But the Phoenix Consortium's long reach had tracked her down for a reason: as a neurogeneticist focused on cellular replications, Tanaka had a talented green thumb. In a way, she'd become a biological creator of life. That's what the Phoenix

Consortium wanted from her: to resurrect this man. To wake Sleeping Beauty.

Vaguely, she knew the Biblical stories of Jesus of Nazareth raising a man named Lazarus and two others from either deep sleeps or still-hearted deaths.

Now Tanaka was asked to apply science and perform a similar modern miracle.

It was not a decision in her power to ignore.

Tanaka didn't fear for her own life, but for her daughter's.

Across the hospital room, a muscular-framed man in a suit held a cell phone where she could see it. The device showed a live image of a college-aged Japanese girl. Bound and gagged. A handgun pointed at her temple.

It was obvious what Tanaka would do next: save her daughter.

And do whatever was required to resurrect a cold-blooded killer from a neurological state of limbo, his physiological imprisonment, his eternal slumber.

SUNDAY, NOVEMBER 29th

DAYS LATER
11:30 PM

The abomination of desolation is not a burned town, nor a country wasted by war, but the discovery that the man who has moved you is an enthusiast upon calculation.
Ralph Waldo Emerson, *Deception*

1
TROUBLE AT HOME

Princeton, New Jersey

Thomas Parker jolted awake from a bone-deep sleep. A half-breath cycled through him before he realized that his newly installed home alarm blared, obliterating the usual stillness of his colonial-style house. He'd dreamt of Kate Morgan, their excursion to the Cayman Islands. His thoughts of her lingered. On Starfish Point, surf crashed over a pair of footprints impressed in white sand, washing away traces of time spent together.

His heart stammered in his chest as his bare feet met the wood floor of his bedroom.

Through his panic, he knew what was happening: someone had broken into his house.

Stumbling, he groped through the darkness, not daring to switch on a light.

His mind charged and grew fully alert, adrenaline fueling clarity.

They were coming for him.

The Phoenix Consortium.

It had been a possibility. Four weeks in the Caribbean gave him time to reflect on his reckless actions. He had destroyed their research facility and their valuable technology, and for all intents and purposes killed their lead researcher, Stewart Richards. Those actions had exposed radical secrets and threatened powerful enterprises.

His home alarm fell silent, its sound replaced by the echoing tread of footsteps on hundred-year-old floors.

Parker peered into the hallway and detected movement approaching fast, coming from downstairs. Retreating to his master bedroom, he quietly shut its door and jammed the back of a chair beneath its knob.

He heard the door's knob turn, slowly at first then more robustly.

A thump signaled that a shoulder had engaged the wood of the door. The improvised doorstop wouldn't hold long.

Parker grabbed a pair of sneakers and slid the double-hung window up, announcing his intentions.

The bedroom door shuddered from an obvious boot strike. The violent battering ram motion continued. Illuminated by moonlight streaming through the open window, the chair brace against the knob slipped a fraction of an inch.

Parker launched himself at the screen covering his window, awkwardly clearing the windowsill and leaving himself dangling half-in, half-out of his two-story home. His sneakers slipped out of his hand, and his gaze panned the backyard below before returning to his tenuous grip on the window ledge. Fingertips and palms ached as he fought for better handholds.

Even though he knew it was coming, the sound of his bedroom door coming unhinged rattled him to the core.

A crisp red laser dot grazed the window frame just above his head, its lethal splash seeking a target. More than a month ago, he'd learned that laser sights led to getting shot.

He took several rapid breaths and knew he needed to move.

Instead of dropping twelve feet and perhaps twisting an ankle, Parker scaled sideways to a drainpipe at the corner of his house. His toes dug against exterior siding for any measure of grip while his hands did most of the work. Fingers latched onto thin layers of trim. Muscles ached as if they were on fire. Pushing himself, he navigated out of view of his bedroom window and lunged at another second story windowsill.

"Outside!" a voice snapped. The word hung ominously in the air. "The doc's outside. Over."

Parker sought a better grip and forced his toes to dig onto of the lip of the first floor window's trim, immediately beneath him. His exposed position offered a tenuous balance at best, while gravity did its best to bring him down to earth.

He felt the sting of the night's chill. Even if he managed to jump without injury, being barefoot didn't help. He wouldn't last long if people were hunting him.

His mind played through limited options. He picked one.

Head up, not down.

Hooking the crook of his elbow into the windowsill, he used his free hand and knuckles to poke out the glass near the latch in the sliding window. The sound of glass breaking was more than he could bear, but he didn't hesitate to thumb over the internal latch and shove up the window.

Parker climbed in and rolled past where he thought shards of glass might lay. The master bathroom and house remained dark, which was a disadvantage if his pursuers had come equipped with night vision. His hand felt wet and he wrapped it in a hand towel. He had no time to inspect a glass cut, and he'd rather die moving than because of caution or inaction.

Unarmed, his only advantage was his house. Dark or not, he knew its layout and contents best.

Parker moved on the balls of his feet and returned to his master bedroom. He slid on a change of clothing and laced up hiking boots before stepping into the upstairs hallway and readying himself for a fight.

He had gotten lucky.

Peering over the stair railing, he heard two voices below. One sounded agitated, the other dismissive. Through the darkness, he discerned movement and the closing of his back door.

One of the intruders had left to join the others looking for him outside, leaving his comrade inside.

If Parker wanted to stay among the living, the moment was now.

Beyond rudimentary cooking utensils and a wood-block knife set from Bed Bath & Beyond, the only weapon he possessed hung on the wall in the bedroom next to his. He passed his unbandaged fingers across the etched brass inscription beneath a childhood gift from his archeologist parents before their untimely deaths: "There are but few important events in the affairs of men brought about by their own choice." Ulysses S. Grant's words rang hollow; Grant himself had rarely worn the cavalry war sword, or even a proper Army uniform, before his promotion to brigadier general of the volunteers.

Parker wrenched the weapon from its mount and gripped it in two hands. He took a calming breath and let the vintage sword lead the way. Creeping low, he avoided moonlight breaking past draperies and headed downstairs.

The intruders were searching for something.

It didn't take much to figure out what the Phoenix Consortium wanted: Parker's research—a neurological interface to the human mind, dangerous technology offering the ability to change global and political landscapes. He knew it as neurological singularity, science's last grand frontier. Over a month earlier, the Phoenix Consortium had tried to acquire prototype versions of his groundbreaking interface, and his home still bore the scars of that extensive ransacking. ANCRI and its governing board, from the Phoenix Consortium, would kill anyone to secure his work.

An outcome worth avoiding.

The remaining intruder rifled through papers on Parker's desk. His back was turned, and he held a submachine gun loosely.

Parker came in low and reached up to twist the man's weapon away, thrusting the blunt pommel of the sword upward. Aged steel contacted chin and bone. The man's balance shifted to his heels. Jerking the weapon from the man's grasp with one hand, Parker followed through with the pommel below the man's chin. Continuing his attack, Parker swept the man's leg with his foot and dropped him hard to the floor.

The body crashed loudly to the floor.

Parker struck the man's face with the butt of the sword again.

The man never cried out as his body went limp.

Parker removed the man's tactical wireless communications, patted down the body until he located a phone and a wallet, and snatched up the submachine gun. Now he had a gun, which went a long way toward evening the odds.

It wouldn't take the remaining intruders long to figure out one of theirs was down. They'd return with a vengeance.

Parker deposited the sword in a wicker umbrella stand, then rolled the unconscious man beneath his desk, out of sight. He inserted the earpiece to the man's comms and clipped the radio to the waist of his pants. Using the man's cell phone, he dialed 911 with the emergency call option.

The 911 operator came on the line.

Parker raised his voice an octave and laid on his best Jersey accent for the recording. "I'm mindin' my own business, but I got to report this. Men with machine guns broke into my neighbor's home and set off his alarm." He gave his address.

The operator started asking questions, and he cut her off. "Sneaking around the bushes, there's no way they're cops. Criminals. Dangerous criminals. Oh, I think they saw me. Get the cops out here."

Clicking off the phone, he tossed it under his desk where the unconscious man lay.

The back door of the house cracked open. Multiple footsteps approached.

Parker gripped the acquired semiautomatic tight, moved out a pair of French doors to his study, and ducked behind a hutch packed with books.

The comms piece in his ear sparked alive. A woman's voice. Assertive. Confident. Their leader. "Arkansas, did you locate the schematics or solid state drives yet?"

Figures stepped past him and gathered in his study.

She was back on comms. "Arkansas, report your location. Over." She waited for a response that never came, then said, "Arkansas, report in. Over."

Parker grinned. *Arkansas is napping. Check back with him later.*

"Damn it, Georgia and Mississippi," she said, not using the comms, "we're on the clock. Tear apart the upstairs. Find the tech. And if you two reconvene with Arkansas, secure him. I'll teach the man not to wander off and go silent." She clicked on the comms again. "Texas and Missouri, return to the house. The good doctor has limited resources for remaining off the radar. He can't hide. We'll secure him by other means. Over."

"Roger that. Tex and The Real Deal Miss returning to the house," another voice said.

Parker counted five states from the conversation—codenames. The leader rounded out the group at six intruders.

They wanted his tech from ANCRI.

Parker risked a glance. Two large and armed shadows—presumably Georgia and Mississippi—headed upstairs, leaving their female boss to pillage his study.

Seizing the moment, Parker dashed in the opposite direction. He cracked open the basement door and ducked into its narrow stairs. He didn't risk turning on lights, and felt along the wall to keep his balance. Unfinished stair treads creaked under his weight—nothing he could do about that.

Where are the police? Anytime now.

At the bottom, in total darkness, he hugged the walls and moved with purpose.

Parker slammed into something around his knees. The second-hand research equipment he'd been meaning to pick up clattered onto the basement's plywood subfloor. Its clamor sounded like thunder. He imagined the noise had reached the rest of the house as well.

From the floor above, movement paused. The house fell eerily still.

"Texas and Missouri, recheck the basement, including crawl spaces," the woman's voice said over the comms. "Make sure there's nowhere for him to hide. Over."

2

THE WINE CELLAR

In darkness, Parker stumbled away from the clutter of equipment strewn about his basement and cursed himself for not cleaning up the junk when he'd had the chance. His nostrils flared, taking in a cool, musty aroma as he sought to calm himself. Identifying the low thrum of a dehumidifier helped get his bearings in a room without light. Carrying the gun he'd collected from the intruder upstairs, he migrated over to the home's boiler in a corner of the basement.

Above, boots trod across hundred-plus year old wooden floors, their sounds unifying and closing in on the basement's stairs.

Parker slid aside plywood panels to expose a bedroom-sized, prohibition-era stone wine cellar. Never had he intended to use the cellar as an escape room. It was a dead-end space with no retreat. Stepping inside, he guided the wall back into place and retreated until his back was flush against cold cast iron, a hand-me-down safe left behind by previous owners.

A storm of flashlight beams and red laser dots pierced tiny

cracks in the walls. The false wall blended inconspicuously into an unfinished basement, leaving thin gaps between joints to match other bare plywood surfaces. Flickers of light penetrated the small confines and fed the adrenaline that fueled his rapid heartbeat. Beside him, wine bottles glowed in wooden racks and redirected the piercing multi-colored light.

He slowed his breathing and aimed his weapon at the sliding door before him.

The earpiece he'd collected crackled to life.

"Heads up. Sheriff deputies just arrived," a man's voice said. "Maryland, you interested in making this a scene? If so, this will get bloody, awful fast. Over."

Parker took a long breath. His emergency call had worked.

"If the doctor thinks this is a stalemate, he's in for a surprise," the woman said over comms. "Texas and Missouri, leave him our parting gift instead. Barricade the storm doors and light up his life."

Parker cupped his ear as the comms went dead. *What?*

Pressing against the false wall, he looked for a change in movement.

No longer overt or stealthy, the intruders' actions changed to loud and pronounced, but he still couldn't tell what they were doing.

A single gunshot made him flinch.

Brilliance flashed just beyond his hideaway door. Expanding warmth radiated through the walls. Squinting through a crack, Parker saw sparks and flashes as knife-like daggers of heat jabbed his skin.

The intruders had set his house on fire.

Trapped, he had no escape as billowing clouds of smoke started to churn. Throughout the house, smoke detectors wailed.

Dread swept through Parker. This was how he would die: by fire.

Kate Morgan flickered in his mind. For weeks, he'd wondered what he'd done to push her away. During a month-long vacation in the Caymans, both seemed to welcome their newfound companionship and romance. Upon their return, her post-trip behavior perplexed him. Kate had gone radio silent. After a week of unanswered calls, emails, and texts, he'd stopped reaching out to her.

The first time he'd met her still glowed in his mind like the swelling heat around him.

Serendipity or mere coincidence had brought her into his life. Now all he wanted to do was tell her goodbye.

Parker had cheated death before, but this predicament seemed inescapable.

Bumping the mass of cast iron behind him, Parker spun to face an antique bank and hotel safe. Running fingers across its door, he felt the subtle details of gold leaf paint beneath his fingertips. A Princeton Bank and Trust bank manager had inherited the safe and moved it to the house after the bank upgraded to a walk-in safe. The former homeowner had finished out the prohibition-era wine cellar as a way to hide the safe. And the safe protected what remained of his game-changing technology, undoubtedly what that the intruders had sought.

The hairs on the back of his neck bristled as a plan formed in Parker's mind.

Through the gaps in the plywood, he studied the fire's intensity, which had spread to the home's early 1900s-era wood structures. Through the haze, the basement stairs were no longer visible.

If he did nothing, death was certain. Staying put meant burning to death.

Unlike the immortal heroes of countless TV shows and movies, he would die if he tried to run through the fire without protective clothing and self-contained breathing. The fire's intense heat and acrid toxicity would sear his trachea and lungs.

Parker had one slim option. And he wasn't leaving without his tech, his impending death be damned.

Setting aside his automatic weapon, he spun the safe's numerical dial several times, then wrenched open the door. Inside a pearl-colored face greeted him—a skullcap formed over a mannequin's head, its fiber optic cables bundled together and patched into a control box. Parker snatched up the head gear and briefcase, and turned to the home's original coal chute, embedded in the stone walls of the basement.

The coffin-sized coal chute was the only route out of the house. The tight fit beat any alternatives.

Still holding his tech, he gripped a hand lever that probably hadn't moved since before he bought the house. Nothing budged. Setting everything down, he put two hands on the lever. Again nothing.

Putting his feet on the stone wall for extra leverage, Parker lay supine in the air and wrenched against the coal chute's interior hand lever. Using his legs as a spring, he put more force and torque against the lever. After straining for several seconds, a rusted iron door swung down, its pinned hinges groaning in protest.

With leverage lost, Parker crumpled to the floor, staring up through the chute. Cooler air fell over him. Peering up, he focused on the yard level outside, where another rusted iron lid led to the outside world.

It was time to leave.

Parker staggered to his feet, collected his equipment and considered how best to navigate the shoulder-tight escape while carrying luggage. It became clear that two trips would be needed: one to open the exterior door, and a return trip to retrieve his things.

A thunderous rumble grabbed his attention, as if the house had been caught in some kind of earthquake.

He peered through the slits of plywood as a concussive blast swept over him, showering his body with blistering needles of debris, heat, and dust. Everything flashed orange as his body flung backward and into the open cavity of the safe behind him.

Parker felt his strength wane as reality vanished into blackness.

MONDAY, NOVEMBER 30th

Nowhere are there more hiding places than in the human heart.
German Proverb

3

CHARRED EFFECTS

9:10 AM, Princeton, New Jersey

FBI Special Agent Kate Morgan wiped away a remnant of tears before stepping out of her car. Her blurred vision stretched past yellow police crime tape and flashing lights on a myriad of vehicles, and locked onto the charred carcass of a 1900s Victorian-style residence.

Princeton. The last place she wanted to be right now.

During the drive up from Virginia, arson investigators had briefed her on a discovery: human remains.

Thomas.

How'd life get this messed up?

Kate fought back a torrent of feelings. As a forensics examiner, she kept her work detached from her personal life. Case assignments were routine. She examined the biological aspects of corpses and causes of death, analyzed physical and genetic evidence, and coordinated cases with other agencies about crimes against victims. Never, ever, had she known the victim, much less been intimately involved with him.

Thomas Parker had been the kryptonite destroying her career. Yet the best thing to enter her life.

Weeks earlier, they'd returned from a month-long trip, where they shared picture-book moments, walked near-endless beaches, and sailed after pristine sunsets. Their Caribbean escape was perfect. The spontaneous tête-à-tête moments with Parker allowed her love again. But that magic had evaporated the moment a bomber attacked the nation's capital; the subsequent trial scarring her in ways that she couldn't express.

Now Thomas was dead, a mere memory.

Time to close this chapter of her life and return to compartmentalizing her world into shareable and non-shareable boxes. Time to act like a federal agent again.

Kate sucked in nervous breaths before retrieving field boots from a gear bag. After lacing up her boots, she slid on a traditional blue windbreaker with its iconic gold lettering. A matching FBI ball cap over long coffee-colored hair tied back into a ponytail completed her attire.

Credentials were flashed to a tired-looking deputy manning the perimeter as she ducked beneath crime scene tape. She cast her gaze across the home's smoldering rubble.

What am I doing here?

The Director had asked her to secure a voluntary deposition from Thomas before other agencies or congressional subpoenas reached him. Influenced by the White House, the Department of Justice (DOJ) had turned DC's three-letter agencies against each other—another fine example of America's beltway politics and political infighting—and the bureau needed to protect its own institution. They needed details on Thomas' research before other interested parties made their moves.

Kate never imagined Thomas would be dead before she returned to Princeton.

Foul play was the only thing that made sense.

Firefighters carrying hoses brushed past her, disrupting her thoughts.

"Looking for something, Agent?" asked an arson investigator.

"Where was the body found?" Kate asked, without offering an introduction. Her words sounded colder, more callous than she wanted. The no-nonsense, compassionless question came from a daily dose of forensics in her life.

"In the study."

"Thomas Parker?" Her gaze tracked over to where she knew the home's study to be. After the crime scene technicians photographed the scene, his body would have been taken to the Mercer County Medical Examiner's office.

"You know him?" The arson investigator had read her like a cheap book, the giveaway her reddened eyes.

"He was involved in the case that I worked last month."

The man's face lit up. "You're that federal agent who rescued those college kids. At that research lab over near Pennington. I saw you on TV. Wow, that was some scary stuff. So, how are those kids? I haven't heard anything about them in the news."

Kate shrugged. The botched mess-of-a-case had turned into a full-blown congressional inquisition. "Justice took over the investigation," she said. "So there's nothing I can tell you." She redirected the conversation. "When I spoke with your office, they said this was arson?"

"Initial indications support that premise. 911 received a call right before midnight. The caller claimed people with machine guns had broken into Mr. Parker's residence. When police arrived, a fire broke out and spread rapidly. When the fire department arrived on scene, much of the structure was already gone, fire well into the roofline. They never had a chance to save anyone or much of the home. And no intruders were found."

Kate swallowed over a knot in her throat. "Where'd the fire start?"

"Witness accounts and burn paths point to the basement."

She handed the investigator a business card and asked to look around, even though the FBI had no jurisdictional connection to a local arson investigation.

The investigator nodded toward the home. "Let me know if you find something important."

Kate nodded back and slid on blue plastic gloves before crossing a debris field that spread into the front yard. The lingering effects of the burnt wood flooded her nostrils. Her boots squished on ash-laden soggy grass. Drawing closer, she studied the blackened lumber rising above an uneven bed of charred remains. At the rear of the house, two nearly intact intersecting walls still stood. The living room's red-bricked fireplace rose above a foundation, and the remnants of crushed and burnt appliances defined the kitchen area.

She turned to the area of the home's study. It had been packed with books and journals.

Burning to death. A horrible way to go.

The two men in her life could not be any more different: Thomas was gone, leaving her with Jack Wright, a former lover who was laid up in a DC hospital recovering from injuries he received when a battering ram of a truck struck his car.

She wiped away more tears before focusing on what she'd come for.

Thomas' death was the exclamation point to her empty life.

Kate ran her gloved fingers across blackened lumber and crushed bits of drywall and concrete. Stepping through where the front door once stood, she noticed that basement stairs had been consumed by fire. An aluminum extension ladder dropped down into a hole filled with the remnants of charred lumber and burnt trash. Latching onto the ladder, she descended into the house's half-infilled basement.

Kate moved through scorched debris, sloshing in mud-like ash that rose past her boots. She saw the remnants of a blackened stone wall that had been built to hide bootleg whiskey a homeowner had sold out of his house during Prohibition. Past the wall, past the remains of a home boiler, her gaze latched onto an empty antique hotel safe. Its door hung open. Kate leaned in to study it.

The technology inside was gone.

A substantive fact: Thomas Parker had died in a tech heist.

4

A TRANSPLANT FOR THE SLEEPING

10:00 AM, NeuroSteps Labs, Glen Garner, New Jersey

Dr. Rikona Tanaka scrubbed in for surgery, something she hadn't done in years—never, outside of Japan. Success determined whether her daughter lived or died. The procedure she was to perform had been attempted only twice, both times by her, a day earlier—on a male cadaver and then a living donor, a mid-sixties Jane Doe. The fully cognizant female never regained post-surgery consciousness. Before those human trials, experiments on primates had produced no successful outcomes either.

And refining her technique wasn't a luxury that time permitted.

The Phoenix Consortium required their lead researcher back— at all costs.

Only a complete cognitive restoration spared her daughter from a death sentence.

Merely a directive: a life for a life.

Tanaka shuddered a breath as she scrubbed her forearms and hands with antimicrobial soap, carefully watching an analog clock to count off two minutes, one for each hand.

Her specialty was green thumb genetics for the brain: mini-brains, cerebral organoids. Her organoid replication technique offered vast opportunities for a plethora of medical treatments, including cell replacement therapy (CRT). Animal-based lab testing showed promise. Neural grafting allowed the damaged brain cells of primates who suffered from a form of Parkinson's disease to be replaced with genetically cultured healthy cells, with only minor tissue degradation or rejection. Her transplant technique allowed replacement cells to form synaptic circuitry with neighboring brain cells. Once perfected, the therapeutic benefits were limitless. As an expert in neurogenetics and biogenetics, cellular replications, Tanaka's cutting-edge work offered tailor-made pluripotent stem (iPS) cell transplant opportunities for patients with irreparable cerebral dysfunctions.

Replace damaged brain cells with new cells.

Revive a host.

A tall order. It had never been done successfully. Any vegetative state would be categorized as a failed outcome.

A failed outcome would kill her daughter.

Finishing up at the scrub sinks, Tanaka backed into the neuro-surgery suite with her wet hands lifted at angles of sixty degrees. A surgical nurse laid out a sterile towel for hand drying and helped her into a surgical gown and mask.

Tanaka studied the hybrid operating room.

Prepped and ready, the patient was covered by sterile sheeting up to his head: Stewart Richards. Barely recognizable. His trademark white hair had been cut off, his scalp shaved clean including his eyebrows. Physiological reference topography, geometric patterns and mapping were drawn precisely onto his head. A breathing tube was the only object taped to a pale, weathered face.

A nurse assisted with the final piece of her attire, sterile gloves.

Tanaka took a solemn breath and stepped to the operating table.

Pivoting to flat screen monitors, she studied high-resolution intraoperative digital brain scans that predicted the optimal surgical pathway based on predictive outcomes. 3D navigation modeling reduced extraneous neurophysiological trauma while anticipating potential areas for hemorrhages and shifting brain tissue.

She reconfirmed anatomical and procedural milestones using a track-mounted donut-shaped 3-Tesla MRI and C-shaped CT scanner. NeuroSteps had given Tanaka every technological advantage available.

All she had to do was pass a straw-like guide through brain matter to a precise location of dead cells deep inside the brain, a destination called the claustrum; laser-remove and vacuum out a four-pinhead-sized dead zone; and insert genetically programmed, petri dish-cultured brain cells.

Simple enough. Theoretically.

Leaning over a comatose Stewart Richards, Tanaka studied his unresponsive face framed in sterile sheeting. She recalled movie dialogue attributed to the World War II Marshal Admiral of the Imperial Japanese Navy Isoroku Yamamoto: *I fear we will awaken a sleeping giant and fill him with a terrible resolve.*

That was Richards.

She nodded to the team around her. "Okay. Time for him to rise or sleep forever."

A series of micro 0.5 milliliter-per-minute pumps sparked to life, circulating donor-harvested cerebrospinal fluid (CSF) into Richard's brain. Needles pierced four quadrants of his skull and delivered CSF past the blood-brain barrier (BBB). During non-REM sleep, the small-molecule, water-like substance carried oxygen and vital nutrients through the tight vesicles and channels inside dense brain material.

Tanaka glanced to Richards' dropping brainwaves.

So far, so good.

As the neurons inside his brain switched-off, those non-firing neurons required less blood flow, creating additional channels for the progression of donor-forced CSF fluid to flush out accumulated metabolic byproducts.

Through a computer console, Tanaka operated an automated robot arm that did the precision work. Two pebble-sized holes were drilled on each side of Richards' skull. Each cavity entry was flushed. Pinhead-sized laser probes were inserted. The precision penetrations reached the brain's claustrum. The dead zones were vacuumed out and packed with pre-growth (iPS) cell transplants and stimulated to invite spontaneous adhering to surrounding neurons.

Two hours later, the procedure wrapped up. The holes in Richards' skull were patched with a bone-like resin. Drainage tubes released any remaining pressure buildup of the inserted CSF liquids.

Post-operative MRI and CT scans showed no neurological deterioration.

Good news.

The brain cell grafts showed signs of anatomical adherence.

Better news.

Exhausted, Tanaka sat on a hard bench outside the OR suite and removed her gown and booties.

She lifted her chin as technicians wheeled Richards down the hallway to a hyperbaric oxygen therapy chamber, where he'd spend the next two hours. The hyper-oxygenated state would enhance healing processes, support anti-inflammatory effects, reduce edema, and help his body purge the lingering effects of anesthesia and other medications.

The first box got checked: Stewart Richards hadn't died.

She sighed. *Not yet.*

Checking the second box was a bigger question: would sleeping beauty awake?

Her daughter's life depended on checking that box. Stewart Richards needed to live.

5

MESSAGE FROM THE DEAD

10:20 AM, Mercer County Medical Examiner's Office, New Jersey

As a bureau forensics investigator and M.D., Kate's duties required her to consult with local jurisdictions on a wide range of autopsies and homicides. A no-nonsense curb sign announced the Mercer County Medical Examiner's Office. The building she sought had pull-through garage doors and an unadorned office front. Kate registered at the front desk and waited for the medical examiner.

A slender man wearing a lab coat came out. Kate handed him a business card. They shook hands. Dr. Merrill Ahmad had a firm yet completely forgettable handshake and an equally plain smile.

He examined her card. "Agent Morgan, what can we assist you with today?"

"I'd like to see the body recovered from the Princeton fire."

"Sure. Come on back." He opened a door and led her down a hallway.

"How many homicides do you get a year?" she asked.

"Forty or so. Another hundred that need determinations of a cause of death."

They elbowed through a wide swing door and entered an exam room equipped with LED lighting, drop cords, stainless steel tables and wash-down sinks. Kate had encountered the smell of death in many forms, and one of them flooded her nostrils. Antiseptics, routine hose-downs, and air filtration systems could not cover up a morgue's lingering stench of death.

Without asking, Ahmad handed Kate gloves and a disposable apron before turning on a digital kiosk. He paged through screen tabs and stopped at a data-populated preliminary autopsy report.

"Cause of death?" she asked, pulling on sterile gloves.

"You tell me." He disappeared into the storage cooler.

Kate scrutinized the medical examiner's in-progress REPORT.

AUTOPSY PERFORMED	YES		DEATH AT WORK	NO
IDENTIFYING MARKS	NO		DENTAL XRAYS	TAKEN
INJURY TYPE	OPEN		DENTAL RECORDS	NEEDED
BLOOD WORK TAKEN	YES		TOXICOLOGY	YES

MANNER OF DEATH		
	NATURAL	
	ACCIDENT	
	HOMICIDE	X
	SUICIDE	
	UNDETERMINED	

CAUSE OF DEATH	1	FIRE
	2	OPEN...ASPHYXIATION / INHALATION
	3	OPEN

SIGNIFICANT	1	LEFT INDEX & MIDDLE FINGERPRINTS
OBSERVATIONS	2	CO2 LEVELS RECORDED AT 54%
	3	SOOT DISCOVERED IN AIRWAY

Most data fields remained blank. The address given was Thomas' home. A case number was listed instead of a name. MALE. AGE was left blank. Anterior and posterior caricature outlines had been circled and simply tagged with SEE PHOTOS.

Kate understood that the deceased had been alive and breathing during the house fire.

Digital photos were attached to the interactive report. Fearful of what she might find, Kate took a breath before tapping on the attachments links.

A burnt and charred body lay naked on a stainless steel table. In her line of work, she'd seen death in countless forms: men, women, children. Outcomes of simple accidents to victims who'd been murdered then had their bodies set on fire in an effort to cover up murder or conceal the victim's identity.

She swiped through the digital thumbnails, skipping photos of black-crusted, blood-blistered skin until she stopped at a face. A man's face.

Kate cupped her mouth to avoid screaming.

"Figure out the cause of death?" Ahmad asked, more as a test than an actual question, as he wheeled in a body zipped up in a white body bag.

"Asphyxiation…" Kate said in an incoherent stream of words. With a swipe of her hand, she grabbed the gurney before he could park it and ripped down the center zipper of the body bag. "Who's this?"

"I'm not following."

"This isn't Thomas Parker," Kate said. The half-charred face staring back at her was that of a stranger, matching what she'd seen in the autopsy photos.

She paced in circles while she ripped off her gloves.

Ahmad crossed his arms. "With Does, dental records and other physical evidence are used to confirm identities, not addresses. I never said this man was the homeowner, if that's what you're implying."

Kate faced the medical examiner. "No. What I'm saying is Thomas might still be alive."

6

THE SHACKLES OF SEDATION

Secured Facility, Unknown Location

The rhythmic movement of Thomas Parker's breath entering a mask mimicked the sounds of morning surf beating against sand along a fog-ridden Jersey shore. The natural pulse of respiration synched to his waking, a life force breaking free of the shackles of sedation.

His transition to consciousness ebbed and flowed as rapid-fire, dream-like images came and went: fire, heat, laser sights, gunfire, intruders, explosions.

Dead. He should be dead.

But the dead didn't dream. At least, Parker didn't think that the dead dreamed.

New memories emerged to drive out the violent ones.

Sunlight breached palm fronds. Gently swaying, he lay in a two-person hammock strung between tree trunks. Beside him, asleep, Kate wore a sundress. Her form pressed against his. Gazing across her, he watched the incoming tide pulse, its cadenced splash cresting sugar-white sand to harmonize with his breathing.

The dead did not dream, nor did they breathe.

That meant he'd survived, somehow.

After a long sigh, he forced his eyes open and found an infinite blackness, devoid of any natural or even artificial light.

Neither life nor death made sense.

He blinked and focused beyond the darkness.

His skin tingled. His cheeks felt flushed, with a cool dampness. A nasal mask covered his face, its presence confirmed by the pressure of face straps. He cocked his head and tried to move, but restraints bound him horizontal.

Parker tried to process the possibilities. The most logical scenario: he'd been taken to Penn Medicine Princeton Medical Center, and placed in psychiatric care isolation or some version of oxygen therapy.

This wasn't heaven or hell or purgatory or any realm in between. He was in a hospital.

"Anyone on duty?" he called through the mask covering his mouth. His voice was raspy, throat hoarse from fire and fumes. "Hey, can I get some help here?"

7

THE RETREAT

Number One Observatory Circle, Washington, DC

Richard Mears, Vice President of the United States, packed two travel bags. It was routine for Mears to manage his personal affairs. He pushed back on the myriad of handlers afforded him, preferring privacy. A desire for personal space overrode his job's suffocating bureaucracy and its extensive security measures. His staff was the smallest since Vice President John Garner's, who'd worked under Franklin Roosevelt. From cooks to butlers to personal aides, Mears retained a staff of eight, excluding his ever-present Secret Service detail and the blend of Department of Defense shadows who lurked nearby in case of a national crisis.

For the next 48 hours, plans would allow him to eliminate his executive entourage, mimicking stunts he'd pulled before during pheasant hunting trips, deep sea fishing, yacht sailing, and the occasional weekend-long Texas Hold'em games with wealthier donors.

Mears added toiletries to a travel bag, then glanced to a honeymoon picture of his wife, Susan, that sat atop one of the master bedroom's dressers. Susan hated the blustery side of Martha's Vineyard this time of year. Her decision to remain behind was best for all involved.

In the photo, a college-aged Susan smiled—something she hadn't done in more than a month, ever since their son, Andrew, had been abducted and placed in a permanent coma.

A man interrupted his thoughts. "How's Andrew, sir?"

Mears glanced at the President's National Security Advisor, Gordon Abbott, who was standing in Mears' bedroom doorway. Abbott was a tall, wiry man dressed in a gray suit who always looked like his disproportioned head was larger than his shoulders should be permitted to carry. Abbott, an indoctrinated think-tank disciple and West Point grad, excelled in both foreign policy and national security matters. The President had hand-picked the party ideologue for the administration's cabinet. And Mears did what all smart Washington hacks did: built an alliance with the president's main influencer.

"No change," Mears said, his voice distant, almost as if a stranger spoke for him. His son, a decorated Navy doctor and accomplished physician working on leading-edge research, lay in a private suite at George Washington University Hospital. There were no known medical treatments for his son's neurological condition. Five, including the niece of Speaker of the House, had been afflicted by the same malaise. "Have the arrangements been made?"

"As requested." Abbott glanced at Mears' luggage on the bed, watching him zip up his last bag. "You sure you want to go through with this?"

"Gordon, the less you know the better."

The man placed an encrypted cell phone on the dresser next to the picture of his wife.

"Nothing more needs to be said, Mr. Vice President. Air Force Two is fueled and ready. Flight time to Joint Base Cape Cod is about an hour and a half. A helicopter will ferry us to Martha's Vineyard from there."

Mears understood that the Martha's Vineyard Airport's runway length was too short for Air Force Two, a Boeing C-32, a modified version of the 757 commercial jetliner. Its Air Force pilots had trained for emergency scenarios and shorter runways, but they'd chosen an intermediate stop at the military base in Cape Cod because it drew less attention.

Abbott reached for one of the bags on the bed.

Mears waved him off. "I'll carry my bags."

8

EMPTY SPACES

Engineering Quad, Princeton University, Princeton, New Jersey

Kate ignored jurisdictional boundaries and called for university police to unlock a fourth-floor lab in the D-wing corridor of Princeton's
Engineering Quad building. She had no time for the plethora of
intra-agency hurdles involved in submitting the requests. The lam-
inated Department of Justice OFF LIMITS sign taped to a gray steel
door reminded her that she had exceeded her bureau mandate.

Thomas Parker's old lab space might hold the answers she needed.

The university officer opened the metal door and waited in the
tiled corridor. An empty space revealed what she already knew:
Parker's university-controlled intellectual property had long since
vanished. Another unsolved tech heist.

On their vacation, she'd asked Thomas about his stolen research.
He seemed bitter, resentful. Understandable, given the countless
hours he'd spent creating a new frontier in science and medicine.

Kate's gaze swept the empty space. She imagined it populated with equipment, supercomputers, cooling systems, and a center-piece chair for terminal integration. Built out, it would've been an academic's dream—cramped, but impressive nonetheless. She knelt and ran her fingers across smudge marks on linoleum tile where equipment had been loaded up and hauled away.

Thomas had proven a worthy standard bearer for a new generation of Einstein-like vision. His Princeton University lab had been the birthplace of neurological singularity.

"Singularity," Kate understood, meant an intersection in time where two paths crossed, a threshold where the mutual function defining two conditions took on an infinite value. For the human species, it was a dangerous point of no return. Technological singularity was the moment when artificial intelligence and computers became autonomous, self-aware, exhibiting a superintelligence surpassing the finite limitations of human understanding. Similarly, neurological singularity was the achievement of synaptic mapping—not just of the brain, but the creation of an interactive map to human consciousness. Parker's radical work had discovered how to decipher complex neural coding—carry on a two-way conversation with the human mind, or even change memories themselves.

And Parker had destroyed everything to keep his core research out of the wrong hands.

Kate's escorting officer cleared his throat and handed her a sealed envelope marked *FBI SPECIAL AGENT KATHERINE MORGAN. EYES ONLY.*

She took the envelope, tore off its end, and slid out a single sheet of paper from a hotel notepad—Princeton | Nassau Inn | Palmer Square. The note read:

WHEN YOU'RE DONE WASTING TIME IN EMPTY SPACES, CHECK IN, THEN TAKE THIS INVITE TO THE BAR. MY INTEREST IS KEEPING THOMAS PARKER ALIVE. WHERE'S YOURS?

9

THE DRAWING ROOM

The Nassau Inn, Princeton, New Jersey

Kate entered the historic hotel, her pulse racing with the thought that Thomas might be alive. The inn and its tavern dated to before the Revolutionary War. Its renovations mixed modern settings with hardwoods and colonial style. She checked in for a single night, then strolled into the tap room, leaving her luggage in her car.

The wood-beamed tavern had a classic college feel, celebrating Princeton University and its famous alumni, athletes and celebrities alike. She passed under a stone arch and located a female bartender waiting on a few patrons. The prominent Norman Rockwell Yankee Doodle mural hung behind glass and a u-shaped bar.

Kate handed the bartender the note.

"I'm told to ask if you're alone," the woman said.

Kate looked around. "Alone enough, wouldn't you say?"

The bartender set down two cocktail napkins and poured two glasses of chardonnay.

"Your acquaintance is upstairs."

"My acquaintance?" Kate leaned into the bar. "Male or female?"

The bartender whispered, "My rent-sized tip is based on keeping our conversation to a minimum."

Kate retrieved the glasses with their napkins. "Thanks for the vino."

Her heartbeat ticked up. Was this mysterious rendezvous something Thomas might conceive? Something inside her doubted it. Not Thomas' style, not after having his home burn to the ground with a stranger still inside it.

Carrying a glass in each hand, Kate navigated the inn's stairs. Her mind was full of possibilities, but none more surprising than the person waiting in the inn's drawing room.

Debra Ford aimed a suppressed semiautomatic pistol at her. The move was brilliant, as Kate was defenseless, each hand occupied with a glass of wine. She couldn't reach her hip-holstered Glock without getting shot.

Kate looked around the colonial-style drawing room, which had been decorated for the holidays. A bar was at one end of the room, a piano at the other. Red-leather chairs and couches were parked on themed rugs filling a long span of wood floors. An antique musket and sword were encased in glass on each side of a gas-fed fireplace. It had four exits.

The master assassin, nicknamed Manea, stood where she could fire a shot and escape if needed.

Kate took a calming breath. "I recall you're fond of chardonnay."

"I indulge, occasionally."

"Oh, you think?"

"Agent Morgan, I can shoot you or we discuss business. Hurry up and mull over your options. I'm rather thirsty."

Kate glanced at the closest exit. She'd never make it before a bullet hit her.

"If I wanted you dead," Debra Ford said, "I would've taken the shot in Virginia, as you climbed off the I-66 bridge."

Kate almost spilled the wine.

"I had you scoped. A very makeable shot, just over 2,000 feet. Well inside my distance."

Kate sat in a grouping of red leather chairs and set the white wine down without a drop spilled. Debra Ford sat opposite, keeping the gun trained on her target. She swooped up a glass with her free hand.

Kate studied the details of her cold-blooded drinking companion, the ex-wife of a dead U.S. Senator. Sipping chardonnay, Debra Ford was mid-fifties, fit enough to pass for forty. She was a natural brunette, but straw-colored hair was pulled back and out of her face. Brown-tinted contacts hid green eyes. She wore a tailored brown barn coat, turtleneck, and black leggings. The black pistol, semiautomatic and suppressed, made her look like a deadly Martha Stewart.

"You must not have many friends, if I'm the best date you can dredge up," Kate said. She hoped she'd pushed a button.

The assassin took a sip. "How's Jack?"

The jab was intentional, personal. Perhaps a sly nugget of goodwill. Only a handful of people knew Jack Wright was alive.

Kate adjusted her poker face. "Recovering from an accident."

"Heard about that. He's lucky to be alive."

"Is this an attempt at being cordial? If so, we can skip the niceties," Kate said. "So, you saw me in DC?"

Debra ignored that. "How bad are his injuries?"

A dodge to her question.

"The hospital moved him out of ICU yesterday," Kate said. "It's nice that you ask about him, Debra. Can I call you Debra?"

"Jack's is quite the resurrection story. Your pretty boy should've died from the two slugs I put in his chest. No one walks away from the shots I take. He won't do it again."

Kate took a breath, then a sip of wine. "Where's Thomas Parker's equipment?"

"Wrong question." Debra Ford chugged down the last of her

wine and shifted her posture, sliding the gun into the open gap of her barn coat.

"Where's Thomas?"

The female bartender arrived with two more glasses of white.

"You're asking as if you actually care about him. How touching." Ford cracked a grin. "You didn't find him at the morgue?"

"No, Debra, I didn't."

"Anything else I can get for you ladies?" the bartender asked, her eyes wide.

Kate shot the bartender an *are-you-kidding-me* glare and reflected on how Ford had choreographed this meeting. Everything was sequenced, including the conversation.

Debra smiled politely. "Perhaps later, dear. Thank you."

They both waited for the bartender to leave the drawing room.

Debra welcomed the second round. "Agent, ask questions that matter most." She had gunned down the bureau's Deputy Director and her ex-husband's lover. The woman's past was littered with bullet-ridden bodies.

"You're a murderer."

"That's not a question, only a statement of fact."

Kate gulped the last of her first glass to keep up. "Debra, you will face justice."

"Morgan, you see the world through a narrow pane of glass. Its size and frame block out other realities. You're a simple doc-in-a-box working with microscopes, chemistry sets, and computers. Occasionally, a case comes across your desk that makes your day relevant. Beyond that your life is rather routine, trite."

"See me so clearly, do you?"

"Perhaps. Now, I serve my country in a different capacity. I exist where the stakes are greater. Protect this nation from threats you don't even know exist. So judge me if you dare. But you too, Katherine Morgan, are jagged and flawed. You pretend to be a saint while secretly hiding away your own sins."

Sins? Kate's mind rewound how their conversation had started. "You saw me in DC?"

Debra took a tediously slow sip, her eyes glaring across the rim of the wine glass. "Morgan, you're smitten by two lovers. For crying out loud, girl, pick one: Jack or Thomas?"

"You're an expert on love? Is that why we're having drinks together?"

"Love. Companionship. Passionate sex. I'm good there. After being faithful in a one-sided marriage and wasting years trying to salvage a broken relationship, my disdain lies in that 'forever' thing. How about you? You faithful to anyone, beside yourself?"

Kate squirmed. "Enough questions about my personal life. Who hired you to kill me?"

"The man you'll want to see after our chat."

"Setting me up on a date?" Kate took a drink, keeping up with her opponent. "What do you want?"

"Sort of a what, but more who. Thomas Parker."

Kate's heart hammered in her chest. She drew a breath. *Thomas is alive.* She wanted to scream *You psycho killer bitch, what did you do with him?* Instead, she snarled, "You burned down Thomas' home just to kidnap him and steal his research?"

"That wasn't me."

"Really? So tell me, where's Thomas?"

"We'll get to that."

"Why do you want him?"

"Because our nation is threatened in ways you don't comprehend."

Kate snorted. "Didn't know you were that much of a patriot. Is that a new angle for you? Saving our blessed country one assassination at a time? Kind of hard to believe."

"It's not important that you do." Debra looked disappointed as she finished off her second glass. "Does Thomas know about Jack?"

"Stay on topic, Debra."

Debra smiled. "Love triangles are such fun." She leaned back in her chair. "I enjoy them. Order us another round."

"No."

Debra flashed a frown. "You familiar with the term 'proof of concept'?"

Kate shivered. She'd learned the term during medical school. POCs were employed by a host of industry sectors, from food and beverage to the military to space exploration. In medicine, POC equated to validating a fundamental tool, technique, or establishing a concept through a repeatable and obtainable demonstration. Pharmacological development broke the process down even further by adding additional steps for "proof of mechanism" and "proof of principle." Parker's radical breakthroughs in neuroscience and mind mapping had already surpassed traditional POC milestones, unless you were a competitor or enemy out to replicate his work.

Kate took out her phone, called the hotel, and asked for the tap room. "Hi. I'm with the lovely, very sweet woman upstairs. You served us drinks. Yes. That's us. Well, we'd like a bottle this time? You can put it on her tab. That'll be fine. Thank you, so kindly."

Debra smirked. "You're interested?"

Interested from the moment a gun was pointed at her. Kate clicked off her phone. "You have my attention, Debra."

"You're naïve."

Kate leaned forward on her elbows. "Where are you getting your intel?"

Debra laughed. "My sources work for me. Not you. Not the bureau."

"You know I can't withhold information on my end."

"Katherine, dear, you want to save Thomas Parker or not? Of course, if you're passionately in love with Jack, then let Tommy boy die."

"Thomas is in danger?"

Debra shrugged. "Pretty much."

The bartender arrived with an uncorked bottle of Beaulieu Vineyard Century Cellars Chardonnay, pretzel bites, and cheese dip. She filled the empty glasses and left after asking if anything else was required.

Debra retrieved her glass. "If you do this, you work by my rules."

"Who will I be meeting?" Kate asked, taking a small sip of wine.

Debra popped a pretzel bite into her mouth. "The Vice President of the United States. But be advised, Richard Mears wants you dead."

Kate swallowed wine down the wrong pipe and coughed. "What?"

Debra raised her glass up to her lips and let its aroma drift into her nostrils. "View it as an opportunity."

Kate shook her head. "You either need me as a patsy or want me to get killed."

Debra took a thoughtful breath. "I work a global stage full of traps. In my craft, if you don't get killed along the way, your reward is a token that permits you to leverage up for a better position. Yes. I'm a patriot. Served multiple administrations, regardless of which political party was in power. Walk this path, you get to save Thomas from what I imagine will be a miserable death. Engage Vice President Mears. Earn his trust."

"You're insane."

"Is that your attempt at humor?"

"No. Not at all." Kate flushed, not sure if it was from the wine or the conversation. As a federal agent, she'd be obligated to report any perceived threat or interaction with the Vice President of the United States. She slid her glass to the center of the table. "Even if Mears wants me dead, for whatever reasons, I'd be stupid to meet him after talking with you."

"Dick Mears needs an ally." Debra toyed with another pretzel bite before eating it. "Tell him that after the current situation is resolved, you'll cure his son."

Kate took a panicked breath. The VP's son was in an incurable coma. The younger Mears was a physician, ex-Navy, who worked for the Pentagon's Defense Research and Engineering for Advanced Capabilities directorate as a subject matter expert. Andrew Mears' mind had been silenced along with five others.

Debra Ford knew an awful lot about recent events in Washington, DC.

Debra continued, "Morgan, your presence serves two purposes. One, convince Thomas Parker to resume his research. If required, use your feminine endowments. Persuade him. Our nation needs functional versions of his tech in a much different way than he might comprehend. Two, if everyone survives this crisis, then both of you can cure the Vice President's son. That, my dear, is where redemption comes to you."

Kate took an anxious breath. The steps ahead seemed simple, but nothing this complex was ever simple. And Thomas Parker might not want to see her—so much had changed between them.

And one thing was certain: the treacherous assassin sitting across from her would surely kill either one of them if they outlived their usefulness, or tried to double-cross her.

10

AWAKENING

Secured Research Facility, Unknown Location

Parker understood that whoever had detained him didn't want to hear from him. Enveloped in darkness, bound to a table or bed, that was obvious. Hours, even days—he had no way of knowing how much time had passed.

As the effects of sedation waned, Parker's head throbbed. A dull pain ran rampant inside his skull. He tried to recall what had happened, his mind jumbled, experiences out of order. Random more than not he thought of the intruders, explosions, FBI Agent Kate Morgan, his graduate assistant Becky Ward, a Princeton University teaching position, lost research.

Parker remembered a nurse and his grad assistant, murdered at the Advanced Neurological and Cybernetic Research Institute (ANCRI). He was responsible for their deaths as much as the madman who'd pulled the trigger.

A clunking reverberation of metal rattled him out of his thoughts.

Light pierced his confines. Parker squinted, adjusting his eyes to the brilliance. Above, lights washed him in a panoramic splash of white.

Craning his neck, he surveyed sterile surroundings. A grid of white plastic walls looked like no hospital that he could recall. He'd been locked down in a single-bed room that resembled a futuristic version of some kind of psychiatric holding cell.

Where am I? Nothing about his surroundings answered that question.

Footsteps drew closer, and a dark-haired woman wearing tan scrubs appeared bedside. Her features revealed Asian ancestry, Chinese or Korean—a nurse, by her apparel. She dialed down the IV drip line that fed into his arm, removed its catheter, then the mask on his face.

Parker noticed that Velcro straps secured his wrists and ankles. He was dressed in a short-sleeved white uniform rather than a patient gown. The flesh of his arms showed no signs of burns.

"I was in a fire," he said hoarsely.

The nurse said nothing. She pressed her fingers against his inner wrist to check his pulse.

Armed Asian men took up positions around his room, their fatigues and bullet-resistant vests not identifying any military branch or law enforcement agency. Each man gripped a laser-sighted assault rifle.

Nothing like being the center of attention among strangers.

A woman wearing a similar austere uniform stepped forward. Her ancestry matched that of her compatriots. Long black hair drifted past her athletically fit shoulders. Her unsympathetic gaze revealed nothing but business.

"Dr. Thomas Parker," the uniformed woman said in an American southern accent, "my name is Dr. Ji-woo Song." She waited for his undivided attention. "You may know me as Maryland."

Memories flashed: intruders, his home, the fire. He'd taken down a man called Arkansas. It had been too dark to see facial features.

The intruders had used southern states as code names. Everyone had spoken in an American southern dialect.

"Let me introduce Texas and Missouri." Ji-woo gestured to two soldiers, who nodded in a show of respect.

The nurse removed his restraints.

"What do you want?" Parker asked, now understanding that the kidnapping had been an elaborate ruse. He looked over the commandos, all Korean in ancestry.

"Your cooperation," Ji-woo said.

A pair of commandos jerked him out of the bed, the no-nonsense grips of their hands sending a clear message. It was futile to resist. When his bare feet touched an epoxied steel floor, coldness shot to his spine. He looked around for a pair of shoes and saw none.

The soldiers paraded him out of his holding cell. Ahead, everything was the like-kind sterile bubble-plastic white. White doors flanked the sides of a long white corridor. The Korean room tags carried no translation.

Ji-woo led the march to a set of double-layered white blast doors that required an RFID card access swipe and a numerical entry. She tapped buttons on the digital keypad.

Ji-woo noticed him watching her keypad strokes. "Dr. Parker, please understand," she said in her Southern drawl, "we hold all of the leverage in this negotiation."

The doors parted open to reveal a bright cavernous room where nearly everything was white in color.

A billboard-sized screen displayed vital signs and brain scans. White elongated coffin-like boxes populated an expansive room. Beside each box stood a person with stubbed hair, wearing a white uniform like his own.

His escorts stepped away, allowing Parker to remain the center of attention.

Parker studied the people dressed like him. He didn't know them by name, but recognized them as a subset of ANCRI's participants.

He flushed, and no longer felt the cool floor.

Ji-woo whispered into his ear. "Refuse to cooperate and your participants will be executed, one by one. Who lives or dies is determined by you, Dr. Parker." Ji-woo dismissed the commandos with a gesture.

Parker thought of when he'd last seen these people. ANCRI had abducted college-aged students to use as guinea pigs in unethical human trials for neurological scientific exploration. He'd helped free them from a hellish imprisonment, only to see them captive again.

Without coercion or manipulation, the participants surrounded him. A face he recognized stood out from the small throng. Dr. Caroline Wang. Her brown eyes were tired, yet focused. Black stubble frosted her head. She reminded him of a cancer survivor who had begun to regrow her hair back. Caroline was the only the person he'd promised to save at the institute.

"What happened? Are you okay?" Parker asked.

Caroline initiated an embrace, as if human contact was essential to her survival. She cupped the back of his neck as her breathing matched the rhythm of his own. As their closeness lingered, her fingers stretched to pull him tighter. The next thing he knew, they were the core of a larger group hug. Youthful human forms pressed into theirs and he felt a swelling presence.

"Thomas. I knew you'd come for us." Caroline's voice was distraught. She took his face in her hands, her gaze clear and intense. "We dream common dreams."

11

THE COMMON COLLECTIVE

Dreams. Common dreams. None of that made sense.

Parker listened to Caroline Wang as they stood in The Great Hall. That had been the name their hosts assigned to their neurophysiology lab. As Caroline talked about concomitant imaginings, he struggled to comprehend the bigger questions. Why were they held captive? Who were their supposed benefactors? Where were they—in a foreign country? Wherever they were, this sterile world and its Great Hall didn't resemble Hogwarts School of Witchcraft and Wizardry.

"None of us have been able to tune out these dreams," Caroline said as she encouraged the others to give them some space.

Parker tried to comprehend this new realm and its encompassing reality. A highly advanced research lab. Fourteen participants. Well-armed, well-funded captors who worked on a tangent similar to his own neurological research. As he scanned the human subjects testing lab, he noticed Ji-woo lurking in the distance, watching him.

He harbored no doubts that her threat of execution would be carried out if he didn't help. At a series of test benches, technicians had already started to integrate his skullcap technology into their own network and compare his hardware to their own knock-off versions, which seemed remarkably similar in materials and methods of construction.

Whoever held them was going to replicate the techniques he'd created at ANCRI.

My tech isn't as plug-and-play as you people think.

Caroline took his hand. "I told them you would come."

"Very clairvoyant of you." He felt her fingers tighten against his. "Caroline, what kind of dreams do you have? How is what you think you see and experience interconnected with the others? Your dreams match their dreams?"

"The experiences appear communal in nature. Similar. But not always. Sometimes it's hard to know if what we're seeing, thinking, or imagining is real. The dreams are lucid, much like I would experience during REM," she said of the rapid eye movement cycles. "Maybe our shared encounters are our brains' ways of transitioning our pasts into long-term memory. I'm calling it our 'common collective.'"

"Sounds ominously like a mindmeld."

Unlike the other participants, Caroline had been ANCRI staff and the whistleblower who'd passed along secrets about the institute's horrors. As the institute's neurogeneticist, Caroline had become the star witness to all of ANCRI's crimes.

"You know, Thomas, we don't blame you."

"That's not comforting."

"Without you we'd all be dead, our bodies incinerated, our ashes disposed of in a Jersey landfill. No one would know about us. But you saved us."

Parker pulled his hand free. "No. I was ambitious. Reckless. Arrogant. Acted without comprehension of my consequences. These aftereffects you're experiencing came from the human-machine interface that I created. I wanted the participants to experience your memories, and Becky's. I thought if everyone witnessed Senator Ford's murder, that that story would be so big that no institution on earth could bury it. I was wrong."

Parker looked around The Great Hall again. They stood dead-center among fifteen white participant pods, body-sized immersion chambers. Pressing his palms against the closest pod, he examined it more closely. The headgear terminals remained incomplete, waiting for the modified skullcaps that the scientists were finalizing. Cables and tubing ran below hard white flooring to a data center of sorts that would be located elsewhere in the facility. The pods weren't as elaborate or as sleek as the ones used at ANCRI. The newer versions seemed to emphasize functional practicality over style or artistic symmetry.

Parker spotted a gray emblem, a symbol etched into a side wall. No wording accompanied the graphic, eight rings bound by a common circle. The opposite wall displayed opposing twin dragons in a yin-yang version of fire and ice.

He racked his weary mind. The images held no meaning for him.

Caroline took a breath. "No matter what you thought of Stewart Richards, he was a visionary. He wrote a white paper on the possibilities of extended consciousnesses. He hypothesized that what we've experienced might occur. Richards called it 'conversational echoes.' But I like my phrase 'common collective' better."

"Conversational echoes?" Parker faced her. "I promised your

father that I would try to save you. So I took risks. Now it seems that my actions have consequences."

"Thomas, we're alive because of you." She kissed him on the cheek. "My extended family is calling us to dinner. Come, join us."

Parker frowned. "You're talking with them now?"

Caroline winked. "Nah, just messing with you. We get fed twice a day around here. You should eat when meals are provided, because there are no midday snacks."

Parker forced a thin smile. "I'll catch up, after I see a woman about a job."

After Caroline left the chamber, he strolled to the woman in charge.

"My house fire was staged—theatrical?" Parker asked.

Ji-woo shrugged. "It was real enough. Provided motivation. We knew your tech was on the premises. We just didn't know where. You just needed to retrieve it for us."

"An elaborate ruse."

"A necessary one."

"Why me?"

"Your intellectual property. Taking you alive wasn't in our original plan. You were supposed to die."

Parker locked his gaze onto Ji-woo's. "But I wrecked your plan when I took out your man in my study."

"Yes. Most unfortunate. The sheriff's department's arrival left us no time to search for our lead neuroscientist. He died in the fire triggering your acquisition. We possessed your specs, but not details of the upgrades to your headgear. Your presence and cooperation ensure that the components will work satisfactorily."

Parker doubted he'd be allowed to live once his hosts had exhausted his usefulness. None of the test subjects would live, either. But he saw no harm playing along, *quid pro quo*, until he gained some leverage.

"Who are you with?" he asked. He pointed to the symbol etched into the wall. "This dragon outfit of yours?"

She shrugged again. "That's a riddle for you to solve."

He chuckled. "Who are you?"

"I already told you."

"Dr. Ji-woo Song. Yes, you did. But I want to know who I'm working with. What's your story? You have a technical specialty? Neuroscience? Medicine? Military?"

"When I was five I was adopted by an American family. I grew up in Baton Rouge and attended Caltech, where I received a Ph.D. in Neurobiology." She pointed to a group of technicians. "Our entire team has advanced degrees from American universities. All within the top ten percent of their classes." She flashed him a condescending smile. "Dr. Parker, you're not very good at small talk, are you? You're hoping to strike up a friendship that you can exploit, a way to persuade me to release participants or get me to say something in confidence that you can later use against me."

Parker rolled his eyes. "Saw through me that easily."

Ji-woo started to walk away. "Keep trying. Maybe I'll enjoy our talks."

"Once we outlive our usefulness, what happens then?" he asked.

She turned to him. "Dr. Parker, if I wanted you dead, you would have never survived the fire. Please, demonstrate some goodwill before I must make some rather unfortunate choices."

Ji-woo dipped her chin as a bow and left.

Parker understood that they were as good as dead.

12
CATCHING A FLIGHT

Chilmark Township, Martha's Vineyard, Massachusetts

Vice President Richard Mears stared at the blustery Atlantic Ocean through the panoramic windows of his family estate. His family had acquired the property after World War II, when wealthy families sold assets to raise cash and expand their businesses in America's post-war economy. The compound had an inkspot-shaped lawn and forested overlook on the Wequobsque Cliffs, above a rugged shoreline and within secured boundaries. For this trip, even though he could not shed all of his handlers, Mears requested that his Secret Service detail be reduced in size. That gave him a traveling entourage of six, excluding himself and the President's National Security Advisor, Gordon Abbott.

"We're alone, sir." Abbott stepped beside him at the windows. "I told the Secret Service that we're playing a round of chess before you turn in early for the night."

His entourage had been housed in the butler's residence, a building detached from the main house. The property was fully alarmed with electronic surveillance on perimeter fencing. "The two shift agents?"

"Watching the Celtics versus the Wizards. They'll make rounds twice a quarter. I estimate that that gives you seven minutes."

Mears took a breath. "And our DoD liaison?"

In parallel to his Secret Service detail, Department of Defense officers accompanied him in case a national emergency arose during a time when the President was incapacitated.

"In the kitchen, reading a Steve Berry novel." Abbott poured Mears a small glass of Jefferson's Reserve Small Batch Bourbon and handed it to him. He crossed to the chess table in front of the room's stone fireplace and arranged the board, taking pieces off and laying down the white king. "Congratulations on your win, Mr. Vice President."

Mears gulped down the bourbon and studied the remaining chess pieces. "It was a close game, Gordon."

"Yes, it was. Have a good night's rest, sir. I'll make sure the kitchen is ready to receive you around eight in the morning."

-|- -|-

Minutes later, Mears slipped past known motion detectors lining the property boundary and walked to cliffs that he frequented as a child. A tight, rugged path led to the thin strip of beach and rocks below, and he descended the narrow trail on the rock face until he reached a sideways plateau. He slipped horizontal for about thirty feet and walked up a new path until he reached the neighboring property. Their estate had a deeper forested stretch to the cliffs, and it was easy to disappear into the trees. Beside their micro-mansion he located a black SUV that had been left for him, its keys on the driver's side rear leaf spring.

The drive to the airport was only five minutes. An access card tucked above the vehicle's visor let him into the private hangar area.

After parking, he grabbed a single carry-on bag and walked the short distance to the flight line. A Cessna Citation Mustang corporate jet was exactly where he expected it. The smaller jet, secured in his wife's father's name, was required because both Martha's Vineyard and his destination had shorter runways.

Mears strode past a no-questions-asked pilot standing beside the plane's stairs and climbed aboard. He took a forward-facing seat as the pilot settled into the cockpit and started the jet's engines.

Gazing out the aircraft's small round windows, Mears reflected on the inordinate risks he was taking. It was simple to conceive a plan to reshape the world, but something entirely different to lead that charge.

By morning, the old world order would have changed.

13

THE FIELD REPORT

Nassau Inn, Princeton, New Jersey

Kate nibbled on a takeout from Teresa's and struggled to complete the half-empty field report on her bureau-issued laptop computer. Her conversation with Debra Ford exhilarated yet troubled her. The former State Department spy and off-the-books assassin had two nicknames: Manea, taken from the Roman goddess of souls of the dead, and The Silent Raven, a label Russian leaders had given her after she interrogated and killed four Central Bank of Russia officials who stole €500 million from a humanitarian aid account. Debra Ford had proved lethal, resourceful, and shrewd.

At the start of their rendezvous, Kate had wanted nothing more than to empty a magazine of .40 caliber rounds into the callous wretch for what she'd done to Jack Wright, the Deputy Director, and to her ex-husband's young girlfriend.

But something Debra Ford said resonated: "I protect this nation from threats you don't even know exist."

What'd that mean?

In some distorted way, the former spy's involvement translated to matters of State—foreign policy—international affairs—complex geopolitical areas beyond Kate's GS-14 pay grade.

An alcohol-fueled fog didn't help Kate connect the dots. The FBI Director had put her into play as a way to engage Thomas Parker. That made sense. The bureau needed his testimony. But did the Director know about Debra Ford? Was the Director making her the backdoor liaison to a known murderer?

That made no sense.

Kate reflected on the bureau's ethics policies. She'd be terminated for not disclosing the meeting with Ford and what she'd been asked to do. For her field assignment, her reporting structure had been streamlined. She submitted field reports directly to the Washington Field Office's Assistant Director in Charge (ADIC), who forwarded any relevant correspondence onto the Director.

She typed up her day's events and ended the timeline with her arrival at the Nassau Inn. Her synopsis highlighted essentials: an arson fire that covered up a tech heist, the likelihood of stolen equipment, a John Doe in the morgue, and the possibility that Thomas was still alive. She needed to say *something* about her mystery meeting with Debra Ford. The last time Kate had been in Princeton, she'd gone way off script. The consequences of that error in professional judgment had included a 30-days-without-pay suspension while the Office of Professional Responsibility (OPR) reviewed the details of the case, her conduct, and the overall circumstances. Jack Wright and the Director himself had interceded to get her reinstated while OPR wrapped up its investigation.

Meeting Debra Ford and not disclosing it, much less failing to disclose a plot involving the Vice President of the United States, would likely result in her firing and facing criminal charges. So in closing her report, Kate did the sensible thing and wrote: *met an informant about a plot to acquire missing technology and engage the Executive Branch. Until matters can be ascertained in greater detail, the informant's identity shall be referred to as Princess.*

She smiled. The woman's ex-husband, Samuel Ford, had once affectionately called Debra "Princess," and she'd hated it.

Princess. If Debra Ford ever wrote a tell-all it would be a stark contrast to *The Princess Diaries.*

Kate hit "send."

Turning out the lights, Kate slid under plush bedcovers, knowing full well that she wouldn't sleep.

How could she?

She had a date with the Vice President of the United States.

14

INVASION

Research Lab, Bader Field at the Atlantic City Airport, Atlantic City, New Jersey

Ji-woo Song felt her chest tighten with anxiety. Early warning systems had detected four helicopters coming in low from the southwest. Screens tracked the inbound aircraft across Shelter Island Bay and Turtle Gut. AI-enhanced predictive defense models had ranked this event as the number one scenario.

The American response was predictable: FBI, ATF, military Special Forces. The actual agency leading the threat didn't matter, only the outcome.

Ji-woo and her team had rehearsed for such developments, and she understood that grave dangers lay ahead. Unifying nations and creating a new commonwealth of people meant that the preexisting monopolies of tyranny would not abandon their positions on the world's stage quietly. Computer models predicted tens of thousands dead. The painful sacrifices were essential and unavoidable.

Moves and countermoves.

Early on, the goal was to limit the loss of life—the sacrifice of operatives, scientists, and soldiers, heroes occupying the trenches on the first day of war.

She reminded herself that their research vessel was never intended to be defendable. It was a gestation destination. A place to create a replicable Dream Weaver program. Only a near-perfect scenario ever included shipping an intact lab and its participants into international waters and delivering the active program to Hong Kong and the shores of North Korea.

Contingency plans dictated the next moves.

Soldiers would engage the intruders while scientists secured the technology for transport. History would note that the Americans discovered the magnitude of their error too late, failing to understand that they'd been a step behind in winning an inconsequential battle in a war that would last decades.

Ji-woo studied a red digital clock in the command post. Numbers cycled down from a minute and ten seconds. She estimated it'd take the Americans another fifteen seconds to reach the main doors on the hull. Another ten seconds to successfully breach the protective doors with explosives.

Stepping out of the control room, Ji-woo entered the Great Hall. Red warning lights flashed overhead. In this moment of crisis, none of her staff had panicked. Carrying out their duties, the scientists collected essential components as fast as possible.

They had prepared two hard-sided carrying cases. The headgear stolen from Thomas Parker's residence was inserted into gray foam padding, and the first case was closed. Hard drives and network cards filled similar padded slots in the second case.

These cases were hers to protect.

Ji-woo felt the burden of sadness. Their six-month operation was never given the opportunity to reach its potential and deliver the Dream Weaver program. They'd come so close.

A communications officer reported that the American forces

had landed on the upper decks. Four helicopters total, each carrying an estimated five soldiers, plus the pilots—an invasion force of twenty. Too many to repel.

The enemy worked their way across the surface decks. An explosion thundered somewhere above her.

Forces were breaching the main doors.

Ji-woo snatched up the cases. It was time to go.

Thomas Parker struggled to silence his haggard mind. His fourteen bunkroom companions had no such trouble. Oddly, the participants had adopted more of a herd mentality, complacent. That was the last reaction Parker had expected them to possess.

Unanswered questions persisted. Where were they? Who held them? How could they escape? None of those answers would come to him if he slept.

Lying on a cot, he focused on the indicator light embedded in the surveillance camera above him. The watchful eyes offered no privacy. After their evening meal, the participants were led to a common bunkroom. Arranged cots matched the pod layout in the Great Hall, with one exception. His cot was closest to the room's single door. Their square-shaped, hostel-like confines were pristine white, like everything else. Exposed to the sleeping area, men's toilets and showers were to his right, women's to the left. Knee-high nightlights along the perimeter splashed their bedchamber with a soft glow.

Parker let his thoughts return to the participants. His software coding at ANCRI must've had undetected errors, or someone had slipped in deviations to test hypotheses that he was unaware of. In his rush to save everyone, he had given no time to validation protocols.

He was solely responsible for unintended consequences, and the damage he'd done to them.

Eventually, his thoughts migrated to Kate: smart, attractive, career-oriented, and sensual when she turned on that part of her persona. In Princeton, they'd had life and death moments together. Afterwards, their tropical escape confirmed that there wasn't anything he disliked about her. They'd spoken about spending Thanksgiving in Virginia where she lived, but the holiday passed without a single word from her. He'd left her voicemails, texts, and emails when he heard about the terrorist attacks.

She'd moved on. It was time for him to do the same.

Parker shut his eyes in a bid to clear his mind.

His bed shook. Outside their bedchamber, distant thunder rumbled, followed by a *clack-clack-clack*—gunfire.

He opened his eyes as the lighting jolted everyone awake.

"Has this happened before?" he asked.

"No," someone said.

Watching the main doors, Parker slid out of bed. His bare feet pressed against the cold floor. They had nowhere to run. They were trapped. Clattering sounds drew closer. They heard shouting voices between eruptions.

From the corner of his eye, Parker noticed a group forming. A hand latched onto his and reeled him toward them.

Blasts peppered the door, separating them from whatever was going on in other areas of the research facility.

The noise subsided. Locks disengaged and the door swung open. Small red beams sprayed the room, seeking targets.

Armed soldiers in camouflage combat uniforms and helmets stormed the bunkroom. As they spread out, Parker noticed the olive-version of the American flag on their right arms.

Without an introduction, one of the soldiers asked, "Dr. Parker, are you okay?"

Parker felt one of the participants squeeze his hand. "You here to rescue us?"

"That assessment is close enough," the soldier said, studying the group. "Everyone here? Everyone accounted for?"

"Yes," Caroline Wang said, behind him.

"Alright. Let's get you people someplace safe."

Conversations were kept to a minimum as the soldiers escorted them through a battered research facility. Scorch marks and bullet holes riddled white walls. Blood was everywhere. Korean soldiers and scientists lay dead on the floors. Ji-woo Song was nowhere in sight.

Barefoot, they were led single file to a large service elevator. A jolt and mechanical sounds announced they were being taken upward.

"Who are you?" Parker asked, studying the man's uniform. He saw only black Velcro strips where he'd expect to see unit logos and military insignia. The man's outfit didn't even display a rank.

"That's classified," the leader of the ops team said.

The elevator clunked to a stop, and doors opened.

"Let's go! Let's go! Let's go!" a different soldier shouted. "Place a hand on the back of the person in front of you and keep moving."

Cool, musty air greeted them as they walked out onto the deck of a ship—a barge of some sort, populated with cargo containers.

The ship's surface was as wide as a football field and twice as long. Three helicopters idled at a safe distance from the fire and flames that pooled around the remains of a fourth. Two covered bodies lay on the deck—pilots, most likely.

On the horizon glowed the lights from a city.

Soldiers led them to the helicopters, the spinning rotors whipping up the night air. Just past the radius of the rotating blades, a soldier stood with cloth bags.

One by one, hoods were slid over their heads.

15

SECURING THE ASSETS

Minutes earlier, Ji-woo Song wrenched down the locking handles to a sealed portside escape hatch. The modified shallow-water barge had multiple levels, and the hatch placement put her four feet up from a berm that made up the north side of Badger Field. It was a long jump, but one she'd prepared to take since the start of her mission.

The clatter of automatic weapons fire from the ship's top deck was reassuring. Her soldiers fought back, sacrificing themselves in order to give her and the others time.

Gripping the handles on the cases tight, she built up runway distance before launching herself through the hatch. Her momentary flight through the air came to an abrupt halt. Bending her knees, Ji-woo rolled forward, somersaulting across uneven rocky ground. Holding the cases as close to her body as possible, she heard them scuff the ground.

When she came to a stop, Ji-woo resisted the urge to look back at the unfolding action. Keeping low, she sprinted east along uneven shoreline.

Ji-woo didn't risk a glance until she cleared runway 22 and reached a camouflaged dinghy. On the floating research lab behind her, weapons fire lit up the night. A rocket-propelled grenade struck one of the helicopters, sending a fireball into the night sky. Three choppers lifted off and banked northwest over the Great Thorofare inlet.

After stowing the cases into the small craft, Ji-Woo shoved the boat into the water. She worked a throttle until the electric engines whirled, and their props drove the dinghy into the channel, toward the northeast.

Ji-woo studied her abandoned research vessel. On the top deck, the fiery carcass of a helicopter burned in the night sky. Explosions bellowed out of lower decks as those who stayed behind destroyed supercomputer networks and the vessel's massive data center.

Violently, the ship buckled and listed starboard in shallow water, sending American soldiers tumbling off the upper decks. The distant gunfire paused.

American forces had begun to reassess their incursion. On the horizon, the remaining helicopters hovered at a distance to avoid any potential surface-to-air encounters—a wise move.

Pulling up a thermal deflecting tarp, Ji-woo slumped low, leaving a slit wide enough to navigate the craft up the intracoastal channel and under the Atlantic City Expressway. Cold musty air washed her face as she watched the water ahead.

She steered the craft's rudder with one hand and unlaced her boots with the other. After stripping out of her uniform, she slipped on a blue dress. Black flats completed a new ensemble.

Silently, her craft glided past canal-side homes, apartments and private docks, then sailed by a water treatment plant. Towering above her, large wind turbine blades slowly swept the sky. The air smelled thick and musty, fragrant from the surrounding marshlands. The short voyage was eerily quiet.

North and west, the skylines were dark. Ahead, few landmarks were available to fix any bearings.

She rounded into the Absecon Channel and welcomed the glow emanating from Harrah's Resort and Casino.

On land, a blue light identified a predetermined landing and Ji-woo Song aimed the tiny craft at the shoreline.

National Geospatial-Intelligence Agency (NGA), Ft. Belvoir, Virginia

In a sixth-floor secured information facility (SCIF), a team of four geospatial-intelligence officers operated workstations as US Air Force and Army liaisons watched a progression of screened activities on a paneled wall. The real-time satellite images tracked the progress of a Joint Special Operations Command (JSOC) mission managed out of Ft. Bragg, North Carolina. A series of clocks logged mission milestones. A tag in the corner of the screens disclosed the operation's codename: DRAGONS DEN.

On a northwest trajectory, four helicopters swept across a darkened landscape marked Pork Island Wildlife Management Area. On the right-hand edge of the screens, the radiating brilliance of Atlantic City came into view. Spaced out, the aircraft touched down on the deck of a shipping barge at the north end of Bader Field on the canal side of Atlantic City. Green-hued thermal images revealed the movement of special mission units (SMUs) as they disembarked from the aircraft. Red-hued images sequenced the exchange of small weapons fire. Small flashes and streaking lines emanated from invading and defending forces.

The Army liaison leaned over and whispered to his Air Force counterpart. "They were expecting us."

"Dragons Slayer," said a GEOINT officer at a terminal, "be advised, four targets are breaking off. On foot. Two due west along the northern shore. One is south on the asphalt and headed to runway 11-29. Your east target has reached runway 4-22. Over."

"Roger that."

On the satellite screens, square target frames tracked each of four individuals who had fled the firefight.

Before the choppers could finish their drop and pop, something flashed from the vessel's port quarter deck. A brilliant orange tail engulfed one the helicopters. The remaining three choppers dipped north of the deck of the ship. The exchange of small arms weapon fire increased, as flurries and volleys ebbed and flowed between opposing sides.

Steadily, more and more red-hued figures slowed and stopped moving. A few green figures were down, mostly those closest to the exploding helicopter. After a brief pause, green-hued figures overwhelmed the remaining red ones.

"The top deck, elevators, and stairwells are secure," a voice confirmed. "Medics are treating the wounded."

"Thomas Parker has been located," a desk supervisor announced. "Fourteen others are with him."

On the screens, the operation changed. A technician swore as below-deck blasts rocked the ship, listing it starboard. Several tagged green figures tumbled off the surface deck and into the water.

The small arms fire subsided as the fight showed momentary confusion.

"The ship was booby-trapped. Hull breeches are being reported."

"It can't sink, but it'll flood." Orders were relayed to secure positions and rescue personnel before continuing below-deck advancements.

On the screens, the tracking frames blinked. In less than a second, all four fleeing red targets had vanished.

"Dragons Slayer, we've lost visual on those loose targets. They've gone dark. Relaying last coordinates. Reacquire by any means necessary. Over."

North Waterfront, Harrah's Resort and Casino, Atlantic City, New Jersey

Debra Ford clicked off her blue LED light. She slid it and a suppressed semiautomatic pistol into a pocket of her long black coat as the dark outline of a small watercraft quietly maneuvered toward shore. She tapped the smartwatch on her wrist and grinned.

Right on schedule.

A Korean woman in a dress beached a dinghy and hiked up the steps to the boardwalk, carrying two metal cases. The woman laid them at Debra's feet and opened the cases to reveal their treasures.

Ford scanned a dark horizon, realizing she'd just hit a different sort of jackpot. "Were you followed?"

"Not that I noticed." The woman's voice carried the dialect of the American South. She pointed to the cases. "As agreed upon, Common InSight."

Ford shook her head. "No. Those are parts and pieces. Hardware. Not the intellectual property or the science behind it."

Ji-woo closed the cases. "We had a deal."

"Not really. We had your tiny version of reality, and then the rest of the world's. I could've just let you and the others die on your boat."

"You should've stayed out of my business."

Ford chuckled. "Dr. Song, what matters is Prosperity. Your Hong Kong-funded microscopic escapades were subordinate to our grander vision. You were destined to fail. I just accelerated that reality. Peace on Earth can be obtained only with sacrifice. You of all people must understand that."

Ji-woo frowned. "If you're wrong, I will kill you, Manea."

"Get in line." Ford shrugged off the alias. She'd been called worse.

She looked over the water. "We'd best leave. Law enforcement will set up roadblocks and lockdown Atlantic City for the night."

She led Ji-woo down a wooden path to a limousine parked along Harrah's Baywalk service drive. A driver waited beside the vehicle. The cases were handed over to the driver, who loaded them in the limo's trunk.

The driver opened a rear door and Debra slid into the backseat. Ji-woo sat beside her, warming her hands with her breath. No words were exchanged as the driver drove a preordained course, picking up Renaissance Point Boulevard and merging with roads leading to Absecon Boulevard, then west across the waterways and marshlands.

Ford raised the divider between the driver and passengers. "What's the status of Thomas Parker?"

"American forces have him and the others."

Ford smiled. The news couldn't have been better. A once-unobtainable Peace on Earth was coming together—an operation that would reset the stage for the United States of America after its years of decline in global influence. The world was far more peaceful when a single superpower controlled geopolitical landscapes.

It was time for the world to go down a new road: A road to war. A realm where the enemies of the State devoured themselves, and fell from within.

She thought of Napoleon's prediction: "Let China sleep, for when she wakes, she will shake the world."

The road to war started with the Sleeping Giant, the People's Republic of China.

TUESDAY, DECEMBER 1st

In studying the history of the human mind, one is impressed again and again by the fact that the growth of the mind is the widening of the range of consciousness, and that each step forward has been a most painful and laborious achievement. One could almost say that nothing is more hateful to a man than to give up even a particle of his unconsciousness.
Carl Jung, the father of analytical psychology

16
MIDNIGHT MOMENTS

Princeton Airport, New Jersey

Vice President Mears watched lights on the horizon as the pilot of his small jet lined up the flight path and touched down. The jet taxied the airport's single runway until it arrived at a vacant spot along the flight line. Smaller, single-engine aircraft flanked the jet, making it stand out from the herd. This stop wouldn't take long enough for anyone to notice. He'd be in the air and back at Martha's Vineyard by sunrise.

The pilot climbed out of his cockpit and swung down the door.

Without a word, Mears nodded thanks and left with his carry-on. As he descended the stairs, he saw an executive Town Car parked on the fringe of the taxiway, its tires more on the grass than pavement. A chauffeur in a black suit and cap opened the passenger's door. Walking closer, he noticed the driver's tailored suit fit the outline of a woman, who wore thick rimmed glasses. Her dark hair was tied back.

Mears tossed his bag into the back and got in. The door shut and the driver got behind the wheel. They exchanged no words, exactly as he'd directed. The all-business driver pulled through the security gate, toward their destination.

When the car cleared Kingston Township, his secured cell phone buzzed. He glanced at the incoming text.

DRAGONS DEN EXTRACTION SUCCESSFUL. VESSEL AND PACKAGE SECURED. THREE SPEC OPS LOST. FIVE WITH MINOR INJURIES. FOUR UNIDENTIFIED TARGETS ESCAPED. NOT SURE OF THEIR WHEREABOUTS.

Mears clicked off his phone and caught the driver's probing gaze through the rearview mirror.

He'd never used this driving service before. It came by referral. The driver looked familiar but he couldn't put her in context, match her to anyone he knew. Through the years, he'd developed the habit of reviewing bios and attendee lists before important meetings, walking in with the advantage of knowing people's names, interests, platforms. The habit fostered a personable and engaging facade, even with adversaries. No doubt she'd recognized him.

That wasn't a concern as long as he kept interactions to a minimum.

The driver picked up Route 1, drove a short distance, then turned onto a private asphalt lane. The Town Car rolled through a heavily armed checkpoint without stopping, as guards armed with assault weapons scrutinized the passing vehicle.

Even in the dark, the expanse of older red-bricked buildings against wooded acreage was impressive. His son, Andrew, a board-level senior consultant for the Phoenix Consortium, had first introduced him to the research-centric, private equity-funded conglomerate. The Phoenix Consortium had created a string of strategic alliances across the globe with the goal of pushing the bounds of medicine and science, while maximizing a return on investment for its private equity stakeholders.

A property monument sign read ADVANCED BIOCORE INTERNATIONAL.

The car tracked on a wide loop and stopped at a three-story, red-brick building. The driver got out. But instead of opening his door, she opened the opposite. Climbing into the back seat, she shoved a semiautomatic into his gut. Removing her driver's cap, she revealed dark hair flowing past her shoulders.

He still couldn't place her.

"There's an open contract on me."

He feigned indifference. "You're pointing a gun at the Vice President of the United States."

"Perhaps that's the smartest thing I've done all day." She grinned. "Be polite, Mr. Mears. If I shoot you, I've got to clean up the mess so I can get the car's deposit back. I'm afraid my government salary doesn't provide that much discretionary income."

Mears took a stalling breath and studied her features, finally recognizing the woman: FBI Special Agent Katherine Morgan. Her single-channel contract had no expiration date, and he had no intention of rescinding it. Having this federal agent dead benefited him tremendously.

Her gaze turned cold. "I'm here to help as part of a trade."

"How so?"

Her eyes warmed a fraction. "My presence affords you plausible deniability. You're doing your best to shelter the President from what happened in Princeton. I get that. I can help there too, although that's not really why we're talking."

"Agent Morgan, you can't offer me anything of value."

"So sure about that?" She lowered the weapon. "I know about Common InSight. Its real-world applications. Peace on Earth."

He shrugged. She was bluffing, and had no idea of what had been set in motion.

"If that doesn't grab your attention, how about this? I can persuade Thomas Parker. Gain his trust. And after we've delivered the technology to implement mass-scale social conditioning, I'll work with Parker to cure Andrew."

His son. Few knew of his Andrew's medical condition, although she'd likely be one of those who did. Now she had his attention. "In exchange for?"

"Neither of my terms are negotiable. One, retract the hit on me. Two, I want in on this research. Assign me as your point person. A liaison, as it were. Someone who permits the executive branch to retain a defendable distance. Specifically, my presence gives you plausible deniability. If all this disintegrates, sacrifice me."

"I don't think so. You've got to give me a better offer than that."

"Your wife, Susan, is traumatized. The nursing staff at GWU introduced me to her in the hospital. Susan's grieving. Broken-hearted. Lost." She took a breath and exhaled slowly. "Mr. Vice President, I'm not here as a federal agent. I'm here because I have unfinished business to take care of. You need Andrew back to make your family whole again, as much as I have some wrongs to right. And by now you've figured out that Thomas Parker gives you the best chance to save your son. I'll help win him over."

17
THE MOST DANGEROUS MAN IN THE WORLD

Advanced BioCore International (ABI), Princeton New Jersey

Parker's rescuers had fitted him, hooded, with earmuffs to silence the helicopter's engine noise. In the dark he had no sense of direction as they flew. Packing the aircraft, bodies he presumed to be other test subjects pressed in against him. Someone leaned him forward as an injection-like pain stung his back, just off-center of his spine. The aircraft banked, then leveled out.

He tried to retain a sense of time. He estimated that thirty minutes had passed before the helicopter feathered its rotors and descended. After landing, he vaguely heard side doors open and the dying whine of blades and engines. Earmuffs were removed, and he was ushered out of his seat.

"Watch your step," someone said. "Hoods will be removed once you're inside."

Unable to see, Parker focused on sounds and voices. Cool air pierced his uniform as hands guided him barefoot across damp grass, then the hardness of pavement or a sidewalk. Ahead, he heard electrical locks unlatch. They stopped on what Parker felt was vinyl flooring.

"Dr. Parker, our apologies for all of this cloak and dagger business," a man's voice said. "It was necessary to keep you and the others safe."

Someone removed Parker's hood.

Sheltering his face with his hands, he blinked to adjust to the light. He stood inside a corporate-style, two-story foyer that arched back. Workers wearing lab coats watched from a balcony.

A corporate logo hung in the lobby: ADVANCED BIOCORE.

Wall-mounted flat screens cycled muted corporate promotional videos. Captions and marketing zingers flashed on the screen as diligent workers hosted mockup business activities.

AT ADVANCED BIOCORE, WE'RE INVENTING AND CREATING A BETTER FUTURE TOGETHER. WE CREATE PRODUCTS AND SOLUTIONS THAT CHANGE THE WORLD.

Around him, the fourteen participants were unhooded and greeted by staff in colored scrubs. Soldiers came and went from a main building entrance.

A dark face greeted him with a broad smile. "It's an honor to meet you," the man said in a thick British accent. He cleared his throat and extended a hand. "Bill Grayson. Your safety was our biggest concern. You must've had a trying experience."

Parker studied the man. The handshake provided was courtesy-bland, warm but not inviting. Like shaking the hand of a car salesman. He was dark-skinned and wore a black suit glued to muscle-toned features. Two security guards in similar suits stood behind Grayson.

"Where are we?" Parker asked, looking back at the building's entrance. Outside, it was dark with no external bearings view as a reference.

Grayson waved for Parker to follow. "We'll get to that."

As they walked, Parker's head was on a swivel. Hallways and intersections came and went. The building was part commercial office, part clinical, heavily geared to research. Card readers defined interior boundaries. When they reached a cafeteria, Parker spotted a stand-mounted U.S. flag. Portraits of the president and vice president hung on each side of the flag. This was a military-sponsored research lab, but no military branch flag was posted beside the U.S. standard. Instincts told him that a covert operations group ran the facility.

The cafeteria had been converted to a triage space where medical personnel checked the participants, logging routine vitals: temperatures, pulses and heart rates, pupil response.

Parker noticed the thoroughness of care. "I have some questions."

Grayson forced a smile. "Those will be addressed during your formal in-briefing."

"Who runs the show here?" Parker asked. "Which branch of military?"

"You see me wearing a uniform?" Grayson asked as he walked away, gesturing for Parker to follow him.

The main building seemed to be composed of internal rings, quadrants secured by a series of controlled access doors. They caught a stairwell up to the second floor, rounded a wide radial hallway and were badged into a secured room. The two guards waited outside as Parker followed Grayson into an arched room.

Once the door was shut, Parker's benefactor flashed him a badge: Dr. William Grayson, Department of Justice, National Security Division.

"Your accent. British English?"

"I was stationed in the United Kingdom until recent events required my services back here in the States."

"Where are we?"

"New Jersey, not far from the rubble that you once called home."

"Am I under arrest?" Parker studied the room, which was split into three sections. The centermost was laid out like a conference room. Computer workstations and cubicles facing a common direction formed one end, and two offices the other. A long, curved, hazed-over window ran the entire span of the small suite of rooms.

"Doctor, you're in a much different situation than that." Grayson handed Parker a bottle of water. "You understand the expression 'you reap what you sow.'"

"How does that apply to me?"

"You went public with technological achievements that didn't belong to you. This mess that you've created is greater than you and couple dozen innocent victims. Your actions have consequences. Global consequences."

Grayson handed him a letter signed by the U.S. Attorney General.

"I have rights. I want to speak to an attorney." He scanned the letter, which declared that the Department of Justice was detaining him indefinitely as a material witness under 18 U.S. Code §3144, section 3142, with justification that Thomas Parker, MD, PhD, was directly connected to a laundry list of federal crimes—treason at the top of that list.

Grayson shook his head like a chiding parent. "You really don't grasp the gravity of your situation, do you?"

Parker slid the letter aside and faced the man. "Enlighten me."

"Per established precedence, upheld by the Supreme Court, Miranda rights can be superseded when it comes to matters of national security. There's an entire set of secrecy orders that apply to your work under the Invention Secrecy Act of 1951."

"Secrecy order?"

"That pretty much means we can take everything that's yours. And frankly, since federal money was partially used to fund your research, the federal government retains all rights to the use of that technology, associated tangents of intellectual property, and all disclosures."

"You're bluffing?"

Grayson cleared his throat. "Dr. Parker, the government considers you the most dangerous man in the world."

Parker felt as if a boxer's jab had struck him between the eyes. He blinked and tried to focus. The most dangerous man in the world? A stunning accusation. The law wasn't his area of strength. He tried to connect the dots from his research and its outcomes, but couldn't see how everything linked.

"Ever hear of Common InSight?" Grayson asked.

Parker shook his head.

"Well, Dr. Parker, you proved its viability when no one else could." Grayson leaned against a table. "We've known about you, your research on cognitive architectures and neurophysiology before your arrival at Princeton. Before the NSA put a mole in your university lab. Long before the FBI stumbled into a mess that they were ill-prepared to handle. We're the ones who guided Stewart Richards your way."

Parker felt his rage swell. "Richards kidnapped innocent people and used them as human test subjects. He murdered people."

Grayson shrugged. "True, Richards was a callous monster. Because of the game-changing promise of what your tech does, our government gave him wider-than-normal latitude and the financing to run the Neurological and Cybernetic Research Institute." He sighed. "There's a label that fits most of us: disposable. When covert field operatives outlive their usefulness, and draw scrutiny upon or bring liability to a central program, they become less relevant. Expendable. Your contributions made Stewart Richards disposable. You did our nation a favor when you put him out of everyone's misery."

Parker snorted. "Which makes me the most dangerous man in the world?"

"His research was floundering. Unwittingly, you proved to be the perfect closer. The person who delivered neurological singularity. Hell, you pulled off a scientific miracle and delivered our end goal: Common InSight, Conversational Echoes, Caroline Wang's Common Collective."

Parked shot the man a hard glare. "I won't help you, if that's what you're headed."

Grayson chuckled. "I'm afraid that makes you and the participants disposable." He clicked a wall button and the panoramic arching window cleared from a crystalline gray.

Parker stepped to the windows. On the upper level, the conference room overlooked a spacious lab filled with experimentation pods. A billboard-sized screen spanned the opposite wall. He was looking at an upgraded neurophysiology lab: the U.S. government's model, eclipsing the Koreans' more academic version and ANCRI's.

Grayson came beside him. "You're the most dangerous man in the world because you're the world's greatest threat. There's no going back. Not for you. Not for anyone. You brought humankind a new space race. A race to control what's inside our heads. The proliferation of nuclear weapons was once seen as the greatest threat to the world: mutually assured destruction. Now the U.S. government has no choice but to sequester all adaptations of similar technologies and forcibly secure you and the participants, indefinitely."

Parker took a ragged breath. "I want to talk to a lawyer."

Grayson shook his head. "If it were up to me, Dr. Parker, I'd destroy every aspect of your work and dispose of everyone involved, starting with you."

18

COVERING YOUR BASES

Kate wondered when Mears would have guards get around to a body search.

Now she knew.

It all happened faster than anticipated. One guard pointed a pistol at her temple. Another hit her with a hockey-style body check. Kate's cheek flattened against unyielding one-way glass, her head shoved hard by a strong grip.

The manhandling sent a message: *Don't mess with the Vice President.*

The covering soldier removed her Glock. The search turned intimate. Her chauffeur's jacket was stripped off. Belt unbuckled and yanked off her waist. Pants dropped. White dress shirt lifted to her armpits. Raking high to low, hands swept bare skin, missing nothing, slipping beneath undergarments, stopping at her ankles. After the guard inspected her belt, he dropped it to the floor and ran his fingers through her hair.

"She's clean," the searching guard said, backing away.

From the corner of her eyes, she saw the covering guard lower his gun.

Without pulling up her pants, she faced Mears.

His expression was hard, calculating. His eyes hinted at a binary decision process: kill her, or accept her offer to help?

"Check the car," Mears ordered. "If you find recording, surveillance, or communication devices, shoot her and ditch her body somewhere it won't be found."

19

HARD CONVERSATIONS

Plain-clothed security guards escorted Thomas Parker and his fellow captives to an upper floor, a locked-down residential wing with a common-use corridor. His third-floor suite was almost welcoming, a mirage inside his institutional arrest. A table at the center of a sitting room held a colorful mix of fresh flowers and a fruit basket with crackers. Sets of clothes had been provided: jeans, t-shirts, and assorted dress shirts. He stripped out of his Korean host's utilitarian whites, showered, and picked a change of clothes at random.

His residence's exterior windows offered a narrow portal to the world. Somewhere near Princeton, New Jersey. Pole lights illuminated a sweeping expanse of grass. A forest boundary lined the distance, about two football fields in length away from the building he was in. Perimeter walls jutted out to the edges of grass, revealing that building structures were clad in industrial-style red brick.

At least his prison came with a view.

His latest hosts had encouraged him to sleep, with a dangled carrot of morning meetings to discuss mutual cooperation. How an engaged relationship might work moving forward.

He didn't want to sleep. Aftereffects of his debriefing with Grayson still lingered.

How'd life get this messed up?

In a span of months, his life had cratered, peaked, and cratered again. He'd lost his university teaching position, most of his research, a best friend and one-time lover, and found and lost an equal, Kate, someone he cared about. In the all the insanity, he'd accomplished the technical breakthrough he'd spent years developing, then destroyed everything—well, most of it.

The best parts of his life were gone. Nothing much remained in its wake.

A light rap disrupted his self-pity.

He opened the door to his room.

Kate stared back at him, her pursed lips twitching slightly. "Can I come in?"

The feelings in his gut worsened. "What are you doing here?"

"Thomas, I'm so sorry." Her eyes revealed nothing. "I owed you responses to your messages. Even saved your voicemails so I could listen to them. I wanted to call, really, but I was afraid. I've missed you."

Parker stepped aside to let her enter. He studied her posture: defensive, insecure, hurt. All of those combined. She wore a black suit, tailored to her midsection and hips, with a white shirt beneath it. He'd never seen her in a suit. All he knew of her attire preferences was lab coats, khakis, t-shirts, dresses, and swimsuits. The suit seemed out of character for her.

"I was given orders. No contact. None."

He'd missed hearing her voice. During their paradise vacation, both of them had avoided talk of love or commitments, anything that extended past tropical boundaries. Their time together had refreshed his soul, which often felt adrift in other relationships. After their return, he'd contemplated leaving Princeton and moving to Virginia to be close to her. He yearned for an embrace.

Kate looked around at the ceiling and walls. "Everything we do is under surveillance."

He shrugged. "Well, that's never happened to us before." She looked like a stranger, not the woman that he'd been intimate with. "Why are you here, Kate?"

Her face stiffened to a mask that protected a flicker of vulnerability. "It's complicated."

"Complicated?"

"Very."

He got to the heart of the matter. "Kate, move past complicated."

"The US government plans to hold you as a material witness."

"That disclosure came with my in-briefing."

"And the participants, too. In terrorism cases, that status can remain in limbo, virtually unlimited. As in forever."

"You're the one who once told me to call them patients, not participants, not test subjects. Well, Kate, they're victims. Damaged goods. People held captive because the government that you work for deems that to be a better situation than returning their freedoms and giving them their lives back—the very lives that were stolen from them."

"I know." Kate lowered her gaze. "What did you do to Stewart Richards?"

"Does it matter?"

"To me, it does," she said, her voice barely above a whisper.

He swung the door open. "You should leave now."

Kate stopped in the doorway and almost kissed him, the gesture feigned but not acted on. Parker watched her leave, hoping she'd glance back and catch him watching her, but she kept walking.

When she was several doors down the hall, Parker said, "They dream. Shared dreams. Experienced physiological changes, neurological alterations. Their condition has several names: Common

InSight, Conversational Echoes, Common Collectives."

She spun around. "I don't understand."

He lowered his gaze. "Kate, I know why you came. Your routine is rather transparent. You came as a friend, a lover, someone to soften me up?" He took a breath. "Let the government kill me or let me live. I don't care. I'm content to rot wherever I'm jailed. So cutting to the chase, I won't help you or anyone else restart my research because I can't do any more harm to them. I took an oath as a doctor: do no harm. And I fell way short of that oath."

Before Kate could reply, Parker closed the door.

20

INTERPRETING THE MESSAGE

Kate struggled to interpret Parker's message as she made her way to the elevators: "They dream. Shared dreams . . . Common InSight, Conversational Echoes, Common Collectives."

That statement puzzled her on so many levels.

At ANCRI, something had gone wrong, beyond the initial memory transfers.

Parker's reminder of the classical Hippocratic Oath to *do no harm* added an extra burden to everything else troubling her. During medical school, a Johns Hopkins ethics professor had explained the evolution of the oath, emphasizing how it morphed over to time to embrace social and institutional relevance. Its original Latin translation had come from Greek: *primum non nocere; first, do no harm.* But the actual treatise in the First Book on Epidemics presented a different angle: *In illnesses one should keep two things in mind, to be useful rather than cause no harm."* Parker had failed the participants by causing harm. She'd done the same in the avenues of her own career, first as a doctor, second as an FBI special agent.

They'd both failed those entrusted to their care.

Kate had thought about Parker since returning from the Caribbean, more than she'd care to admit. Lonelier without him, she was aware that he'd become kryptonite to her career at the bureau. He'd done everything right: called, left voicemails, sent texts, showing concern over her well-being during attacks in Washington, DC. By freezing him out, her stone wall of silence had become a feeble defense that fostered brooding and confusion.

Thomas Parker was entitled to feel hurt. He'd deserved to hear from her before now.

Life weighed heavy. What she'd learned about Parker during her last case made it impossible for her to see him the same way before their tropical vacation. But the voice inside her head previously telling her to steer clear of Parker no longer existed, muted by her conversation with Debra Ford. "Pick one."

Thomas Parker—a genius-level neurologist with a caring heart—and a man who had stirred long dormant feelings inside her.

He'd risk his life to save others, and wouldn't rest without making amends.

Parker had chosen to be *useful*.

That was her leverage.

He needed redemption. She needed it as much as he did.

What she was about to undertake was a calculated risk. If successful, redemption was the prize. If disastrous, it was a risk that could get everyone killed.

Kate hit the elevator's down button.

In Advanced BioCore's Neurophysiology Lab—the cathedral, she'd heard staff call it—Kate stepped into view of the Vice President. As his driver, she waited on the periphery while Dr. William Grayson wrapped up a cursory presentation of the facility. A month earlier, she'd seen a much larger version at ANCRI. This latest technical achievement had doubled down on the sophistication of earlier genesis trials funded through a different private entity, the Phoenix Consortium.

Kate understood her role more clearly now. Domestic espionage was a new realm for her, and completely outside her bureau duties. Debra Ford seemed determined to maneuver her way into a dangerous game, something she'd undoubtedly done many times over in different countries and foreign venues. Ford's declaration that she was protecting the nation from threats that others didn't know existed was downright bone-chilling. Regardless of the current political fallout from the complete disaster at ANCRI, the executive branch was staying fully invested in the mindreading business, nation-building, and Common InSight.

When Mears finished with his tour, he walked out to the waiting Town Car.

As his chauffeur, Kate opened the car door. Mears got inside. She climbed behind the wheel and drove past the security gate.

"Will Dr. Parker champion the program?"

Kate glanced at the Vice President through the rearview mirror. "He's assessing his options, which are limited."

"But he'll see things our way?"

"I believe so, if I'm on the team."

"And after we've accomplished our work here, you two will help my son?"

"Yes. We'll work on a treatment to bring back Andrew."

Mears sighed. "I'll give you 'til noon tomorrow to convince Parker. Do that and you're in—no bounty, and broad operational latitude. I'll make arrangements for the DOJ to secure your services indefinitely. And saving my son is paramount."

"Understood, sir."

An uncomfortable silence hung between them as he watched

her in the mirror. "Agent Morgan, fail to make this work and you won't survive the week."

"Message received."

Mears leaned forward and over the driver's seat. He had something in his hand.

She took the object and studied it. It was black and round, like a hockey puck. The device had no identifiable markings, only a small universal power port.

"What's this?" Kate asked.

Mears smirked at her through the rearview mirror. "I'm told you're bright, resourceful. Figure it out."

21

AWAKENING

5:10 AM, NeuroSteps Labs, Glen Garner, New Jersey

A faint touch of skin against his forehead woke Stewart Richards from a prison of slumber.

"How are you feeling?" a woman asked, her voice reverberating across the hemispheres of his mind. He couldn't recall the last time he'd heard someone speak. The echoes of her words grew more intense, like ripples shooting back at him through a narrow chamber. Words overran words. She followed up with another question. "Are you experiencing any discomfort?"

He swallowed over a raw throat and forced open heavy eyelids. The scene around him was blurry. Dim lighting focused on his bedside, not the room. A Japanese woman in scrubs studied monitors that displayed his vitals.

Richards blinked and forced himself to assess his surroundings: someplace mocked up to feel hotel-like. Through window shades, it appeared to be dark outside.

She brought a capped cup to his mouth and slid a straw between his lips.

"Drink." Her voice continued to ripple in his mind, the cascade of echoes gaining distance in frequency. "Your throat will burn for a while because of the intubation tube."

He took a sip. Apple juice. The liquid felt cool on his raw throat.

"Can you understand me?"

Richards nodded, slowly. Something wasn't right. His head felt heavy, like he was wearing a helmet. Warily, he touched the knitted cap on his head.

"What do you remember, Dr. Richards?"

Remember? An odd question.

He closed his eyes as thoughts flooded his mind, as if pure adrenaline was injected directly into his heart and he was waking from a horrific trance.

"Where am I?" he croaked.

"Someplace safe."

"That's not an answer."

"Okay, you tell me where you're at."

He looked around the room. "I've never seen this place before."

"Tell about the last place you do remember."

"Not here." Neurons sparked in his mind, all screaming at once. He winced, feeling shockwaves of sluggish thoughts break free simultaneously. "ANCRI. Dr. Rikona Tanaka from the Kyoto University. You were a sponsored fellow at RIKEN Brain Science Institute. A neurogeneticist. Talented in your field of expertise. That's why I recruited you."

He watched Tanaka almost smile.

"You're no neurosurgeon." He touched his knitted cap again. "What did you do to me?"

Tanaka's lips tensed. "Brought you back to the living. Be grateful that I didn't kill you."

22

MORNING IN MARTHA'S VINEYARD

5:20 AM, Chilmark, Martha's Vineyard, Massachusetts

After an uneventful flight back to Martha's Vineyard, Vice President Richard Mears retraced his steps back to his family's compound. Slipping past the property's perimeter sensors, he reentered the main house with enough time to allow a few hours of sleep.

But thoughts of his son shadowed him.

A proud father, he'd been impressed with his son's career accomplishments. Then over a month ago, Andrew had been abducted and neurologically maimed, placed into an incurable coma by a madman.

Modern medicine offered no hope, no recovery. Andrew was alive, yet lost to Mears and his wife, Susan.

No parent should lose a child.

Instead of washing up, Mears undressed and slid under the

bed's covers. He stared at the ceiling. His mind cycled through the options before him.

After a Princeton ghost site focused on medical research had been compromised, Mears feverishly worked to deflect attention away from the President of the United States of America. Behind the scenes, he'd arranged for others to take the blame. Eliminating FBI Special Agent Katherine Morgan was critical to carrying out that plan. She'd become a multi-front threat: to the executive branch and the presidency, to a medical frontier offering cognitive control of people and species-changing research, and to the New World Order vision that Mears championed.

How could Morgan have learned about the contract hit? It had proven providential that an assassin missed an earlier window of opportunity. Only one person knew that detail: a Founder, Debra Ford—Manea—a former State Department spy and diplomatic assassin. Somehow, though, Morgan and Ford had forged common ground.

A disturbing revelation, but Morgan had stepped forward with a message of hope: Andrew could be cured, awakened.

Undoubtedly, Morgan had seen the damage in Andrew's MRI films. A hole scorched deep inside his son's brain, a third the size of a cigarette ember. Her influence in pushing Parker to reengage his research and save Andrew could make her an indispensable ally.

-+- -+-

Three hours later, after a shower and shave, Mears headed downstairs. The National Security Advisor, Gordon Abbott, had laid out a generous breakfast spread. A pairing of Secret Service agents ate at the breakfast niche that overlooked the neighboring house.

"Sir, I didn't know what you might have a taste for so I whipped up a bit of everything."

Mears poured himself a cup of coffee and said his good mornings.

"How was your evening?" Abbott asked, cocking his head to a television that was on but muted.

CNN ran a scrolling caption. BREAKING NEWS. U.S. ARMED FORCES TRAINING EXERCISE DISASTER AT THE OLD ATLANTIC CITY AIRPORT. More info buzzed on the lower screen while video footage shot from a helicopter played. A shallow water freighter listed in the water. The charred wreckage from a helicopter was visible on the top deck. Three confirmed fatalities. Names were being withheld pending notifications to their families.

Mears pointed to the TV. "A bit restless, but I managed a few hours of sleep. What is the Pentagon saying about that?"

"They're investigating, sir. Details aren't in yet about the cause of the accident."

Mears nodded, for the benefit of the Secret Service detail. A DOD liaison had briefed him on the flight back to Martha's Vineyard. It had been no accident. A rocket-propelled grenade had hit the helicopter. The JSOC teams that hit the freighter were the best in the business. Any deaths were regrettable. Still, the mission was a success.

With his back turned to the agents on duty, he exchanged cell phones with Abbott, sliding the borrowed one he'd been given into a potholder beside the oven. A note taped to the device requested a full background, financial, and communications check on an agent with the FBI. The President's National Security Advisor had plenty of resources at his disposal to execute such a request.

Abbott pointed. "Your morning briefing is on the table, sir."

Mears took a sip of coffee. "I'll join everyone for breakfast after a call."

He stepped into the hallway, away from his handlers, and cycled through his phone's directory until he found the number for the U.S. Attorney General, John Custis.

Custis answered after several rings.

"Good morning, John," Mears said. "I'd ask this in person, but I'm not in Washington at the moment. I need a favor."

"Sure. What can I do for you?" Custis asked, his voice reserved.

"You know that FBI agent who tracked down and killed that terrorist?"

"Yeah. Law enforcement's newest celebrity. Katherine Morgan. You either hate what she did in Princeton or love what she did in DC. I heard the bureau doesn't quite know what to do with her—it goes back to Hoover—the bureau disapproves of agents who become limelight hounds. I stopped by GW when she was getting treatment to offer my gratitude. The entire bureau came through that day. She risked her life to save others."

"Reassign Morgan to Justice. Permanent or via intra-agency loan. Whatever it takes. Frame it as a career opportunity."

"Gonna tell me about this opportunity?"

"Don't think I will. Not yet."

"Well, I'm sure the Director and I can come to some agreement. When do you want the reassignment to take place?"

"Today. Before noon."

23

GIFTS

Wearing a suit, tie, and color-matched knit cap, Stewart Richards swung open French doors to a second-floor balcony overlooking a sandstone piazza. Sunlight grazed the tops of a wintery mix of oaks, elms, and maples. His overlook glowed. Cool air washed his cheeks. An icy touch invigorated his senses. While frail, he was gaining strength by the minute. His brain, though, felt sluggish, as if idling in neutral rather than allowing streams of consciousness to pass without interruption.

Seeds of doubt were germinating. His cognitive recovery might take more time than he had patience. Recovery times for brain injuries varied according to age and brain plasticity. Some injuries healed in months, most within two years. Some brains never recovered. He vowed to push his recovery envelope.

During his morning's post-operative exercises, Rikona Tanaka briefed him on his surroundings. The State of New Jersey had granted a twenty-year lease on the site of the former Hagedorn

Psychiatric Hospital in exchange for facility renovations. ANCRI's parent company, the Phoenix Consortium, had gutted Hagedorn to create a state-of-the-art neurological research lab complete with an operating suite and a data center populated with supercomputers.

NeuroSteps Labs. That explained where he was, but not why.

"Dr. Richards," a woman said from behind him. He turned to see a woman holding up a smartphone. "A photo, if you'd be so kind."

He stood taller. She tapped the device's glass.

"Who are you?" he asked.

She ignored the question while she worked her phone, doing something with the photo. When finished, she said, "I'm the one who orchestrated your awakening."

She did not offer a hand to shake, but gestured down the corridor, stone-tiled with floor-to-ceiling windows.

Taking her cue, Richards walked ahead. The corridor ended at a room designated as the Director's Library. He stepped through a pair of solid oak doors. Plush carpet. Classical wood trim. Vintage hardcovers lined shelves; he recognized them as classics from Europe, Russia, early America. He passed a reading table adorned with gold-leafed editions of H.P. Lovecraft and Edgar Allan Poe. A baby grand piano occupied one corner.

Hagedorn's former director had good taste in furnishings.

The woman pointed to an ornate oak desk, where two equipment cases were open for inspection.

He moved forward to look. Inside the cases, pressed into gray foam, were components from his old research lab: Thomas Parker's headgear and network hard drives. Essential components to resume his research.

"What did you say your name was again?" he asked, studying her closer.

The sandy-haired, middle-aged woman had a determined but disarming smile. Her eyes held an intensity that he couldn't put a finger on. She exuded confidence. A long black overcoat shielded a body he suspected was toned. She was no scientist, that was sure.

"I didn't. It's Debra Ford."

He cocked his head. "How did you acquire this equipment?"

"None of your concern, if you put it to use."

Richards frowned. "And what do I owe you in exchange for my life, Ms. Ford?"

"More than you can imagine." Ford brushed past him to place her fingers on a pearl-faced mannequin's head wrapped in high-tech headgear. Her touch on the face's forehead seemed a sort of mind-meld. "Dr. Richards, a revolution is coming. And your contribution will move that era forward in time."

Rikona Tanka rotated spherical cultured cerebral organoids from one bioreactor to another, mixing in oxygenated stabilization gelatins to mimic the body's own complex physiology.

Her processes had developed ways around the metabolic stress that cultured organoids often experienced. This particular batch of mini-brains, floating in pink Jell-O-like stasis, could mimic the neural activity of a preterm infant.

A door to her lab opened and she looked up. Her heart almost stopped when she saw the woman, Debra Ford.

"I have good news," Ford announced, smiling. "I convinced the consortium to release your daughter. Your contract on Richards is fulfilled. She'll receive safe passage and money."

Tanaka nodded. "Thank you. But—?"

"You must remain at NeuroSteps. Be my eyes and ears. Can you do that?"

Her daughter was safe. That's what mattered. "Yes. For how long?"

Ford considered the question. "Stick to our agreement. Do that and I'll get you home so you can be with your daughter."

Tanaka bowed. "Understood."

24

THE OFFER LETTER

8:30 AM, Advanced BioCore International, Princeton, New Jersey

Parker controlled his emotions. Wearing jeans, an Oxford dress shirt, and loafers, he sat at a conference table and studied the document in front of him. Dr. William Grayson sat opposite him as Kate waited nervously in a corner of the room, avoiding eye contact.

Grayson pointed to the multi-page letter. "Instead of holding you completely against your will," he said, "the U.S. government is prepared to offer you an opportunity: the lead research position at Advanced BioCore."

"Not interested," Parker said, trying to decipher the document—part offer letter, part non-disclosure agreement. The legalese protected the U.S. government more than the person signing the document.

Grayson shrugged. "No problem. There are plenty of dark, unpleasant holes to put your ass, Dr. Parker. Places a lot worse than here."

"I want an attorney."

"As I mentioned, that's not going to happen." Grayson disclosed the government's leverage in detail: Parker was a material witness, a person with information alleged to be material concerning a criminal proceeding. The authority to detain material witnesses dated back to the First Judiciary Act of 1789. The government had been using the federal material witness statute since 2001 to detain suspects without charge for indefinite periods of time. The Supreme Court had weighed in on aspects of the statute in a case called Ashcroft vs. al-Kidd, giving the government wide latitude in material witness declarations.

"You expect me to believe this?"

Grayson flashed him a painted-on, broker-like smile. "That doesn't matter, Dr. Parker. You're in legal purgatory. And as we speak, a federal grand jury is determining whether or not to bring multiple charges against you. Our case is clear. You're the prime suspect in the new age of domestic terrorism."

Parker took an anxious breath. "What I did saved lives."

Grayson leaned forward on his elbows. "That's not a legal or ethical justification for your actions. Certainly not defensible in court. Listen: you subversively released sensitive technology secrets into public forums, which empowered foreign state actors to engage you. Evidence will demonstrate that you delivered trade secrets to enemies of the state. Serious acts classified as treason. Terrorism. Separate from those charges, you unlawfully violated the civil liberties of how many people? Thirty-one? If that's true, that's thirty-one counts of prosecutable physical assault."

Parker understood the point. He glanced at Kate, who looked away.

Grayson folded his arms and leaned back in his chair. "Keeping up on the math? At ten years for each assault and twenty added years for treason, that's, what, three-hundred-thirty years? With good behavior, an early release on parole is often granted at fifty percent time served—after one-hundred-and-sixty-five years."

Parker shook his head. "My answer hasn't changed. No."

Grayson shook his head and sighed. "Even if the DOJ doesn't take action, the State of New Jersey will step in with its own criminal prosecutions. Oh, and then there's the civil side: ambulance-chasing lawyers building class action lawsuits on behalf of the families and victims. The only way out of your criminal and legal entanglement is to accept this deal."

Parker hadn't considered state or civil implications, or any statute of limitations.

"Thomas," Kate finally said, "don't sign it."

Grayson glared at Kate then tapped the document. "Dr. Parker, this is the best deal you'll get from the US government. Sign it."

Kate handed Grayson a slip of paper. He looked at it, got up from the table, and left the conference room.

When they were alone, Parker said, "Your good cop, bad cop routine is good."

Kate sat across from him. "Grayson isn't messing around. The firestorm is growing, and the internal investigations will be endless. Power brokers in Washington are nervous. The agencies that know about your research and its possibilities are spooked. The U.S. government needs a patsy, a fall guy. If you don't negotiate some sort of deal and sign onto the program, that person will be you." She put her face in her hands. "A month ago I never would've imagined it would have come to this. I'm sorry, for everything."

Parker shook his head. "Kate, I'm struggling to believe you."

She nodded. "Thomas, I know. I owe you more than an apology. I want things to go back to the way they were between us. I want to be more than friends." She wiped a tear away. "I'm a borderline wreck, but I need you to trust me. Everything that is going on is bigger than the two of us."

Parker struggled with a reply.

Unlocking her cell phone, Kate brought up a photo and showed him the screen. He knew the man: Stewart Richards.

Parker shook his head. *Impossible.*
"He's awake, Thomas."

25
SECOND CHANCES

NeuroSteps Labs, Glen Garner, New Jersey

Richards was wary of Debra Ford, yet she'd come bearing gifts and seemed to have played a considerable role in his resurrection. He lifted the pearl-faced mannequin's head with his skull-capped headgear out of its metal case onto the oak desk. The face had no defined features. A fiber-metallic, spinal cord of dreadlocks streamed from the headdress to terminals still fitted in the gray foam inserts of the case.

Thomas Parker's creation was genius.

A headache spike made him cringe. When the pain subsided, he asked, "Who do you work for?"

Ford shrugged. "That's a very dangerous question." She strolled to the library's windows, leaving him alone with the headgear. "Let's say I have influential benefactors."

ANCRI. Its funding mechanism was a parent group called the Phoenix Consortium, which had its own Board of Directors. Their tentacles were far-reaching and vast.

"You spoke about a revolution, insurgency," Richards said. "What do you want from me specifically, Ms. Ford?"

"You're my contingency. In case others fail. You want this neurological frontier and all the accolades that go with it." She turned to him. "I need you to get beyond theoretical. Deliver a working neurological interface. Simply put, complete what you started."

That's what all of this is about. Music to his ears.

He stared into the goddess-like face. "And what will you do with this dangerous watershed of technology once I deliver it?"

Ford placed a firm hand on his shoulder. "Establish a nationalized consciousness. Build a platform to deliver social conditioning on a global scale. The people I represent want a person to go left instead of right, and then use their influence to convince others to take that same left turn. We're not interested in taking over the human race, merely persuading them to unify into a Common Collective." She wanted to use his magical frontier to build a cognitive virus.

Richards studied the pearl-face more closely. Energy surged through him, and he no longer felt weak or frail or old. Instead, he felt a deeper sense of purpose, as if he'd just been given a second chance to showcase a bold vision.

26

THE AGREEMENT

Advanced BioCore International, Princeton, New Jersey

Parker struggled to find the right words. Murder? That was no longer an accurate label. Perhaps there were no right words to justify secrets and lies and malice, but Kate deserved to hear the truth about what really happened to Richards.

Closing the photo on her phone, she sat across from him. Her hands started to reach across the conference room table, then withdrew.

He took a nervous breath. "Part of me felt ashamed, yet at the time full of rage. You're an FBI agent. How could I tell you? The man deserved to experience what others felt, saw. I don't know if I would do things any different."

"Thomas, I care about you." She sighed. "Please know that. I had plenty of chances to ask what happened to Stewart Richards. But I didn't. I didn't want to know. It was better if I didn't know what you did to him."

A security guard opened the conference room door. "Dr. Parker, the participants are ready to see you now."

Parker pointed to the document on the table. "Should I sign it?"

Kate's face grew somber, as if she was escorting him to the gallows. "Yes."

Silence lingered between them.

Signing the document would likely destroy his career, as a physician and a researcher. His mind searched for an alternative, but came up blank.

He looked at Kate, who nodded. The gesture was absent of affirmation or warmth.

Initialing the bottom of each page, he reached the end of the agreement and scribbled his signature on the final line.

"Give me your hand," he asked, extending his.

She hesitated before reaching out.

Their eyes locked. Gently, he touched the back of her hand to see if she'd pull away. She twitched, but her hand remained still. She seemed to hold her breath an extra beat. Turning her hand, he drew a symbol on her exposed palm.

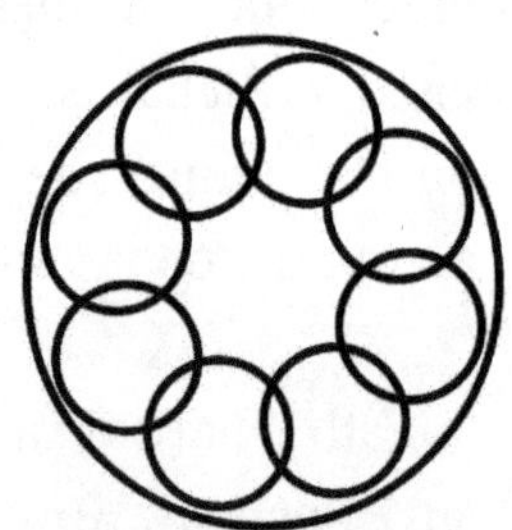

"Find out what this means," he asked.

She looked at where he'd drawn the symbol, then closed her hand. "Of course."

He rose and walked to the door, turning to look at her, hoping she'd say something.

With a closed hand, Kate shifted her posture ever so slightly and broke eye contact.

That was all the affirmation he needed.

Parker followed the guard out, leaving her with the document that would destroy his life, his career, and his love for her.

Kate hated the charade and watched a man she cared about leave the room. Since security cameras in the ceiling monitored every movement, she'd need to act quickly. She grabbed the signed document and pretended to thumb through it and check the bottom of each page for initials. She stood and turned her back to the camera while folding and tucking the papers into her jacket pocket, then laying a completely different agreement on the table.

Her sleight-of-hand trick had given Parker a comprehensive get-out-of-jail card with substantially better legal terms and absolution without retribution. The substitute carried Parker's signature, initials, and even fingerprints.

How Debra Ford had known the terms of the original agreement was a mystery. She seemed to be playing her chess game three moves ahead of everyone else, and orchestrating moves with brilliance.

Damn scary.

"You get him to sign it?" Grayson asked, entering the room.

Kate handed him the replica agreement. "Dr. Parker wants a copy, for his records."

Grayson shrugged. "Like that's going to matter."

"He's working for us now. His options are limited. He knows that."

Grayson flipped through the pages. "The doc's a tool. A means to an end. When our job is finished here and we have what we need, he's disposable. Is that understood?"

She took a ragged breath.

Grayson raised his head. "Morgan, you're on board, right?"

Kate nodded. "Don't start lecturing me. I know what needs to be done."

27

GROUP THERAPY

Standing in an observation booth, Parker watched group therapy through one-way glass. College-aged men and women with short, month-long hair stubble sat in plastic chairs and wore green patient wristbands. Caroline Wang led the session. Her band was yellow.

After a night's sleep, they'd received an array of casual clothing: jeans, t-shirts, sweats, leggings. Comfort clothes. Nothing institutional. Advanced BioCore wanted their fourteen participants to feel at ease. In need of test subjects, ANCRI had the University of Miami students kidnapped under the guise of a boating accident, where no bodies were ever recovered at sea. Wang rounded out Advanced BioCore's group at fourteen participants.

A chair in the discussion group was vacant, reserved for him.

Questions flooded his mind. Twenty-eight participants had survived ANCRI's original house of horrors. And somehow Advanced BioCore had acquired half of that population as their next generation of test subjects. Where were the others? The missing fourteen?

In hiding from the government? Taken by the menacing Korean contingent? Dead? Or worse, test of subjects in parallel, secretive research program?

Before, time didn't permit learning names, except Caroline Wang's.

Sensing the participants needed to express their feelings, Caroline had volunteered to run the open forum, safe haven therapy moment. Provide a place for people to talk about their feelings, struggles, and nightmares. They'd been through hell together.

The students missed their lives: families, friends, lovers, university life.

Dreams. Reflections. Exchanges between non-modeled, non-associated consciousnesses.

That was never part of his plan. An accident delivered by fate. He listened to them take turns, sharing.

A young woman was talking. "I see details in our lives, even those who aren't with us. I wish these visions I have would go away."

Caroline shrugged. "That may never happen."

"Other people's memories. Not mine. The dreams I relive seem so real."

Caroline sighed. "They're real. Were real."

"That doesn't make them dreams. That makes them memories."

Another participant wrung his hands. "I have moments in my life that I want kept private. I don't want to share those. Yet to everyone here I'm an open book."

A young man said, "I'm haunted by those who aren't with us. Anyone else feel haunted?"

Placing her elbows on her knees, a woman leaned forward. "Not me. Sure, I relive the torture and murder. Pain. Fear. Loneliness. Vulnerabilities. Vile, dark moments. But now in a way, this acquired intimacy makes us family. Maybe we remember for a reason because it's best not to forget." She paused and broke a smile. "I know her as Becky."

"Me too," someone added.

"Ward," chimed in another participant. "Becky Ward. Becky wore a red dress to impress Dr. Parker."

In unison, everyone chuckled.

"She'd rocked that outfit."

"Becky loved him."

Parker's skin tingled. It was strange to hear people talk casually about his life. Rebecca Ward, an undercover NSA field operative, had worked for him at Princeton as his grad student. Two years of buildup had led to a night of bad judgment on his part. He'd never know if Becky's feelings were real, or part of her secret agent act to get what she wanted—his tech.

"Girls are such geeks," one guy said sourly. "You romanticize everything. Her behavior was never about love. It was old-fashioned greed. Becky sold Dr. Parker out. She traded money for a night of sex and betrayal. How'd that work out for her, huh? Dr. Richards turned her into one of us, then killed her to make a point."

The therapy session fell silent.

"Thanks for being a jerk," another guy said.

"What? Did I say something that wasn't true?"

Parker took a calming breath. It was time to take his seat and join the conversation.

"How about we talk about something other than my pathetic love life?" Parker said, helping himself to coffee. He allowed the plastic cup to warm his hands before taking his seat in the group. "'Saying I'm sorry'... just empty words. Nothing I can do or say can make anyone whole again. I naïvely thought that by exposing you to Dr. Wang's memories, making you witnesses to crimes, that I could save you. I was wrong."

"We don't blame you, Dr. Parker."

"Maybe you should."

"We'd be dead without you."

Parker sucked in a breath. "Tell me about these dreams. When did they start?"

"Memories," a participant corrected him.

"Let's run with that. Memories."

They spoke all at once. Caroline intervened and redirected the conversation counterclockwise, as if to unwind time. In this setting, she was the group leader, a substitute matriarch for their interconnected consciousness.

Intense emotions filled their voices as they conveyed shared experiences.

Fascinating, from a psychological standpoint.

It was a stretch, but if their neurological conditions weren't physiological in nature, then their cognitive associations and behavioral manifestations mirrored mass psychogenic illnesses. Their group behavior was puzzling, reminding Parker of mass hysteria cases, phenomena of collective suggestion or associative social influencing.

Shared behaviors suggested self-preservation, a move to unify and build strength in numbers and a self-convinced indoctrination into a common belief system—an alignment of individual social constructs with a shared traumatic experience.

Parker understood people could convince themselves of any number of perceived or imagined experiences. Their absorbed reality infected others. Groupthink mindsets could multiply like organisms, viruses. Human history was littered with the discarded baggage of rejected social norms and misguided group conformity.

Sweeping his eyes counterclockwise, he studied the participants' expressions and listened to memories that weren't their own.

Accidental or not, he'd really messed up their heads.

He'd originally called the program Applied Mind. At ANCRI, he'd turned over the software side of his neuro-modeling interface to a researcher named Talib Makara, who led a brain trust of artificial intelligence (AI) programmers. Stratospherically brilliant, Makara was without a doubt the crudest prima donna he'd ever met. But the man excelled in quantum mechanics, neuromolecular algorithms, theory of the mind (TOM) applications, and self-awareness artificial intelligence (SAAI).

To complete Parker's mammoth task, Makara's team would've used pre-constructed, modular algorithms combined with autonomous AI bots to build code. That approach likely polluted essential coding schemes with unintended SAAI DNA wetware constructs. To shorten the development phase, corners were cut—beta testing skipped—the only viable outcome was to make the impossible, possible.

Applied Mind had gone live the moment Parker hit the button. *Reckless? Worth the risk?*

Only twenty eight people knew the answer to those questions.

Parker remembered a conversation he'd once had with a colleague about the myth of Pandora. Zeus had been a jealous god, seeing human evolution was a sin. Every bit of knowledge gained made them less respectful to the gods. When Zeus gave Pandora a beautiful box as a wedding gift, he'd told her not to open it. But of course Pandora couldn't resist. Opening the box released all manners of plagues and hardships. The human race suffered. Realizing her mistake, Pandora closed the box and unwittingly trapped its remaining contents inside—the Spirit of Hope.

Original Greek tales had a vase instead of a box—a vessel that might've stored lamp oil, an essential fuel for light. Light, no different than knowledge, was an energy force that drove out darkness. The same could be said of the trapped gift, Hope, an internalized mindset, expectation, or desire that had the power to inspire humankind and drive out darkness.

His vanity, ignorance, and lack of foresight had released this latest plague upon humankind. And the participants had paid for his sins.

Yet his return had brought them Hope.

28

A MESSAGE FROM THE GRAVE

Like a shadow, Kate entered the observation room after Parker had joined the round-robin, share-the-deep-secrets-of-your-life therapy session.

Through one-way glass she watched him. A collection of voices came across speakers in the ceiling. He needed this moment as much as the participants did.

A typical professor-like introvert, Parker didn't fit any check-the-box molds that Kate knew of. Brilliant yet oddly earthy. For most of their careers, his parents had been tenured archeologists at the University of Colorado. They spent most of their time excavating dig sites in Central and South America. They'd taught him to sail, scuba dive, rock climb, hang glide, and camp. Homeschooled, he'd gone with his parents on countless research trips. His father taught him languages. Besides English, Parker was fluent in Spanish and Portuguese. On a bet for a thousand dollars, Parker taught himself

Latin. His mother mentored him in the sciences, including physics, chemistry, and biology.

If Kate used dating apps, she was convinced she'd swipe right. What drew her to him? A complete mystery. Debra Ford had been right to call her out.

Pick one.

If only life was ever that easy.

Career destruction withstanding, it would be Thomas Parker.

Kate knew about Parker's fling with his grad student. Academia discouraged such relationships. Rebecca Ward had been offered a ten-million-dollar payoff to ditch her undercover National Security Agency mandate and hand over Parker's university research. Becky never received a nickel.

Parker would carry the burden of Becky's death with him for the rest of his life.

His technology ushered in a radical future: mind reading, an advancement worth killing for. Any number of federal agencies, foreign countries and their state actors, or criminal organizations would risk human collateral in order to grab the tech and use it to expand their influence in the world.

After ANCRI, Kate had become acutely aware of the U.S. government's historical and current malfeasance: unethical medical initiatives under the direct oversight of the Department of Defense, and covert sponsorship of illegal human experimentation via private sector proxies. The U.S. government understood that societies noticed less when test subjects were drafted from the indigent, homeless, slaves, prisoners, soldiers, or the mentally ill. Dead college students seemed to be a new spin on the principle. In a world of instantaneous social media and 24/7 news, governments and global corporations had evolved to construct physical disassociations and plausible deniability when it came to sponsoring illegal research.

A raised voice interrupted her thoughts.

"Secrets," a woman snapped at Caroline Wang. "That's what this is about."

"What kind of secrets?" Parker asked.

"Power. Greed. Corruption," someone else said. "We're just pawns in our government's efforts to develop mind-reading applications. Aren't we?"

Caroline lowered her head. "Yes."

Parker shrugged. "I doubt there's any other way to sum it up."

"Are you here to help us? Get us out of here?" another person asked.

He squirmed in his seat. "You've been taken from your families, friends, people who care about you. Tortured. Violated. Experimented on. As Americans, your constitutionally protected rights have been suspended. Those who hold you against your wills, those who are enabled or sponsored by the U.S. government, will continue to do so until they get what they want or they're forced to release you. We're being held under statutes for material witnesses." Parker shook his head. "I'm playing catch up to what's going on. But I promise to get everyone out of here."

"It's about the control of the secrets that we know, isn't it?" a woman asked.

"I suspect those holding us want everything," Parker said.

A man said, "Common InSight—the research program that Senator Samuel Ford was investigating. He was attacked in his girlfriend's condo. Upstairs. In a bedroom. A woman, his ex-wife, questioned the senator about it. When he failed to answer her question—"

A woman completed the memory. "She shot his girlfriend twice."

Kate's hands covered her mouth. The participants had witnessed an abduction and murder—through the eyes of Samuel Ford himself. Crime scene details few knew. Kate had been at the senator's Georgetown love shack when his coed lover's body was found in a bathtub. Debra Ford had gunned down her ex-husband's girlfriend and orchestrated the abduction, eventually handing off Samuel Ford to ANCRI.

If ever admissible in court, Parker's technology offered law enforcement a new range of tools to solve crimes, if a victim or suspect were willing to subject themselves to memory probing and crime scene reenactments.

The flashes of déjà vu contained a dream-like hook—a surreal discussion and grisly walk down memory lane—a piece to a grander puzzle. Debra Ford was after Common InSight. As if a ghost spoke from the dead, Samuel Ford had returned to the living through his shared memories.

At ANCRI, Kate considered Caroline Wang to be "the singularity witness." That conjecture was wrong. The star witness had proven to be Samuel Ford.

The hair on the back of Kate's neck tingled. Debra Ford had played matchmaker by bringing her back to Thomas and connecting her with the Vice President. All along, Debra Ford would stop at nothing to get hold of Common InSight.

Kate glanced at the palm of her hand and the image that Parker had scribbled on it.

Secrets.

Conspiracies.

The world needed to learn the secrets that Samuel Ford had carried with him almost to the grave, even if that meant that the participants needed to relive those horrifying moments again.

The world needed to hear his story.

Torturing people to extract memories was not only illegal, but highly unethical.

Crazy thoughts, Kate chided herself, *but not wrong ones.*

29

ALLIANCES

NeuroSteps Labs, Glen Garner, New Jersey

Alone, Richards strolled into a boutique-style neurophysiology lab. He'd returned home.

He faltered, not physically but cognitively.

Time stopped then restarted.

The sensation lasted what he suspected was seconds, and he shrugged it off as being tired. Walking among the living took more energy than he'd remembered.

Refocusing, he looked across the compact footprint. No floor space in the two-story lab was wasted. Rows of egg-shaped, space-aged capsules filled the room's center. The uninhabited containment pods were nearly identical to the ones used at his lab at ANCRI, with a notable difference. Glass canopies enclosed the units, much like a protective shield covering the cockpit of a small aircraft. The enhancement wasn't logical. The neuro-stimulation and response units (NSRUs) didn't fly and the occupants weren't exposed to any environmental threats. Perhaps some technician thought windows made the units look more stylish. He made a mental note to have the glass lids on the pods removed.

Walking the lab's perimeter, he noticed that each of the four walls was actually a billboard-sized LED screen, stretching from floor to ceiling. He was used to a single front-facing interface called "The Wall of Knowledge." The same applied here, times four. If all of them lit up at once, their intensity might drive him back into a coma.

He needed to be careful and not turn all the screens on at once.

Richards understood that the Phoenix Consortium, the private equity arm of his former lab, had vast resources and access to original equipment specifications. In case he failed to at ANCRI, the company had hedged its bets and built NeuroSteps as a fallback site.

Regardless of the number of participants, this kind of research required a football field-sized data center. He'd never consciously listened for the noise, but he heard it now: the mechanical sounds of a central plant, massive pumps, fans, and chiller systems. Essential components to supercool a state-of-the-art data center. The low, constant thrum was faint, but ever present.

Richards turned his attention to the eighteen empty pods. His frontier would require a new generation of participants.

⊹ ⊹

From a corner of the room, Rikona Tanaka studied Richards. At ANCRI, she'd never worked with the lead team, the hand-selected, popular crowd. For security reasons, a limited few worked inside the ANCRI's neurophysiology lab and directly with the participants. Neurogenetics and neurosurgery were her niches, relegating her to lesser seen, back-of-house duties.

But she'd heard stories.

Stewart Richards was a monster, a maniacal tyrant who had complete disregard for the value of human life. Cold-hearted, the bastard sacrificed his daughter as his program's first participant in order to reach a technical milestone and create a baseline cognitive model.

There was no telling what Richards' second coming would bring the world.

What's worse than a monster?

The answer terrified her.

"Dr. Tanaka, your patient survived his procedure," a woman said, gesturing to Richards. "Is he healthy enough to resume his duties?"

Tanaka turned to look at the two women standing beside her. She recognized Debra Ford. The other, a Korean woman, had just arrived. Neither wore lab coats.

Tanaka bowed slightly. "Post-procedure tests need to be run, but Dr. Richards appears to demonstrate full cognitive functions."

Ford gave her a tablet. "Your daughter, as promised."

An agreement upheld. *Akiko.* Tanaka watched a short video on the screen.

On the bow of a ferry half a world away, her daughter's rich black hair fluttered in a breeze. Akiko smiled, appeared happy. Ferries worked as everyday transportation among the several thousand islands of Japan, a place that was thirteen hours ahead of U.S. Eastern Standard Time. The screen showed the lush mountainside of Kushima along Shibushi Bay towering behind her daughter. Akiko's features were bathed in a sunset's warmth, suggesting that the video had been taken only a few hours earlier.

Akiko's name meant *bright child.* It couldn't be more appropriate. Exceptionally bright, Akiko had followed her mother's footsteps into medicine at the University of Tokyo.

Tanaka watched as her daughter pressed her fingers against her lips and blew her mom a kiss. The video ended.

Akiko's alive.

"I want to speak to her," Tanaka said, a demand rather than a request. "Hear my daughter's voice. I need to know that she's safe, completely free."

"That will be arranged," Ford said, "Your daughter can resume her life as long as you continue to support our initiatives."

Tanaka nodded. *Message received, loud and clear.*

"Are your specimens ready for delivery?" Ford asked.

"Tomorrow." In labs elsewhere in the facility, Tanaka had resumed her original ANCRI mandate and created defined batches of organoids. Mini-brains. Carefully engineered organs capable of being bench tested as part of neuro-stimulation models. She'd been instructed to cultivate a separate collection for an outside research entity.

"They'll be ready tomorrow." Tanaka passed back the tablet. "I should return to my duties," she said. "Is there anything else?"

"Not at the moment. Dr. Tanaka, you've done well."

Raising a monster from a metaphoric grave in exchange for Akiko's life.

Tanaka would have done far more than "done well" to save her daughter.

✛ ✛

Debra Ford watched the neurogeneticist leave the lab, before turning her attention to Stewart Richards, who inspected the stimulation pods populating the room.

Standing beside her, Dr. Ji-woo Song spoke. "Sacrificing my research station so you could consolidate work under this man was counterproductive. Foolish. Our Hong Kong investors lost a billion dollars in that raid. And I lost talented staff."

Ford shrugged. "Our government needed a small victory. A contrived enemy to focus on. Your team's sacrifice provided essential misdirection. And trust me when I say this—no matter how promising your research, it had little chance of success." She pointed to Richards. "He'll deliver what our benefactors want."

"And Thomas Parker?"

"Familiar with baseball?"

"Dodger Stadium was fifteen minutes from Caltech. I was known to have taken in a few games. What's your point?"

Ford opened an application on the tablet then handed the device to Ji-woo. "Parker serves a parallel purpose—one that yields dividends, but in a much different way. He's our long game, all nine innings. Stewart Richards is small ball. Base hits strung together to set up manufactured runs. Unless your goal is to swing for the fences, it pays to execute both to win."

Ji-woo studied the digital photographs, a mix of men and women. Names, official titles tagged each image. Chinese nationals who worked for their consulate in New York City.

Her next targets.

Prospects for a new army.

In her mind, she called them acquisitions. In Ford's baseball analogy, they'd serve as base hits and were essential to Richards' small-ball strategy of bringing in runs.

She glanced at Ford. "When?"

"Tonight. Manhattan."

Ji-woo cast her gaze to Richards, who continued to inspect his new laboratory. Even at a distance, she sensed that the haggard man was a mere shell of his former self, even if he was a genius. "We're betting a lot on him," she said, knowing she would get no response.

30

RETURN TO WASHINGTON

Washington, DC

In the realm of American politics, Vice President Richard Mears understood that the phrase "hell to pay" was often nothing more than empty threats. Politics from two ideological extremes churned eternally beneath the city, regardless of which party held the White House or the two chambers of Congress. Whenever there was blood in the water, sharks weren't far away. And more people than usual were gunning for the President.

He'd been summoned back to Washington, DC. Not entirely unexpected, he supposed.

Mears stepped out of a Suburban and entered the West Wing through the north lobby. The National Security Advisor, Gordon Abbott, walked behind him as his Secret Service detail dispersed.

The public disclosures were difficult to deflect, Mears thought—the cold-blooded murder of a Senator from Oklahoma and government-sponsored illegal human research trials conducted on citizens of the United States. Convenience more than anything else made one person the target of public ire: the President.

Although the news and social media were churning out conspiracy theories about what occurred in Princeton, the Executive Branch—the Department of Justice and the Attorney General, Department of Defense (DoD), and the Department of State—formed a unified front around the President of the United States.

But rallying around the President wasn't enough. Time had come to go on the offensive.

Both chambers of Congress demanded hearings. When the DoD, Justice, State, and FBI refused to comply with the barrage of subpoenas based on national security concerns and ongoing investigations, Washington politics heated up.

The President's Chief of Staff greeted him. "Everyone is present. The President will join you shortly." On the phone, they'd agreed to an informal meeting as a way to downplay the situation.

Across the hall from the Oval Office, the Roosevelt Room was a versatile meeting space named after two distant cousins: Presidents Theodore and Franklin Delano Roosevelt. Mears left the Chief of Staff in the lobby and sat in a brown leather chair at the center of the table, leaving the opposing seat on the other side open for the Commander in Chief. This small group of individuals routinely saw each other so no handshakes were exchanged, only verbal greetings.

As the National Security Advisor, Abbott sat at the end of the table. Flanking Mears were the Directors of the FBI and CIA. The Attorney General and the Chairman of the Joint Chiefs of Staff sat next to the reserved seat in the middle. The only notable absence was the Secretary of State, who'd been dispatched to New York and the United Nations.

This meeting had no secretaries, no scribes, just "eyes only" personnel. The fewer people who were part of the discussions, the better. Nothing would be recorded or written down. Thin briefs complete with photos and recaps lay in front of the occupied chair.

Mears held onto the advance copy he'd received when his

plane touched down at Andrews Air Force Base. On the drive to Washington, Mears had studied the mission recap and focused on answers to the questions the President would ask.

Paper shredders stood next to each of the two room exits. Prepared by DoD intelligence teams, nothing printed would be leave the room.

The Oval Office corridor door swung open. The President entered. Everyone stood until he gestured that they should sit.

"Peace on Earth?" The President took his seat and rapped his fingers on the brief before him. "How about calling the program the Destruction of a Presidency?"

"On the contrary, Mr. President," Mears said, careful not to exaggerate the facts. The Commander in Chief needed digestible, relevant facts. Nothing more. "Thanks to the outstanding mission cooperation between DoD and the FBI, we now have a target. Identified state actors that we lacked a month ago. The press won't have any choice but to echo that target. Congress will redirect as well."

"How'd the North Koreans sail under our radar and onto our shores?"

Mears had anticipated the question, since the North Koreans were a surrogate in this upcoming war. He gave a firm nod to the Attorney General, Frank Murphy.

"Mr. President," Murphy said, "Treasury has linked this billion-dollar floating research lab to the People's Republic of China. Our people are working with CIA to confirm the source of the funds, which we believe were channeled through Hong Kong from mainland China."

The Chairman of the Joint Chiefs added, "The ship has been identified as the *Norvana*, with a Hong Kong registry. A month ago, it entered U.S. territorial waters and the Gulf of Mexico. This North Korean operation was planned out well in advance. Before the fiasco in Princeton. Once in the Houston channel, the vessel cleared customs and swapped out its transponders and universal shipboard automatic identification system. The replaced system transponders came from a dry-docked U.S. freighter called the *San Jose*. External markings and country of origin were altered to make the *Norvana* a clone of the *San Jose*. From Houston it sailed to Atlantic City as an American vessel."

The President asked, "If the Chinese funded this snatch and grab operation, how was North Korea involved?"

The Director of the CIA leaned forward on her elbows. "North Korea is the false front. A proxy. Perhaps the initial strike force. In case their operatives and scientists were captured and interrogated, there would be no direct link to mainland China. Hong Kong's role was the financial facilitator, the clearing house for the operation."

The President sat back in his leather chair. "What have we learned about their tech?"

Mears grinned. "Not as good as ours."

"These dream chambers will bring us peace on earth?"

Mears nodded. "Yes. Mr. President."

The President took a breath. "Is it true that Chinese, Russians, and British are working on their own versions?"

The CIA Director said, "That's what field intelligence tells us. But this Hong Kong-funded enterprise appears to be closer to our own research efforts. Somehow they secured classified information. But not enough to replicate what was done in Princeton."

"Will the story of a military training exercise hold up?"

"If we keep it simple," the Chairman of the Joint Chiefs said. "Mechanical failures. Four service members lost in the accident. We have total control of the *Norvana*."

The Attorney General spoke next. "Since the research debacle in Princeton, interagency cooperation is strong—Pentagon, DOJ, FBI, CIA, NSA, State—we're on the same page. Operationally everything runs through a Justice operations task force, supervised by my office."

The President pointed across the table. "I want Dick involved in key decisions. He's the designee for the Chief Executive."

Mears nodded. Exactly what he wanted to hear.

The President rose from his seat. "Eventually, the media will learn that Atlantic City was no training accident. How will that be handled?"

Mears stood along with the others. Each administration had different methods for leaking sensitive and classified information to the media and not getting caught. Some Presidents figured out that process better than others.

Mears held up his hands to make sure no one spoke out of turn. "Mr. President, we're now on the offense. We'll dictate how things play out. We've been provided an enemy we intend to fully exploit."

The President picked up on the cue. "When will the media focus on the North Koreans?"

Mears smiled thinly. "Tomorrow, sir," he said, having put that initiative into play already. "Through back channels at the United Nations. It'll take the media a couple of days for the message to propagate, but we're confident the media will redirect."

"Dream chambers," the President said with a sigh as he turned to leave. He cast a scrutinizing look across those in the Roosevelt Room. "We'd better be the first to get this tech functional to support special operations and deployment. If we don't, we'll lose this war and the world. The last thing I want is to fail at bringing the world our version of peace on earth."

31

SEEKING ANSWERS

Advanced BioCore International, Princeton, New Jersey

Kate entered a curved conference room that overlooked the neuro-physiology lab and activated the hockey puck-style satellite hotspot the Vice President had given her. She linked her phone to the device and typed in a phone number. While she waited for the call to connect, she studied the research space filled with pods through the span of windows. Below, technicians had begun final preparations.

This well-funded knockoff of ANCRI was readying the pods to be occupied. The government wasn't changing course. They sought what only Parker could deliver, and no person or entity would stop that from occurring.

Grayson had said no one would outlive their usefulness, starting with Parker. That would include the participants, any witnesses. She wondered if it applied to federal agents as well.

After several rings, a man answered. "Identification?"

"Katherine Morgan, FBI." Someone had intercepted the Vice President's phone. Not surprising, considering the clandestine nature of what she was calling about. Mears would be careful to maintain a defensible distance from any criminal activities. "Who am I speaking with?"

"That's not relevant."

"Let's try this again," she snapped. "Who are you? Spit it out or I hang up."

Seconds passed. "Gordon Abbott."

It took a moment to recognize the name as the President's National Security Advisor. Abbott was no run-of-the-mill switchboard operator. He had to be supporting the Vice President's cloak and dagger operation. Kate wondered how extensively the Executive Branch was involved in Advanced BioCore.

"Mears?" she asked.

"In a meeting."

Kate clicked off the phone and deactivated the satellite hot spot, sticking the device in the pocket of her suit jacket. She mentally reviewed her options. Leading solo field investigations and covert operations was outside her specialty, but the practice was becoming routine.

Turning on her heels, she spun away from the windows and went looking for answers. She'd memorized the facility's general layout from the fire evaluation placards mounted in public corridors, and headed to the facility's security operations center (SOC).

A uniformed guard with a holstered sidearm stood outside doors that were part of a continuous curved glass wall. Beyond the Advanced BioCore International corporate logo etched into the glass, Kate spotted security staff at a series of workstations.

She flashed her bureau identification at the guard.

"If you don't move," she said, swiping her hand against her suit jacket to reveal the Glock clipped to her belt, "I'll shoot you."

The guard cupped his ear and glanced to her hand, which rested on her service weapon. She hadn't noticed that he was wearing an earpiece.

The guard nodded and stepped aside as an electronic latch to the doors clicked.

"Wise choice," she said pushing past the guard.

Inside, she saw a corporate-style integrated combination crisis and tactical operations center, not unlike other corporate command centers. The ADVANCED BIOCORE logo stretched above an enormous two-story curved video wall. The display was active with various screenshots, although none were medically based. Corporate-branded personnel occupied workstations with multiple monitors. A side wall of monitors was dedicated to the major news networks: China was exerting its control over Hong Kong and clashes between protestors and military raged in the streets.

A video wall dedicated to a cargo freighter named the *Norvana* caught her attention. Images showed a simplified neurophysiology lab, research spaces, and a heavily damaged data center half-flooded with water. The image Parker had sketched on her hand was under analysis.

Grayson handed her an ID card attached to a lanyard.

"Your FBI credentials won't work here," he said in his heavy British accent. "Wear it at all times. It's your facility access." He faced her to make sure she got his point. "Be smart. Draw within the lines. Don't go out of bounds. Not here. Don't blow anything up, either. Our security is real good at what they do."

She donned the lanyard and pointed to the image. "What does it stand for?"

"Not sure." He gave a quick rundown of the SOC and its functions. "We're classified as a national asset resource team that directly supports IC initiatives and programs," referring to the seventeen member agencies of the US intelligence community. "Our integrated communications patch us into most networks except the CIA's. They denied our network request."

"And you need the CIA's help to identify the symbol?"

"We know the ship's port of origin, potential sources of international funding, even have a lead on its crew. American citizens, North Korean children adopted by families here in the States. None have discernable ties to foreign governments or state actors." He took a long breath. "Right now, the intelligence circles are calling the symbol the Eight Rings, until they figure out something more substantive."

Debra Ford would know, Kate thought.

Grayson noticed the change in her expression. "You know what it is?"

Kate shook her head. "No. But I have a contact who might know. I'd like to interview the crew of the research vessel."

"I'd grant your request, if that were possible," he said. "No one survived the raid."

"You're kidding me, right?" The time she'd spent with the Vice President had kept her from getting the whole story. "So who botched the op? Who was the rescue team?"

"Justice ran the show with USSOCOM support," Grayson said. The United States Special Operations Command directed Joint Special Operation Command (JSOC) teams. Although the Defense Department was generally prohibited from conducting direct exercises on American soil, JSOC teams routinely supported security measures for the Olympics, Super Bowls, Presidential inaugurations. Grayson pointed to the video wall. "Advance BioCore had no role in the rescue operation. We were just observers."

"Is it possible to see any recordings?"

He nodded. "What we have, I'll make available."

She smiled. "Thank you."

He handed her an envelope. "A copy of Parker's contract with the federal government. How'd you ever get him to cooperate?"

She slipped the envelope in her jacket. "That's between me and the Vice President."

Grayson chuckled. "The doc better come through."

"He's one person on board. Now the hard part. How's the government planning on getting voluntary signoffs? Patient consent? Not sure kidnapping, coercion, and holding people hostage will work for a new round of human trials."

He flashed a grin. "Agent Morgan, you'd be amazed what leverage the U.S. government holds."

32

LIGHT READING

When Parker returned to his three-room dormitory suite for the evening, he was surprised to find takeout from La Messaluna and a bottle of Crown Royal XO next to a centerpiece of freshened-up flowers and a restocked fruit basket. After talking with the participants earlier, he'd made a mandate about ordering dinner from the Princeton Italian kitchen, in part to see how far his demands would go. Advanced BioCore seemed intent on catering to his every whim.

He tossed his company-provided badge on a table, grabbed a glass from the kitchenette and filled it with ice, and doused the ice with a generous amount of the Canadian whiskey. He peeled off the cover to gnocchi bolognese and inhaled its aroma before sitting on a couch and clicking on a television to see what news he'd missed. Talking heads cycled through various stories, from riots in Hong Kong to the President's upcoming trip to Europe.

As Parker sipped the whiskey and enjoyed his meal, he noticed a laptop on the coffee table. Taped to the device's cover was a passcode. Who'd left the surprise gift—Kate?

He wondered what she was doing. In only a short time, she'd become one of the few people he was comfortable with. He had acquaintances, colleagues and researchers, associates in the neuroscience and medical professions, but few close friends. Kate had checked several boxes in his life. He missed her.

Now he wasn't sure he could trust her, or whether it was wise for him to let his guard down around her.

If she'd left him the computer, it was because she wanted him to do something with it. Setting aside his meal, Parker fired up the machine.

An Advanced BioCore interface screen appeared. Parker opened the menu options and chose a research database.

He typed **THOMAS PARKER** into a search bar and hit enter.

Nothing.

Next was **APPLIED MIND**, the neuro-link program he'd co-created at ANCRI to transfer memories. He doubted Advanced BioCore was oblivious about the application.

Again, nothing.

He repeated the process for **COMMON INSIGHT**.

The query result was the same.

Parker dug his fingernails into his scalp and thought about the participants. Advanced BioCore needed the participants—why? The government could always go out and kidnap a new batch college students to torture. Keeping this select group of test subjects together was important—why? Caroline Wang had mentioned that Richards had written a white paper on extended consciousness and **CONVERSATIONAL ECHOES**. He entered the query and an archived version of the document popped up on screen.

Air felt trapped in Parker's lungs as fear swelled. Richards had hypothesized that ANCRI's participants might experience what Caroline had called a Common Collective, an overflow mindmeld encounter in which an uncontrolled barrage of thoughts and memories were transferred from one person to another.

Embedded blue network links took him to a series of video files. The files were arranged in two columns under the heading THE NEW HUMAN ARTIFICIAL INTELLIGENCE:

INFLUENCING CEREBRAL OUTCOMES   HOW MATTER BECOMES MIND
SYNAPTIC SHUNTS TO DEFUSE PTSD   PREDICTIVE NEURALNET MODELING
RETRAINING NEURAL NETWORKS   CONVERSATIONAL ECHOES
PREDICTING COGNITIVE OUTCOMES   STABLIZING SEGREAGATION
WEAPONIZING THE MIND   NEURAL GENESIS THERAPIES
FORMING COGNITIVE DOMINANCE   PATCHING COGNITIVE GAPS
CREATING ALLIGNED ASSETS   SYNAPTIC TRANSPLANTS

The left-hand topics seemed to align with Defense Department initiatives and the portfolios of any number of military-led agencies, including the Defense Advanced Research Projects Agency (DARPA). The right column themed with typical medical and neuroscience research areas.

Parker used his cursor to choose SYNAPTIC SHUNTS TO DEFUSE PTSD and clicked.

A video popped up, showing a podium in front of a banner with logos for ANCRI and DARPA. The title of the session was THERAPIES ON THE HORIZON. A younger Stewart Richards walked onto the stage. A vibrant, long-haired brunette handed him a microphone.

It took Parker a moment to recognize the woman. Daddy's little girl had followed her father's footsteps into neuroscience research.

Parker had only seen the woman only once, in a photo.

Caroline Wang had taken a photo as evidence before Amy Richards' emaciated body was cremated to conceal her death. Before taking her last breath, Amy had endured months of torture at the hands of her father. After his daughter's death, Richards repaid her by placing her brain in a jar and displaying it on a shelf in a conference room.

Parker studied the video more closely, wondering if Richards had known all along that he would sacrifice his daughter for a chance at the technical breakthrough his research needed.

Richards was a predator, a monster.

In the video, Richards flashed a broad smile and said, "Erasing traumatic events in the human mind to cure PTSD is akin to cognitive censorship. Right now pharmaceuticals, counseling, and mind-body physical therapy are the best treatments for those who suffer from post-traumatic distress. But what if there was a new approach? What if new horizons in medicine offered long-lasting cures—a rebalance of the mind, as it were? As most treatments do, cognitive censorship will have side effects. Going down that rabbit hole will require sacrifice, not in cognitive capacity or abilities, but in deciding which memories to blunt and embracing the hard fact that the treatment will have an associative cascading effect on other memories."

Parker got the gist of Richards' logic.

"Dimming the horror-filled memories," Richards continued, "will have a countering impact on joys as well. Brushstrokes can gray down absolute darkness. But those same strokes fade the brightness of light as well. The time is coming for us to make bold choices. To choose what to keep and what to vanquish."

Parker hit the pause button. Richards was talking about more than how to medically treat PTSD or other mental illnesses and psychological disorders, like bipolar disorder, schizophrenia, compulsiveness, depression, or aggression.

He took a swig of whiskey and fast forwarded to the end of the video.

"Ladies and gentlemen," Richards said, "we are embarking on a new frontier. Soon we will have the technical ability to dissect and adjust neurological physiologies to cure those who are afflicted. We will be able to help those who suffer. Yes, without a doubt concerns linger about cognitive censorship, but sacrifice is required to make the necessary repairs and make a person socially and individually whole again. The techniques and technology on the horizon will help us rewire and retrain the brain. Cure mental illnesses. Reverse the debilitating impacts of diseases and injury. Even increase the intellectual capacity of our species. The day is coming where we will be able to decipher a memory from scratch and carry on a two-way conversation with a total stranger. Tonight, our minds have been enlightened, opened to new discoveries. Enjoy your evening."

The audience applauded. Richards nodded his thanks.

Parker understood that he'd been schooled by a madman. Without realizing it, he'd executed cognitive censorship, playing the unappointed role of judge, jury and executioner.

He had put Richards into a coma as a way to save the lives of his subjects. No one influenced his actions or forced him to inflict that trauma.

He turned off the video and finished his glass of whiskey. Before the night was over, he'd need several drinks, just to forget.

The first time Parker had met Richards, when he was teaching at Princeton, their conversation had ended with eerie questions similar to the speech Richards had given: "What would it take to read an unmapped mind? Decipher a memory from scratch? Carry on a two-way conversation with a total stranger?"

Parker felt a chill.

A moment was coming in the not too distant future, a show-down—a point in time when he would have to kill Stewart Richards all over again.

33

DECONSTRUCTION

Director's Library, NeuroSteps Labs, New Jersey

Stewart Richards feared that if he slept, he might not wake—a logical neurosis, given that he'd just emerged from a coma.

Still, exhaustion overtook him. It had been a long day among the living, and his body was weak. It needed rest.

For several hours, he sat at his director's desk and matched program code to neurological processes in an effort to deconstruct Parker's methods for memory propagation.

A nurse in the hallway cleared her throat. "Dr. Richards, please."

Ten minutes earlier, he'd waved the woman off, but she refused to leave. The presence of a babysitter annoyed him.

"All right," he snapped. He put a digital pin into his modeling application as a bookmark for his spot in the coding structures. He got up from the desk and tucked a laptop under his arm.

The nurse escorted him to his residence.

At his door, she pointed to the laptop. "I'll need that, sir."

He wanted to resist, but it would be embarrassing to be subdued by a nurse on his first night back. He surrendered the computer, entered his hotel-like accommodations, and discharged the nurse before she did something awkward like tuck him in for the night.

Rather than washing up and heading to bed, Richards sat down at a desk to transcribe a series of notes, sketch out flowcharts for systems progressions, and create a detailed agenda for the next day. Before he knew it, he'd filled five pages of a notepad, front and back.

On the sixth page, he documented a set of procedures that he wanted to focus on.

Heading the list was the **PROGRESSION OF ENERGY TRANSFERS.**

He understood that every object in the universe was bound by mathematical constraints, the laws of physics and chemistry. Unique in its existence, the vastness of the human mind was contained by a one gallon paint can-sized organic host. In fact, neither the mind nor the brain could function without the other. He recalled a quotation from Aristotle that Parker had once cited: *The energy of the mind is the essence of life.*

Energy—physics and chemistry.

Mind reading—a physical task of intercepting states of energy that propagate across a cerebral landscape.

Cognitive mapping and extraction of the human consciousness stood as one of the last great medical frontiers.

He'd come so close to reaching and proving the validity of neurological singularity—the point where the brain could be unhinged to expose the essence of energy trapped deep inside. Once exposed, the human mind could be read, rewired, or changed, over and over again.

Thomas Parker had cheated him out of that discovery.

Now NeuroSteps would give him a chance at redemption.

34

AN EVENING AND A CONCERT

8:00 PM, The Beekman, Financial District, New York City

Ji-woo Song recognized that a night like this was no time to start an international incident, but that occurrence would come along soon enough.

She'd been to New York City on many occasions, but this was her first visit to The Beekman. Originally constructed as the Temple Court, the building was one of New York City's original skyscrapers, completed in the same year as the Brooklyn Bridge. Remodeled into a hotel, the structure was an architectural icon that combined modern, eccentric art with its nineteenth-century lineage.

The hotel and its vast spaces were hosting a private event, a black tie Prosperity gala sponsored by the United Nations Food and Agriculture Organization. Dignitaries from the United Nations, Manhattan financial executives and their guests filled the hotel. A digital display in the hotel's main lobby tracked fundraising efforts northward of eight million dollars.

Wearing a long, open-shoulder black dress, Ji-woo loitered along the third floor inner balcony, which overlooked the main floor. The semiautomatic strapped to her inner thigh forced her to awkwardly stand with her legs apart, to prevent the holster and weapon from chafing her skin. Tiered balconies with hardwood railings and white ironwork rose above and below her. People huddled along the inner corridors to watch the festivities below.

Dispersed through the crowds were various security details protecting the U.S. Secretary of State as well as the Chinese Ambassador to the U.N. and the Chinese Consul General. It took little training to identify the U.S. Secret Service and Chinese Consulate Security teams blending in.

She'd entered the gala as a guest, having to clear metal detectors and security screening. Her gun came from a night stand in an upper-level hotel suite, where she'd armed the rest of her team with similar weapons.

Her perch offered an excellent vantage point.

Below, the center of attention was the only daughter of the Chinese Consulate General in New York, a violinist. Her music resonated through the seven-story atrium. The young girl's animation added a deeper layer to her performance, and reminded Ji-Woo of the classical violinist Sarah Chang. A teen of similar age played a piano offset to a main stage. Proud parents sat in the front row to the left of the performance. The Secretary of State sat opposite on the right. The American representative looked tired, pale, and struggling to stay present in the moment.

The teen ended her performance to applause, recognition well earned. She and her accompanist made bows to the dignitaries in attendance. A proud mother presented her daughter a bouquet of Chinese roses. People formed a line around the girl, the Secretary of State near the front. More bows were exchanged along with handshakes. Eventually, the lead officials greeted one another. After the first wave of greetings passed, guests returned to enjoying complementary refreshments and hors d'oeuvres.

Ji-woo watched Secret Service agents consolidate around the Secretary of State as he left the hotel. Other dignitaries followed suit. The remaining contingent of security belonged solely to the Chinese Consulate.

Ji-woo and her team made their moves, dispersing to fill voids in the crowd with the sole purpose of guiding hand-selected attendees who possessed gold plastic cards to a roped-off set of stairs. The NO ADMITTANCE sign blocking off the downstairs was removed to permit the small contingent to pass.

The group of Chinese consular service officers and their companions made their way into a peculiar basement area called The Alley Cat, the hotel's former cellar and mechanical room that had been transformed into a small-group theatre and lounge, reminiscent of Tokyo's side-street bars and classic American cocktail clubs. The lighting was dim, but the club's eclectic nature stood out. The pre-selected guests mingled and sipped drinks. Music played softly to set the mood.

Ji-woo brought up the rear and made a final headcount. Fourteen: all targets present and accounted for, including a few bonus guests.

Servers refilled drinks and exchanged the cards that each guest carried for a gold-wrapped box.

Ji-woo picked up a glass from the bar and rapped it gently with a fork. When everyone's attention fell on her, she raised a spare gift box so everyone could see it.

"*Wǎnshang hǎo*," she said in Mandarin. *Good evening.* "*Nǐ de lǐwu, qǐng dǎkāi.*" *Your gifts, please open.*

Those holding the gold boxes seemed anxious as they broke ribbons and tore away wrapping. The servers pressed their advantage while the guests were distracted, jabbing pre-filled syringes into exposed necks.

The immobilization was instantaneous. Partially opened boxes clattered to the floor. A few guests momentarily struggled before succumbing to the chemical cocktails entering their bloodstreams.

The servers did their best to guide each person to the floor rather than having them collapse hard.

Ji-woo unholstered the pistol strapped to her leg then checked her wristwatch. Hotel security cameras would drop offline for a limited duration. Her team had less than five minutes to get fourteen people to the hotel's loading dock, located in an underground garage.

Wrists and ankles were bound with nylon restraints. Sedated, none of the fourteen stirred.

In the garage, advance crews cleared hotel staff and ensured that no gala attendees were straggling nearby. A catering van awaited the Chinese nationals, a mix of men and women. An array of cots allowed for twelve to be stacked and racked like rolls of carpet. The two bonus prizes were laid side by side on the floor.

Ji-woo climbed into the back of the van and nodded to the driver. The snatch-and-grab operation had gone off without a hitch.

With its cargo loaded, the van exited the garage into Theatre Alley before merging with evening traffic. The quickest route out of Lower Manhattan was to take the Brooklyn Bridge. Expansion joints in the pavement rumbled beneath tires until giving way to the sounds of tread traveling across the bridge.

Two medical technicians checked each captive's vitals, logging the results into a computer. Ji-Woo unclipped her thigh holster, slipped out of her evening dress and donned a new set of clothes: pants, pullover top, leather jacket, and hiking boots. Her semiautomatic went into an inside pocket of her jacket and she climbed up into the passenger seat and checked the vehicle's side mirrors. The two escort vehicles were trailing as expected.

Once across the bridge, the driver took the Brooklyn Queens Expressway to the Long Island Expressway. A navigation and traffic app on the driver's phone logged the route. Before reaching 678 North, the driver exited the freeway and drove the final half-mile to a junkyard without car lights on. The industrial area was dark and virtually unoccupied.

The front gate to an unlit junkyard had been left open.

When the vehicle approached a portable single-bay shop, an automated overhead door opened to allow the van inside.

The Willets Point stop was the first of several before the final destination. Once authorities realized Chinese nationals were missing, law enforcement would scour any and all available resources, including traffic camera feeds, toll plaza cameras, and satellites to track any possible clues to the mass abduction. The three-card monte maneuvers away from the city would make tracking them impossible.

Inside the shop, Ji-woo and her team got out of the vehicle. They stripped off peel-away plastic sheeting to give the van an entirely different look, changing it from white to dark blue. They mounted a tool rack to the top of the van and changed the license plates.

She checked her watch: on schedule. The stop took just over fifteen minutes. While their trek wasn't an expeditious route back to New Jersey, it was the one least likely to attract attention.

The blue van wound back to take the Whitestone Expressway across the East River. Different lead and trailing escort vehicles picked up their caravan to run interference, just in case.

The medical technicians returned their attention to the Chinese nationals, setting IV drip lines and catheters in their arms to ensure a uniform sedation. The last thing the operation needed was for anyone to wake up and create a disturbance.

Ji-woo typed in a text message into her cell phone

14 IN 3 HOURS.

She hit send. Excitement surged through her.

She was one step closer to creating a new nation.

35
DAILY REPORT

Kate swept her dormitory suite for surveillance devices. After finding nothing obvious, she showered and changed into a bureau t-shirt. She felt closer to normal, better. Rarely required to wear a suit, she was glad to get out of anything considered dress clothes.

Standing in silence, she stared out her third-floor window, across a u-shaped bricked patio to the residence wing that housed the participants. She could see Parker's windows from hers. Window coverings were drawn closed and she couldn't discern inside movement.

Kate wondered what he was doing. Research, most likely. A constant reader, he was a technical journal junkie, a hard-wired geek.

Part of her wanted to beg him to leave this insanity behind. Forces beyond their control and the world at large seemed to demand otherwise.

Their time in the Caymans seemed an eternity ago. She wondered if they could ever get back to that kind of escapism, a place and relationship without mad science or law enforcement duties.

She glanced at a clock on the wall, sighed, and turned on her computer. It was time to make her required bureau-assigned log and submit it to the Assistant Director in Charge (ADIC) of the Washington Field Office. Her write-up stuck to the thin facts, without a deeper dive into areas of substance that she could neither explain in detail nor conjecture about without factual data.

She submitted the report and closed her laptop.

After washing up, she slid her Glock beneath the adjacent pillow in her queen bed, and turned out the light for the night. Her head barely hit the pillow when her cell phone rang. Her hand swept in the dark to the device chiming on her nightstand. She tapped the green answer icon, squinting at the tiny illuminated screen. The caller ID read UNKNOWN NUMBER.

"Katherine Morgan," she said.

"Your field report wasn't very thorough," a man's voice said. "You need to provide more detail."

Kate wasn't surprised to get the call. Sitting up, she turned on a bedside lamp.

"I didn't think you wanted me to," she said to Vice President Richard Mears. "How can I help you, sir?"

"You called earlier."

"Yes. I wanted to pass on that Dr. Parker is on board. He met with the participants to discuss their neurological conditions. He's concerned about them, that something adverse happened to them during their previous memory transfers."

"Understood."

"Sir, I need to see that ship. The *Norvana*."

There was a long pause. "Work through Grayson. Report anything you discover that we haven't figured out yet."

"Like what the eight rings represent?"

"Especially that."

The phone went dead.

Kate tossed her phone onto the nightstand, turned out the light, and buried her face in a pillow. Tomorrow would start early.

And she needed to be awake before Thomas Parker.

WEDSNESDAY, DECEMBER 2nd

History is written by the winners.
Alex Haley

A modified version of Alex Haley's declaration is:
The draft of history propagated to the masses is a version censored by the victors.

36

ESSENTIAL ARRIVALS

12:25 AM, NeuroSteps Labs, Glen Garner, New Jersey

Debra Ford watched the headlights of an office furnishings freight truck stop at the facility's front gate. Security teams inspected the vehicle for tracking devices before allowing it through.

Two years earlier, Ford had stumbled on a National Security Agency (NSA) brief about research being done in a barebones engineering lab at Princeton University. That brief had been the germination of a program called Common InSight.

Her multi-prong, government-sanctioned operation had its ebbs and flows, and ill-conceived interferences from rival agencies. Her dream of forging new global alliances while vanquishing enemies of the state was now within her grasp. But the costs to fuel liberty's bright flame had been heavy. Time and again, history had proven that sacrifices were necessary for causes that changed the world forever.

She recalled a quote from Washington, not her favorite president: *Liberty, when it begins to take root, is a plant of rapid growth.*

Over the past several hours, Ford had tracked the elaborate hide-and-seek exercise as Ji-woo and her strike team drove counterclockwise out of New York City to the north and then into New Jersey. Route times and stops had been scripted. No gas stops. No driving through areas with dense surveillance. Swap vehicles had included four different vans and this final cargo truck. Lead and lag cars had been reshuffled every thirty minutes.

Common InSight was about to change the world and bring liberty to the globe.

Ford could finally see Ji-Woo's face through the windshield. Pulling the collar of her jacket tighter around her neck, she waved for the driver to park under a tall canopy.

Rear doors opened. Inside the truck's cargo space, medical technicians attended to fourteen unconscious people.

Ford smiled. Each Chinese consular attaché had been selected based on a required skillset. The group was mix of consulate officials and their guests, the guests having the simple misfortune to be at the wrong place at the wrong time. To help keep them from being missed, the Chinese Consulate's office of Personnel and Oversight had already received internal requests to grant the consulate workers five personal days off after the gala.

If Stewart Richards held up his part of the bargain, none of the abducted would be missed.

Ji-woo climbed out of the truck's cab.

"Anything you didn't get a chance to report?" Ford asked.

"Nothing," the woman said, reaching back for a small duffle bag. Her face showed concern.

Ford held her up. "We're a step closer."

Ji-Woo pulled away. "The PRC"—the People's Republic of China—"won't give up without a fight. They'll go to war with any nation that confronts them. As President, Xi Jinping will defend himself if for no other reason than to save face. China will not retreat from the world stage. It's not in their nature."

Ford turned her attention to the medical prep team unloading the Chinese nationals. The newly acquired were transfered to gurneys, and IV bags hung on poles above them. In the triage area, fourteen victims were stripped out of their fancy gala clothes and prepped for a thorough hygiene regimen.

"Every war needs foot soldiers," Ford said. "Yesterday we had none. Tonight we have fourteen. In weeks we'll have ten thousand. In a year, millions. In two years a new nation, a place where Communist China no longer exists."

Ji-woo turned away. "I would've preferred to do this covertly, in the shadows."

Ford sighed and shook her head. "No. The time was now. This window that we've been given is open for a very short period of time. We need a bold statement. One with damaging repercussions. China will no longer be able to dismiss the consequences of their aggressions as western media propaganda."

Ji-woo lowered her head. "You'd think I would be ready by now."

Ford put a hand on the woman's shoulder. "In two years, maybe sooner, you'll lead a new nation. One that unites old and new worlds. We will bring Prosperity to the planet."

37

THE LIMITS OF REFUGE

5:10 AM, Advanced BioCore International, Princeton, New Jersey

Parker tried to sleep, but spent the night tossing and turning. His mind refused to surrender to slumber, energized by the challenges that lay ahead. Finally yielding to frustration, he got out of bed, showered, and dressed for the day.

He plucked an apple from his complimentary fruit basket, left his room, and walked over to the research areas. He half-expected to encounter movement restrictions, but the few guards he encountered took no action to redirect him.

He stopped at the doors leading to the Neurophysiology Lab.

Parker used his ID access card to enter the lab's anteroom. Air equalized between corridor and lab spaces. Doors opened and he went inside. The dimly lit lab was a large space. Unoccupied pods dotted the floor. The surrounding observation rooms on the second level were dark. The Wall of Knowledge and its headwall mixture of interactive screens were off. Gauges and tiny LED lights from unattended workstations filled his periphery like colored stars watching him from a close horizon.

Wandering without a particular destination in mind, he dragged his fingertips across the contours of the vacant stimulation pods. Parker stopped at a pod in the first row, gripped its handholds and climbed inside. As he submerged into its grave-like world, the machine's sidewalls of sensors and terminals cut off all light and sound. He snorted and flexed his shoulders and hips against the vinyl padding that supported his weight.

Alone.

The weight of past failures pressed in on him, following him into the imprisonment of blackness. The claustrophobic tightness didn't bother him. In fact, he welcomed its refuge. During a year-long excavation that his parents had led in Toniná, in the Chiapas highlands of southern Mexico, he'd frequented nearby caves and underground fissures. Spelunking became more than a pastime, it was an escape from the drudgery of life in tents on a pre-Columbian archeological site.

Parker closed his eyes and let his mind drift.

Darkness. A place, at least for a moment, where secrets were unimportant.

The capsule he occupied was never intended to protect secrets, but rather extract them from the depths of quiet minds. His legacy to the world—a place without secrets or refuge or solace—a place where quiet escapes no longer existed.

He imagined he was lying on the floor of a cave. Droplets ticked as mineral water passed from stalactites to ponds. Gravity was at work. *Tick. Tick. Tick.* The rhythmic progression grew louder, more rapid, as if influenced by an impending watershed.

An intruding voice broke nature's cadence. At first it was muffled, without clarity.

He was no longer alone. Opening his eyes, he saw a face break the boundaries of his shelter.

"A penny for your thoughts?" Kate asked, staring at him through the opening of the capsule-like pod.

Parked huffed. "It costs more than that."

"You're up early."

"Couldn't sleep." He took a long breath. "Spying on me?"

"Worried about you."

A dodge to his question. Kate wasn't a morning person by choice. On their month-long vacation, she'd slept in whenever she could, when he wasn't rousting her out of bed to go diving or embark on an early morning hike. He missed feeling her form press against his during the night, something he wasn't about to admit.

"What are you doing?" she asked.

He shrugged. "I was wondering what it was like. To be one of them. A participant. Alone. Afraid. Not in control of your own thoughts."

Kate's dark hair dangled past her shoulders to frame her face. The faint ambient light from the surrounding lab gave her features a tinted glow. He missed waking and seeing her next to him. Something else he'd avoid mentioning.

"Thanks for ruining the moment," he said.

"I can leave if you want."

The ticking sounds he'd heard had been the heels of her shoes, first on the tile floors and then clicking together like a knock on a door.

Kate offered a trace of a smile. "Or I could join you."

His view of her reminded him of when they'd first met. He'd been shot. Her figure had crouched over him as he lay on a slab of cold concrete. Then he'd been moved to the dining room table of an NSA safe house. Special Agent Katherine Morgan had saved his life, in more ways than just one.

"I'm a monster," he said.

The clicking of her heels stopped as she shook her head, her dangling hair pulsing in an oval motion.

"I don't believe that." Her lips twitched. "You can tell yourself that, but it's not true."

He swallowed over a knot in his throat. "What I've done to these people—"

"Don't do this to yourself."

Kate climbed over the edge of the pod to squeeze into his chamber of solitude. Her presence blocked out any remaining ambient room light. Warmth pressed upon him, dispersing the weight of his sins. Pinned against the bottom of the pod, her form molded over his, knees, arms, and elbows adjusting to fill crevices and voids. Their lips met. They kissed. Her fingers reached beneath his neck and drew him closer.

Her mouth pressed against his cheek. "I'll do it."

"I haven't asked you yet." He could feel her trying to calm herself. Kate feared few things, but she did struggle with claustrophobia. During their vacation, he'd convinced her to get dive certification and go shipwreck diving. She did the training and open water diving easily enough, but refused to swim inside any sunken ships resting on the bottom of the ocean.

"But you will," she said. "The way I treated you, you deserved better. Thomas, life for me got pretty messed up when I returned to DC. I didn't intend to put distance between us. I was afraid that I wanted things in life that I shouldn't have. A normal life. Life with someone who wasn't law enforcement for a change. I thought about you. A lot. I missed you."

He croaked out a laugh. Making love in the box-like space would prove challenging, if not impossible. She responded with a laugh of her own and kissed his neck.

Parker sensed the spontaneous incursion wasn't about intimacy as much as it was about seeking forgiveness without actually asking. Her breasts rose and fell against his chest, her breathing balancing his.

"I'll do it," she repeated, kissing him, drawing his lips deeply into hers.

Kate had volunteered to go someplace that he hadn't been ready to consider even going himself.

38

MOMENTS OF TRUTH

6:00 AM, White House, Washington, DC

Richard Mears entered the West Wing to receive the morning's executive briefing. The President had left Andrews Air Force Base at 4:00 AM to conduct a series of meetings with the Group of Seven, universally known as the G7. Unless the two were together, the administration's tradition had the President's daily brief (PDB) occurring earlier, giving presenters time to make requested adjustments before the VP received it. The President received his PDB the moment Air Force One lifted off for its flight across the Atlantic.

Mears managed a sound four hours of sleep then felt compelled to start his day early.

The PDB focused on the incursion of Chinese state actors into U.S. boundaries and the set-up of a floating research lab in Atlantic City. The blatant escalation of kidnapping, theft of intellectual property, and espionage signaled a preemptive strike by the People's Republic of China. The three-letter agencies around Washington were working on forensic and financial evidence to link China to the covert operation before releasing the news publicly. Those killed on the ship during the military-led operation were confirmed to be U.S. citizens, all North Korean child refugees and adopted by American families in good standing. This led the intelligence communities to speculate about North Korean or Chinese moles in the U.S., akin to the Operation Ghost Stories investigation that led to the arrest of two Russian sleeper agents in 2010. Russia had been trying to infiltrate the U.S. since the 1950s. North Korea and China were no different.

Of course, proxy espionage and theft of government, industrial, and commercial technology and trade secrets were nothing new: China, Russia, Japan, Turkey, India, Israel. For nearly eighty years, U.S. domestic policy had been reactionary, tolerant of intellectual property theft. China state-sponsored espionage campaigns had targeted Silicon Valley, the Department of Energy and its national labs, NASA, New York's financial districts, military bases, and genetically modified agricultural products.

Atlantic City raised these attacks to a new level.

National Security Advisor Gordon Abbott wrapped up the briefing. "We know where the data and evidence will eventually take us, but we're still missing critical facts."

Mears thanked everyone and turned to the phone that had started ringing on his desk.

"Good morning, Mr. Vice President," the President's Chief of Staff said over the phone. "I have some unfortunate news to relay." The woman cleared her throat. "We learned late last night that Ambassador Peter Tang passed away the day before last."

Mears leaned against the side of his desk. "What did he die of?"

"A heart attack."

Mears sighed. Peter Tang had been a friend since Georgetown Law School. They had ventured into different aspects of politics. Fluent in several languages, Tang took the diplomatic and international law route, eventually serving several administrations to be the U.S. Ambassador to Thailand and then the senior diplomat and *de facto* Ambassador to Taiwan. While Tang was always cautious about expressing Asia-Pacific Rim views in public forums, privately was a different matter.

Secretly, Tang was a proponent of creating a new landscape for Asia. Tang would've declared himself an anarchist if that meant neutering China. He considered the Handover a move that would ultimately lead to the coldest of wars. Britain's transfer of sovereignty over Hong Kong in 1997 should've returned the land to the people of Hong Kong. The one-China policy had been a failed idea concocted by international neophytes and ignorant fools. Communist China's grand strategy and ambitions for global expansion had put the autocratic country squarely on a collision course with the United States, which would eventually bring about another Cold War.

"The memorial service is scheduled for Saturday," the President's Chief of Staff continued. "In Georgetown. The Ambassador's family wants to know if you can attend."

"Of course. Clear my calendar. And send a card and flowers to his wife, Szu-Wei." Mears thought for a moment. "Please inform the Secretary of State, if he hasn't already heard the news. He's been good friends with the Tang family for years. I'm sure he'd want to pay his respects as well."

39

DECONSTRUCTION

NeuroSteps Labs, New Jersey

Richards opened his eyes. He was staring facedown at the desk in his hotel-like suite. It took several blinks to shake his stupor. He must've fallen asleep while sketching out notes, which meant that he never made it to bed.

He glanced at a wall clock: 6:30 AM.

He'd slept the entire night at his desk.

Steadying himself, Richards stood and worked to clear the fog in his mind.

After a shower, shave, and a change of clothes, he felt better. The nurse from the night before checked on him and arranged for breakfast. Scrambled eggs, toast, orange juice, and black coffee. Rested, nourished, and with notes from the previous night in hand, he was ready to resume his research.

Richards entered NeuroSteps Cybernetics Lab and found a team of engineers and technicians dissecting and analyzing Thomas Parker's original hardware, his neurological interface and headgear.

A team in a neighboring lab had already uploaded programming code from solid state hard drives. As the components were dismantled, the team methodically passed each piece of equipment to the next stage-gated workstation. The systematic precision's only goal was reverse-engineering the mechanisms.

Directed by project leaders, teams tracked the deconstruction matched to five functional cybernetic areas: physical system components and human-machine hardware interfaces, software and artificial intelligence wetware solutions, human cognitive modeling wetware solutions, computational analysis and enhanced machine learning targeting predicted outcomes, and integrating optimization and continuous improvements.

Richards grinned. NeuroSteps engineers were not just replicating Parker's equipment, but working to build a better mind-reading mousetrap.

Consumers rarely understood that it was routine for companies around the globe to deconstruct competitors' products—anything from automotive parts to foods and beverages, to chemicals and pharmaceuticals, to consumer electronics, to advanced computer systems.

On one set of monitors, logs tracked commercially available substitute components. Another tallied custom parts and proposed how to build suitable replications most efficiently.

Richards twitched as an unfamiliar sensation grew. His mind froze. Time moved forward without him. Minutes later, his sputtering mind broke free from a transient stoppage.

Something isn't right.

His brain struggled to stay conscious, a symptom of a larger problem.

He couldn't solve this dilemma immediately. He remembered the notebook he carried, and the notes that he'd drafted the previous evening.

Stay in motion and try not to stop again. Just keep thinking.

Richards approached one of the research leads and presented his hypotheses, laying out the critical path procedures for action.

The NeuroSteps way of conducting business emphasized flexibility and adaptability. On the fly, arrangements had been made to bring together an entirely new team conscripted from members of other teams. The new initiatives team was dedicated solely to the tasks that Richards had prioritized.

Richards felt energized, empowered.

NeuroSteps would deliver his Frontier.

40

SECRETS WRITTEN IN THE PAGES OF A DIARY

Advanced BioCore International, Princeton, New Jersey

Kate hated everything about this déjà vu in the worst way.

Her head was wedged between white foam blocks. A face mask restricted her head movements. Confined within the sounds of a demonic clamor, vibrations rattled her, sending tremors deep into her bones. Even knowing the science behind functional magnetic resonance imaging (fMRI), it still took all her strength to go through the process voluntarily. There was nothing natural about having your hydrogen atoms jiggled. Too much jiggling, and you cooked to death from the inside out. Perspiration painted her skin as she forced herself to take long, drawn-out breaths and calm her mind.

"Kate, you're doing great," Parker said through a speaker somewhere near her head.

What a lie.

The last time she'd taken an fMRI for Parker, he tricked her into freaking out.

Kate considered volunteering to do something she was deathly afraid of as equating to stupidity, even if the experience wasn't going to maim or kill her.

Stay on task, she told herself. The more she thought of other things, the more noise would infiltrate Parker's neurological baseline model.

Noise was bad. Noise corrupted system routines. Mind-wandering and daydreaming during evaluation testing created excess noise.

Colored images cycled through the goggles that covered her face, progressing from simple to complex, then letters of the alphabet, then whole words and phrases, and finally images of well-known destinations and famous people. Kate focused on each image, repeating each unique name silently in her mind.

Elsewhere in the facility, she knew, real-time simulations were being run in parallel to match brain activity to the neurophysiological architectures that Parker had established as target points for cognitive associations. This time around, Parker had added complexities to the set of assessment metrics, and the procedure was taking longer than Kate wanted.

She wanted to ask aloud: *Are we done yet?* That kind of unauthorized thinking translated to noise.

So she asked it again: *Are we done yet?*

-+- -+-

In a cramped control room, Parker sat at a console populated with terminals and monitors. Neurological scans, biodata, and images filled the screens. Through the viewing window, he could see the fMRI unit. The imaging room was dimly lit to create a more calming experience. The lower half of Kate's body and feet stretched down a white mobile table. Her head and shoulders disappeared inside a large white donut.

The last time he'd subjected her to an imaging experiment, she eventually melted down and threw a tantrum. He couldn't blame her. He'd tricked Kate into a fight-or-flight response, a series of cognitive functions closely tied to emotion.

Fear, a powerful primal human emotion, could cripple or empower.

The deception had worked.

Kate's original scans gave him a clear neurological baseline, a template for tracing the migration of neurotransmitters, micro-electro-chemical reactions, and ion transfers across synaptic gaps in the brain. In practical terms, the simplest thought of a two-dimensional colored shape required a half-trillion neurons to fire and billions of simultaneous transmissions to propagate through the brain. Complex shapes, objects with complexity, required greater neural signal propagation. His neurological templates and modeling had the ability to factor down the micro energy transfers to tens to hundreds of thousands of signals, creating simplified ratios like the lowest common denominator in math. The example he'd used with students in his classes at Princeton was searching for one quarter placed on a single seat inside a 100,000-seat football stadium. From a simple square-footage exercise, it was an enormous task that might take all day long. But if the placement quarter could be constrained to a certain section of the stadium, finding the silver-colored object might take only thirty minutes.

That was what Kate's original brain scan offered: a way to reduce the mind's geographic regions. A baseline template for a smaller search area. Then a supercomputer could be tasked to focus on relevant bio-chemical energy transfers in the mind and know which regions of the brain to ignore.

He took a frustrated breath.

This time around, Kate was subconsciously resisting the exercise.

Her scans and developing cognitive model told him that she was holding back. Thought suppression.

Secrets.

As an FBI agent, she constantly compartmentalized thoughts and experiences. Went with the job. In the 1980s, researchers conducted a series of studies to better understand the cognitive dynamics of holding back feelings, neutralizing distressing thoughts, telling lies, or revealing secrets. Suppressing thoughts often created other behavioral issues and stress. Researchers had categorized thirty-eight common secrets, hypothesizing that on average a person held onto thirteen secrets.

What were Kate's thirteen secrets?

What was she holding back?

He couldn't help wanting to know. Accessing someone's thoughts without permission was akin to reading their diary and learning their deepest, darkest secrets. He felt that slippery slope tugging at him.

Parker reprimanded himself for being selfish, and changed course. He timestamped her developing fMRI scans and enlarged a translucent, three-dimensional model. A walnut-like topography bristled with a sparkling luminescence of tiny hot spots and revealed deeper fibrous regions inside her brain. Descriptive tags highlighted high-level organ structures.

Bringing up different visual streams, he moved Kate away from random associations and simple cognitive structures. On the screen, he uploaded pictures of Stewart Richards. Parker shuffled his gaze between screens.

Kate started to focus harder as her mind lit up with new associations.

Doubling down on the complexity that he beamed into her mind, he released pictures of Oklahoma Senator Samuel Ford, on Capitol Hill wearing a variety of suits and looking very much like a civic champion and then more personal ones in everyday life. The final image in this string showed Ford standing beside his ex-wife during an award ceremony.

Bingo. Now he was getting somewhere.

Kate's mind blazed with cognitive associations. Without realizing it, she'd freed herself of the subconscious shackles holding her back. In a way, secrets were being accessed.

Somehow, Kate knew the senator's ex-wife in other contexts.

For years, MRIs had been used as potential lie detectors, far surpassing what polygraphs measured in terms of stress evaluation and emotional responses. Around the world, for-profit companies marketed the ability of MRIs to turn the pseudoscience of lie-detection into commercial authentication services, claiming accuracies above ninety percent.

Parker fidgeted in his seat, then he gave in to the urge.

He typed in a line of text and flashed it to her.

WHAT'S YOUR SECRET?

Kate's brain sparked new cognitive associations, ebbing and flowing under the illumination recordings of the fMRI. A University of Pennsylvania psychiatrist and neuroscientist, Dr. Daniel Langleben, had tracked the progression of blood flow in different parts of the brain when his test subjects lied. Kate's anterior cingulated cortex, the dorsal lateral prefrontal cortex, and the parietal cortex regions grew more active. Deception. When a person lied and knew their statements were false, their brain often worked harder than if they actually had told the truth.

Secrets.

Parker was tired of dancing around how he felt. As he released the final string of images, moving to personal associations, he knew this had nothing to do with helping the participants.

He did it anyway. *Secrets be damned.*

In three-second increments, interrelated images flashed to Kate for a specific context: a sailboat, a sunset, a stretch of sand, a pair of footprints in sand and leading to a horizon, silhouettes of a couple on a beach holding hands.

Kate didn't pick up on the change in testing until it had happened.

She grasped enough of Parker's neuromapping process to understand that she'd been manipulated, without her consent.

Within a few hundred milliseconds, her mind acknowledged harboring secrets and feelings well before she could have verbalized them.

The new sequence of images pierced her visual cortex to spark a new wave of thoughts. She shuddered as a spike of adrenaline rippled through her body, sending her pulse racing and flushing her skin. The otherworldly vibrations engulfing her seemed to grow louder. She shut her eyes, knowing Parker wanted a particular biological response from her.

The last set of images—a sailboat, a sunset, footprints in a stretch of sand, two silhouettes holding hands—reached past her mind's defenses.

That was its intended purpose. He'd used her vulnerability to elicit specific emotions before. Manipulated her.

Previously, it was for the greater good. Now she wasn't so sure.

Kate almost shouted: *Get out of my head!* Instead, she did the opposite, focusing on an imaginary ice cube sitting on a cold white counter. *Cold. Nothing melted. Ice and a hard surface.* Slowing her breathing, she clicked the edges of her front teeth together and harmonized the action to a rhythm with the MRI unit.

Seconds passed and swelled past a minute.

Breathe. Ice. Counter. Cold. Breathe.

More time passed.

Suddenly, like a tremor preceding an earthquake, Kate shuddered. She felt the mechanical suffocation of the MRI machine's noise closing in on her. Her concentration on *ice, counter, cold* broke.

Flushed and flustered, Kate said, "Thomas?"

No response came.

Her heart jumped, causing her hands to shake.

"Thomas, answer me. Please. Say something."

He exhaled, revealing his frustration. "I wanted to know."

Kate couldn't hold back any longer. "Turn off this damn machine! And get me out of here!"

41

OUTSIDE CONVERSATIONS

Parker decided his next best course of action was to give Kate space.

Provoking her during a moment of vulnerability, he'd intentionally flustered her. He'd asked, without asking: did she love him? There was no right or wrong answer. He just wanted to know where she stood on their relationship.

The neurological responses from her mind were inconclusive, yet her physical gestures indicated a resounding *no*.

At least *no* was an answer. He could live with that and move on.

Parker was about to return to his residence when a guard intercepted him.

"Dr. Parker has been located," a woman said into a microphone attached to a radio. "Bringing him up front now."

"If this is about the incident with Agent Morgan—"

"Sir, your contract with the U.S. government prohibits the transfer of materials in all forms. At Advanced BioCore, you must follow these agreements. Intellectual property must remain secure at all times."

He was about to argue with her when she nudged him to start walking.

Confused about what his latest infraction might be, she directed him to the facility's front lobby, a space he'd recognized from his arrival at Advanced BioCore.

Atop the reception desk was a hard-sided white and red plastic container displaying a red medical cross. The label on its side read: HUMAN ORGANS FOR TRANSPLANT. HANDLE WITH EXTREME CARE. DO NOT FREEZE. A decal below the label documented the container's contents: human tissue.

Attached to the handle of the cooler, a tag read:
DR. THOMAS PARKER, NEUROLOGIST, ADVANCED BIOCORE INTERNATIONAL.

After he signed for the package, the receptionist handed him an envelope.

Parker extracted a card and read the message left for him.
TIME SENSITIVE. DELIVER THESE SPECIMENS TO YOUR BIOGENETICS LAB THEN WALK OUTSIDE. ALONE. ON THE EAST SIDE OF THE PROPERTY PAST THE FOUNTAIN. TEN MINUTES. YOUR CLOCK IS TICKING. DON'T BE LATE.

Parker pocketed the card and checked his watch, wondering when his ten minutes had actually started. He snatched up the organ transport container and returned to the research wing. Entering the Biogenetics Lab, he ignored the red tape striping on the floor, a line that separated non-sterile from sterile areas. Technicians and researchers started barking at him for violating protocols. Ignoring their complaints, he broke the container's seals, cracked it open, and studied its contents.

Set within cooled gel inserts, six spherical plastic balls contained light-brown organs immersed in pinkish liquids. Organoids. He could see veins and folds in the clumps of tissue.

Cerebral organoids. Mini-brains, to be exact. Well-developed mini-brains. Nothing fit to be transplanted, but rather studied and stimulated.

Parker backed away from the organ box.

A curious biogenetics researcher peered inside.

Parker checked his watch. "Don't touch," he said. "We'll talk about what to do with those when I return."

Jogging, he left the research wing and navigated corridors to the east side of the building. His access badge let him out the last series of secured doors. Surprisingly, the exterior exit door opened without adult supervision: no security, no babysitters, no federal agents pretending to be his lover.

Still, surveillance cameras would watch every movement he made.

An open breezeway led to a campus-like setting. Cool morning air invigorated his senses. East-facing lawns stretched away from tightly clustered facility buildings. Sunlight pierced winter-barren treetops, spraying him with warm rays. Squinting through the brightness made him think of the movie *Poltergeist*: "Do not go into the light. Stop where you are. Turn away from it. Don't even look at it."

That was exactly the opposite of what he needed to do.

He entered the light.

Parker trekked down brick walkways to reach a wide-open spread of grass. The turf beneath his shoes felt squishy, as if groundskeepers had recently watered. The sunlight gave him an energy that he hadn't possessed minutes earlier.

To the southeast, the sunrise cast shadows across the grass. Trunks and limbs cascaded across a tapestry of green, not unlike a spread of neural pathways.

A pulsing reflection caught his attention, at the boundary of the adjoining forest.

The snap of light grew more brilliant: a signal.

At the property's tree-lined boundary, on the other side of a wrought iron fence, a woman wearing a rustic-looking brown coat tucked a mirror and hand-sized binoculars into her coat pocket. She'd been watching him from the shadows, waiting for him.

Parker glanced around. They were alone.

"You deliver the organoids?" he asked, drawing closer.

Fifty feet out, she said, "Just another doc in a box, aren't you?"

As he walked, he studied the woman. Wide-lensed sunglasses covered her eyes and didn't permit him to get a read on her age. North of forty. Dark hair, chocolate-colored. Below the semi-bulky coat she wore, black leggings stopped at a pair of running shoes.

He had the sense they'd met before. "Do I know you?"

"Don't think so."

"But you know me?"

"For a doctor, you're not particularly bright."

"Excuse me?"

Her lips pursed for a second. "Dr. Parker, you're expendable. And if you keep pretending you're the victim here, people are going to die. This quest—let's call it what it really is—Common InSight, is bigger than you." She took a vigorous breath of cool air. "In order to secure it and set *your* terms, construct a viable solution before Stewart Richards beats you to it."

He stopped at the edge of the trees. "Who are you?"

The woman feigned irritation. "I've said this to others. Stop asking the wrong questions." She removed her sunglasses to reveal intense hazel brown eyes. "What you did at ANCRI was admirable. Blow up the lab to hide evidence and data. But now you're stonewalling the inevitable. You're taking a neutral stance in a negative-sum game. If you don't win, you're irrelevant. Richards gains by default. Any competition to his work will be eliminated. You. Caroline Wang. Those college kids. Everyone dies. Token collateral damage erased from the history books. That'll be your legacy."

Parker grasped the challenge set before him, but doubted its validity. "You've got me at a disadvantage. How do you know this? And why do you care?"

"I have my reasons."

"Why should I trust you?"

She smirked. "I'm not saying you should. But you can't just blow up this lab like last time. You'd be dead before you try."

Parker chuckled. "You must've read a report on what happened. That's how you knew that my modeling needed mini-brains to stimulate: sensory inputs for pyramidal neurons, voltage gradients, harmonic interactions, ion action potentials. Thanks for the gifts but I don't need any more dubious alliances."

"Anyone figure out that you're going to try and save the participants?"

He'd never verbalized those sentiments, but somehow she knew.

"Dr. Parker, in my profession the key to making the world yield to your will is deception. Powerful misdirection. Deception creates illusions, projected perceptions. So, who to trust? If you don't trust me, people you care about will die. Then you'll follow them to the grave."

He doubted he could trust this stranger, even if she pointed out a path to be taken. His thoughts circled back to the participants.

"What do their dreams reveal?" she asked.

He'd given that question a lot of thought. This was no time to reveal the only cards he held. He corrected her instead. "They're not dreams. Memories. Shared memories."

"Memories layered with dangerous secrets. Powerful secrets that afford you the leverage you're so desperately lacking. Learning those secrets gives you influence, powerful leverage."

He understood the statement and suddenly felt small, like a field soldier in someone else's war.

"Ever ask yourself where the other fourteen are?"

ANCRI had acquired thirty participants. Two were killed. Twenty-eight survived. Of those, fourteen were now human test subjects at Advanced BioCore. Somewhere else were fourteen others, presumably possessing a similar set of shared memories.

"I can take you to them," she continued. "All you have to do is trust that I'm protecting your best interests, at least on some level."

"What do you want from me?"

"When the time comes, give them what they want. What the government wants. It's okay. People want to know what Senator Samuel Ford knew. Share it."

"I'm not following."

"Dr. Parker, if you don't, people will die."

The woman put her sunglasses back on and edged sideways, sheltering her figure in the shadows cast by tree trunks. Her brown coat and black leggings turned into camouflage. Her attire was its own deception.

In the distance, someone called for him. It was Kate.

"Morgan is manipulating you," the woman said bluntly. "Of course, you know that, don't you? Do you trust her? With your life? With other people's lives? Ask the federal agent about DC. Why she dumped you after your trip. Dr. Parker, you're a means to an end. And Morgan's secrets are so deadly that you won't survive them. Trust her if you will, but be prepared to lose your life if you do."

His mind reeled. Instincts told him this woman was neither his advocate nor benefactor.

But she probably wasn't wrong. Not entirely.

Kate called to him again.

Cocking his head, he glanced at Kate, who ran to make up the distance between them.

"Let's say for argument," he said, "that I buy into this delusion that you're peddling. You're invested. I lose, you lose. Tell me I'm wrong."

The woman flashed a handgun, holding it low, pointed at the ground. She cracked a half smile and stood behind the trunk of a tree, leaving only her face and the gun visible.

"I can kill Morgan, if you'd like?"

Parker frowned. "No. Leave Kate to me."

The woman drifted further into the woods. "Suit yourself, Thomas Parker."

"Come on, cerebral organoids? Not much of a gift between strangers. I can tell you're no delivery person. You came here for a reason. So, make this conversation between us worth my time."

She chuckled and withdrew deeper into the woods, until she was almost invisible. "Use your Magical Mystery Tour. Ask your participants about Common InSight."

He recognized the Beatles reference. The LSD-inspired psyche-delic soundtrack wasn't his favorite from the Fabulous Foursome. He disliked Lennon's "I Am the Walrus" the most. A filler song on the same record, "The Fool on the Hill," was actually about wisdom unseen.

Parker understood that he might be that fool on the hill.

He cupped his hands around his mouth and whispered, "I need more than that."

A voice drifted through the trees in a way that didn't let him triangulate its location. "Manhattan. Last night."

Parker tossed a pair of open palms at the woods. "You kiddin' me? What kind of clue is that?"

Kate slowed and thrust her hands against her hips. Out of breath, she said, "Thomas, what are you doing out here?"

42

MISSION ACCOMPLISHED

Debra Ford missed the adrenaline rush associated with clandestine field work.

Even harmless covert shake-and-release meetings—like meeting Thomas Parker—energized her. They always had. Years earlier, the State Department had removed her from case assignments and pushed her off the books. For ten years running, she'd delivered State's top covert field results, although none of her classified case assignments would see the light of day. The Russians had given her two nicknames and still had a bounty out on her. As the State Department grew more politically correct and negotiated with terrorists and dictators, her field methods were deemed aggressive without warrant. State had asked her to step away peacefully. Not quite her style. To break up the doldrums of retirement, she'd accepted an occasional side job as long as it lined up with her end goals.

Those goals had brought her to Princeton, several times now.

Trekking a previously scouted path, one that traversed firm ground, Ford left no footprints and reflected on what she knew about Thomas Parker.

She'd read an NSA psychological profile on the neurologist, researcher, and Princeton professor. That detailed report had been compiled by his former graduate assistant, Rebecca Ward. Based on his personality profile, Ford had devised a set of motivational triggers geared to advancing him in an essential direction. In an extra twist, she convinced the DOJ to label Parker the most dangerous man in the world. If he failed to cooperate, her backup option was a wild roll of the dice, a resurrection of sorts—Stewart Richards.

Her recommendations to both the DOJ and the Pentagon classified Parker and the twenty-eight participants as national security threats. The tactical move shielded the executive branch from additional fallout from ANCRI, and left the dreams of Prosperity and Peace on Earth intact.

For the short term.

Congress still demanded hearings on covertly funded research, abductions, dead senators, and illegal human research. Preemptive court filings, national security warnings and restricted access, and old-fashioned stonewalling had the intended effects. The hearings were delayed. In less than a week, a new set of threats would snatch Congress's attention and everything that happened in Princeton would shift to the back burner.

Ford cut through a gap in perimeter fencing and kept to treed boundaries, making her way southwest until she came out on Washington Road.

As she climbed into her car, Ford thought about how predictable Parker had turned out to be. The psychological profiling had been spot on. In a way, that made him a reliable, persuadable asset.

The race was official: Thomas Parker versus Stewart Richards. Whoever lost would die for his country.

And neither of them could do anything to change that outcome.

43

WHEN WORDS HURT MORE THAN KNIFES AND DAGGERS

Winded from running, Kate stood beside Parker at a cropping of deciduous trees, an odd place for him to be wandering alone.

From his posture, she gathered that he was mad.

She'd blamed him for entrapping her, asking questions that she didn't want to answer. Since returning to Princeton, seeing Parker again, she'd struggled to rekindle their flame, unsure if the disconnect was her or him. He'd changed. She'd definitely changed. Not for the better.

Her impression of him was fractured, which was not his fault at all. Her outlook on life, even love had changed.

"Thomas, please say something," Kate said. She reached for his hand, not knowing how to break the barrier between them.

He jerked his hand away.

She'd seen him vulnerable, at his worst. During their vacation, she'd felt comfortable and yearned for that part of their relationship to return. It was hard when secrets and even evil pushed them apart.

In many ways, they were so alike. Independent. Stubborn. Perceptive. Smart in the sciences. Medically trained doctors. Precise at whatever they focused on. People who struggled with moral rights and wrongs, intertwining ethics.

Without acknowledging her presence, Parker headed back to BioCore's buildings.

The unspoken jab was warranted, in a way. Frustrated, she kicked a shoe at the grass, struggling to find the right thing to say.

"Thomas, stop! Please… just stop."

Halfway across the lawn he turned around.

Kate allowed distance and silence to do her initial speaking.

"What?" he asked.

"So, you want to know if I love you? Flashing me silhouettes. Images portraying what? Love? Friendship? Companionship? Until death do us part? You knew I was trapped. Yet you asked anyway. Lovebirds on a beach. People holding hands. A pair of footsteps in the sand." She stormed across the grass. "Have the guts to ask me, face to face. You might be surprised at what I say."

She bumped his shoulder hard to put an exclamation point on her statement and marched to the facility.

"It's best if you leave," he called back at her. "Today."

Kate slowed her gait, but refused to turn around. She lowered her head to stare at the brick walkway she'd just stepped on. A tear dripped onto her cheek and she fought to ignore its descent.

"I do love you, Thomas," she muttered beneath her breath, not loud enough for him to hear. "I just needed you to ask differently."

He was solving a problem in his heart with his head.

She was struggling with the same.

Parker had four problems. Kate reckoned her small sacrifice in the fMRI unit solved one of them. He needed a baseline. She checked that box. Her mild sacrifice had worked previously, at ANCRI.

Second, he'd need to construct an interactive neurological model using her brain as a baseline template. It was impossible to complete neural network modeling forecasts without a foundational map. That was where building on her brain scans fit in. He needed a volunteer for that. The participants had too much noise—voices, memories mired in their heads—to transition to reliable, accurate templates. The most logical solution to those wetware substrates was Kate. He knew it. She did too.

The third problem was entirely hardware-related. His missing headgear was unique. He'd built the original interfaces through trial and error. Out of paranoia, he'd never documented the components. No blueprints for replicating the device existed. He'd have to build those from scratch.

Finally, there were massive amounts of program coding to develop. BioCore had an extensive team of software engineers to write software applications, as long as Parker overcame his three other problems first.

Kate took a breath and turned around as another tear streaked down her cheek.

"I won't beg." She'd never beg anyone for attention or beg to stay when she wasn't wanted. She decided to use the only leverage she had. "How are you going to build a neuromap to use as a baseline template? I dare you to use anyone else but me."

She wiped the tear from her cheek and sniffled.

"When you stop being an ass," she said, "just talk to me."

Kate left Parker standing at the edge of the grass, a bit stunned.

Badging back into the facility, she prayed that she'd pushed the right buttons rather than say the wrong thing and drive him away.

44

SACRIFICE IS NEEDED

NeuroSteps Labs, Glen Garner, New Jersey

Ji-woo Song had prepared herself for a moment like this since she was five years old. Her entire life converged on a date on a calendar, except she'd never know when the date would arrive.

Nevertheless, it was time to fulfill destiny. Perform whatever was asked of her, even if that required sacrifice.

Wearing a white uniform, she bowed and allowed a technician to guide her to a chair.

She stepped through clouds of black hair across the floor to take her seat. She looked at her bare feet, and saw that her toes had disappeared in the trimmings of hair sacrificed by the soldiers conscripted to join her in building a new nation.

Technicians pulled back her long hair as electric shears sparked to life. Efficient hands touched her neck and scalp. Before she knew it, a pass had been made. A sheaf of black hair fell away. Then another and another. She saw the stripping of her hair like tossing coins into a wishing well, a payment made to lighten the burdens of many.

Hope was coming to the world.

Closing her eyes, Ji-woo accepted the transformation. The next step was wet shaving of her head to produce a clean scalp. When she opened her eyes, her bright brown eyes gazed back at her through a hand mirror, crested by arching eyebrows.

She saw resolve in her expressionless face. The face in the mirror was that of a leader who supported a cause greater than herself.

She was a Founder.

Richards stood outside NeuroSteps' interactive imaging suite. He hadn't been told who his baseline participant would be, only that it was a woman who was fluent in English, Mandarin, and Korean.

The three languages were essential to the required application.

The Korean-American introduced to him as Dr. Ji-woo Song rounded a corner, escorted by technicians. She wore a white jumper and slippers. As he'd instructed, her head had been shaved and marked with the geometric patterns, electrode points.

He knew little about this woman or about the other participants who would join her as participants.

"Dr. Richards," Ji-woo said with a bow, "let's go to work."

Richards gestured to the fMRI unit beyond an open door. "After you."

She nodded and entered the high-tech imaging suite. A warm hue washed over the 10 Tesla, ultra-high-resolution machine. She climbed onto the table connected to the unit. A technician positioned her head between vinyl-covered blocks and closed a plastic facemask over her head.

Richards stepped into the radiologist's control room. In an adjacent room, different technicians studied preloaded brain functions and neuromapping templates on various workstations. Elsewhere in the facility, everything was networked to quantum-based supercomputers. As images were generated, technicians tagged the results. Once tagged, programmers wrote neural-interrelational predictors—reading how brain signals propagated across the mind.

This functional MRI suite was custom-built for research. The scanner was similar to technology built for the Helen Willis Neuroscience Institute at UC Berkeley. Normal resolution in high-imaging MRI units could only get close enough to see 100,000 neurological neighborhoods in the brain, about the size of a grain of rice. This newer version had a neuron granularity down to half-the-size of a poppy seed, roughly 6,000 neurons. The result was astonishing clarity. The clearer the image, the less the supercomputers had to guess and approximate gap parameters.

The technician running the fMRI machine ran Dr. Song through a sequenced, scripted routine, having Ji-woo give responses, first in English, then in Korean and Mandarin. The testing started with simple assessments and graduated to more complicated ones.

Richards had instructed the technicians to replicate the process Parker had developed. Once scanning finished, supercomputers form-fitted her scans over a baseline neuromap.

He strolled to the viewing window.

Anticipation stirred in him. This computational modeling exercise brought him half-way, a step closer to neurological singularity.

Ji-woo had been briefed on the mental gymnastics required of her. Using three languages, she worked through a series of elementary objects, phrases, written language, complex objects and images, photos of people and places, short segments of video, and saved for last were the leaders of Hong Kong, both Koreas, and Beijing. Silently, she spoke the name of what she saw, visualized the object, and finally spoke the name what she visualized.

Other than being cold and having to put up with the constant thrum of the machine, the testing process fell into a routine. Thirty minute breaks were given on the hour, where she hydrated and rested in a dark room.

Six hours later, she'd completed the gauntlet of tests and returned to her room where dinner awaited.

Every time she passed a mirror, she couldn't help but think a stranger was accompanying her. Baldness was necessary. Two mannequin heads on a bathroom vanity displayed different Asian-haired wigs.

Cutting hair was part of the human rights violations of forced labor in Xinjiang, China, Ji-woo knew. As part of its campaign to subjugate and assimilate minorities and lockdown dissidents, the Chinese government had built concentration camps as a funnel for mass-scale forced labor. Those who survived or escaped the camps told stories about women's heads being shaved when they arrived, as a statement of their servitude and a donation of the last value they possessed.

Hair taken from slaves and prisoners was sold for wigs.

Ji-woo forwent the hair for now, considering her new look a badge of courage, a rite of passage. Her baldness emphasized her face, the passion behind her brown eyes.

Richards returned to the director's library and read through progress reports generated by the task force teams assigned to the project.

What he had witnessed exceeded his expectations. Rather remarkable. He'd seen what Parker had achieved on shoestring budgets, which put those accomplishments into perspective. He compared those earlier efforts to getting three astronauts to the moon. NeuroSteps' expanded set of human trials would deliver an army of men and women to Mars in the same amount of time it would've taken to get to the Moon.

Richards understood the future NeuroSteps would bring. It was a deal struck with the devil.

Decades earlier, he'd been a runner-up for a Nobel Prize for Medicine. Years later, the Phoenix Consortium offered him a chance to lead ANCRI. NeuroSteps' terms would be different. He could champion the technology, but would never gain recognition for the actual achievements. Instead of being the face of the enterprise, he'd been relegated to the position of a ghostwriter. He would lead accomplishments that would never be credited to him.

We knew the world would not be the same. It was what Robert Oppenheimer had said about the Manhattan Project. It would be true in this case as well.

Once Richards finished his work, NeuroSteps Labs would control the technology. He'd read up on the for-profit corporation, a worldwide conglomerate with multiple facilities focused solely on medical and biological research. Results from his neuromapping work would be shared with other labs for decoding and replication: one in London, another in Japan, and the final one in India. Each facility tackled a unique aspect of computational quantum biomechanics. The contribution delivered a days-to-minute (DTM) approach for probabilistic neural programming (PNN) of large organic systems.

The tenets of modern forecasting methods dated back to the Manhattan Project and early Monte Carlo simulations. Advances in evolutionary artificial intelligence and genetic algorithms had provided a new level of interpretability to large-scale neural architectures.

As a ghostwriter, he was on the verge of unhinging and deconstructing the human mind, the most complex bio-machine ever.

Richards rubbed his forehead against the painful pulsing in his head. A lingering side-effect from brain surgery, no doubt. Rising from his desk, he walked down the hall to the balcony overlooking a courtyard, hoping fresh cool air would relieve his pain. He pushed open the balcony doors, staggered outside and clutched the railing with his hands.

Closing his eyes, he inhaled long, deep breaths of cool air, which did nothing to alleviate the pain. He touched the cap on his head and gingerly felt the bandages beneath.

His legs felt weak. He stumbled to a bench just beside the balcony's door.

Wrenching his eyes shut, he let his mind drift. He felt the presence of others—an arrival of sorts, inside his mind. Individuals. Moments of time in other people's lives. Images flashed through his consciousness in no particular order. He was taken places. Birthday parties. Family parties. First kisses.

The eureka moment pulled at him, took him to open water. City lights dotted a distant horizon. People rode on the trampoline of a large catamaran. Laugher. Music. The ebb and flow of the ocean. The smell of ocean brine filled his nostrils. A girl grabbed his waist. Drew him close. She was college-aged. She kissed him, deep and passionate.

She shook an empty paper cup. "Fetch me a refill."

He kissed her, grabbed the cup, and trotted off, heading below deck. The music grew muffled. Footsteps clattered on the deck above. The churn of the vessel's engines vibrated through its fiberglass hulls. Walking with the rise and fall of ocean's waves, he reached the galley. A full self-serve bar was packed. He snatched ice cubes out a bucket and poured one-third rum and two-thirds Coke into the cup. Before heading up, he stopped to check his appearance in a mirror. His hand combed through a ragged mop of dark hair. He was young. Early twenties. And badly in need a shave to scrape off the grunge of stubble on his face.

The boat jostled, causing him to spill the drink. The music went silent. Screams echoed through the vessel. Footsteps rumbled. Boat engines died.

Richards grasped the importance of what he was experiencing.

An invasion force had overtaken the catamaran as it motored off the shore of Miami on an evening cruise.

He was reliving a young man's memories. This was the moment when twenty-eight college kids had been kidnapped to become ANCRI's Phase 2 participants.

Footsteps drew closer and he tossed the rum and Coke to the floor. He searched for somewhere to hide. Before he could move, a man stormed below deck and kicked him in the sternum, sending him to the floor of the galley. Clutching his chest, he staggered to his feet. A syringe came out of nowhere clutched in a hand. A sharp pain struck the base of his neck. He flailed furiously at his attacker before a wave of darkness swept over him.

Richards awoke to find his nurse standing over him. He'd fallen unconscious on the bench. She was talking to him, and it took a few seconds for him to realize what she'd been saying.

"Dr. Richards, are you okay? Should I call someone?"

He shrugged her off. "No. I was… resting. Came outside for some fresh air, and laid down on the bench and closed my eyes. That's all. If you'll excuse me, I must return to my work now."

She guided him to his feet and he dismissed her, heading back to the director's library.

Richards took an anxious breath. *What a rush!* The reflected moment from someone else's life felt so real, painful, intense.

Trepidation followed. Somehow, he'd inherited an encyclopedia of memories and experiences. Richards had experienced similar visions when Thomas Parker forced him into a neurological stimulation response pod and ran a memory transfer routine. These new episodes invigorated him with insight.

At a computer, he pulled up a network directory and cycled

through archive files. And there it was: his own white paper on the possibility of extended consciousness.

Conversational Echoes.

In a way, he'd predicted the possibility of shared memories.

45

THE FUNCTION THE BODY

Advanced BioCore International, Princeton, New Jersey

In the Biogenetics Lab, Thomas Parker studied cells that would be found in a neocortex, while other scientists transferred the remaining golf ball-sized mini-brains floating in pink artificial cerebral fluid to larger containers for continued growth and analyzing.

He massaged his forehead and thought about where he'd left things with Kate. Their exchange of words dug at him, burning like a pulled muscle. Not visible to others, but under his skin it hurt. Telling her to leave wasn't planned or intended. She seemed committed to staying. Not a bad thing. In the past, he'd cured the periodic loneliness in his life by submerging himself in research. The busier he was, the less he thought about not having someone in his life.

At Advanced BioCore, the refuge of work was a mirage.

He remembered words from Thomas Edison: *The chief function of the body is to carry the brain around.* Parker would add to that: *the purpose of the brain is to carry the mind around.*

If only he could get his mind right.

His thoughts returned to the participants—what they'd experienced, their shared memories. It was impossible to study the mind without factoring in the terrain of the brain itself. The brain was the host of the mind. Neither existed without the other.

Under dual viewing eyepieces an inverted microscope, he examined a tiny sample sliced from a cultured mini-brain and compared it to what he knew. The magnification of the pinhead-sized sample was 400 times closer than normal microscopes. Next to him, a monitor projected what he was seeing. This tool permitted him to see the rolls and folds and stretches of the cellular structures. To get closer, he'd need an electron microscope or a technique called expansion microscopy to view pyramidal neurons and neuronal circuits at a nanoscale resolution.

What he saw was healthy vessel structures, clusters of cells. Someone had gone to great lengths to cultivate this cerebral organ.

Hospitals, pharmaceutical companies, medical research centers, universities worldwide took on the academic exercise of creating organs, organoids, anything from skin to livers and kidneys to lungs to cerebral organoids. Regardless of the ethics behind lab-cultured organs, this biogenesis industry technique was essential to finding new pharmaceutical treatments and medical breakthroughs. Around the world, labs grew designer organs for injecting with cancer or other diseases, and then treated them with potential cures. All without the need for human hosts or animal testing.

Mini-brains could be stimulated to send and receive micro-signals, brainwaves. At two months old, mini-brains could emit sparse electrical activity at a single frequency. At ten months, mini-brains produced regular brain wave activity across a range of frequencies, similar to the brains of older fetuses or infants. Swiss teams had discovered that modern human brains matured at a slower rate compared to other species: primates, mice, swine, and even Neanderthals. Science was moving rapidly to a moment where most anything could be grown in a lab. Yet none of the artificial organs were thinking brains—instead, they were akin to reactionary brains. Way too primitive to support science fiction's notions of brain transplants.

Parker double-checked cell clusters under his viewing lenses. He'd needed a deeper view into the organ in order to track and qualify energy movements, record the voltages and ion charge change states passing between synaptic junctions and feeding axons and dendrites.

He glanced across the lab at the scientists working with the organs.

The mystery woman in the woods had come bearing not just physical gifts, but instructions, warnings. He doubted he'd ever figure out her Manhattan clue. The mini-brains were essential, which not only explained the delivery but the timing of the delivery.

The woman's warnings had proven essential as well. If he failed, people would die.

He leaned forward and peered through the biological inverted microscope again.

Brain cells.

An epiphany hit him. He understood how Stewart Richards had awoken from his slumber. Only one person could have cured Richards: Dr. Rikona Tanaka, the biological creator of these brain cells.

46

THE NORVANA

Badger Field, Atlantic City, New Jersey

Kate welcomed the time to think as she rode in a bureau helicopter to Atlantic City, the only passenger. As a special agent, she'd ridden in helicopters, but had never been a fan. They were small, bumpy, and loud.

Her hearing protection muffled the noise of rotors and whine of the engine.

She reflected on how she'd left things with Parker.

After leaving him standing on the grass, she'd gone to BioCore's command station and logged into security feeds. Video recorded earlier showed a box being delivered to the front desk by a local delivery company. She'd managed to zoom in and read the package's decal: HUMAN ORGANS FOR TRANPLANT. After receiving the package, Parker had taken it to the Biogenetics Lab, then walked outside. No security cameras covered forest boundaries.

It was obvious. Parker had met someone.

She knew only one person who could stir things into a frenzy—

and she wanted to put a bullet through that woman's forehead.

Debra Ford.

Kate watched pieced-together footage until she saw herself run to catch up with Parker. She'd checked with scientists in the lab and learned that the organs weren't transplantable. Cerebral organoids. Mini-brains. Not her area of expertise. She'd seen them once at ANCRI. Cooked up by a doctor named Rikona Tanaka.

The delivery was a way to push Parker forward in his research.

She wondered how much Debra Ford pitted everyone against each other: her, Parker, Richards, Tanaka, whomever had taken Parker hostage, the bureau, Justice, the Vice President. Yet she understood what the organoids represented: a two-fold message.

First, Parker needed the biological material, real neurons, to collect micro-electrical energy states so that he could use that data in neuromapping models. Second, it was a clue, for her and Parker. If Stewart Richards awoke from a permanent coma, he'd need an organ transplant. That was where Rikona Tanaka and her green thumb entered the picture.

Kate had seen MRI scans of the Vice President's son and other hostages rescued in Washington, DC. Each victim had a rice grain-sized hole burned into their neocortex, punching holes in their claustrums. With their brain cells destroyed, the victims had no way of waking. The thin sheet of neurons worked as a gateway, the claustrum functioning like an on-off switch for human consciousness. Doctors at George Washington University had made the discovery by implanting electrodes into a woman's brain, a patient who suffered from seizures, and stimulating her brain with micro-electrical currents. What they discovered was that their patient could be frozen in time through a process that stopped conscious functions.

Tanaka must've grown specific replacement neurons and successfully grafted those regenerative cells into Richards' brain. If true, Tanaka had not only brought Richards back, but given medicine a way to surgically treat people who suffered from severe neurological ailments and brain trauma, anything from Parkinson's to Alzheimer's to tumors to strokes.

The relevance of the moment was significant. Now Parker had a way to cure the Vice President's son.

The exhilaration Kate felt evaporated like drops of water sprinkled onto a hot summer sidewalk. Alive, the deranged scientist had access to Parker's work and would undoubtedly restart his research to finish what they'd started.

Debra Ford had fielded to two teams for the same quest.

Whoever wins gets victory, whoever loses dies. If Richards secured Common Insight first, Parker and the participants would become disposable. Grayson had said as much.

The delivery of the mini-brains leveled the playing field, kept the game competitive. That also meant that Richards was likely ahead in the research game.

Kate struggled with how to sum this up in her nightly field report. Inquiring minds would want to know these details.

The helicopter banked, causing her to realize she'd lost track of the aircraft's progress. From the north, they'd entered the boundaries of Atlantic City.

She checked her watch. Thirty minutes had elapsed. On a strip of land hugging the ocean, the casino town was separated from the mainland by long shallow marshes, which were wider than the actual footprint of the gambling Mecca itself. Through the helicopter's windows, she saw the strip of casinos and a thin stretch of sand that touched the ocean. The discontinued airport they approached was a small triangular patch of land north of the I-40 freeway. A minor league baseball stadium had been built on part of Bader Field. A couple of abandoned asphalt runways intersected. A freighter was docked on the north edge of a rocky shore.

Kate noted the charring on the deck of the ship. Tugboats pumped out flooded decks and ejected water streams back into a bay. It would've been a tight fit, but the shallow water freighter must've arrived at Bader Field under the I-40 bridge. The ship was docked in a manner that hid it from the city, in a way that few would even asked about it. A research vessel hidden in plain sight.

The helicopter landed on a section of cracked asphalt. A man wearing a familiar blue and gold jacket greeted her as she got out.

"Craig Stern," the man called as they both ducked and shook hands, "from the Newark Field Office. I'm a crossover who assists the Atlantic City Resident Agency and supports Justice from time to time."

They walked past the radius of the rotors as the pilot cut power.

"Tell me about the ship." Kate said over the dying whine of blades whipping the air. She was surprised by how much dust the churning metal knives had raised.

On shore, a diesel generator ran. Power cables stretched across dirt and up to the ship. Unmarked and marked cars were parked in rows. Lots of government license plates.

They headed up a makeshift gangplank.

"The *Norvana*," Stern said. "Its home port is in Hong Kong. Once in territorial waters, the ship entered Houston." He pointed down the stretch of the craft's hull. "The name was painted over with *San Jose* to mirror an American freighter in dry dock for repairs. A stolen transponder made the *Norvana* look like the *San Jose*. Once back at sea, this was the *San Jose* to anyone who cared or tracked maritime shipping. Seems that ships in dry dock aren't monitored. Stealing transponders and a simple paint job in a couple of places made for the perfect camouflage. Not hard to pull off at all."

On deck, walking was awkward because of the ship's list, about a ten degree angle. Kate could see charring caused by a fire.

Stern noticed her focus. "One of the spec ops choppers took a hit from an RPG. Both the pilot and copilot were killed. Two others wounded. We removed what was left of the aircraft to keep it out of public view." He gestured to an elevator. "This way."

Kate could see where bullets had peppered metal and paint. A few blood stains marked where people were hit, too. Numbered yellow cards tagged those locations as part of a larger crime scene.

"You mentioned the *Norvana* is from Hong Kong. What about the people funding the operation? Running it? Those responsible for abducting Thomas Parker and the others? Did we capture anyone?"

Stern shook his head and hit the down button of the elevator. "Being captured wasn't an option for them. Four escaped and have not been located. The rest fought to the bitter end. Not a single person survived."

"Who were they?" she asked as doors closed.

"American citizens. Every one of them. North Korean by birth, but brought to the States as children through a legitimate refugee adoption program."

The freight elevator descended. Doors reopened.

Whatever was normal about the freighter topside had changed.

Below deck, the *Norvana* was all research. Bullet sprays marked up what normally would've been sterile walls. Everything was white and bright. Random yellow crime scene cards populated the floors where dried blood remained.

Bureau crime scene techs worked in various rooms, their familiar khakis and branded blue shirts comforting to see. Other agencies had joined the evidence-gathering teams.

Stern led the way. "Everyone wants in on this action. There are reps here from just about every agency: Justice, Homeland, CIA, NSA, Pentagon, DARPA, even some guy working for the Joint Chiefs of Staff who leads a Chemical, Biological, Radiological, and Nuclear Defense task force."

Instinctively, Kate kept a hand extended as she crossed uneven flooring, wanting to catch herself if she slipped. The ship's list turned simple walking into a challenge.

Kate asked, "How'd someone finance a mobile lab?"

"The CIA and Treasury believe the funds passed through Hong

Kong, with the suspicion that the source of the financing came from mainland China."

She stopped in her tracks. "China?"

Stern grinned and hit a button. "Yep."

A pair of doors slid apart to expose a sterile, white two-level room. Whatever fight had occurred elsewhere on the ship, it left this core room untouched: a neurophysiology lab.

She counted fourteen stimulation pods dotting the floor, one for each participant. It was more of a boutique, simpler than ANCRI's or BioCore's versions. All of the scripts for controls and consoles were in Korean.

Her gaze tracked to the opposing symbols etched into the walls. They were like corporate markings rather than government branding or flags.

The first matched what Parker had drawn on her hand: a circle binding eight smaller joined rings. No government slogan or propaganda statement accompanied the image. The image looked incomplete, awaiting final artwork. The other pictogram showed smoke-like dragons forming a circle, yin-yang style twins.

"Any idea on what these mean?" Kate asked.

Stern shook his head. "As of yet, no one has linked the images to foreign actors, country, or historical reference." He pointed to the rings. "A couple of symbology experts provided initial feedback. The larger circle, a backdrop represents unity, a common bond or philosophical platform. The eight rings, member units, are linked, each equal in size and shape."

"Sort of resembles the Olympic rings." Kate rubbed her chin. "Well, it's not a representation of China. Their flag is one large gold star with four smaller stars arcing near the main star." She thought. World history and foreign affairs weren't an area of strength for her. "The flag of Hong Kong is red. A white flower is pasted in the middle of it."

"We're still piecing things together."

She examined the closest pod. The first time she'd seen the contraptions, unconscious people in head-to-toe style space suits occupied them. On the *Norvana*, the final wiring and tubing terminations remained incomplete, as if the knockoff units had been constructed on the fly. Scaled down, compared to the units at ANCRI or Advanced BioCore. Until she'd joined Parker inside a pod, she'd never actually been in one.

"The Korean term for this lab," Stern said, "is a Dream Chamber. After Princeton, numerous foreign governments want this tech, from allies to enemies, including China and North Korea. The leading theory is that China made a proxy move through North Korea to secure the intellectual property, funding the covert operation through Hong Kong so that nothing could be linked to the People's Republic of China."

Kate thought of *The Wizard of Oz* and the man behind the curtain.

On the surface, the simplified foreign affairs entanglement and conspiracy angle seemed logical. Both governments had overt ambitions to rule the world. Eight rings, joined in uniformity, conformity, without individual separation, were bound by a larger ring. That sounded a lot like socialism, communism, authoritarianism—a place where China ruled the world.

"What do we know about Common InSight?" Kate asked.

"Nothing that we can discern so far from any translations or material."

She nodded politely. Either Stern knew and wasn't willing to say, or he wasn't the right person to ask, just another uninformed tour guide.

She tried a different angle. "Does the Peace on Earth Initiative mean anything to you?"

He shook his head. "No. Should it?"

Kate strolled to a test bench where neuro-interface headgear had been hastily abandoned before final assembly. An unexpected chill shook her as she remembered what Debra Ford had said: *I protect this nation from threats you don't even know exist … work a global stage filled with plenty of traps … served multiple administrations.* Ford had implied she knew where Parker was, and knew about the *Norvana.* The former State Department assassin was working a position to enable the Koreans or oppose them, all while supporting the Vice President of the United States.

Richard Mears wanted Dream Chambers, Common InSight, and Peace on Earth. Not unexpected for a career politician who probably wanted to become the next President of the United States.

Undoubtedly, the same went for the bureau, which was why the Director had requested that she reengage Parker. The Vice President and the Director seemed to have an alliance built on a common interest. The bureau, Justice, CIA would all prosper from a working version of this technology, even if it meant overriding a person's civil liberties.

This technology would become an unfathomable weapon.

Kate lifted the headgear from the table. It was heavier than she remembered. Slowly, she slid the skullcap over her head. A set of fiber optic cables, spaghetti-thin cooling tubes, and wires draped behind her and ran down her back like an umbilical cord. The device's weight pressed on her head and strained her neck muscles. Definitely something to wear only when lying down.

Closing her eyes, she remembered the first time she'd worn such a device. Exhilarating. Magical. In a Holographic Immerse Simulation Room, a 3D virtual spectrum of her brain revealed the inner workings of her mind, accessed through the headgear. A collage of images peppered her thoughts. Shapes. Words and language. Faces. People. Events in history. Parker had stimulated her brain as a way to build a neurological template, a neuromap. Once he'd built a map, Parker used it as a pathway to access other people's minds.

"Dreaming about anything, Agent Morgan?"

Kate opened her eyes. Stern was staring at her like she was crazy, or an idiot.

She smiled thinly. "If you only knew."

"Hey," one of the crime scene technicians shouted, "put that down. It's evidence that hasn't been logged yet. Take it off."

Kate rolled her eyes. "Not the first time I've touched stuff and got busted for it." She removed the headgear and returned it to the table. "Can I see the data center?"

Stern smiled. "Come on, this way."

She followed him down a series of slanted corridors and angled flights of metal stairs. The world of plastic white walls and floors mutated into utilitarian gray. They passed a bulkhead and stepped into the bowels of the ship.

From end to end, blocks of supercomputer cabinets filled the metal can of a space. The systems were dormant, with only overhead lighting functional. Blast holes in the ship's exteriors had been welded over and repaired. The flooded space had been recently pumped out. Whoever had operated the ship destroyed the supercomputers to take the equipment out of the hands of the U.S. government.

At one end of the massive vault-like room, NSA personnel wearing shirts marked with FORENSICS AND INVESTIGATION worked beside DoD personnel wearing fatigues as the teams disassembled computer equipment for inspection.

Stern pointed to the cabinets. "Here's what we know. It's quantum-based, similar to what the RIKEN Center for Computational Science in Kobe, Japan, runs. This data center may not look like much, but it surpasses what the DoE runs at Oak Ridge. In another room, chillers liquefy nitrogen and pipe it through cooling tubes."

She was familiar with the concept. "This stuff isn't available at the local electronics store. It's custom equipment. Have we tracked down who purchased it?"

"The CIA tells us that the supercomputer components came from Japan. We've found that there's a fine line to walk when demanding that an international conglomerate release the names of their top clients."

Kate pictured how the data center looked when operational. Anticipation surged through her, knowing that she needed to make amends with Parker to get BioCore's systems up and running. She needed to win back his trust in her. Whatever Parker was planning, she needed to be part of it.

Common InSight was about revealing secrets, an event that she needed to stop.

47

MNEMOSYNE

NeuroSteps Labs, Glen Garner, New Jersey

Richards joined NeuroSteps' programmers in their weekly meeting. In a large conference room, he sat at the head of the table, an obvious newcomer to the way NeuroSteps conducted its business. Monitors and cameras around the room video-conferenced in teams across the globe. Introductions were made. Teams closed out old initiatives before moving to new work.

The program lead jumped into the company's critical path project, codenamed Mnemosyne, named after the Titaness of memory and remembrance. "Dr. Richards," he said, "requires large-scale system applications. Updated filtering parameters have been released to your team leads."

Sighs filled the room, exhausted engineers and programmers allowing their frustrations to be heard.

"Dr. Richards, please expand on the premise of the filtering."

"Conversational Echoes," Richards said, reading from prepared notes, "are essentially noise. If a room full of people speak all at once, even the most cognitively proficient person can track and comprehend only a couple of simultaneous conversations. A person's auditory system, sensory funnel, becomes overwhelmed. But that doesn't mean your mind cannot discern more than it can recall and decipher. Similar sounds, quieter amplitudes and distant voices, get cancelled out. Yet closer, more distinctive tones and inflections resonate better and are more efficiently processed by the primary auditory cortex. If we stimulate multiple participants at once, using the listening analogy and permit them to speak out of turn, cross-contamination of memory transfers will occur. The clear messaging that we mean to focus is overridden by noise pollution."

The lead programmer flashed up a flow chart on a screen, showing highlighted stage gates inserted into original coding to filter participant's inputs.

"Based on the adjusted protocols that Dr. Richards has provided," the program lead said, "we can control the conversational flow and exchanges of memories, adjusting the direction and flow to match our forecasted execution paths. These filter sequences act like traffic lights, controlling who speaks and who receives information."

Richards leaned forward on his elbows. "Without this filtering, the participants will become neurologically impaired, inundated by a circus stream of unwanted voices, which will have significant cognitive repercussions. As I understand our mission objective, we may only get one chance at this, so it's best not to spoil the entire batch all at once."

"Perhaps we should test one participant at a time," a programmer said, speaking with a French accent over a video screen. "This tells me that we need to slow the human trial phase down. We're nowhere near ready for live action experiments."

Richards leaned back in his chair. "We're on a deadline, are we not?"

The program lead said, "Program delays are not an option. If we had all the time in the world, Mnemosyne would be executed from

New Jersey." He looked sternly at those in attendance, including the staff on video-conference. "Get these updates incorporated into the wetware applications. You're not authorized to change testing protocols or timelines, so no more complaints. Yes, we're operating on an aggressive schedule, but our job is to make the impossible possible. And I don't want to hear after the fact that teams bypassed quality control and commissioning metrics. No one cuts corners just because workload increased. Figure out what needs to get done, and do it."

After staff left the conference room, Richards approached the program lead. "Thank you for allowing me to join your meeting."

"Everyone just received double the workload without a corresponding deadline slippage. That means people will be working through the night."

"This filtering will improve cognitive outcomes."

The program lead nodded tiredly. "Our people will deliver Mnemosyne by the time you need it up and running."

48

A CUP OF TEA

Chinese Tuxedo, Chinatown, Manhattan, New York

Debra Ford arrived early for a late-afternoon meal. She'd learned the trick to surveillance was to arrive well in advance, before the targets themselves arrived, and, in her case, not drink too much tea. She paid in advance for a table at the front of the restaurant that offered a wide view. The attire chosen for the occasion was a gray business suit with vest and pants, something a female partner of a Financial District law firm might wear. She wore a long, dark-haired wig and dark-rimmed glasses. While she paced herself through a sweet potato spring roll and a Caesar salad, she read the day's *Wall Street Journal.*

On time, the U.S. Secretary of State and the U.S. Ambassador to the United Nations entered. Both were escorted to a booth in the back of the restaurant. Their Secret Service entourage split up and sat at peripheral tables. The tables surrounding the American dignitaries were left empty, displaying reserved signs. They had room for a private conversation.

Ford tapped her earpiece. She'd met and chatted with both individuals on several occasions, although she doubted they'd recognized her in wig and glasses. The microphone buried in the palm plant beside their table broadcast a clear conversation.

"Susan, thank you for joining the meeting on such short notice," the Secretary of State said. "This business will get out of hand if we don't take action. After today's meeting, relay similar discreet messages to the British, French, Germans, and Japanese."

Ambassador Susan Kirkpatrick nodded. "Understood, sir."

The Secretary drew a labored breath. "Your fervent commitment is required to see this through. You're in line to replace me when the time comes, so be a good steward of our office."

The doors to the restaurant swung open, grabbing the Secretary's attention.

"Let's greet our guest, shall we?" the Secretary continued, wobbly and weak-kneed as he stood.

The Ambassador rose as well.

Asian men in suits entered. The leader of the foursome walked to the back of the restaurant as his security detail scanned the space for threats. The men quickly noted the presence of the U.S. Secret Service.

Ford could feel the surge of testosterone in the restaurant: different security teams, men skilled at protection and threat elimination, carefully accessing threats and problematic scenarios.

Tung Tsang, Commissioner of the Ministry of Foreign Affairs of the People's Republic of China in the Hong Kong Special Administrative Region, bowed. The Secretary and Ambassador followed suit.

"Peace," Commissioner Tsang said as he slid the sleeve cuff of his white dress shirt up to expose the inside of his wrist, which bore a tattoo of eight equal circles looped together in a chain.

"On earth," the Secretary said, drawing up his sleeve to reveal the same marking.

"And goodwill," Tsang replied.

"Towards humankind," the Ambassador said, revealing a tattoo matching her male companions.

"Please be seated." The Secretary gestured to a chair. When everyone sat, he continued. "It's troubling that the one country, two systems mindset deprives Hong Kong of a voice at the United Nations. China won't stop until Hong Kong is subservient to the mainland. It's unfortunate that your lot has come first. Macau and Taiwan will not be far behind. China's imperialistic expansion must be subverted."

"Then the time for Prosperity has arrived," Tsang said, pulling down his shirt sleeve.

The Secretary sighed. "It has." He slid an envelope across the table. "The Ambassador's memorial service is Saturday. In Georgetown. It would be an honor if you could make it. It would mean a lot to his family."

Tsang opened the envelope. "Yes. I heard the news. Peter Tang was a good friend. A skilled diplomat. I could count on his thoughtful guidance when I needed it. The world is a lesser place without his presence." Tsang tucked the envelope into his suit pocket. A pot of tea was brought out. Small cups were distributed. He poured hot green into the cups and raised his. "I wouldn't miss the memorial service for the world."

The three dignitaries toasted and finished their tea.

Commissioner Tsang rose, bowed to the Secretary and U.N. Ambassador, and left the restaurant with his security team.

Debra Ford raised the newspaper that she was pretending to read, while dropping a black silk scarf onto the floor as the Secretary of State pulled himself up from the booth, leaving the U.S. Ambassador by herself. Measuring his footsteps, he walked to the front of the restaurant, stopping beside Ford's table.

"Madam," the Secretary said, bending over. After rising, he fluffed and flattened a black scarf, obviously dropped from the table.

He nodded and returned it to Ford. "I believe this is yours."

"Thank you for noticing." Ford smiled and felt the invitation cards tucked inside the fabric. "Have a good day, sir."

The Secretary returned a smile. He joined his pair of Secret Service agents and left the restaurant.

Ford cast a casual glance to the rear of the restaurant, where she noticed Ambassador Kirkpatrick peel the fake tattoo off her wrist and discard it in the tea cup that she'd just toasted with. The woman held up a finger to the Secret Service pair who'd accompanied her and placed a phone call.

Ford tucked the scarf and her newly acquired memorial service invitations into the inside pocket of her suit. She left the newspaper on the table and walked out of the restaurant.

Doyers Street in Chinatown bristled with people and traffic. Ford walked down to Chatham Square to hail a cab, thinking that she'd waited her entire life for a chance to shape a new era of history and sow the seeds of democracy in the dark reaches of the world where it wasn't wanted.

49

THE IMPLICATIONS OF
BEING A PATRON SAINT

Advanced BioCore International, Princeton, New Jersey

Parker didn't believe in the notion of fate, chance, but yearned for a sign. Wanted a sign. A simple preemptive incursion from an immortal spirit or angel—or even a demon from the depths of hell, for that matter. Essentially, any gatekeeper with the symbolic keys to the treasure and knowledge he sought. In lore and stories, adventurers seeking treasure were often required to make a payment or provide a sacrifice.

He was willing.

He'd studied Richards' white paper on Conversational Echoes and struggled to piece together its prophetic riddle. There had to be a way to pay his penance and make things right.

Standing in the Neurophysiology Lab, he stared at a dark Wall of Knowledge devoid of data and previewed a small script of benchmark testing routines that scrolled though at intervals. If he successfully ventured down this path, the screen would abound with real-time neurological data from fourteen test subjects.

Caroline Wang strolled up next to him. "Thank you for doing this."

He took a solemn breath. "These memories you share with the others could get magnified, much worse."

"We're willing to take that risk."

He shook his head. "It's not so easy for me to accept that."

"You doubt?"

"I doubt a lot of things."

Caroline walked a checkerboard path, cutting through the rows of unoccupied pods. "You know whose face I first saw when I was brought out of one of these?"

Parker lagged behind her. "Don't say mine."

"The moment I saw your presentation in Princeton, I knew Richards' quest for this neurological frontier would become reality. You took us where we needed to go." She glanced inside the capsule-like space, hands reaching inward and running along the tube and wire-filled walls. "I was unconscious when they suited me up and dumped me inside. Had no memories or awareness of what would come. Until you woke me from a drug-induced slumber. A soulless fear overwhelmed me. There was no escaping the fiery energy that you poured into my mind. Everything happened so fast. Memories. Lights. Ghost-like steps of my past. I saw what you told me to see, experienced what you needed me to re-experience, felt what no one else could, told the world where I'd been and what I'd done. I wasn't in control of my mind, you were."

"I'm sorry, Caroline."

"Don't be." She leaned over the pod's edge and took a deep sniff. "It smells like a new car in here."

He laughed. "You know that's the off-gassing of plastics, the release of volatile organic compounds and oil-based liquids from the embedded materials."

She gave him a curious look. "Does Katherine Morgan find you humorous?"

He shrugged. "She did for a while. Now, I'm not so sure."

"She could do worse than you, I'm just saying."

"You see more in me than you should."

She leaned against the closest pod, over the edge of its coffin-like chamber, and arched her back until she faced the ceiling. "When I was disconnected from tubing and wires, intravenous lines, it was like waking from a premature death. The outer room was bright, noisy. Yellow strobes flashed like bolts of fire belting from the sun." She faced him, taking his hand in hers. "My father taught me to have faith in nothing except science, and now I know why."

He felt her hand squeeze his, her fingers intertwine with his.

Caroline barked out a laugh and rubbed the stubble on her scalp. "You're a damn lousy patron saint, Thomas Parker."

He gripped her hand a bit tighter. "I'm no saint, but if I were, it'd be the advocate of lost causes."

She smiled. "Hah! Not too lost a cause, I hope." Tugging his hand, she pulled at him to walk behind her. "You know, I don't know how much others have seen of my life. What I've done. Those I've betrayed. The choices that I've made to get ahead. I only know what the others say they saw. There are secrets in my life that I don't want to relive. Like watching Richards kill his daughter when I did nothing to stop him. As her friend, I betrayed her."

"I know what that feels like, Caroline."

"When you woke me, my mind felt like it was on fire. I sensed the presence of others filling me in a way that I couldn't shed. It was like being possessed."

She led him into a corridor and used his lanyard to badge them outside.

Sunlight had faded past the buildings to the west and they stepped out onto a bricked breezeway, not far from where he'd walked left the complex to meet the mystery woman in the woods.

Caroline let go of his hand and soaked up the outside air, her arms and hands drifting lighter beside her as she walked. She closed her eyes and breathed deeply, as if she was trying to psyche herself into a trance.

He realized she'd just used him to escape the facility.

"You know," she said, craning her neck back, "in those last moments of a common collective, I felt Richards' presence. You didn't mean for him to join us. But, in the end, he did. I became a mirror that reflected the malice he'd shown his daughter, the way he treated her, the way he'd murdered her. And he felt no remorse."

"I never meant for that to happen. That wasn't intended programming."

"It was mine," she said bluntly, opening her eyes and staring at a cloud-filled sky. "The moment I felt his presence, I wanted him to see what he'd done to his daughter."

"You felt his presence?"

"Took you long enough to ask." She thought for a moment. "How long can we be outside?"

"As long as you want, Caroline. As long as you want."

She drew in deep breaths of fresh air. "I need a break when this is over."

He liked the sound of that.

She looked at him inquisitively. "You figure out the filtering that you need?"

"No." He scrunched his forehead and frowned. "Not yet. I've read the papers, but I don't know how to make everything work."

Caroline laughed. "Perhaps I can help with that. It seems that you put the bastard inside my head. You want to know how Stewart Richards would go about creating filtering based on his premise of Conversational Echoes? Okay, let's find out, doc, shall we?"

50

UNANSWERED QUESTIONS

Kate stepped out of the helicopter after it landed on a small pad at Advanced BioCore. Bill Grayson met her beyond the reach of blades churning in the air.

"What'd you learn?" Grayson called.

She reached back into the chopper and yanked out a section of headgear, dragging its cord behind her.

"Not enough," she shouted back.

"What's that?"

"Evidence, from what I'm told." Kate repositioned her fingertips beneath the curvature of the skullcap, yanked up beside her hip, and started walking. "Find Dr. Parker. Tell him to meet me in the Cybernetics Lab."

Once she was clear, the helicopter banked away and flew out.

Grayson snatched the umbilical end to keep it from dragging on the grass. With his free hand, he clicked a radio and called for assistance, then asked for Parker's location. Technicians loaded the headgear onto a cart and wheeled it off to the Cybernetics Lab.

Kate let Grayson chase down Parker, while she took out the hockey-puck satellite hotspot and dialed a number.

After several rings, the Vice President answered. "Find what you were looking for, Agent Morgan?"

"Not exactly. What do we know about that ship?"

Mears confirmed what she'd learned from Craig Stern, but provided no new information. Kate wondered whether Stern's report had been politically scripted.

"And the relevance of those symbols, the twin dragons?"

Mears sighed. "We don't know yet."

"Don't know or won't say?"

"I answered your question correctly the first time."

Kate decided to poke the bear. "Does your answer change if I tell you I think we have a way of curing your son?"

Silence fell for several seconds. "No, it doesn't. But that's good news, Agent Morgan. Very good news indeed." The bear had hardly flinched.

Kate took a breath. "Yes, Mr. Vice President, it is good news."

"Anything else you have on your mind?"

"What does the government want with Common InSight? What do we plan to do with the technology and the application? Is there an overarching program that should be disclosed?"

"That answer is above your paygrade, Agent Morgan. Perhaps we can talk about it later, when and only when you have a medical treatment for my son, Andrew."

The call disconnected.

Kate clicked off her phone and reflected on what she knew of the government's ambitions and secretive research programs. If history was building a case for a watershed moment, it seemed to be building it on a mammoth scale.

One thing was clear: the executive branch was out to turn Common InSight into a weapon.

51

THE MINDS IN A
COMMON COLLECTIVE

Parker considered a communal mindmeld approach unconvention-al.

But who could argue with results?

In the group therapy room, the participants sat in a circle. Parker stood in the middle. Lights were dimmed to enhance the experience. Behind the participants, tables had been erected. At each table, a programmer worked feverishly at a keyboard. Behind the programmers, panoramic screens displayed streams of code and 3D function blocks. Behinds the scenes and unseen by those in the room, deep learning artificial intelligence bots managed by massive supercomputer networks executed quality control measures and provided real-time progress tracking.

Based on Richards' memory transfer premise, the participants guided the software engineers through a series of added filters in neural wetware modules and master control planes.

The shared insights were astonishing.

Parker knew his fair share of programming conventions, but had never experienced anything like this—groupthink on steroids, a common interactive collective—a group of people putting their minds together in order to build a bigger brain.

Flowcharts logged the rapid application development progress and highlighted the 80 completion percent mark.

Parker couldn't explain the secret sauce style magic being displayed or the stark fact that only two of the participants actually knew programming, yet the entire group seemed technically proficient on neural network modeling. Searching their minds for inter-related memories on conversational echoes, they had demonstrated the ability to extract abstract memories and form new cognitive relationships. If one person had a gap in their knowledge, someone else filled in that void.

The symbiotic showcase sent chills down Parker's spine. Unwittingly, Stewart Richards had made these strangers into overnight experts in the field of neurological architectures.

Caroline Wang was next. "Based on Dr. Richards' tagging sequence, a filter addition is recommended to eliminate neural replications in the Balance Node 210, Base Segment 12. Clip that sequence back to the same access node as the adjacent segment."

A programmer raised his hand. "Hold up." Head down, he typed at a keyboard and studied a screen next to him. "What does this filter accomplish?"

A young woman said, "It reduces cross-contamination and allows the neuromapping to mate with a discussion host rather than assimilated unauthorized memory exchanges. Essentially, it keeps us sane rather than making all of us crazy."

The participants exchanged chuckles, as if they were the only ones who got the joke.

From the corner of his eye, Parker saw Kate enter the room and linger on the periphery.

He held up a hand. "Okay, let's take a break and let our engineers catch up. You've put a lot on their plates."

Grateful for the timeout, the participants dispersed. After thanking Caroline for leading the groupthink, Parker approached Kate, who'd been watching the session.

"What's all of this about?" Kate asked, all business.

He hadn't known her long enough to see through her façade.

"Kate, perhaps we can start over. Get past what's keeping us apart."

"I know about the delivery this morning. The organoids. You met someone outside, near the woods. A woman, I suspect. Probably told you that you couldn't trust me."

Parker understood her point. "This line of questioning isn't starting over."

She smiled ruefully as the investigator behind her eyes stepped back. "They weren't questions—more observations, conjecture. Yes, Thomas, let's start over."

52

IT STARTS WITH A DEMIGOD

NeuroSteps Labs, Glen Gardner, New Jersey

In the building's basement, Ji-woo Song strolled the corridor between makeshift jail cells. Behind thick meshed fencing were the Chinese nationals abducted in New York City, each occupying cages the size of a bathroom. They were unconscious, lying on cots. IV bags filled with a chemical cocktail of propofol and thiopental fed sustained sedatives, similar to the therapy that kept patients in induced comas. Monitors tracked vital signs. A team of nurses at the entrance monitored them electronically and on video screens.

These fourteen conscripts, a good mix of men and women, would join her in a new war as foot soldiers, *buqu* soldiers. Ji-woo selected the name *buqu* from China's rich history, the class of hereditary soldiers with a proud lineage dating back to the country's original Three Kingdoms. Each *buqu* would be endowed with a carefully constructed destiny.

Ji-woo had come to study their faces, to gain enough familiarity to be able to spot them in a crowd. She stopped at the first cell, a man in his early forties with naturally short, black hair, meaning no shave or haircut would be required. A senior network security analyst for the People's Republic of China in their New York City consulate. A Communist Party ideologue. His consulate role supported Chinese attachés at the United Nations, hacking and tracking the communications of other UN members. Unwittingly, he was essential to the plans that lay ahead. The secrets that he'd return would unravel a nation from within. In her mind, she gave this man a new name: Fuxi, in honor of one of the Three Sovereigns, a demigod mythological ruler in ancient northern China.

She moved to the next cell, and the next. As she passed the cages, she gave each *buqu* soldier a codename that would act like a homing beacon, an unconscious trigger to align their focus and start a series of thoughts and commands.

Satisfied that she could distinguish any one of them in a crowd, Ji-woo returned to her residence, where she showered, ate a small dinner, and mentally prepared for the neurological training that she'd lead the next day.

Stewart Richards never feared the arrival of death—an inevitable, inescapable state of existence befalling all living creatures, the permanent cessation in which the electro-chemical magic in the body just stopped working.

He had no notion of an afterlife, no spiritual recycling of his existence, no particle dispersement where his soul returned to an eternal creator in the cosmos.

Death was merely the binary opposite of life.

Dispensing a non-binary, one-sided justice, Parker had neither killed him nor permitted him to live, only sidelined him in a metaphoric purgatory. Counter to those actions, fate's intervention had proven ironic, fortuitous. Tanaka had thrown him a lifeline, albeit a short one.

The brain scans that Richards studied told him that he was living on borrowed time. He had days, weeks, perhaps months. Then his brain would end his conscious existence.

Richards had spent the past two hours in NeuroSteps' fMRI, first following the protocols used by the participants, then recalling memories that weren't his at all. Seated at a desk filled with consoles, he studied the clarity in the 3D models of his own brain. Tracking logs recorded how his brain functioned during imaging.

The infilled holes of his brain held the telltale signs to his future.

Scans of the claustrum, thin bilateral structures connecting the pre-frontal cortex and subcortical regions including the thalamus, showed the blood flow via the middle cerebral artery. Within the patch job itself, the claustrum functioned normally except for faint signs of perimeter deterioration. He'd read Tanaka's pre- and post-surgical reports. Her replacement cells were a mix of Type 1 cells, large neurons covered with spiny dendrites as core organoid material, with interspersed groupings of GABAergic interneurons.

Obviously, Tanaka's biogenetic alchemy had limits.

His brain was working but not entirely whole.

His scans revealed an impending death sentence.

A prophesy.

A return to purgatory.

He'd become a dead man walking.

Ultimately, the lack of neuronal adhesion would lead to additional cellular breakdowns and neurochemical disruptions. His claustrum relayed brain signals and neutral transmitters that facilitated consciousness and awareness. Damaged, impaired, or diseased, the gateway would eventually succumb to an inactivation syndrome.

Richards rose from the consoles and absorbed the revelation. What had Einstein said? *Time is an illusion.*

Plato said it better: *Time is the moving image of reality.*

Reality stopped when a body of matter ceased its course of motion, conceding to the continual erosion of time.

If his diagnosis translated to the shortest of life sentences, days or even weeks, Richards vowed to use whatever time remained to return the favor.

Thomas Parker had cheated him out of the world-wide recognition that he deserved.

And Parker would pay for that crime with his death.

53

CRAFT BEER AND A BENCH

Morven Museum & Garden, Princeton, New Jersey

Parker had convinced Grayson to secure a spontaneous, yet private event for the participants at Morven, a stone's throw from Advanced BioCore. Lit torch poles lined garden paths that led to the rear of the property, where an entertainment tent had been set up. Modern jazz played softly in the background. The chef at The Peacock Inn had prepared an evening meal. A few docents supported the quiet affair, providing tours of the main house and answering questions about the historic estate, originally the home of Richard Stockton, one of the signers of the Declaration of Independence.

Nightfall brought a cool breeze. The participants had coats and jackets. Rimmed fire pits offered warmth and a place for conversation without the oppression of house arrest lurking over everyone.

Parker believed the momentary escape from institutional lockdown would help with everyone's mental well-being, and he'd vouched for the group's good behavior. Grayson was concerned about escape attempts and unauthorized contact. Cell phones were prohibited, including those owned by the museum's docents and catering staff. Hovering at a distance, armed security guards oversaw the festivities.

He wrapped up a conversation with Caroline, encouraging her to get the others to talk about their lives outside of institutional imprisonment.

Casting his gaze across the property, he tracked a run of torch poles to a wrought iron bench. Kate sat alone, away from the participants, next to a sign marked the Great Lawn. An obviously rule-breaking BYOB six pack of beer sat on the ground beneath her bench.

He headed her way, noticing the can of beer she drank from was from a local brewery—Troon, Keep Your Distance Milk Stout. The bench was open for a drinking companion. Before sitting, Parker studied Kate for a long moment. She was smart, independent, but not invincible.

"Ask me anything, Thomas," she said, taking a swig of the craft beer.

He hesitated, not sure whether her invitation was sincere or a ploy. He chose sincere.

"What happened?" he asked. He sat next to her in a way that let him keep a distant eye on the participants.

"I feel like damaged goods," she said. "After our vacation, I returned to DC and became the centerpiece to those bombings and that terrorism case you saw on the news. I got roughed up. Bad. People I cared about got hurt. Good agents were killed. That twenty-four hours taught me things about my life that I never knew existed."

"Do you love him?"

"No. Not anymore. But that doesn't mean I don't care about him."

"Jack Wright?"

"The one and only." She took a troubled breath. "Randy Wang

got hurt too, that NSA Colonel who helped us at ANCRI. Caroline doesn't know about her father's condition, what he went through. Reconstructive surgery on his voice box. The doctors say his voice will return, but it'll take months."

She passed him a beer. They clinked cans.

"I didn't return your calls because if there was fallout from that chaos, I didn't want to drag you into a quagmire not of your choosing. I wanted to spare you from the meltdown called my life. In a way, I was afraid of normality—with you—with us. I'm not offering any excuses, nor do I want sympathy. Bureau leadership told me to steer clear of you. I'm an agent. I listened. In a way, you're kryptonite to my career. Putting distance between us was reflex. But I read every text, email, and listened to every voicemail. After a while I was afraid to respond. Then the Director asked me to return to Princeton and secure your deposition."

The resentment and melancholy that had taken root inside him lightened.

He didn't expect a simple "ask me anything" would make a difference. It had.

He forced a smile. "You found no one home."

Her lips twitched. "I thought you were dead."

Caroline made her rounds, taking a moment to sit with the participants who'd broken out into small groups. The garden, music, and food seemed to put everyone at ease, as much as could be expected since they were all technically prisoners of the government. She picked a trio sitting in a small group. She handed the closest boy— they were still only kids, boys and girls—a digital tablet displaying a consent form.

"How are you guys doing?" Caroline asked, studying each one of them, a boy and two girls.

"I miss my family and my boyfriend," a girl answered without hesitation.

"I miss my family, too," Caroline echoed.

The boy glared at the guards on the perimeter. Caroline could tell what he was thinking before he even spoke.

"Why don't we overpower a few of them, make a run for it? I can take out one, maybe two."

She sighed. So many of their memories had been shared. First kisses. The first time they had sex, or not. Who they loathed or loved. Self-esteem. Doubt. This twenty-two-year-old boy had lettered as a high school wrestler. In college, he switched to competitive judo while pursuing a degree in finance. He possessed the confidence, size, and skill to take out at least one of the guards.

Caroline shook her head. "This isn't the time. It's not worth getting someone hurt. Plus, where could we hide? Where our own government won't find us? We know too much."

"But we'd be free," the boy countered.

"If no one dies trying to escape, we'd be fugitives. For how long? Days? Weeks?" Caroline pointed to the tablet held by one of the girls. "That is the best option. Maybe our only option. I won't lie. There are risks. But we'll be free. No longer of interest or value to our government."

Parker regretted pushing Kate earlier. He yearned to hold her close, take in the smell of her hair, but resisted the urge, needing the "ask me anything" moment to continue so he could get a better read on her sincerity.

Kate checked her emotions. "The woman you saw this morning contacted me, too—Debra Ford."

He took a long swig of beer. Senator Samuel Ford's ex-wife. "She said a few things about you."

"Like don't trust me."

"Among other things."

"She wants, our government wants, this tech that you and Richards created."

"If she's the one who propped up Richards, why does Advanced BioCore need me?"

Kate shrugged. "Insurance. In case Richards doesn't or can't deliver."

"So I'm the insurance policy."

"The government wants proof of concept. Real-world applications. Either to weaponize it or use it in foreign affairs, or both. Peace on Earth. It's a no-holds-barred tech race endorsed by the White House."

Parker was puzzled. "So, who cured Richards?"

"Dr. Tanaka, I presume."

"No, I meant who put her up to it. After what happened at ANCRI, Tanaka wouldn't help him or attempt neural grafting without being coerced. Who put her up to it?"

Kate exhaled slowly. "I have theories. Those who abducted you were American citizens, originally children rescued from North Korean camps. Adopted by families here in the States. They attended US colleges. Must've been indoctrinated into becoming sleeper agents. We don't know who they are yet. And I saw the eight rings logo that you showed me in their lab. The ship is called the *Norvana*. Their financial backing came from mainland China. I walked the *Norvana* and brought something back for you to look at."

"What's that?"

"A version of your headgear. Thought you might want to inspect it."

Some of the disclosures matched what limited information he'd gleaned from Ji-woo Song. "China's behind this?"

"It's no secret, really. China dares the U.S. to catch them, and puts up a stink when we do. For years they've conducted espionage on U.S. targets: Department of Energy, national labs, universities, Silicon Valley, Wall Street, pharma, agriculture. Earlier this fall, attachés from their consulates infiltrated military bases. Besides working tech, our enemies want what's been sensationalized as Dream Chambers."

"Dream Chambers?" Parker tensed. "Common InSight. Mind-reading."

"Think bigger. Brainwashing. Cognitive manipulation. Interrogation. And where the Chinese are involved, the Russians, Israelis, and Europeans won't be far behind." She frowned, realizing her can was empty. "Debra Ford is a former State Department field agent, a spy, an assassin, although our country would deny the latter. Maybe she's working angles to sell the tech to the highest bidder."

Parker understood the larger problem. "She said that if I gave the government what it wants, she would take me to the rest of the fourteen, the other participants."

"An incentive."

"She knows I want to save them."

"And what exactly did she tell you to give our government?"

"What Senator Ford knew."

Kate' mouth fell open. "What's that?"

Parker finished his beer. "I don't know. But the participants will. That's how things circle back together. I exposed the participants to what Senator Ford knew. Secrets. Probably powerful enough to destroy a nation. Perhaps bring down a presidency? Your guess is as good as mine."

Noticing his can was empty, she reached below the bench and grabbed another TROON. She popped open the can and passed it to him. She did the same for herself. "What else did Debra Ford tell you about me?"

He took a sip. "That you're manipulating me. Your secrets are so deadly I won't survive them."

Kate took a swig and choked on her beer. "Did she tell you that a very influential person hired her to take a shot at me? I'm not sure Manea is entirely trustworthy. She's a cold-blooded killer. Good at what she does." She glanced at him. "Her best leverage occurs when she sows discord, seeds of doubt, between us."

Parker smiled and took her free hand. This long-sought exchange was rekindling thoughts he'd had about Kate during their island vacation together.

"All right, time to wrap up," one of Advanced BioCore's guards called. "We're leaving in five minutes."

Kate squeezed his hand. "What are we going to do?"

He gave her a mischievous smile. "We're going to find out what Senator Samuel Ford knew and figure out how those secrets can save the participants."

54

UNIVERSITY LIFE

NeuroSteps Labs, Glen Gardner, New Jersey

Richards returned to a session in the fMRI unit, lying on the table with his head and upper torso inside the scanner. The machine mechanically churned like a jackhammer as its gradient coils pulsed to produce magnetic fields and cycled on and off.

A radiologist guided him through a progression of pre-listed questions.

Richards focused on memories, searching his mind for someone else's life.

Rebecca Ward, Becky, Parker's graduate assistant for nearly two years. A National Security Agency (NSA) and Central Security Service (CSS) field operative, Becky was inserted into Parker's university research so that the government could track his progress.

Richards felt electricity surge through him, inner rumblings of static that signaled an avalanche of thoughts. The point of view confused him until he saw Thomas Parker walk past her in their cramped university lab. It was a fourth floor, two-level setup with metal platforms above. Hand-me-down supercomputers executed data analysis. Super-cooling micro-tubes and bands of cables were strung everywhere. A chair-like centerpiece with skeletal framework was the focal point of the room.

He focused Becky's attention on a stainless steel test bench.

Parker had disassembled sections of electrode-studded headgear, his brain-computer interface. The same device that Debra Ford had delivered on the day he woke from his coma.

"How much clarity will the new fiber optic microchips sensors provide?" Becky asked, leaning closer to the contraption.

"Enough to get past the skull's impedance," Parker said, swinging a magnifying glass over his work to enlarge the components, "and target the synaptic energy transfers that we're looking for. The aspect ratio will be a hundredfold."

"You think we've done it?"

"We're one step closer, Ms. Ward."

"I'd love to write this up for publishing. We can co-author an article."

Parker reached for a jeweler's screwdriver. "No. I'm not ready."

"You need to publish for tenure. If you had an article in submission, maybe the tenure committee will give you some latitude. This is an earthshaking achievement."

"Drop it, Ms. Ward. My answer's not changing. This won't get written up."

Parker was a stubborn fool, resistant to the credo of publish-or-perish. If the man would've simply published and filed for a patent, his career trajectory would've been different, dramatically different.

Richards closed his eyes, focused harder. He fast-forwarded through the next six months of Becky's dual life, as an NSA spy and a university research assistant.

He stopped at the morning of Parker's show-and-tell at

Princeton. Richards' pulse quickened so much that he could feel his hands tremble.

High school students packed a small observation room.

A high schooler named Amanda sat in the chair. Images flashed on a board, reflections from the girl's mind. Crystal clear proof that Parker's techniques worked on the simplest of levels. Becky ran the demonstration like a game show. Students cheered at answers to the questions she asked. Through observation room windows, Richards saw himself standing behind the throng of high school students who'd come to watch the science day presentation. Caroline Wang packed herself into the crowd as well. On a monitor, Parker shared the real-time neurological activity that the girl in the chair was experiencing.

Richards could feel his lungs flush with oxygen, his breathing deepen.

This was the day he'd asked Parker to come to ANCRI. It was the last day Parker's lab equipment had been seen, before it was stolen.

He closed his eyes to run out her day.

Becky had showered, changed into a red dress, and added perfume. The fragrance was sweet, inviting. She put on lipstick. A gold necklace draped around her neck swung above her dress' neckline. High heels and a black shawl covering her shoulders completed her ensemble.

She was not a dress-up kind of girl, but this was her payday night.

Becky walked to the Ivy Inn, a bar down the street from Princeton's engineering quad. In the back of the tavern, she staked her claim to a red vinyl booth and settled in. The usual band of Monday night football junkies, pool players, and social gatherings filled the place. On televisions, pregame activities were in full swing for a Giants-Cowboys football game.

Two bottles of Sam Adams were ordered and placed on coasters at her table.

Becky's cell phone buzzed. A text message came through, from someone called Manea.

WHERE'S YOUR DATE? WE NEED TO MAKE SURE THE DOC STAYS OUT OF THE LAB ALL NIGHT.

Becky worked the digital keys of her phone.

I KNOW HE'S LATE. IT'S NOT MY FAULT. HE'LL BE HERE. AND OUR AGREEMENT SAID NOTHING ABOUT HURTING HIM!

Frustrated, Becky silenced her phone.

"Thomas Parker will pay his tab," she whispered to herself as she pushed up her bra, then flattened her dress to accentuate curves, "cause he's my damn fireworks."

Richards inhaled deeply to evaporate the memory that he'd just experienced.

Manea was the person he needed to learn about. A behind-the-scenes opportunist. The person who'd orchestrated the clearing house effort for Parker's university lab. That person was also the last one in possession of Parker's early-generation research, something Richards sought to acquire when the chance arrived.

With that early tech, Richards would be unshackled from the Phoenix Consortium, ANCRI, and NeuroSteps, and well positioned to take his research into the light where worldwide fame and recognition awaited.

THURSDAY, DECEMBER 3rd

Progress is a nice word. But change is its motivator.
And change has its enemies.
Robert Kennedy

55

WHAT A WHISPER CONVEYS

5:15 AM, Advanced BioCore, Princeton, New Jersey

Thomas Parker stepped out of the shower, dried off, and wrapped a towel around his waist. He peered through the bedroom doorway. Asleep, Kate's long dark hair flowed across a pillow and bare shoulders. What was not covered by bedding left an impression. He'd learned that she was a heavy sleeper, opposite to his biorhythms in many ways. It felt good to have her back in his life, even though he was trying to get his head around whether he could trust her.

After all, Katherine Morgan was a Special Agent with the FBI—with a job to do, and a deposition to take on what occurred in Princeton.

The government was likely building a legal case against him. A talk with a lawyer was in order before he made any statement regarding what happened at ANCRI.

Even though their Advanced BioCore living accommodations were identical, they decided it was best if she stayed in his room rather than him sharing hers. He was segregated with the participants, not lodged with on-site scientists and engineers. They'd joked about not knowing the limits of BioCore's surveillance measures. If security watched on closed circuit monitors, they'd gotten an evening show.

He thought about when they'd first made love, the night after ANCRI. His home had been ransacked and left in shambles by people searching for his tech, so they spent several intimate nights at The Peacock Inn before flying to the Cayman Islands.

In some ways, you're kryptonite to my career. Her "ask me anything" openness weighed on him.

Quietly, he drew the bedroom door closed and glanced out the window shades, noticing how dark it was still outside. Sunrise wouldn't arrive for a couple of hours.

Time that he could use to get work done without interruption.

After a cup of coffee, Parker got dressed, left Kate a note, and headed to the Cybernetics Lab to check out what she'd brought back from the *Norvana*.

Three hours later, Kate awoke and shrugged off any notion that she'd made a mistake.

Sunlight streamed through a slit in the window shades, splashing the bed. A pillow still bore the indentation of where Thomas slept.

She embraced his pillow and buried her face in it. She could faintly smell his scent. From their brief time together, she'd learned he slept light. A chronic workaholic, something always was on his mind. He started his days early. In that way, they were opposites. She slept in whenever allowed.

Shoving the pillow aside, she slid her bare figure out from beneath the covers. A quick scan of the floor and discarded clothing came up with a shirt. His, not hers. Snatching it up, she slid it on.

Barefoot, she looked through the suite for him.

A handwritten note was parked against the coffee maker in the kitchenette.

I'VE MISSED SPENDING TIME WITH YOU. LAST NIGHT BROUGHT BACK GOOD MEMORIES. IN THE CYBERNETICS LAB. THOMAS.

She smiled.

Thomas Parker was her mission.

And she was glad to have it.

Parker was astonished how fast the time had elapsed. Immersed in bench testing and calibration, he back-checked Advanced BioCore's replica headgear against what the Koreans had manufactured. Both versions followed his work, with few deviations, yet neither exactly matched his university prototype.

Becky must've passed on old schematics to whoever had paid her for them.

A mix of wires, fiber optic cables, and super cooling micro-tubes stretched across test benches as signals from the headgear passed to oscilloscopes and electro-chemical wave generators. Monitors revealed a rainbow tapestry of results. At Princeton, he'd invented comparison neurological mockups to superimpose different artificial walnut-like topographies. The variances were subtle, but recognizable to a person who knew what to look for. Each skullcap had a crowded matrix of SQUID wafers—superconducting quantum interface devices, capable of detecting weak magnetic waves and ion current transfers passing across synaptic junctions inside the brain. The SQUIDs required liquid micro-cooling, composed of liquid hydrogen, helium, and nitrogen. The different liquid temperature states of the compressed gases tuned the devices. With precision tuning, different depths inside the brain could be recorded. Without the superconducting fluids and near-resistant-free electrodes, the headgear would be nothing except a clunky helmet tied to a fairly useless parlor trick.

He checked the monitors again for final confirmation. The replica brains pulsed with a neon-like brilliance.

He hated to admit it, but the Advanced BioCore version was more refined and easier to calibrate. They'd really done their homework to make the equipment plug-and-play.

"Whose mind are we reading this morning, Dr. Parker?"

He glanced up to see Caroline Wang smiling, her head cleanly shaved to eliminate the black and gray stubble that had grown back over the past month.

She handed him the tablet that she passed around to the participants. "Everyone signed. They're ready—for whatever happens."

He sighed. "I'm not making guarantees. They know that, right?"

Caroline nodded. "They understand this is their best chance. They want their lives back."

Setting aside the tablet, he faced her. Her eyes never wavered. Parker broke off his gaze and leaned close to whisper. "How much do you want to remember?"

She drew him closer and slipped an arm around his neck. Her lips touched his earlobe.

A whisper was her response. "All of it. I want to be the only one left. The last Singularity Witness."

✛ ✛

Kate entered the Cybernetics Lab to find Parker and Caroline Wang intimately close. The woman had her arm around his neck and her lips pressed to his ear.

Kate fought her instinctive response.

The two of them shared a lifetime bond. Caroline's shaved head gave her a different look.

Gazes met. Caroline abruptly stepped away. The woman nodded and left without anything said.

Parker's expression was easy to read: a masculine innocence.

Nothing happened.

Kate shook her head. "What was that all about?"

He handed her a tablet from the table. "Patient consent forms. Fourteen total. Caroline convinced them to sign last night."

She scrolled through the documents, which explained Caroline's hair loss. She'd been first in line to volunteer.

The investigator inside her wanted to ask more questions.

Nothing happened.

Not nothing.

Parker was planning something. And Caroline was in on it.

Instead of asking, she draped her arms around his neck and kissed him.

56

HOLOGRAPHIC MODELING

NeuroSteps Labs, Glen Gardner, New Jersey

Richards was pleased. His day started with a string of project updates right out of the gate with team leaders video-conferenced in from around the globe. NeuroSteps' vast resources had paid dividends.

Previously, his hands-off management style led to him being cut out of the successes that he'd deserved. This time, he was central to the evolutionary outcome.

Adrenaline coursed through Richards' system, fueling the natural emergence of psychosomatic butterflies.

A preparatory test was scheduled for midday, only hours away.

He walked to a technical space that he'd once considered a lesser contribution to the whole. The sign beside the door read VIRTUAL REALITY IMMERSION SUITE.

Electric doors parted to reveal a gateway.

The VRI world was black, dormant. As he entered, sensors triggered minimal lighting that revealed an arched fortress above. Mounted to the skeletal dome of structural rigging, a cosmic-like boundary dotting the curvature of the theater held a thousand tiny glass eyes, their pupils as blue as a tropical ocean. Instinct wanted to call the off-body VR projection cameras the stars in heaven.

But the spiritual notion of heaven existed only when God was present.

Today, he was God.

Since awakening, Richards had given the VRI theater a great deal of thought. As a global science and medical research company, NeuroSteps had branded their interactive hologram realm with a catchy marketing label: MindScape.

Parker had proved resourceful in using ANCRI's space as a surrogate stimulation pod. He'd follow those same footsteps.

"Dr. Richards," a woman's voice said behind him, "I'm ready."

He gestured to a stool anchoring a spread of phosphorescent lines and patterns that dissected a circular floor into geometric quadrants.

Ji-woo Song took her perch.

While the tan hues of her facial features seemed to glow, her eyes divulged apprehension.

"Relax, Dr. Song," he said, retrieving a pair of silver tipped VR gloves from a workstation. "This won't hurt. You might even find the activity enlightening."

After slipping on the gloves, he mechanically lowered headgear over her shaved head. He moved his tipped fingers so that she could see them, mimicking touching the keys of a piano. Ten slim reflections displayed subtle movements hovering in darkness.

Tapping his fingers, he launched a holographic interface. The world around them exploded in varying shades of light and depth, generated by the VR cameras enveloping the room to create a truly cosmic experience.

He chuckled at the astonishment on Ji-woo's face.

A computer-generated female voice spoke. "Welcome to MindScape, the most state-of-the-art virtual experience available.

Brought to you by the brilliant minds at NeuroSteps Labs."

A holographic, semi-transparent display panel materialized in thin air.

"This VR console provides preconfigured interfaces," the AI personal assistant said. "To access custom applications, select that menu option at the bottom of the screen. If you have questions or require assistance, please ask. My name is Cassiopeia. Cass if you prefer a nickname. I am available as your resource—"

Richards laughed and rubbed the knit cap on his head. "Cassiopeia, we'd prefer to conduct our work without input. Mute all interfaces, verbal and visual. No assistance is required. Initiate now."

"Understood," the AI voice said, and vanished.

Richards typed on the virtual console hovering in the air. Cycling through menu options, he studied its numbered, pre-populated options. Not seeing what he needed, he entered custom commands.

"How does a holographic interface help?" Ji-woo asked. "I was never briefed on its value or importance, so on my research team we never included its function."

"Trust me, it's not essential. There are other ways to demonstrate the same techniques. This off-body virtual reality works like a three-dimensional interface, a way to see inside your brain but not specifically access your mind, thoughts. That occurs in the Neurophysiology Lab." He enlarged an aspect of the floating console to concentrate on a specific feature. "Programmers uploaded your neuromap this morning. Like individual files stored inside a file cabinet, your logged brain activities are akin to case studies that are available for inspection. Artificial intelligence case managers have decoded and structured your psychological models as visual applications."

Only one participant was logged into the system: Ji-woo Song, identified as NS-001.

He thought back to ANCRI. His own Phase 1 efforts had begun with his daughter's sacrifice as the Genesis Participant. From the moment she climbed into a pod as the first test subject, Amy's physical body degraded, well before her mind did. Even knowing that Amy was gradually dying, he refused to cease experimentation. The sacrifice that Amy made was too valuable to waste the value gained. Later, Oklahoma Senator Samuel Ford occupied Amy's pod, and he provided similar value.

Thomas Parker's insertion of FBI Special Agent Katherine Morgan as an extra participant to ANCRI's pool of test subjects had been a clever move. Unanticipated. Creating a holistic neurological backdoor into the testing applications. Morgan's cognitive interface became part-template, part-virus.

"Let's see the stars inside your mind," he said. "Shall we?"

Richards activated an application called Centaurus, borrowing the title from the astronomy's brightest stars, a trio of spheroids of plasma making Alpha Centauri, the closest stars to Earth.

Ji-woo gasped. "What am I seeing, feeling?"

Above, a cosmic brilliance of tiny dots and pulses rained like the aurora borealis painting a darkened sky. A universe of tiny green, blue, red, and orange migrations throbbed to life.

Richards grinned. "Your brain, or at least reflections of it. Synaptic junctions, pyramidal neurons, streams of neurotransmitters."

The coursing phosphorescent brushstrokes changed the moment he placed gloved fingers against her exposed cheek.

"Memories are activated in a number of ways," he continued, while touching her skin. "Through smell, touch, emotion, situational circumstances." He withdrew his hand, then slapped her. His tone changed. "What do you want with Common InSight?"

Ji-woo winced and shot him an angry look. The tapestry above percolated with shifts in her neural firings, recognition of being struck and how that activated other aspects of her memory.

"I don't know what you're talking about," she snapped.

"One thing I didn't tell you about this virtual experience is that it doubles as a lie detector." The statement was untrue, but she didn't know that. Fear of the unknown worked as leverage. "So lying and concealing facts from me are impossible. Virtually impossible. So, I'll ask again. What is your agenda?"

The rise and falls of her changes in breathing were obvious. Behind tight lips, Ji-woo Song was figuring out what to do.

With her strapped into the headgear, he hardly feared an attack. She'd likely stumble off the stool and dangle while she flailed in vain to free herself. Not quite strangulation, but it'd be a difficult situation for her.

He shrugged. "Okay, have it your way."

On the holographic console he uploaded a new application: Topic Override.

Ji-woo shivered uncontrollably, her body consumed with muscular spasms similar to the reflexes of a person in hypothermia. The mild convulsions streamed from her skull to her feet. Teeth chattered. Speech slurred. Eyes widened in fear. The temporary neurological stimulation disrupted her ability to string together thoughts and created mild paralysis. She felt no pain.

The spread of Ji-woo's brain impulses filling the room turned disjoined, chaotic, showing signs that her brain was short-circuiting, confused. Bands of yellow and orange dots swelled, drowning out the normal hues of green and blue.

Richards counted off seconds, wanting a sensation of helplessness to seize her.

After twenty seconds, he closed the application.

Ji-woo groaned and cringed, not in pain but an inability to fight back.

Slowly above them, her brain activities returned to a normal pattern, congested dots of yellow and orange yielding to blues and greens.

"What's your plan for Common InSight? What do you want with the application?" When she gave no immediate answer, he waved a hand over the holographic panel. "We can continue this adventure until you lose bowel control and need to be carried out of here on a stretcher. It'll take days to recover."

Her gaze locked onto where his hand had stopped in midair. A red button hovered inches below.

She yielded. "Foot soldiers. A few at first. Then an army. Assassins to put in the streets. *Buqu* soldiers. Allies who will first sow discord, trigger events that lead to building a new nation from old ones. Our campaign will bring together peoples around the world who want Peace on Earth based on one united, democratic Asia. We call it Prosperity."

The declaration of nation-building caught Richards by surprise. The tension charging his muscles faded, and he lowered his hand.

At its core, NeuroSteps' version of Common InSight was nothing more than high-tech brainwashing, socially conditioning people into sterilized mindsets, accumulating outlooks and perceptions on life, establishing conformity in belief systems, and creating a technical format in which to spread indoctrinated political views to the masses.

A global scale of groupthink.

She swallowed over a knot in her throat. "What are you going to do now that you know?"

He understood Ji-woo's place among the participants. She was the biological origin of a larger symbiotic consciousness, the bicameral mind, the inner guidance to those who were to be indoctrinated.

Dr. Ji-woo Song represented the future of what was to come.

"Help you." Richards took a solemn breath and stared into her eyes. "But I'll need a favor in return."

57

WHAT THE EYES SAW

Advanced BioCore International, Princeton, New Jersey

Kate had been summoned to the facility's Security Operations Center. The two-story ops center buzzed with conversations and activity. The curved front video wall beamed screenshots of on-site and off-site locations. Work stations were populated with corporate-branded security personnel. Side wall monitors ran the major networks and the daily news programming.

In a breakout room, Grayson waited for her, alone.

Carrying a tablet, Kate entered and noted that the monitors that he watched relayed different angles of the same event: Thomas Parker in the Cybernetics Lab.

The recordings were looped.

On a workbench, Parker worked on his skullcap and headgear.

Caroline Wang entered the lab. The short continuous stream of events happened fast.

"Whose mind are we reading this morning, Dr. Parker?" Caroline asked, handing him a tablet. "Everyone signed. They're ready... for whatever happens."

He sighed. "I'm not making guarantees. They know that, right?"

Caroline nodded. "They understand this is their best chance. They want their lives back."

Parker set aside the tablet and stared at Caroline, his gaze searching hers.

He pressed into her, his body almost merging with hers, and whispered in her ear. The lab's audio didn't pick up what was said. Caroline reached around his neck and pulled him close, her lips pressed to his ear.

Quiet words were exchanged. Nothing microphones could capture.

Kate saw herself enter the lab.

The surprise on Caroline's face said it all as the woman backed away from Parker. The shock on Parker's face was a readable expression as well. Caroline left without saying anything.

Grayson stopped the video at the point where there was a clear gap between Parker and herself.

She knew what they'd said and what came next.

Grayson cleared his throat. "Are those two planning something? Something we should know about?"

Kate shrugged. "I doubt it. Why do you ask?"

He cocked his head at the video. "I'm well aware of what happened last time. People died. Most of the research was lost, destroyed. Such a scenario will not happen at Advanced BioCore." He took a breath. "It's important that I know what was said between them."

Kate handed Grayson the tablet Caroline had provided. "Dr. Wang collected patient consent and volunteered to participate herself. There's nothing more that you need to know."

Grayson studied the electronic forms, noting the fourteen finger-sketched signatures.

Kate strolled closer to the monitors. "You really don't know what's about to happen here, do you?"

Grayson chuckled. "It's not my business to know. My national security mission is to get whatever I'm assigned executed. I serve this country as a soldier. And I deliver results. The philosophical judgments, physical context, and means and methods of what gets done here or elsewhere are irrelevant if they get in the way of the mission."

She studied the expression on Parker's face. He'd been caught in the act.

"Are there are cameras in the residences?" Kate asked.

Grayson laughed. "Just the ones we need to keep an eye on."

Anxiety rose inside her. Blushing, she crossed her arms.

Grayson gave her a devilish grin. "Your rendezvous provided a hell of a show for the third shift. As I hear it, certain physical endowments didn't go unnoticed."

Kate glanced away, trying to think of a scathing reply. When nothing came to mind, she said, "We're in a relationship."

"Evidence would suggest that. Yes."

She drew her arms tighter into her body. "Even Advanced BioCore must have privacy restrictions. Surveillance limits. Correct?"

He shook off the question. "Special Agent Morgan, are all federal agents so cavalier with their objectivity?" When she did not answer, he added, "The security recording contained no particular relevance to Advanced BioCore, and, as a result, I found no reason to retain any embarrassing footage. Word to the wise. Because of our federal obligations, a great number of people have network access. Our premises aren't Vegas. What happens here may not stay here."

Grayson left the breakout room, taking the tablet with consent forms with him. Kate was alone with the frozen video of her and Parker standing inside the Cybernetics Lab.

Message received.

58

UNFORGETTABLE

Parker took the calibrated headgear into the Neurophysiology Lab and turned over his commissioning results to hardware technicians. Advanced BioCore's corporate rules prohibited him from making the modifications directly to the pods, so he gladly passed them off to others.

Fourteen pods were a day's worth of work. A small team could complete the retrofits in four hours. And he required only a single functional acceptance test for a pod. That meant others could retool the remaining pods while he ran testing.

He glanced up at the Wall of Knowledge. It was dormant. *Not for long.* Shifting his attention to the engineers working their magic in the confined space of a centrally located pod, he watched them unhook and reroute terminal connections to integrate his headgear solution.

The lab's main doors whooshed open. Kate entered, looking troubled.

"Is everything okay?" he asked.

She looked up at a wall-mounted security camera mounted in the anteroom and nodded. "I'm fine."

"If you'd rather not, we can do this later."

"No."

"We're ready, Dr. Parker," the technical supervisor called. "It's all wired in."

Parker extended his hand, which Kate took in hers.

"Let's get this over with," she said, her voice edgy.

"You can't do this if you're upset. You'll throw off the metrics." He turned her so that she faced him and smiled. "Think of me, if it helps you relax."

She cleared her throat. "That won't help."

"Kate, you need to have a clear mind."

She shrugged. "I know."

He led her to the completed pod. A medical tech holding out electrocardiogram leads awaited her.

Kate stopped short of the pod and withdrew her hand from his. "I want just the two of us present. No one else. No one to watch."

Parker noticed that Kate was scanning the lab filled with staff.

"Sure." He turned to the others in the room. "Okay, folks, take a break. We'll do this in private. You can complete retrofits when we're finished here."

Kate took ECG leads from the med tech and studied the color-coded set. Parker could tell she was trying to recall the 10-lead VRL electrode placement from medical school.

One by one, staff disengaged from their work and left the lab.

When they were alone, she unclipped her holster, slid off her belt, and placed everything on a table. When she started to self-administer the lead placement on her torso beneath her shirt, he activated the pod. Electric motors angled the coffin-shaped capsule to a sixty-degree position, vertical enough to allow an occupant to step into it rather than climbing up and over the sides.

After giving him a peck on the cheek, she leaned backward into the confined space. Her eyes looked nervous. Twitching lips revealed the same.

"Close your eyes," he said. "You'll do fine."

She nodded, the gesture insincere and without a hint of conviction.

He put his hands on her hips to press her into a self-forming body mold, bound her wrists and ankles with Velcro straps, and slid the headgear into place. Placing his mouth into a small place where metal and gadgetry did not cover her jaw, he kissed her, letting his lips linger on hers for more than a breath.

After connecting ECG leads to a terminal, he lowered the pod horizontally.

He understood her apprehension. In some ways, Kate had a right to be afraid. In the wrong hands, both of them knew, this radical technology could kill a person by scrambling their brain.

The first time he'd used Kate as a baseline participant, he'd done so using a virtual reality theater, a place that did not have the same power as a stimulation pod. Since Advanced BioCore didn't have a holographic theater, a pod was the only mechanism available to create a template.

Parker adapted his approach to the tools that were available, but that didn't mean it was without risk. Miscalibration, corrupted programming and neural net coding, improper data exchanges—those dangerous scenarios were real.

He would've selected Caroline Wang as his baseline, but her mind was cluttered with other people's memories and a great deal of excess noise, mental stuff that would require filtering before her core mind could be examined or used as a template.

Kate proved the perfect specimen, his own genesis participant.

Sitting behind a console, he fired up the machine and followed a prescribed set of routines. He slipped on a headset and adjusted his audio.

He could hear her breathing. "Are you doing okay?"

The short response told him otherwise. "Don't ask."

Immediately, the Wall of Knowledge blazed with data. The ECG data box appeared along with other graphical readouts. A 3D model of Kate's brain showed her neurological activities. Nerves spoke where silence reigned. Her heart rate was elevated, a symptom of claustrophobia and anxiety.

Everything else tracked as expected.

"Think of a solid blue circle. It's cool like ice," he said.

He glanced between the monitor and the big screen. Having done this before, Kate knew the drill. Her mind was thinking, but she was struggling to concentrate. She was distracted. Her pattern of breathing had rigidness to it. Emotional and cognitive stress created abnormal ECG waves.

He took a different approach, knowing that Kate needed to warm up. "Slowly, turn the circle orange. It's warm, vibrant. Sunlight. You're on a boat called *Sabbatical*." He figured she'd understand the reference. It was a 40-foot monohull sailboat that he'd chartered during their vacation in the Grand Caymans. They had all the sunsets they wanted to themselves. For nearly a month, she was happy, without a care in the world. "You're bow-side, forward, facing the sunset. Warmth splashes against your body. An endless sea is calm."

The monitors and brain scans registered neurological changes.

Anxiety waned. Breathing fell normal.

From his console, he couldn't see her mouth but hoped she was smiling.

Kate had found a small sliver of peace inside her mind.

A sunset.

With nothing but a simple suggestion, the power demonstrated was all hers.

Minds are like parachutes – they only function when open. The quote came from Dewar, the Scottish whisky distiller. Before beginning to cross-reference a neuromap using Kate's mind, Kate had to open it first.

Her real-time neurological scan ebbed and flowed with normal activity across the walnut-shaped topography. As an organ, human brains shared common genetic and atmospheric structures, yet each mind inside was exclusive to its host. Where Kate placed memories and learned structures was unique yet similar to the participants.

At Advanced BioCore, Kate's original mapping came from the fMRI process. With the contribution of quantum-based and neural net supercomputers, this exercise cleared any remaining unknowns to refine a base template.

He flashed a 2D image of a star into her visual cortex, white against a black background. The image replayed on the big board. She thought about the image, then silently said the word in her mind. The process was repeated before graduating to complex shapes, then on to people, settings, language, and videos. To layer in complexity, he spent a several minutes feeding her auditory cortex clips from famous speeches: Ronald Reagan, the Apollo landing, Martin Luther King, Oprah Winfrey, and a TED talk by telecommunications entrepreneur Tan Le about her headset that read brainwaves. Completely unrelated to the testing and to close out the process, he piped in Natalie Cole duet's mix *Unforgettable* with her late father, Nat King Cole.

"Thank you, Thomas," Kate said across her speaker. "The sunset with you made all the difference."

"I didn't know I was there."

"Right beside me."

Parker sighed. "You're unforgettable, just wanted you to know that."

She laughed. "Yeah, right. How about you get me out of here? I've suffered enough already."

59

NEWS

Eisenhower Executive Office Building, Washington, DC

Richard Mears walked to the windows of his ceremonial office over-looking the White House's West Wing. Most Vice Presidents used the set of offices to host token meetings and press interviews. Mears was different in that manner. Buffered from the daily noise and activities of the White House itself, this secure space had evolved into a perfect temporary command center. Along the central room's conference table, workstations had been setup to access select government-funded research labs around the world.

Mears had dismissed the staff for the day, leaving him alone with Gordon Abbott, the President's National Security Advisor. Getting rid of his Secret Service was a different matter entirely. While the President traveled abroad, his Secret Service presence increased. Unyielding mandates offered no opportunity to scale back their watchful gaze. But since the Executive Office Building was a secured area, he could require the agents to stick to the corridors.

While he waited for the calls to come in, he strolled into his ceremonial office and slid open the center drawer of the Vice President's ceremonial desk. The drawer was empty. Plexiglas protected its bottom. As a farewell gesture from each preceding Vice President, users since the 1940s had signed the drawer on their way out of office.

The drawer didn't contain his name.

Not yet.

Mears closed the drawer and smiled. Someday it would have his name added, but not until he'd been elected to the highest office, that of President.

An instant messenger sound pinged from one of the workstations.

Abbott accessed the secured computer terminal.

Mears joined him as a multi-frame video popped up, split between Advanced BioCore's Neurophysiology Lab and the company's security operations center. William Grayson, a liaison from the Department of Justice, National Security Division, stepped in front of a camera. The veteran agent had been handpicked for his assignment and embedded inside the international company.

Mears' son, Andrew, had recommended him. Both joined the Navy in the same officer class, except Grayson yearned to become a SEAL. The rigorous program ran an enlisted-to-officer ratio of 10:1, and Grayson eventually washed out of the brutal training. A fortuitous call from the Research Director at the Naval Research Laboratory (NRL) offered Grayson a different career path. He finished at twenty years, then joined Justice.

"Evening, Bill," Abbott said. "We're interested to hear how things are progressing."

"Good evening, Mr. Vice President and Mr. Abbott." Grayson flashed a smile. His accent was the result of too much time spent in the United Kingdom, despite the fact that he was a U.S. citizen. "A great deal of progress has been accomplished in a short period of time."

"And where do things stand with Dr. Parker?" Mears asked.

"I was skeptical at first. Our leverage on him was… questionable. I expected him to be an impediment, but he quickly eclipsed all of our researchers. Metaphorically, we play hobby chess. Parker is the grand master who can play chess blindfolded. Patient consent was secured without coercion. Hardware and software development are on track. An initial neuromap and baseline templates have been constructed."

Hopeful glances were exchanged.

Mears' eyes were drawn to the video showing the lab. Only one person was visible in the lab, with what appeared to be someone inside a stimulation pod. "When can we get a demonstration?"

"Milestones put us at a couple of days out."

Mears sighed.

Abbott showed concern as well. "Bill, that makes for a tight timetable."

"Tell us what's going on in the lab," Mears said. "Is that Parker?"

"Yes. He ran the FBI agent through a series of diagnostic checks. We call it commissioning. The two of them have a connection on how to make this tech work." Grayson provided a quick brief of what the recorded video displayed, including close-up shots of brain scans.

Mears asked the most relevant question remaining. "What's the chance of failure?"

Grayson shrugged. "I don't have that answer, sir." He collected his thoughts. "This is a complex undertaking and Parker's rapid progress is substantial. To back him up, everything is checked for accuracy to make sure this application works."

Mears nodded. "And Morgan?"

Grayson grinned. "She's brought assets to the table that we weren't likely to find elsewhere. Her presence has certainly nudged Parker in the right direction."

Abbott's cell phone buzzed. He recognized the number and showed it to Mears.

"Bill," Abbott said hastily, "we need to jump on another call. Keep us updated."

Abbott clicked off the workstation and unlocked his phone, placing it on speaker mode.

"Mr. Secretary," Abbott said, "how are you today?"

"Well enough, Mr. Abbott. Thank you for asking." The voice sounded tired, the opposite of well.

Mears knew the Secretary of State had health issues. A patriot to the bitter end.

"The Vice President is with me. We're alone."

The Secretary's voice perked up. "Well, good evening, Mr. Vice President."

Abbott seemed anxious to cut to the chase, so Mears gestured for him to drive the conversation.

"Mr. Secretary," Abbott said, "how did your ground work in New York turn out?"

"Future events look favorable."

They exchanged glances again. The agreement among the three of them was to compartmentalize field and research initiatives in case one aspect of the missions was discovered. Their covert investment was like secretly running domestic sleeper cells inside the borders of America.

The Secretary had suggested early on that they communicate in cryptic statements and avoid specific details whenever possible, in case someone outside the group of nine overheard parts of a conversation.

"Twin Dragons?" Abbott asked, using the codename to a covert, under-the-table funded political renaissance that had no official connections whatsoever to the U.S. government. Operation Twin Dragons was Common InSight put into action.

Very few even knew of the impending watershed movement—and for plausible deniability reasons, certainly not the President.

"Underway as we speak."

Mears asked, "And the upcoming festivities?"

"All signs point to a Saturday delivery."

Mears took a breath. "Will you be joining me?"

"I wouldn't miss it. It should be quite the show."

Mears never considered a memorial service much of a show, even an Irish wake.

"Will guests be joining us?" Mears asked.

"Confirmed."

Mears wanted to ask who, but decided against it. Communist China's overseer of Hong Kong was essential. Other envoys and dignitaries would be the icing on the cake.

The Secretary cleared his throat. "Changing the subject, if I may, I feel that I should bring this up. You two are the first to hear it. I'll inform others including the FBI and DoD. It has come to my attention that several Chinese consular attachés and their companions did not return to their consulate after festivities Tuesday night. We cannot confirm whereabouts or what the Chinese might be up to. Our people took an accurate headcount at the Beekman in Manhattan when people arrived for the fundraiser. Fourteen fewer left the premises."

Abbott frowned. "What does that mean?"

"State is unsure."

Abbott followed up with another question. "Do you think the Chinese are taking their nationals off the grid?" Abbott asked. "Do they have an op underway?"

"Not enough intel at the moment. My people will draft scenarios and predictions. I also want to reach out to CIA."

"Good idea," Mears said.

"If you two will excuse me," the Secretary said, "I have to meet several interested parties tonight before I turn in."

Mears smiled, thinking that the Secretary of State was a dedicated public official who rarely took a night off from his duties.

60

PHOSPHORESCENCE

NeuroSteps Labs, Glen Gardener, New Jersey

Stewart Richards realized he'd never been this close. Ever. Standing alone in the Virtual Reality Immersion Suite, he restudied the scans and analysis on his new genesis participant, Dr. Ji-woo Song. Her mind was strong, active, making her a brilliant choice for a baseline template, a perfect neuromap.

In front of him a holographic panel floated in mid-air and displayed the current time: 17:20 military time.

Above, a world of neon colors consumed the room, a digital replay of Ji-woo's brain matched to the testing she'd undergone. From where he stood, Richards estimated that he was inside her temporal lobe, specifically the entorhinal cortex, an area that functioned as a network hub for memory, navigation and the perception of time. This world could be touched. All around him neurons bristled, synaptic junctions sparked on and off, and neurotransmitters streamed. The moment was mesmerizing.

A remarkable aspect of NeuroSteps' Common InSight application was its accuracy—over 99 percent—in predicting what Ji-woo Song would say or think in terms of the next closest cognitive tangent. Machines had constructed behavioral patterns, futuristic predictors. Supercomputers could pre-determine what she'd do next.

Richards blinked as a raging pain swept through his skull, starting at his ears and migrating into his frontal lobes. Time stuttered for a long moment, then longer. The brightness of the holograph enveloping him dimmed.

Everything froze. Time. Movement. Thought.

"Dr. Richards," a woman's voice echoed in his mind, her tonal inflected heavy with a southern drawl, "can you hear me? Dr. Richards, are you okay? Dr. Richards."

His headache subsided, leaving him disoriented.

Beside him he found Ji-woo, her expression a mask of concern.

"Dr. Richards, are you okay?"

He blinked then nodded, not quite sure. He glanced at the time on the holographic console: 18:42.

Rubbing his brow, he gathered himself after several breaths. An educated guess told him what had just happened. Dr. Rikona Tanaka's neurological patch job was degenerating as predicted. His mind had frozen for an hour and twenty two minutes, leaving him in a state of cognitive limbo.

"Just tired," he finally said.

Ji-woo placed a bread loaf-sized tool bag on the room's stool and motioned for him to open it. Inside, he discovered a black semiautomatic pistol with a threaded suppressor, two magazines stocked with 9mm hollow point ammunition, and an identification card with his photo on it. The facility was Advanced BioCore International, its Princeton campus.

He'd never heard of the company, but obviously Advanced BioCore was the competition.

Richards turned to her. "Thomas Parker's there?"

She nodded. "Deliver my *buqu*. After that, what you do is none of my concern." She squared up to him. "Know how to use a gun?"

He grinned. "I've done so a few times."

She shrugged off his firearms awareness and walked to the boundary of the hologram, lifting a palm to brush the outer edge of her frontal lobes, allowing a finger to follow the contour of the longitudinal fissure separating her right and left cerebral hemispheres. The tiny projection cameras streamed beams of light that coated her hand in such a way as to make it look like she'd slipped her hand inside a jellyfish.

"Enter using the loading dock," Ji-woo said inspecting the phosphorescent glow. "Head straight to the Security Operations Center. The SOC is the facility's corporate command post. Guards will be armed. Eliminate anyone who opposes you. Once you weaken their SOC team, I would suspect finding Thomas Parker will be rather straightforward."

Richards zipped up the tool bag. "This stays between the two of us?"

She retracted her hand from the hologram. "Do you know how long you were frozen?"

Reluctantly, Richards nodded. "Yes."

"Is that a side effect of this process? Will it affect me?"

"No." He cleared his throat. "It's a burden that I alone must endure. It has nothing to do with you or the others or Common InSight."

⊹ ⊹

Ten minutes later, Richards returned to his residence. Taking out the bottom drawer to his dresser, he stashed the bag provided by Ji-woo in the hidden cavity beneath the drawer, a simple void to secret away tools that he'd need when his work at NeuroSteps had wrapped up.

61

HOME

7:30 PM, Princeton, New Jersey

Parker couldn't tear his gaze away from the charred rubble. His home of the past five years was a wasteland. Crime scene tape stretched around the property on all sides.

He got out of the Advanced BioCore-provided car and walked the short stone sidewalk to where his front door once stood. Kate lingered a few steps behind, giving him space to take it all in.

Using a flashlight to illuminate the scene, he surveyed what was left. Not much. A total loss. The closer he got, the stronger the smell of ash and burnt lumber. At the rear, an intersection of walls still stood. The brick fireplace towered above what remained. The kitchen held the carcasses of appliances, like log stumps poking out of a mud-laden swamp.

At night, sifting through the garbage would be a futile effort. He'd search for hours and wouldn't recover much. He'd possessed few heirlooms from his parents, mostly archeology artifacts and trinkets from past expeditions. He would've lost the Civil War Era sword given to him from his father, the one he'd used to take down one of the Korean intruders.

He felt adrift. With no home or faculty position, nothing kept him bound to Princeton. Once the business was concluded with Advanced BioCore, he was free to go wherever life led him next.

It would be a hell of an insurance claim.

He glanced to Kate, unsure if she understood.

Dropping his gaze, he sighed.

At his feet was an olive wood box. A band wrapped around it secured the lid. It was artistically etched with charred lettering. Burgundy, France. Large enough for a couple of bottles of wine and accessories. The kind of box that was sold as a gift set. The box's writing was French. Fluent in Spanish and Portuguese, he could make out some of the wording. A winery from Coche-Dury Grand cru vineyard of Corton-Charlemagne. A paper logo identified the State-side retailer: Manhattan Wine Company, West Chelsea, New York City.

"What's that?" Kate asked, swinging down the blaze of her flashlight. She picked it up. From the way she examined the box, he could tell that she had an idea who delivered the gift. "Wine."

He eyed her cautiously. "Not a bomb?"

"Not Debra Ford's style." She shook it. "I wonder if it's expensive? I bet it's expensive. It has to be expensive. I hope it's expensive."

She ran her fingers across the surface of the wood, tracing her fingers along the pyrography and letters. Her hands stopped at a symbol in the cover's corner.

Parker shrugged. "How do you know it's from her?"

"A hunch." Setting the box on the sidewalk, she removed her car keys and flexed the metal band, stretching a joint enough to create slack. She slid the band off and cocked her head. "Moment of truth. Shall we?"

Reluctantly, he kneeled.

"Want to do the honors?"

He shook his head as Kate cracked the lid. Nothing happened. She grinned and flipped the cover off. Inside there were two bottles Coche-Dury Corton-Charlemagne, Grand Cru Chardonnay bedded in straw, crystal glasses, wood-inset corkscrew and cutter, stopper, and crackers and cheese.

A thick card was tucked next to the wine bottles.

Parker retrieved it. There was no envelope, just the card.

The wording on the card was manuscript.

THE REMNANTS OF ASH AND RUINS CAN ALWAYS BE WORSE. YOU COULD BE WITHOUT BREATH, LIFELESS, AND CONTRIB- UTING TO WHAT IS GONE. DF

Kate chuckled. "I didn't know Debra Ford was sentimental."

He cast his gaze across the rubble of his home. The point was noted.

Plucking out a bottle and the corkscrew-cutter, Parker walked over to a step in the sidewalk and sat. He cocked his head for Kate to join him. Snatching up the pair of wine glasses, she plopped down beside him. Trimming off the foil, he threaded in the corkscrew and pulled out the cork. She held up the glasses and he filled them halfway.

As they clinked glasses, Kate asked, "I wonder if drinking un-chilled white wrecks the aromas of expensive wine?"

Parker smiled. "We have two bottles to find out."

"Don't forget the cheese and crackers."

They took sips.

He laughed. "I'm not sure my taste buds would know what quality wine should taste like."

"Two glasses," she said. "I wonder if Debra's secretly rooting for us."

Parker held his tongue, thinking that Debra Ford had offered to kill Kate.

62

THE SYMBOLOGY OF WINE

Advanced BioCore International, Princeton, New Jersey

Back in her dorm suite, Kate washed up for the night before sliding under the covers on her side of the bed. Shirtless, Parker leaned against pillows to prop him up while he read progress reports on a tablet. Turning on her side, she studied his features. Fit, with unexpected muscular definition, opposite of what she believed to be the mold for most professor and researcher types. Immersed in reading, he had the peripheral awareness of a gnat, not bothering to notice her coming to bed.

She frowned. The professor was too into his book.

Learning of the extensive reaches of voyeurism, she insisted they spend the night in her room rather than his. She didn't have the faintest idea if her residence had hidden cameras, but thought it was a safer bet.

The image of an orange sun formed in her mind, the one that he'd asked her to concentrate on when she was in the stimulation pod. A sunset. The sunset observed from a deck of a boat calmed her when few other thoughts would. The best thing about their Caribbean escape was that neither of them had brought the baggage of work and unfinished business to paradise. In the time they'd spent together, he saw things in her that perhaps she didn't want to acknowledge, a glimpse into her soul.

Rare things for her to share.

Now she was fearful of what Parker saw.

Watching the rise and fall of his chest, she wondered what he was thinking, pondering. In the time she'd known him, she'd learned that he saw past physical boundaries to solve quandaries that few even considered.

Thomas saw the world more differently than anyone she knew. He'd agreed to continue his research at Advanced BioCore not because she asked him to, but for the people he needed to save.

Parker had a plan to do something, which he didn't want to share. He'd withheld information from her at ANCRI, and it made all of the difference—details and information that she didn't want to know then or now.

She ran her fingers across his torso, tracing the definition of muscle beneath skin.

He smiled and glanced at her.

The spell of endless work and unfathomable commitments had been broken.

Beneath the bed covers, Kate slid closer. She could feel his warmth. They kissed, slow and gentle at first then deeper, more passionate. His breath smelled of mint toothpaste.

She pushed the tablet out of his hand, causing it to clatter to the floor.

They laughed.

He peered over the bedside to check on it. "Nothing's broken."

"Well, then I didn't try hard enough."

Before he could retrieve it, Kate climbed on top of him, using her palms to pin him down. Stretching out, she brushed his chest with extended fingers. He ripped the pillows out from behind him and lowered himself. Hands found the outside of her thighs and rode up beneath the t-shirt she wore. She bent to kiss him and could feel him pulling her closer, their bodies melding together as one. She sighed, closing her eyes. His fingers moved to the small of her back. His lips were moist. Their kiss sent a sensation radiating through her that stirred up more feelings.

In the other room, her cell phone rang.

She cocked her head, sensing the poor timing of the interruption.

His lips caressed her neck. "Kate, don't answer it."

"No. I have to." Breaking away and sliding out of bed, she folded down her t-shirt as she ran barefoot into the small living room of her suite. "Hold those thoughts, Thomas. I'll keep this short."

She heard him groan and imagined him reaching for his tablet.

Snatching up her phone, she swiped the call icon and hoped that it hadn't gone to voicemail. "Morgan."

"You didn't file a daily report last night." The voice belonged to Vice President Mears. She noticed that the hockey puck satellite hotspot had activated and automatically transferred the call to her cell phone. The number on the device's screen read RESTRICTED. "And one wasn't submitted tonight, either. I'm calling to know why."

Kate walked as far from the bedroom as possible and leaned against an outside window sill. Keeping her voice down, she said, "Both have been busy days in the lab. Long days. Very long. Several technical hurdles were overcome. I got caught in—"

"I shouldn't be getting intel from Grayson when I should be getting it directly from you, Agent Morgan. You work for me. That was our deal."

"Yes, sir. Understood."

"I need to know that you're still invested. Committed to what's at stake. We need to know that you're not withholding information, from your own Director, from Justice, from the Office of the President."

She cleared her throat. "Nothing has changed on my end."

"If you violate our terms, this deal of ours is off. There will be consequences to failing to support our initiatives. Remember, I told you that you wouldn't survive the week. Don't cross us. Keep that in mind."

The call ended.

Kate swore. She thought about calling the Assistant Director in Charge in the bureau's Washington Field Office to explain herself, but decided against it. Bureau leadership hadn't officially contacted her about her unfiled field reports. On an operation this important, surely one or both of them were in constant dialogue with the Vice President and or the Attorney General. Obviously, Grayson had filled in the blanks for the VP.

She glanced to the bedroom.

Parker had turned out the light. His way of sending a message: take care of business.

She wondered what version of events Grayson had submitted, and whether his report included video attachments.

Huffing, Kate decided to file her delinquent report in the morning. Setting her phone next to the chardonnay gift box, she returned to the bedroom.

Her phone rang again.

Backtracking, she answered it. "Morgan."

"The rest are in solitary confinement at a mental health in-patient facility in Maine."

She recognized the voice. Debra Ford.

Kate rubbed her brow. "Say again, Debra?"

"I promised Thomas Parker that if he did his job, I would tell him where the remaining participants were held."

Kate snatched a notepad off the counter and scribbled down

what she'd just heard. "Where in Maine? What's the name of the place?"

There was a bit of a chuckle. "Not so fast. I'll take him there. After he delivers what they want."

"Delivers? Who? What do you mean? Who's after what? Common InSight?"

The chuckle changed to edgy laughter. "Agent Morgan, you're afraid Thomas is keeping secrets from you? Especially after last night?"

Kate glanced around the room and wondered if she was being watched. She became aware of air touching her bare legs beneath the hem of her t-shirt. Grayson had obviously lied about deleting the video.

She crossed her arms to pull the cotton shirt tighter to her body and let silence be her response, hoping Debra Ford would divulge more.

"How was the wine?"

Kate grimaced. "You spent too much. Could've got the same thing cheaper at a liquor wholesaler." She glanced at the wine box. Besides the French winery's wording etched into wood, she noted the symmetrical symbol branded in the corner, a post-purchase artistic addition. The distributor's label was on the opposite corner: Manhattan Wine Company, West Chelsea, New York City. "Debra, it was a thoughtful gesture considering that Thomas lost everything he owned in the fire. So, what were you doing in Manhattan? Visit there frequently?"

"Running an errand, nothing more."

"Really? And the symbol on the box? An emblem for Common InSight?"

"Prosperity, dear."

"Prosperity? Is that important?"

"Depends on how you view it." The subject was changed. "Was the wine good, dear?"

Kate rolled her eyes. "Delightful, Debra. Send more when you can."

"I might."

She took a breath before cutting off the chit chat. "Since it's just us girls talking, what do you want? What's your end game? Spell it out for me."

The response came out blunt, matter-of-fact. "Implantation. To transfer thoughts from one person to another, and so on. Common InSight."

Kate shook her head. "Manea," she said, using the goddess of the dead nickname that Ford had been given. "I have no idea what that means."

"Know how I got that name? Did any of the files you read on me say?"

Actually, she'd never read any of those EYES ONLY reports, which were classified above her security clearance level. An NSA spymaster she knew had provided a verbal synopsis.

"Not really. Is this important?"

"Listen up." An loud exhale came across the phone. "I watched a good friend get gutted from her legs to her throat, slowly, painfully. Just because she protected a sister who worked as a finance executive at an international humanitarian organization. The killer, a corrupt Italian nicknamed the Butcher, had lineage from old Italian families. Original Mafia families. And to expand his territory, the Butcher joined forces with a crime syndicate in Russia. When he tracked down the sister, he did the same to her. An inch at a time—the sister's torture lasted a full day. The Butcher and his team of hackers stole 500 million Euros. The humanitarian organization was wiped out. Because of his family connections, INTERPOL wouldn't touch the Butcher. So I went off the books as it were. An eye for an eye. I dispensed justice on behalf of my friend and her sister. I showed no mercy. It was brutal. The Butcher and his closest associates were eliminated. Through persistence, I tracked the stolen funds to Sberbank in Moscow. The four Central Bank of Russia officials laundering the money were treated the same. I did not stop until most of the funds were restored to the European Central Bank and the nonprofit."

Kate collapsed in a chair, struggling to grasp the details of the story. "So when you're not working for the State Department, you're a dark-of-night vigilante?"

"Katherine, dear, I have the scars to prove it."

She nodded. "I bet you do." She considered her next question carefully. "So how'd you get out of Russia? I'm sure that wasn't easy after killing those bankers."

"An American living in England helped me with logistics."

"Why tell me this? The few glasses of wine we shared make us such good friends?"

"Because, Morgan, you are so quick to judge my motives. Our world is changing. Rapidly. Wars are coming that you don't know exist. Somebody has to take action when no one else will."

"What wars? Fill in the gaps for me. Tell me about the eight rings. The symbols I saw on that ship, the *Norvana*."

"Eight rings? Look closer." A long exhale came across the phone. "By now, Thomas is asleep. Must've got tired of waiting. The story of your life, I bet. Well, in any case, that frees you up to enjoy another glass of chardonnay."

The call ended, leaving Kate staring at her phone.

63

MORE TO THE STORY

In a breakout room in Advanced BioCore's Security Operations Center, Debra Ford stood next to William Grayson and watched monitors display footage of one of the on-property residences. On screen, Kate Morgan stared at her phone before turning her attention to a wine box.

Ford grinned. Morgan had begun to piece together the clues.

Both calls had originated from the same number, and the federal agent had been spoofed into believing that the first call was from Vice President. What Morgan didn't know was the latest commercially available application program interface simply synthesized the Vice President's voice, making it only sound like him, even embedding the person's natural intonations and emotion. Modern technology had grown so sophisticated that software could replicate anyone's voice with about a minute of original recorded audio. As an elected official, Mears had hours of tape for synthesis. In the future, audio files alone would no longer be admissible in court as evidence because anyone with a standard computer could say anything from anyone, without any residual forensics traces to discredit the recording or prove what audio was real and what audio had been fictionalized.

The timing of both calls had ratcheted up the pressure.

The results were instantaneous.

Morgan picked up the wine box to study it.

"I wish you wouldn't have mentioned me," Grayson said.

Ford eyed him wearily. "I never said your name, Bill. And she's new to global espionage. I doubt she's clever enough to connect you and me and Moscow." She strolled to windows facing the ops room and de-energized the frosted glass to peer at the action displayed on the big board. "Morgan needed spoon-feeding. The story served a purpose."

"Not if it blows my cover."

She turned to him. "Bill, dear, you've been paid to see this through. Twenty million. Half up front. Over the years, I've made you a very rich man. So don't complain."

"I'm not." He glanced at the monitor. "I don't see why she's needed now that Parker's on board. Just another obstacle to get rid of in the end."

She smirked. "How do you know I'm not grooming Morgan for a future role?"

"Got things planned that far out, do you?"

"You might be surprised."

64

PROSPERITY

Kate tempered her anger, knowing her deep-seated surveillance paranoia had been validated. Big Brother was watching. Big Brother's representative was none other than William Grayson. Kate stared beyond an open doorway and into a dark bedroom. Ford couldn't have known that Parker went to sleep without Grayson's involvement.

That meant Grayson was not just working for the Vice President but also Ford.

Instincts told her that the Vice President and Ford were not on the same team.

If Ford was preparing for battle, what was the Vice President doing? *Warfare is based on deception*, she thought.

Secrets. Lies. Conspiracies.

Puzzle pieces. Small sections and shapes, almost unidentifiable at first, but when combined, disclosed the entire picture.

"Enjoy another glass of chardonnay" echoed in her mind.

Ford was pushing her onto a path of discovery, telling her something without actually telling her. A scavenger hunt leading to a destination, of which "implantation" was only a small part. "To transfer thoughts from one person to another, and so on. Common InSight."

The box, not the wine, was important.

Hauling it over to a table lamp for better illumination, she inspected the pyro-crafted prosperity symbol burned into olive wood. Simple. Symmetrical. In some ways the symbol was an ambigram, symbology that contained visual perception, allowing the object to be viewed the same or discovered in different ways, like yin-yang, the Star of David, swastikas, a Cross Barbée.

Twin arcing dragons and eight intersecting rings fit that mold too.

As an expert in forensics, she was trained to see details that other people didn't. The symbol's scoring was different than the French winemaker's etchings, providing a clue that it was added after the box was purchased.

Firing up her bureau laptop, Kate searched the Internet for like images. Sure enough, it was there: Lu. The Chinese pictorial represented prosperity, good fortune, or good luck. Imagery linked to the trio of Chinese "star gods." Prosperity was associated with the Chinese New Year tradition.

Prosperity.

What did that have to do with a box of wine?

Grabbing a notepad, she sketched out her puzzle pieces as

boxes. Each box carried a title: PROSPERITY, EIGHT RINGS, TWIN DRAGONS, CHINA, MANHATTAN, HONG KONG, NORTH KOREA. Drawing lines between the boxes, she connected what she could.

The Internet's best match for EIGHT RINGS was a thoroughbred racehorse. Debra Ford had told her to look closer, so she sketched out the rings again.

There were NINE RINGS, if the outside diameter was counted.

Each internal ring was of equal size, bound to another. A web search for NINE RINGS came up with Tolkien references. Nine Rings of Power given to the most powerful kings of men, and the possessors of the rings became Ring-wraiths.

She doubted any symbolic ancestry traced back to the evil servant warriors and Tolkien.

Debra Ford wasn't making this easy.

Mad that the dots weren't magically connecting, she flipped the note pad page and started over, focusing on just PROSPERITY, CHINA, and MANHATTAN.

Thirty minutes into a string of new Internet searches, she hit pay dirt.

The Prosperity Gala in the Financial District of Manhattan had been held days earlier. The fundraising event was sponsored by the United Nations Food and Agriculture Organization. Dignitaries from around the world attended, including representatives from China.

Several international newspapers ran small stories on the gala but none were as intriguing as *The Vigilant Patriot*, an anti-Chinese government newspaper based in Hong Kong. An English translation to the website was available. She clicked on it. The newspaper's logo was twin yin yang smoke-like dragons, exactly what she'd seen on the research vessel, the *Norvana*.

The article defined the contrasts between what China publicly said and supported at the United Nations and what its authoritarian actions demonstrated. One country, two systems was an illusion. A failure. The people of Hong Kong were under siege by the oppressive regime of the Communist Party. Because of the West's one-sided commitment to remain hopeful on one party, two systems, the UN had fallen to communist rule. China was a permanent member of the UN Security Council and bought political influence on the cheap. China was the second-largest monetary contributor to the UN, only behind the US. Its hegemonic ambition was to reshape the UN in its own image. Under its subversive power, China obstructed Hong Kong from any formal recognition. Technically it wasn't a nation, just property. Hong Kong held no autonomy. It had no international voice. The world had turned its back on the people of Hong Kong, giving China *carte blanche* to use invading forces to slaughter anyone who stood against them. China was imprisoning everyone who stood against them.

The article talked of prosperity delivered by two dragons—twin dragons—fire and ice.

Peace on Earth could not be suppressed any longer. A revolution was coming.

The article bolstered its revelations by citing unnamed sources at the United Nations with firsthand knowledge of the plans. The story closed by describing how the People's Republic of China had gone on the offensive, setting out to assassinate any Peace on Earth rebellion before it could start. The article's sources revealed that fourteen Chinese nationals had gone underground after a New York City Prosperity Gala to carryout China's preemptive strikes.

Kate gathered her thoughts. Questions formed around a single focus. If article wasn't just hopeful propaganda meant to feed a shrinking population of resistance and influence—the people of Hong Kong—and if the article was factual, it predicted a coming war. A civil war. A war Hong Kong stood no chance to win.

Unless the abandoned nation had allies—twin dragons. A new age of soldiers to champion their cause.

Kate thought about Debra Ford's story about her, the two sisters, and the Italian Butcher.

"Somebody has to take action when no one else will." Ominous words.

Twin Dragons. Fire. Ice. Yin-Yang. How was Debra Ford helping the people of Hong Kong defeat a mammoth empire like China?

Ford would use Common InSight to build an army that would deliver Peace on Earth.

Kate's last thought surprised her: if Debra Ford obtained the technical power behind Common InSight and possessed the ability to foster democratic thoughts inside the minds of the oppressed, should she even be stopped?

FRIDAY, DECEMBER 4th

Technological progress is like an axe
in the hands of a pathological criminal.
Albert Einstein

65

THOSE WHO PROVIDE THE AXES

Parker reached beside him. The form he searched for wasn't there. Rubbing his eyes, he checked a bedside clock: 4:30 AM. He clicked on a light, slid out of bed, and entered the adjacent living room.

She'd been there all night.

Asleep on a couch, Kate had her FBI windbreaker pulled over her as a blanket.

Scattered across a coffee table were notes. He sorted the papers filled with sketches, a grid of linked associations, and conjecture.

Kate had puzzled things out.

Nine Rings represented a new nation, one that absorbed the identities of its contributors, eight member states. Ji-woo Song and the *Norvana* were funded by Hong Kong, not North Korea. China had released fourteen assassins into New York City to stop Peace on Earth from starting.

The direct associations noted in graphic was troubling.

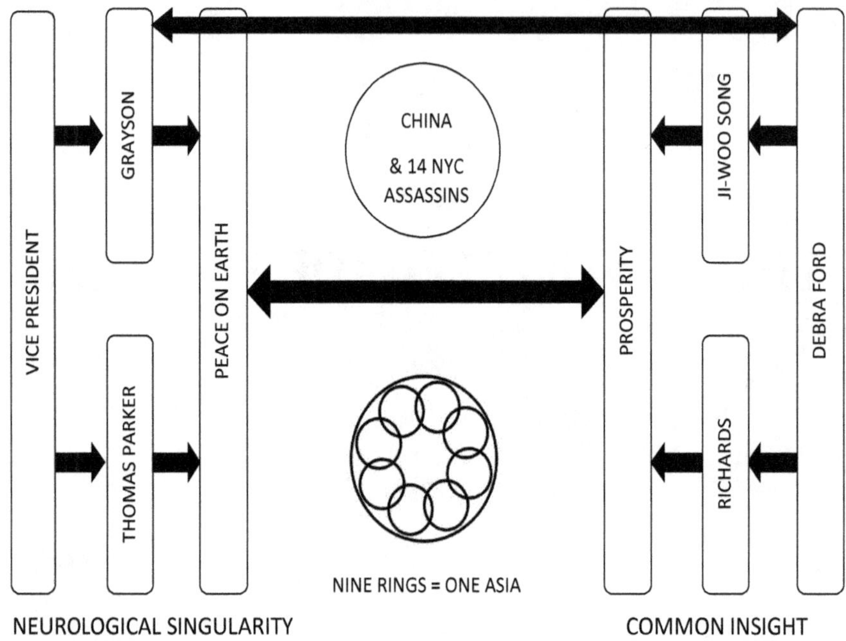

Her notes hit home.

PARKER'S TECH DELIVERS THE SWORD OF JUSTICE AS COMMON INSIGHT. PEACE ON EARTH IS THE COVERT PROGRAM THAT COUNTERS CHINA'S ADVANCES IN THE WORLD.

On the bottom of the last page, Kate pondered two questions:

SHOULD I STOP DEBRA FORD?

WHAT DO I DO ABOUT THE VICE PRESIDENT?

Both went unanswered.

Parker backtracked in the notes, following her logic. She'd surmised that China was an imminent threat to Hong Kong, Taiwan, even Macau. In its quest for territorial expansion, China would not stop until it met an opposing force. Unchecked, China would position itself to take over the world. The only way to stop China was an Asia united, One Asia, the Nine Rings.

Parker stopped reading the notes and glanced at Kate, who was still sleeping. He wondered what she thought of him, and whether she held him responsible for this mess.

Inside, he felt hollow, as if he'd given the world technology that was far worse than the atomic bomb. Mutually insured destruction had kept nations in possession of such weapons in check since the bombing of Nagasaki. That would not be the case with neurological singularity. Empowered with Common Insight, nations would prey on nations, people on people, until individual autonomy and democracy no longer remained. Humans couldn't live without the fear of cognitive influence by those with the power to control their thoughts and change their minds.

He thought of Eric Arthur Blair, the novelist better known as George Orwell, who'd written *Animal Farm* and *Nineteen Eighty-Four* and given the world a host of neologisms, like Big Brother, Thought Police, memory hole, and doublethink. The man's literary projections had become manifest in wide aspects of modern politics and social structures—capitalism, communism, socialism, totalitarianism, and quests for world domination.

Human existence had just acquired a new doomsday clock.

He thought of what Einstein had said about technology: "Technological progress is like an axe in the hands of a pathological criminal."

Parker understood that he'd become the reckless fool responsible for handing out axes to the lunatics and fanatics. More innocent people were going to get hurt, and he didn't know how to prevent that from happening.

Kate hated the deception. Playing possum. She kept her breathing shallow and pretended to sleep on the couch, while Parker read her notes. He needed to understand the bigger picture. See how the pieces of the puzzle connected. How he fit into the illicit schemes of others.

Parker struggled to check his emotions.

Setting aside Kate's notes, he watched her sleep.

Within a span of a few months, he'd gotten lost, absorbed in the broader initiatives and the flow of other people's business.

He never wanted this.

None of it.

Almost none of it.

His thoughts of her had grown complicated.

Trust was a fickle thing, difficult to hold onto when its fabric was tattered, worn.

Kate's repose took him back to when he first saw her. Barely knew each other then, unsure of the other's motives. Yet they'd found a way to make it work, build trust. Each needed the other. Now he wasn't so sure.

He yearned for simpler times at Princeton—teaching, working on ideas not yet realized inside a make-shift lab. If Stewart Richards hadn't manipulated him into leaving Princeton, he would never have met Kate. Their paths would never have crossed. Neurological singularity would have remained an elusive dream.

Parker left Kate sleeping and went to shower.

A minute later, a turn of the faucet yielded warmth and steam. Discarding his clothes, he stepped under the spray of water and allowed it to bring his skin alive. Early in life, he'd been deprived of such luxuries—an archeology vagabond, or at least a son to a pair of them.

Under the hot water, he thought of his parents. He missed them. He'd lost them in a plane crash years ago. Nothing of them remained but memories. No mementos. No pictures. Not even artifacts. At times, the latter had been more important to a pair of archeologists than their son.

Everything connecting him to them was lost when his home burned.

He never blamed his parents for raising him in an endless string of summer camp tent-style adventures. Archeology was their life. He was a simple addition to it. Their quests were to dredge up other people's pasts. Rocks. Dirt. Trinkets and treasures that most of the time had little or no monetary value. Bones and human remains. Origins of people and animals long gone. As tenured archeologists, they lived to do what they loved. Diggers to the core. During early childhood, he'd grown up living more outside the United States than inside it. The amenities of modern life—functioning plumbing, running water that you could count on, and hot showers—didn't exist for him. Not until his teen years, when he pushed back and demanded civilization, did the luxury of a consistent shower arrive, an event not connected to a tent or a dilapidated trailer.

Even though he claimed to be no traditional archeologist, he was in a way. As a physician and neurologist, he was a facsimile of his parents, evolved to become a neurological archeologist. While they had searched for biofacts of the past, he searched for biofacts within living beings, memories.

He was a digger, a neurological digger.

He finished his shower, toweled off, shaved, and put on clean clothes.

Walking out of the residence, he glanced at Kate, who still slept. Kate was different from his parents in almost every way.

She would've liked his parents. They would've loved her.

66

WHEN EVERYTHING IS GONE

In Advanced BioCore's Security Operations Center, Bill Grayson fixed his attention to a span of monitors in a breakout room and watched Kate Morgan's residence. Moments earlier, Thomas Parker had left her room to start his day in the labs.

On the screen, he enlarged a camera shot of Morgan's sitting room to zoom in on handwritten notes. She'd appeared to have purposely left the notes out for Parker to find.

During the night, security techs couldn't enlarge imagery to identify what the notes actually said. It wasn't until Parker set them down in such a manner as to allow security to get a closer look at the pages.

The news was troubling.

Grayson put his cell phone on speaker when the call went through.

"You know what they say?" the voice asked over the phone. Vice President Mears seemed to be taking the news rather calmly.

"One page, yes. Bits and pieces of the rest. It's not good."

On screen, Morgan rose from the couch, glanced at the notes, then headed into the bathroom. Through an open doorway, a shot showed her reaching for the knobs of the shower. Audio confirmed that water was running. Morgan shut the door.

"She's getting into the shower." He checked his watch estimating how much time that he had. "You want me to grab them?"

"Clean her out. Take everything. And I mean everything." Mears paused. "Scan the notes and forward them."

A minute later, Grayson and a team of guards entered Morgan's residence using a master key. Carrying black plastic bags, they collected everything: clothes, shoes, computer and cell phone, case notes, wine box and bottles, and even her FBI credentials. The room's hardwired residence phone was removed, as was her semiautomatic stuffed under the bed mattress. Everything went into plastic bags.

In less than five minutes, nothing personal remained.

As Grayson left, he taped over the door's peephole and set the door's locking mechanism to quarantine mode.

Only security could open her door now.

Kate stepped from the shower, dried off, and used her towel as a wrap. Heading into her bedroom, she opened a dresser drawer in search of clothing. The drawer was empty. Spinning around, she realized something was different.

Someone had entered her room. Thomas? She wanted to call out for him but decided against it.

Kate reached for where she'd stashed her Glock. Tucked below the mattress. Nothing. Pulling up the mattress, she reached deeper inside the gap between the mattress and the box spring.

Her .40 caliber semiautomatic was gone.

She searched the rest of the residence.

The raid had netted everything: clothing, shoes, badge, phone, satellite hub, computer, and notes. Debra Ford's box of chardonnay treasures fell missing in action. They'd even removed the residence's hardwired phone.

Grayson had left nothing but the towel she wore.

Easy to do, when your subject was under surveillance.

Someone in the operational chain of command disliked what she'd written: Debra Ford, the Vice President, Grayson himself?

Kate gritted her teeth and paced while she figured out what to do next.

Circling the room, she stopped to look through the peephole in the hallway door. Black. Taped over. She wrenched the door handle. The lever moved, but the handle failed to disengage the lock. It was as if she'd been confined to quarters.

Kate tossed a glance to the outside windows. Generic glass with aluminum frames. It was still dark outside, with sunrise still more than an hour away.

A plan formed in her mind. It was time to break the shackles of imprisonment.

Bedding would work as makeshift clothing. Utensils from the kitchenette and anything else that carried a point or edge would be her weapons. Her academy training had failed to provide a course on prison facility escape tactics or the art of making shanks, but the exterior windows offered an escape route.

Of course, with the advantage of surveillance, Grayson and his thugs would be waiting outside. She moved through the suite, searching for anything to use to her advantage. When she looked up, she noticed the sprinkler heads. By themselves, fire sprinkler heads weren't particularly helpful. But smash out the glass vial or lead link holding the sprinkler's mechanism in place, water would flow. A lot of water. Once that happened, flow switches in the sprinkler mains would trigger fire alarms and send a signal to the fire department.

Eisenhower Executive Office Building, Washington, DC

In his makeshift command center, Mears studied scanned documents. His cell phone had Grayson on speaker mode. For an experienced intelligence officer and current executive running a for-profit research site, the man was more nervous than the situation warranted. Perhaps Grayson was demonstrating the limits of his capabilities.

Morgan was locked down, contained.

Beside Mears, Gordon Abbott enlarged Morgan's hand sketch on the monitor. "She clearly doesn't know everything."

Mears shook his head. "Close enough."

Abbot shrugged. "Fact-less conjecture." He turned to the Vice President. "A lot of moving parts have to come together for us to pull this off. And Morgan could mess things up. What do you want to do?"

Mears cleared his throat. "Indoctrinate her."

Abbott scoffed. "Well, that's damn reckless."

Advanced BioCore International, Princeton, New Jersey

Still in nothing but a towel, Kate turned out the residence's lights to work in the dark, believing the complex's surveillance systems lacked infrared capabilities.

Tearing bed sheets into wearable-sized fabric, she prepared a new ensemble, one configured as part-toga, part-hobo dress. She tore up pillow cases to function as an inner top and skirt.

Her plan was simple: go on the offensive.

She'd trigger the sprinkler heads and go out the window when the fire department arrived. The distraction would divide Advanced BioCore's security teams and better her odds. Once outside, she'd circle back to overtake a security guard with prison-style, home-made weapons.

Get a gun. Take down Grayson. Call in federal reinforcements. Shut everything down.

She'd let her higher-ups manage the fallout of another illegal human subjects program. At least she could take out half of a grander Peace on Earth.

Somewhere down the line, Debra Ford would be next.

Kate understood the lethal obstacles ahead, but she considered the course of action better than waiting around for Grayson to figure out that she was better off dead. She'd learned one thing about herself in recent months: she hated being the victim.

Someone knocked on her door.

She thought of Thomas, then realized that it could be anyone— including security, ready to haul her off somewhere dark and put a bullet in her brain.

Entering the living room, she grabbed a chair and carried it to the door, readying herself to use it as a weapon. She peered through the door's peephole. Light appeared rather than darkness. The tape had been removed. The hallway looked clear enough.

One hand grasped the handle. The other gripped the back of the chair, ready to swing wildly if anyone burst through the door.

The handle went down without resistance. The door lock disengaged.

Kate cracked open the door.

The hallway was empty.

At the foot of the door was folded clothing beside her boots. An envelope stuck out of one of the boots.

Accepting the offering, she swept up everything and closed the door. What she held went on the kitchen counter. Pants. Shirt. No undergarments, no socks. No Glock, either. Tucked inside her boots were her badge and a sealed envelope. *PEACE ON EARTH* was scrawled on the envelope.

Kate felt a clump inside the letter-sized envelope. She tore it open and slid out an electronic car key and a paperboard card with an address in New York City.

67

INHERITED MEMORIES

In the Neurophysiology Lab, Parker worked at a console to add one last programming insert to the coding stream that Advanced BioCore's software engineers had compiled overnight. The night before, he'd scrutinized the final assembly and testing logs, ensuring the wetware algorithms were on track. In parallel efforts, the pods and headgear had cleared all quality control milestones.

Now, only one final commissioning step remained: an actual test drive on a human.

Caroline Wang had offered to be first, and the last.

As with Kate earlier, he worked alone with the participant.

She touched his shoulder. "It's going to work."

He shrugged. "Clinically, you're insane, you know that, right? Hear voices. Have visions. Inherited memories not your own. You've seen secrets that can destroy nations. In most societies that's bad."

Wearing blue surgical scrubs, she smiled and rubbed her bald head. "If this was the late seventeenth century and I was in Salem,

Massachusetts, the Puritan magistrates would claim I was smitten with the devil. They'd call me a witch."

It was good to see her smile.

"What are you going to do when this is over?" he asked, tilting up a pod so that she could strap into the contraption.

Stepping backwards, she leaned into the body-tight compartment. Her brown eyes radiated conviction, clarity.

"Never do anything like this again." She shuffled her shoulders to fit into the body mold and centered her head. He lowered the skullcap. Part of her face disappeared behind an optical interface that covered her eyes.

She reached out and touched him, feeling for him like a person who'd lost her sight. "Thank you, Thomas."

"It's premature to thank me for a lobotomy."

She chuckled. "That's not funny."

He took her hand. "I thought it was sort of funny."

"Not at all."

He placed her wrists and ankles into Velcro restraints, precautions to keep her from accidently bumping components that if damaged might kill her. After lowering the pod to a horizontal position, he initiated the start sequence.

Through a headset he spoke. "What's on your mind?"

"Nothing you care to see, I'm sure."

He chuckled. "If only that were the case."

He entered a predefined script and followed the sequences he'd used for Kate. Caroline's brain scans and bio-readings stretched across the Wall of Knowledge from one side to the other. 3D neurological maps tracked neurological signal progressions. Her mind was entangled with noise, corrupted with overlapping memories. Replication algorithms tapped into neural pathways that mirrored real-time feedback. Yet it was difficult to discern which memories were hers and which had been accidently implanted by the others.

A modeling algorithm on a screen next to his console station constructed real-time patterns and distinguished the roots to her thoughts and how the overlapping noise of other memories complicated things, like a trunk of a tree hidden in a grove of vines. Slowly, modeling profiles reached a pivotal moment of clarity.

What Caroline saw, so did supercomputers running elsewhere in a data center.

Gradually, he increased the complexity of images beamed into her brain.

Parker moved the sequencing images that Caroline saw in her mind to a central screen.

Memories.

A young child sat at a dining room table. In front of her was a birthday cake. Eight lit candles. Streamers swept down from a ceiling. Proud parents and grandparents sang "Happy Birthday."

"Make a wish and blow out the candles, dear," her mother said.

Caroline leaned close to the cake and blew. Fire-tipped candles flickered before going out. Her family clapped and embraced her.

He grinned. The moment was magical.

Common InSight.

And a first step in memory recall.

Over the next two hours, Parker moved beyond eight-year-old birthdays and peered deeper into Caroline's mind, focusing on select memories tied to ACNRI, Stewart Richards, Samuel Ford, and finally the other participants. Inherited memories were categorized and evaluated differently so that computer algorithms could dissect the cross-associations that had been shared among participants.

The process was messy and required several attempts to find the metaphorical tree trunk hidden in a thicket of vines. In and among themselves, the vines weren't irrelevant. The progression required tracing origins and clearing the vines away with a scalpel rather than a machete.

The data collected would take even the fastest supercomputer hours to digest.

At the conclusion of the calibration process, Caroline was fatigued, mentally and physically. Her face showed the stress she'd undergone, a mask covering tired eyes. She'd aged during the process. He lifted her from the machine and placed her into a wheelchair. An IV was strung on a pole to administer electrolytes and a sedative.

Caroline needed sleep without dreams.

Time to allow her mind to recover.

68

STICKING TO THE SCRIPT

Manhattan, New York City

Noticing a trio of cars that tailed her in varied formations, Kate stuck to the script and drove to the Manhattan address provided. A fresh-off-the-lot, generic white sedan with dealer paper tags and no license plate awaited her as she walked out of Advanced BioCore's front doors.

The smart key she'd been provided engaged the ignition. A GPS mounted in the dash assisted with navigation.

With a full tank of gas, she'd debated making a run for it—driving like a bat out of hell and heading either to the closest police station or to one of the regional FBI Field Offices, of which she had three to choose from: Philadelphia, Newark, or a satellite office in Atlantic City.

Even when floored, though, her gift car couldn't out-accelerate a bicycle speeding downhill. She assumed this was the reason they'd chosen the vehicle—so she couldn't shake her three-car tail. If she deviated, she'd be intercepted and probably shot—or taken back to Advanced BioCore, and then shot.

With no wallet, money, cell phone, or gun, she was handicapped. The only weapon she had was a powder puff of a car. Easy pickings for armed pursuers.

She considered the Manhattan address an opportunity. Once in New York City, a plethora of options would present themselves. The address provided was damn close to the bureau's New York Field Office—a ten-minute walk on foot, five minutes if she ran.

Morning rush hour traffic heading into the Big Apple had turned an hour's drive into three. She sped through the toll plazas without paying, knowing that the New Jersey Turnpike and New York State Thruway Authorities would capture the vehicle's license and a picture of its driver. She encountered three different sets of automated buzzers and camera flashes. Each time she held her FBI badge against the windshield to provide identification. At least authorities would know who was behind the wheel and log a record of the car itself.

Darkness yielded to dawn in a city like few others.

Weaving through the quagmire of Manhattan traffic, she followed navigation directions and parked illegally outside the Temple Court Building and The Beeker Hotel. The relevance of the address had become clear.

She looked around for the cars that tailed her, and saw none.

Gathering her bearings, she mentally pictured where she stood with respect to the bureau's New York Field Office, just several blocks north. Even if a trio of pursuit vehicles blocked off major streets, it was close enough to run for it.

She filed that away in her mind.

Entering the hotel, Kate headed to the concierge's desk. She barged past a customer and shoved her badge in the face of the customer service clerk, in no mood for subtleties or politeness.

"The manager. Now."

Before the stunned expression of the service clerk and customer could fade, a man cleared his throat and stepped forward.

"How may I be of assistance, ma'am?"

Kate studied a balding man in a suit, his annoying expression bright yet borderline condescending, in a how-may-I-serve-you manner.

"Who was the manager working the night of the Prosperity Gala?"

The suit glanced to the customer being served and apologized for any inconvenience, then gestured to see her credentials.

She obliged. "Special Agent Katherine Morgan, Federal Bureau of Investigation."

He studied her badge and ID. "I can read." He returned the credentials. "I have something for you. I'll be right back. Can I get you something while you wait? Bottled water? Coffee?"

She shook her head and took in the glamor of the posh hotel. White and black tiled lobby. Dark hardwood walls and high ceilings. The front desk was covered in ornamental throw rugs. Nearby, a bright green-walled seating area had no core ceiling, instead it rose up several floors. A picture of Edgar Allen Poe was the prominent piece of art on display. Tall, ornate glass-doored bookshelves provided a boundary to separate the seating space from a corridor.

"Agent Morgan, your party is waiting for you."

He handed her an envelope, a lot like the one she'd been provided at Advanced BioCore. It contained the same handwritten phrase: *PEACE ON EARTH*.

Kate thought for a moment and lightened her tone. "Does the hotel have a courtesy phone that I may use?"

"Of course. Hardwired or cellular?"

"Either will be fine. Oh, a couple of other things. May I have a writing tablet and several pens?"

"Anything else?"

Kate fingered the paper-thin envelope, unsure if anything was actually sealed inside. "Not right now, thank you."

The manager reached behind the service counter and retrieved stationery branded "The Beekman, A Thompson Hotel" and two stenciled pens.

He motioned for her to follow him and guided her to a set of stairs barricaded by a thick velvet rope strung between two brass anchor points. The downward-leading stairs had been corded off for privacy.

The manager unclipped an end of the velvet rope and said, "One of our guest associates will bring a phone."

She nodded. "Thank you."

As she headed down, she prepared herself for anything, including an ambush, although that seemed unlikely given the elaborate meeting place. A man and a woman wearing matching black suits greeted her at the bottom of the stairs. The man held a black semi-automatic where it could be seen.

"Turn around." The woman said, matter-of-fact. "Hands against the wall."

Kate understood what was coming and faced a glass-blocked wall. A palm was shoved between her shoulder blades to drive her closer to the wall. Feet were kicked wider apart. The woman's hands swept below her shirt, washing bare skin. Without a belt or under-garments, nothing was missed as the woman moved groping hands off her breasts and thrust them deep into her pants. Intimidation was the intent of a pointless body search. Fingers brushed her hair, her ankles, her boots.

The woman spun her around to make eye contact.

"Should I thank you for the… attention?" Kate asked.

"Next time. When I'm off duty." The woman winked. "She's clean."

The man holding the semiautomatic holstered the weapon and slapped his colleague on the back as they went upstairs.

Kate studied the odd-looking dungeon. A riveted metal wall

arched around to an entertainment space. A headless female mannequin greeted her. A sign called the location THE ALLEY CAT. The space was a mockup of a prohibition-era underground speakeasy.

In the back, in a U-shaped leather sitting area, was an old man sipping tea.

The Secretary of State.

The cozy bar setting was unattended. They were alone.

Obviously, the two bodyguards were Secret Service agents.

"You're looking for answers?" he asked, his voice tired, burdened.

Frail was an understatement of the man's appearance. She'd seen plenty of photos of the career public servant. He'd lost significant body weight. His eyes appraised her and revealed a keen mind at work, even if his body countered that impression.

"How long do you have, Mr. Secretary?" she asked.

"Weeks." He poured her a cup of tea in a gold-leafed cup with oriental markings on it.

"Prostate?"

"Stage Four."

A death sentence. The second leading cancer in men explained his significant weight loss. He would've undergone chemo and radiation treatments to extend what remained of his life. Nothing but a long, grueling string of suffering ever led to a Stage Four cancer diagnosis.

"Sit, please." He slid the cup of tea over along with a plate of sliced cheese, crackers, and grapes. "I heard you didn't have time for breakfast. You must be hungry."

Kate set the envelope provided to her face up on the table, set aside her note tablet and pens, and picked off a couple of grapes. Not hungry, she was famished.

"Milk?" he asked, holding out of creamer cup. "Sugar?"

"No, thank you." She cleared her palate to make room for more grapes. "How high does this go? Does the President know?"

The Secretary sipped his tea. "You don't expect me to answer that, do you?"

"Then why are we talking?"

"To see how much you know." He sipped his tea. "Now that Thomas Parker is on board, you've outgrown your usefulness."

Kate sipped her tea. Earl Grey. Bitter without the addition of sugar. The Secretary drank his with milk, like many in Britain did. A small demonstration of the refined tastes of a well-traveled man.

His threat didn't go unnoticed as she sipped more tea. She offered no reply.

"You have discoveries to share?" he said, pointing to the tablet.

Kate recreated the sketch that she'd completed earlier and added a larger box around everything that was tagged SECRETARY OF STATE.

From his suit, he retrieved a photocopy of what she'd drawn. Obviously he'd received a scan, from either Grayson or the Vice President.

"How close am I?"

"Close enough to make you dangerous."

She took another sip of tea and eyed him across the rim of the cup. "To who?"

"Those high and low."

"Does Dick Mears know Grayson works for Debra Ford too?"

The Secretary refilled his tea cup. "Thanks to you, he does."

"And how does Senator Samuel Ford fit into all this?"

"He became a threat."

"How much did the Senator figure out?"

"Enough. Much like you, Special Agent Morgan."

She swallowed over the knot forming in her throat. "To who?"

"Those high and low."

"So you had Debra Ford kill him," she said as a statement, not a question.

"Manea put her ex-husband to better use."

"No it sounds like she gave him a Stage Four death sentence."

The Secretary nodded. "All mortals have death sentences. You. Me. Ford. Dr. Parker. The participants, as you call them. So now that you know, what do we do with you?"

"Mr. Secretary, who's we? One Asia? Twin Dragons? This syndicate that you're running?"

"Well, I've never considered us a syndicate." He exhaled. "Let's just say those high and low."

The female Secret Service agent who'd strip searched her appeared and set a courtesy cell phone on the table. A sticky note provided the device's passcode.

The Secretary dismissed the agent.

Kate glanced at the device, doubting she'd actually be allowed to use it.

They sat in silence. Her mind was filled with questions that she doubted she'd get the answers to, but she fired off a series anyway.

She started with what had brought her to Manhattan. "Prosperity. What's its relevance?"

"Balance. An equal distribution of mass. Value for all who cherish it."

"Secretary, is there a civil war coming?"

"It's already started. You're just a little late to riddle that out."

"Is this war you've launched about China invading Hong Kong?"

"China's aggressions into Hong Kong are mere a microcosm of a grander infestation. Their nationalistic appetite will consume the world until there is no opposition remaining that threatens their Wolf Warrior diplomacy, their worldwide conquest."

"Peace on Earth and Prosperity are about restoring balance in Asia?"

"No. The world."

"You and the Vice President are out to forcibly exploit Thomas Parker and Stewart Richards into using their neurological technology to deliver your esoteric cause. Debra Ford called it implantation.

Common InSight. Mind control. You plan to brainwash people into fighting your cause."

The Secretary took a breath. "'Conscience is nothing but social conditioning.' A quote attributed to the Hindu goddess of wealth, love, and prosperity. Since the beginning of human existence, those in power have indoctrinated their armies, equals, and servants in defined constructs of social conditioning and mindsets. This war of mental slavery has occurred long before the arrival of neurological singularity. If we don't secure the technology and applications first, our enemies will. And when our enemies have this power, they will not hesitate to use it against us. If we don't act with a preemptive strike, the world we know and our country will be lost."

Kate thought about the Chinese nationals who'd disappeared after the Prosperity Gala, a strike force of assassins willing to take on their enemies within the borders of the United States.

"Mr. Secretary, as a federal agent, you know I can't hold my tongue about what you just admitted to." She took a breath and recited the oath she'd taken on the first day of her academy training and again when she completed it. "I'm a special agent sworn to support and defend the Constitution of the United States against all enemies—foreign *and* domestic. I bear true faith and allegiance to the same. I take this obligation seriously, without any reservation or purpose of evasion. And I faithfully execute the duties of the office that I serve."

The Secretary shrugged. "Morgan, you're an idealist." He took a thoughtful breath. "I guess that is something we share, even if the protective veneer that we carry as our coat of arms is often cracked and flawed."

69

COMMISSIONING TRIALS

NeuroSteps Labs, Glen Gardener, New Jersey

Inside the Neurophysiology Lab, Richards oversaw final commissioning, which tracked well ahead of schedule. The first series of cognitive transfers would occur within hours.

He determined that this final protocol was an acceptable deviation from his plans.

Instead of transferring memories as planned, the participants would inherit transformative reconditioning, cognitive transplants—a genocidal experience that caused the death of free will. The hub and spoke process used Ji-woo Song and her Korean-American colleagues as master hubs and controlled the fourteen Chinese participants by radiating neurological transmissions downstream. On the abstract level, the parasitic process was similar to immunology and computers, where a virus invaded host cells with the sole intent to control and replicate.

Richards called the process "turning."

At the fifty-thousand-foot level, the premise was to hijack a person's mind and transplant a new belief system with actionable constructs. An extension to his end goals he hadn't even considered, with the limited forethought of achieving memory transfers and thought control.

In *turning a person*, a hub forcibly reshaped a spoke, taking over their target from the inside out. Not a novel concept, the core concept of a long string of alien invasion and dystopian literature and films: *Venom, The Host, Alien, The Invasion of the Body Snatchers.*

He watched the last of the participants, Ji-woo, put on her bio-suit and slip into her pod.

"See you on the other side, Dr. Richards," she said, her face set as she disappeared into a realm of metal, wires, and tubing.

"Yes, we will," he said with a nod.

Technicians had already brought her bio-readings up on display boards. Vitals. Neurological signals. Stimulation feeds.

"Can you hear me?" Ji-woo asked in English, her southern drawl clear and distinctive.

Richards grinned and slipped on a microphone. Ji-woo hadn't actually spoken; the computer had created her voice, using tonal inflections created by mere thoughts.

"Loud and clear, Dr. Song," a technician said. "Language check. Same phrase. Can you hear me?"

"*Nae mal deullini,*" repeated Ji-woo's voice translation. A dedicated panel on the big board tracked her neural associations and displayed the Korean translation in a transliterated text, rather than the script form. The visual display was easier for the non-language speaking technicians to follow. Below the first translation appeared Ji-woo's Mandarin version: "*Ni néng tīng dào wo ma.*"

He'd initially underestimated the challenges of language barriers in cognitive thought transmissions. Because NeuroSteps was a global operation, its depth of resources and engineers had kept up with the challenge and delivered solutions.

And Ji-woo Song had proven herself an extraordinary visionary.

Her Korean-American companions spoke next, each relaying a rehearsed set of phrases and mental imagery, working as a true Common Collective. Learning from his previous failed attempts, Richards had programmers institute priority control sequences, like parental controls, to ensure that one hub spoke at a time. Each spoke end, a Chinese participant, was connected to each hub, where each hub was responsible for a precise series of indoctrination projections.

The participants were a mix of Chinese nationals and Korean-Americans, which meant that English was not the best common language for communication protocols. Each of Ji-woo's team members spoke fluent Mandarin in addition to Korean and English. Not all of the Chinese nationals possessed enough English for it to be the baseline conversational language.

Ji-woo Song had used neurological singularity to build an army, *buqu* soldiers. In this case, Mandarin proved the language of engaged thought.

Richards considered that a fair trade, compared to what he got out of the deal.

A technician pointed to one of the screens. "Spokes are coming out of deep sedation. Five to seven minutes until cognitive readiness is available. On my mark. Three, two, one. Sedation reduction is commencing."

Richards sucked in a few breaths to steel himself. If everything followed the current trend, this neurological frontier would be his greatest masterpiece yet.

70
PREDICTIONS

Advanced BioCore, Princeton, New Jersey

After making sure that Caroline was resting comfortably, Parker sequenced each of the remaining participants through a reduced set of calibration checks one at a time, careful not to exceed an hour with each person.

The tedious process substantiated a common set of neurological outcomes: memories. Experiences that weren't theirs.

Using the same closeout method, Parker ran through memories associated with Richards, Samuel Ford, and the night the participants themselves had been abducted off a catamaran in Florida. This common backdrop told him how each person cognitively structured their experiences. Learning how each person stored memories was essential to his end goal.

A protocol he called Synaptic Touch was part of complex computer algorithms. AI bots were being trained on where to look inside each person's brain in order to trace and target certain memories.

Revealing the right memories would free them all.

Grayson entered the lab and stood on the periphery, keeping his distance while he watched Parker up close. The man was at ease, a consummate technician, precise, and efficient with time. If the neurologist delivered the secrets they sought, Peace on Earth was well within reach. Advanced BioCore was a step away from reading minds, learning what each person knew and how much they knew.

When Grayson had first learned of the unproven science, he was skeptical. Now he was mesmerized by what he saw. Computer applications had extracted memories from inside people. The extensions of the technology were limitless: medical, scientific, space exploration, military, and political.

Debra Ford was right. Those who had the access and the ability to control dangerous secrets could dominate the world.

Parker's technology was worth billions to those who controlled it, and Grayson saw no reason he couldn't peel off a bit of that action for himself.

That was good for business.

His brand of business.

71

NEW YORK

The Beeker Hotel, Manhattan, New York City

Kate sensed something deeper missing from their conversation, something the Secretary of State was reluctant to disclose. Without a watch, she had no idea how much time had passed—an hour, perhaps. The skilled diplomat's manner was almost warm, inviting, like talking to a grandfather. Their conversation wandered. She finished the grapes and sipped a second cup of Earl Grey, this time adding sugar to cut its bitterness. She understood the cleverness of his chit-chat. He was still fishing for how much she knew. They talked about her time with the bureau. What she knew about Thomas Parker, Stewart Richards, Debra Ford. The conversation even touched on what she'd gone through in Washington weeks earlier.

She finished her tea and glanced at the cell phone that had been delivered. The device would display the time at least, even if she wasn't permitted to use it.

"May I?"

"By all means."

She clicked the phone. The time display read 11:15 AM. Using the code provided on the sticky note, she accessed the phone. No service bars registered. The basement of the hotel had blocked cellular signals.

"Trouble?"

Kate sighed, and felt light-headed. "Perhaps."

He refilled their teas and took a sip of his.

Kate looked at the spread on the table. Something wasn't right.

Her lightheadedness became a heavier fog. She tried to blink it away, and looked at the Secretary.

"Feeling okay, Agent Morgan?" he asked.

She dropped her gaze back to the table. Something had been spiked. It wasn't the tea. Not the grapes. She'd seen him eat one. The sugar? The Secretary took no sugar with his tea. The bitterness of Earl Grey had prompted her to add a couple of teaspoons.

Sedative? Lethal agent?

Her sluggish mind recalled what she'd learned in medical school about poisons, toxins, and venom, and tried to match what she was experiencing to a rapid onset of symptoms. The sugar's sweetness and the tea's bitterness masked the taste of whatever she'd been given.

The female Secret Service agent who'd frisked her set a wooden box in front of her. The ornate box was etched in gold leaf, in a nautical theme. Central to the charts, compasses, and seafaring icons were a pair of twin dragons.

The same smoke-thin dragons she'd seen on the *Norvana.*

Kate tried to stand and fought for balance. The woman shoved her back into her seat. Muscles throughout her body surrendered their strength.

The Secretary glanced at a gold watch on his wrist. "Leave us for what time remains."

The agent dutifully left.

"Open it while you still can," the Secretary said, setting aside his tea.

Kate bobbed her head and took a frantic breath, fingering up a brass clasp to hinge open the box. Inside were a semiautomatic pistol and a magazine set into felt inserts. A Glock 23, like her bureau-issued service weapon.

"There were eight of us when we started this revolution," the Secretary said. "We call ourselves the Founders. One champion for each of the eight rings, for each nation. When our work is done, one of us will lead a unified nation. Two of us have died. Six remain. After I am gone, our ranks will be five."

With hands as heavy as stone, Kate removed the gun and popped the magazine into the weapon. She cocked back the slide to chamber a round and aimed the Glock. Her finger moved to the trigger. Using a two-handed grip, she targeted the Secretary's chest.

"What did you give me?" Kate asked, her mouth numb, lips tingling. "A toxin?"

The Secretary squared up his chest to give her a clear target. "I could dive into a monologue about a particular tradecraft that both the Russians and Chinese excel at. But that would run out your remaining time. Instead, I want you to make a choice."

Her head bobbed. The gun in her hand sagged. Eyelids felt heavy. Her skin tingled.

The Secretary snapped his fingers in front of her face to grab her attention.

She lifted her chin and the gun. She repositioned a steadying hand below the weapon to act as a brace, pulling her elbow against her stomach. The Secretary stood unwavering in the Glock's notch and groove sights.

"With my dying breath, I will fulfill the oath I took as a Founder. Peace on Earth will be realized. Common InSight is a vehicle to change the world and its inhabitants. You took a similar oath, Agent Morgan. So ask yourself, with your last breaths you take on this planet, are you prepared to stop me? You've been given a gun. Make the choice."

Not an easy answer. He was unarmed.

Coldblooded murder wasn't her brand of revenge.

Kate felt defeat overtake her. Closing her eyes, she lowered the weapon and let it fall from her hands.

The Secretary walked beside her.

The growing pull of gravity was strong, forcing her to slump sideways.

The world around her winked in and out, her rapidly fading vision focused on the outline of the Secretary's face. She tried to grab him, but the muscles in her body couldn't move. Gravity had won.

Before she blacked out, his words dropped her to the icy depths of a frigid lake.

"Welcome to the Common Collective of Prosperity."

72

AN OBSTACLE OF SECRECY

The Mansion on O Street, Dupont Circle Neighborhood, Washington, DC

Debra Ford understood a return to the cesspool called Washington, DC, was essential. Hardly desired. As the daughter of a career diplomat and ex-wife of an Oklahoma Senator, she'd had to make the nation's capital a second home for most of her life. Those who lived and worked in DC saw a far different world than the throngs of tourists who stopped in for a few days: a high cost of living, horrendous traffic, crowds, deteriorating government buildings, entrenched political mindsets that led to endless bureaucracy.

A return to the swampland required a touch of luxury and discreet accommodations.

The executive Town Car she'd rode in parked at a curb a block west of Dupont Circle. The brick row house-style structure matched much of the urban landscapes in Washington, except for one major difference. The Mansion on O Street was an eclectic blend of surreptitious lodging and museum. Essentially, everything in the hotel was for sale except secrets. A pair of lions guarded a red door. Other than a placard dedicated to Rosa Parks, very little identified the property. A simple sign read INN DOWNSTAIRS. The word-of-mouth, 100-plus room hotel offered themed lodging, 85 secret doors, hidden passageways, and private chefs. The hotel's slogan paralleled the Vegas theme: *what happens at the mansion stays at the mansion.*

The ultra-private accommodations catered to those who carried secrets.

Everything a woman flying below the radar required in a stay.

The chauffeur carried her large, soft-sided bags to a front desk, where a week's stay had been paid in advance. She received a room key and carried her own bags to the Monterey Suite, a spacious residence with windows that optimized sunshine, separate private entrances, and reserved parking.

On an entry table, in a decorative bowl, was a car's key fob. She swept a quick glance across the suite. Exactly how she remembered it. Bright. Lots of windows. Large kitchen. Beige and white with wood trim. Part-soutwestern, part-Victorian. No secret doors or passages unlike other areas in the hotel.

Ford checked her watch. Time was getting tight.

Not bothering to unpack, she set her bags on a Victorian bed and retrieved a leather portfolio off a desk, freshened up, and headed outside.

In the reserved parking spot, she found transportation: a BMW 230i sedan matched to the keyless starter. She placed the leather folder on the passenger's seat and navigated the streets of DC until she picked up the George Washington Memorial Parkway, heading south. The drive was reasonably short. She arrived in Alexandria forty minutes later and parked in a garage adjacent to the United States Patent and Trademark Office (USPTO) headquarters.

In the interior atrium of the USPTO's Madison Building she met a pair of patent lawyers, liaisons to an expedited process. They escorted her into a conference room, where the agency's Deputy Director and a case manager awaited them.

Unlike most federal agencies, the USPTO operated entirely on the collection of fees rather than taxpayer dollars. Unknown to most, an expediting process was available to select patent filers who had the funds to pay for premium services.

Ford had selected the expeditors based on their credentials. Both had worked for the USPTO and were familiar with the procedures for streamlining the process. Their firm specialized in corporate patents, trademarks, infringements, and international litigation. Their preparatory work had included multiple patent searches, trademarks, and clearing the field of patent squatters and patent trolls.

Introductions were made. Everyone took seats around a table.

Ford opened her leather portfolio and withdrew prepared filing submissions, complete with schematics and electronic documentation on thumb drives.

The case officer set five applications side by side and scanned the top forms, checking for accuracy and formalities.

"You're filing on behalf of Thomas Parker, M.D.," the case officer said, noting the name listed on the applications.

"That is correct," Ford said. "He's the inventor and technical owner of the processes."

"You're filing five different versions?"

Ford glanced to her attorneys. Their technical teams had advised her to submit all versions—the similarities more prominent than deviations—regardless of who actually possessed the tech. The five detailed submissions included the one stolen from Parker's Princeton University lab, which was now in France; ANCRI's; NeuroSteps'; Advanced BioCore's; and the inadequate startup attempted by Dr. Ji-woo Song's researchers. In the patent and trademark world, what mattered was who filed first and whether that filer possessed the technical documentation to substantiate their claim. By filing all versions, Parker had cornered the market, locked down derivations of the technology, and essentially short-circuited potential reverse engineering approaches.

"That is correct," one of Ford's lawyers said. "Our filings disclose that Dr. Parker created the multiple hardware and software interfaces, along with the logistics that were essential to the technology."

"This will require a third-level security review."

Ford had been briefed on that requirement. Federal law required the Commissioner of Patents to refer any application that might be detrimental to the interests of national security to an appropriate defense agency for review. The inspecting agency would subject the patent and its applicant to a secrecy order, officially confiscating the legitimacy of such a patent. The problem with the one-sided mandate was the U.S. did not have authoritarian oversight over foreign nationals, international corporations, or other governments.

Her attorney nodded. "This is a medical application, and submitted as such. However, the reason our clients are expediting this process is to get ahead of foreign state actors who are trying to patent-squat on his technological solutions. Time is of the essence. An extended third-party review permits our country's enemies—the Chinese, Russians, Turks, and North Koreans—to outmaneuver Dr. Parker. If they do that, the numerous fields in American medicine will be irrevocably harmed. It's in our nation's best interests and our citizen's well-being not to let that happen."

The case officer removed a declaration page from an application and scanned a list of names. "Applied Mind, Synaptic Touch, Neurological Singularity, Neuromapping, Common InSight, Mind Sight, Dream Chambers. That's a mouthful." He ran his finger down a longer list of terms and abbreviations related to the filing. "I'm sure we can support Dr. Parker in this process."

Debra Ford smiled. If Defense Department hurdles could be cleared under the guise of medical research, Parker would be the sole controller of the radical world-changing technology, the father of global civil wars, and a contributor to the deaths of millions. With the patents all in his name, Parker would acquire a bullseye the size of Rhode Island, having legal control over the technology. He'd become the sole possessor of tools that could destroy nations, religions, and organized crime. Neurological singularity threatened those in power. In order to deal with the immediate threat, nations would label him a criminal, an international terrorist.

Parker would have nowhere on earth to flee. If those in power couldn't secure his tech for their own benefit, they'd want him dead. A war was coming, and, unwittingly, Thomas Parker was central to it. He was the distraction, the misdirection, the dupe to the game at hand.

While the world focused on him, a new democracy would take over Asia, starting with the Sleeping Giant.

73

DISCOVERIES

NeuroSteps Lab, Glen Gardener, New Jersey

Released from her grueling calibration procedure, Ji-woo took a break and entered the director's library still wearing her biosuit. In the Neurophysiology Lab, she'd turned over the remaining indoctrination to her Korean-American brothers and sisters, who finished charging the minds of the Chinese participants.

As requested, a meal and an electrolyte-enriched drink awaited her. As she perused the library, she stumbled across Richards' notes, equipment drawings, and sketches. A bound book was labeled *MEDICAL JOURNAL*.

Sipping on her electrolytes, she perused the journal.

It was a memoir of sorts, a diary of what he'd experienced since awakening.

He'd been having episodes that he termed "time outs." Richards had documented the results of his two MRI scans, noting the degradation of his neurological implants. Unless he could repair the damage or reseed his brain, his self-diagnosis was terminal. He doubted he had longer than days or weeks.

The general erosion of the artificial replacement in his brain was not reparable. As his condition declined, he wrote, the best scenario would transform him into a dead man living—a ghost inhabiting a human form. An existence akin to those who suffered from a neurological syndrome called *Encephalitis lethargica*, which had been the subject of a book and a movie based on the work of Dr. Oliver Sacks. Forty years after they'd been ill during a 1920s sleeping sickness epidemic, several patients responded to L-Dopa drug experiments. Sacks's patients suffered from neurological sequelae, a brain condition that left its victims with an akinetic disorder, without the ability to move or speak. Richards held no hope for such a pharmaceutical miracle to cure his condition. Eventually, time would fade and he'd no longer be able to wake.

Richards wrote that being a neurological transplant pioneer equaled the significance of Seattle dentist Barney Clark, who in 1982 became the first human to receive a permanent artificial heart. Clark survived 112 days on the mechanical replacement organ. Richards hoped to surpass Clark's stretch of longevity, but wasn't sure of his odds. He considered another round of neurological transplants a low probability for long-term success about as successful as a full brain transplant.

Someone knocked at the door.

"Dr. Song," a security guard said, "your presence is required downstairs."

Ji-woo returned Richards' journal to where she found it, snatched up her turkey club croissant and drink, and followed the guard.

✦ ✦

From her Biogenetics Lab, Rikona Tanaka saw a throng of staff standing along a spread of exterior windows. Curious, she set aside her organoids and joined the crowd.

"I tell you, it's her," a front office clerk said. "That FBI agent who rescued those college kids. I saw her on the news. And when I was out on break, someone drove up with her in that van. The driver asked me for who was in charge. That's when I saw her. I tell you, terrible things are going on in our labs. That's why they don't let us in that big lab or downstairs where they keep people locked up in cages."

Tanaka jockeyed for position to see outside.

"Shut it," a woman snapped. "You're always gossiping. Everywhere you look you see conspiracies. Nothing weird happens here, except the wacky things going on in your head."

Below, in a canopied courtyard, a gurney had been rolled out to the van.

Attending physicians wearing scrubs hopped into the vehicle and carried out a woman.

A dark-haired, unconscious woman was placed on the gurney.

The clerk pointed. "I told ya."

"That could be anybody," the woman said.

Outside, doctors covered the woman with a sheet.

Tanaka had met the woman once—at the Advanced Neurological Cryogenics Research Institute, a place she'd hoped not to remember.

✛ ✛

Ji-woo followed the security guard outside and under the canopy that had served as the triage area for the Chinese participants a few nights earlier. A generic white van drove away, leaving a team of doctors in scrubs standing beside a gurney.

Another security guard blocked the doctors from taking the new arrival inside.

Ji-woo studied the body beneath a sheet. The general shape

contours of the fabric told her it was a woman. An ornate wood box sat on top of the body.

"She's exposed out here," one of the doctors said, pointing to a span of upper windows where staff had congregated. "We need to move her inside."

Ji-woo held up her hand and studied the box that sat on the abdomen of the woman beneath the sheet. Encircled twin dragons in gold leaf adorned the box.

Lifting the sheet up, Ji-woo looked at a woman. Caucasian. Brunette. Late thirties, early forties. Out cold.

Something chimed inside the box. Ji-woo dropped the sheet and opened it. Inside, beside a semiautomatic pistol, were car keys, credentials, and a ringing phone.

She activated the device and noticed the identification: FBI Special Agent Katherine Morgan. She had no idea who that was. Didn't care. She held the phone to her ear.

"You get the package, Seondeok?" a voice asked. She recognized the caller—another Founder. His codename was Zhulong, after the Torch Dragon. He also went by another title: Secretary of State for the United States of America.

Each Founder took on a representative name from Asian history to demonstrate Prosperity's commitment to the balance between the past and present. The relevance usually matched a historical element to one of the countries making up the eight rings. Her appointed name was Seondeok, the first female ruler of the Three Kingdoms of Korea, Queen Seondeok of Silla. Two Founders had died before witnessing the rise of Prosperity. Six remained to decide the fate of the world.

She glanced at the doctors and guards around her. "Leave our guest to me."

After everyone departed, she looked at the weapon in the box: Glock 23 Gen 4 Austria, 0.40 caliber. A pistol used by numerous law enforcement agencies, including the FBI.

Ji-woo understood the device she spoke on was a run-of-the-mill burner phone, paid for with cash. The over-the-counter purchase made it difficult for third parties to track the caller if no financial accounts were linked to the device. This conversation would remain anonymous between the two Founders.

Ji-woo frowned. "I don't have time for extracurricular activities. There's a schedule to adhere to, for both of us."

"You're telling me there's a problem?"

Ji-woo took a breath. From her point of view, there were a lot of problems.

"I want her involvement," the Secretary said.

"That action requires a vote from majority, not a single Founder."

"I have four votes, including yours." Four represented a majority, where a simple majority ruled. The Secretary knew how she'd vote before even placing the phone call.

"I don't like this. It's dangerous. And we don't need her."

"Agent Morgan's contribution will pay dividends," the Secretary continued. "I've provided instructions that must be followed without deviation."

Ji-woo glanced inside the box. Beneath the weapon were instructions. She read through them. "This woman hasn't been vetted for this reality. She could be a disaster waiting to happen. Any number of anomalies will arise if we insert her."

"Seondeok, you will lead a new nation," the Secretary said. "An opportunity presented itself. One that we must take advantage of. Your guidance will give Katherine Morgan a warrior's mentality. Her involvement adds another layer of legitimacy. An unsuspecting distraction."

Ji-woo clicked off the phone, removed its back cover and took out its battery in case the phone had been tracked. Dismantled, the device went inside the box. She closed its lid.

She felt bitter, but not much.

This last-minute addition was unwarranted.

On such a momentous eve, inheriting this added burden was the last thing she needed. Yet, as the Torch Dragon, the Secretary's voice often guided Ji-woo to a broader awareness of their shared cause. Not this time though. Now she considered the Secretary's instructions as requests, not demands or requirements. Alterations would be required to bring everything together without traceable flaws.

This was her moment to step forward as the leading Founder.

Gripping the handles of the gurney, Ji-woo shoved it toward the facility.

74

THE OVERRIDING MESSAGE

Kramerbooks & Afterwards Café, Dupont Circle, Washington, DC

Debra Ford absorbed the consequences of her actions.

She'd overstepped her role as a Founder.

A simple majority of the remaining six ruled, making any dissenting vote irrelevant.

The message on a phone's screen came across loud and clear.

NOW THAT YOU KNOW, YOU'RE EITHER WITH US OR AGAINST US. NO MORE GAMES. NO MORE INTERFERENCE.

Ford clicked off the disposable phone and checked her emotions.

That was her downfall in this particular instance.

Emotions.

Things had gotten sentimental.

Slipping the phone into the pocket of her barn coat, she continued to peruse books on overcrowded shelves inside the independent book shop. The shop catered to locals and celebrities alike, anyone from rock stars to politicians to presidents shopping with their daughters. The day's business brought in the usual crowds searching for their next read. She stopped at a section dedicated to Staff Picks and recommended reads, and noticed a nonfiction book with a glowing, cracked Liberty Bell on its cover.

Liberty.

A dangerous notion.

Existence without the oppressive restrictions imposed by governing authorities. Those who considered freedom and liberty essential to living were opposed by those who considered the two notions chaos and lawlessness.

Human existence had rarely managed to balance individual freedom with a functional governance framework that served everyone. Even the most utopian ideals of governing eventually grew soiled by greed, inertia, and the physical requirements of enforcing rules on people who wanted to be free.

As a Founder, she understood that delicate balance and saw what needed to be done. Liberty often required sacrifices.

But that didn't mean she had to endorse such a sacrifice.

Pushing Morgan to remain a step behind had been risky, and the agent's abduction was only one of the consequences. Ford had pieced together what the Secretary of State did not mention: Grayson had told the Vice President about Morgan's connecting the dots, and the Vice President had consulted with the Secretary of State. Two of the six Founders. The third vote came from the Founder who represented Macau. Ji-woo Song, who routinely followed the Secretary's decisions, had cast the deciding vote.

Returning to New Jersey and rescuing Morgan was not an option.

Intervening from long distance wasn't possible without an intermediary.

Contacting Thomas Parker for assistance was counterproductive.

Now that others had decided the FBI agent's fate, Debra Ford resisted the urge to comtemplate what fate that might be.

75

AN ARMY FOR ALLIES

5:30 PM, NeuroSteps Labs, Glen Gardener, New Jersey

Stewart Richards thought he was drinking from a fire hose. So much was happening so fast, and the predictive algorithms on the big screen astonished him. Post-event modeling projected a ninety-five percent adherence rate among the participants, a remarkable outcome. NeuroSteps engineers, scientists, and programmers had delivered a weapon like no other.

And Dr. Ji-woo Song had used the technological platform to hijack the consciousness of strangers. If the transformative reconditioning forecasts held, they'd successfully "turned" over a dozen people. One day the participants were Chinese consulate officials. The next they were soldiers conscripted into a different army, *buqu* soldiers complete with new belief systems and actionable ingrained directives.

Early in his career, Richards had built up his credentials by working for military-focused research think tanks. Back then, he'd never considered these tangents. What the US government wouldn't give to have this new age weaponry to backfill the CIA's notorious Project MK-Ultra mind control program.

The screens translated Chinese thoughts into English so that Richards could follow along with the cognitive transplants and neurological conditioning process.

Ji-woo Song had interlaced cognitive evolutions with historical elements derived from a broader Asia. A unique mission assignment was implanted in the mind of each *buqu* soldier, known only to them and none of the other participants. The last concept seeded into the *buqu* was the notion that their Korean-American mentors were the reincarnation of ancient China's Four Guardians: the Azure Dragon of the East, the Vermilion Bird of the South, the White Tiger of the West, and the Black Tortoise Warrior of the North. The compass-aligned warriors protected a greater Asia.

The *buqu*'s duty was to serve the Guardians by purging Asia of greed, corruption, and communist rule. If the *buqu* fulfilled their mission assignments, they'd be promoted to kings and queens in a new world order. Then, and only then, the Yellow Dragon would return to unify people and complete the transformation of a new nation.

The brilliant depth of their indoctrination played on China's ancestry, heritage, and perceptions of nobility.

Choosing a woman at random, Richards elevated the first *buqu*'s pod while the others remained under sedation.

Medical technicians unhooked her from the intense gadgetry and assisted her out the pod. Lucid, the woman scanned the room. The guardians, minus Ji-woo Song, surrounded the woman.

"*Ni zhīdào women shì shéi ma?*" asked one of the Korean-Americans asked in Mandarin. *Do you know who we are?*

The woman studied them, then bowed. "You are the Guardians," she said in English.

"And who are you?" another guardian asked.

"*Cáo de nǚ'ér,*" the woman said. "A daughter of Cao. A *buqu*. My lineage goes back to the noble warriors of the Three Kingdoms. I serve the Guardians. I serve our eight Founders. I serve Prosperity. I am a *buqu* warrior."

Richards glanced beside him and was startled to see Ji-woo Song holding up a phone to record the initiate's outcome.

He looked at her more closely. "You're a Founder in this new world order?"

She nodded. "One of eight."

He said the obvious: "China will have objections about being overthrown."

"I harbour no such illusions. But soon, Prosperity will have millions of *buqu* and modern China will fall from within the ranks of the Communist Party itself."

He gave her a suspicious nod. "And what does America get out of this oncoming war?"

"Peace on Earth," she said, her voice cold.

"I was unable to see your role as a Founder during their mental conditioning. What do you get out of this?"

Ji-woo kept filming and didn't flinch. "I am the Yellow Dragon. My evolution transforms eight nations into One Democratic Asia. A place where Prosperity rules. A place where people are united without the threat of tyranny, imprisonment, coercion, or fear. The scales of the global world stage will be rebalanced for the benefit of all."

Incredible, Richards thought. "Then my work here is done."

Still recording the questioning of the *buqu* soldier, Ji-woo nodded toward the entrance to the Lab.

Richards turned and saw a sheet-covered body. On top of the body was a box.

Strolling over, he looked inside the box. A semiautomatic pistol. A badge. Car keys.

He pulled back the sheet to reveal a face.

No introduction was necessary: FBI Special Agent Katherine Morgan, unconscious.

He'd hoped their paths would cross again.

76

INFLUENCING OUTCOMES

6:10 PM, Advanced BioCore, Princeton, New Jersey

Parker resisted the temptation to contemplate Kate's eureka moment hypothesis until baseline testing and commissioning steps closed out, the last participant was released, and the results had been uploaded to the main networks for further analysis. Returning to his residence, he wondered where Kate had gone.

One of the security staff intercepted him to pass on a message. *THOMAS, GOT CALLED AWAY TO PROVIDE CRIME SCENE SUPPORT ON THE NORVANA. LEADS CAME IN THAT NEEDED MY FORENSICS SUPPORT. I'LL BE AWAY FOR A COUPLE OF DAYS. LOOKING FORWARD TO SPENDING TIME TOGETHER. GOOD LUCK WITH THE TRIALS. KATE*

The message was written on the same paper as Kate's earlier notes. As a federal agent, Kate had returned to her element, back to where she belonged in contrast to the tagalong medical research that he'd put her in.

He wondered what Kate had done with her sketches and diagrams about who was who in this undertaking. Debra Ford had been clear: he was competing against Stewart Richards to secure a technology that would fundamentally change the world.

He thought of the twin dragons, yin yang reflections, and the power brokers they represented. The Vice President of the United States promoted Peace on Earth. Debra Ford, Prosperity. Because of his position, the Vice President would bind him to the Department of Defense and federal agencies like DARPA. Debra Ford's background was aligned to State Department endeavors and probably the CIA. Mears wanted neurological singularity to build a better army. Ford, a world of super spies. Different ends of a power spectrum that supported a common cause: global domination.

Starved, he ordered delivery from The Brick House Tavern and Tap wondered if Kate's FBI could be trusted. Not likely. No entity or agency could be trusted with this kind of power.

Something else troubled him.

Concerned that he'd overlooked critical information, he accessed the computer in his suite and logged into Advanced BioCore's medical library where he'd originally found Stewart Richards' white paper on Common Collective. Bringing up a menu, he scanned the military research-aligned topics again.

INFLUENCING CEREBRAL OUTCOMES	HOW MATTER BECOMES MIND
SYNAPTIC SHUNTS TO DEFUSE PTSD	PREDICTIVE NEURALNET MODELING
RETRAINING NEURAL NETWORKS	CONVERSATIONAL ECHOES
PREDICTING COGNITIVE OUTCOMES	STABLIZING SEGREAGATION
WEAPONIZING THE MIND	NEURAL GENESIS THERAPIES
FORMING COGNITIVE DOMINANCE	PATCHING COGNITIVE GAPS
CREATING ALLIGNED ASSETS	SYNAPTIC TRANSPLANTS

He clicked on INFLUENCING CEREBRAL OUTCOMES. A series of video files and articles appeared. He selected a scholarly article bearing the same title, published by the National Defense Industrial

Association (NDIA) Business & Technology Magazine. NDIA's emphasis was to support decision-makers in the defense marketplace, whether that was industrial applications or government stakeholders.

That article focused on the rapid advancements in neuroscience and corresponding technologies, and how such tools would benefit military endeavors. The National Research Council of the National Academies of Science had co-sponsored the article.

In medicine, pharmaceutical companies, device manufacturers, and healthcare systems ruled the world. Their business models focused on keeping corporate cash registers ringing and on controlling supply chains. By itself, big pharma would seek to destroy Common InSight or at least discredit it by declaring it so dangerous that no private sector company should use the tech.

That left governments to be the competing players, for defense initiatives and nation building efforts. He doubted DARPA would use the tech to treat the mental health aspects of soldiers suffering from PTSD and depression when the agency could use it for grander ambitions. Behind the scenes, DARPA developed weaponry over medicine. That matched the initiatives of weaponizing the mind and building better soldiers and spies.

Common InSight was the weapon that delivered Peace on Earth.

He reflected again on Kate's hypothesis.

Facing government takeover and the power of cash registers, Parker reckoned the only course worth pursuing was to be the doctor who focused on those who needed the help: the participants.

77

BAGGAGE FROM OTHERS

NeuroSteps Labs, Glen Gardener, New Jersey

Stewart Richards shuddered, startling himself as if waking from a bad dream. His skin tingled and he swayed, needing to extend a hand for balance. He grabbed onto a gurney. His brain was degrading more quickly, switching off without notice and leaving him standing like some sort of paralyzed zombie.

In front of him, the FBI agent still lay unconscious, and he understood that her sedation would be wearing off soon.

Freed from his trance, he turned around to take in how much time had elapsed.

Ji-woo and her team had performed a post-event assessment on the last participant. He'd timed out for nearly ninety minutes.

Ji-woo oversaw the transition of the participants as they came out of the pods. The progression had them separated from their peers.

Remarkably, their cognitive enhancements produced no anomalies, and each was receptive to their new role, even if that meant leaving their past behind.

Fourteen recruits had evolved to become *buqu* warriors.

The depth of their compliance stunned her. Post-event evaluations indicated that not a single participant would turn rogue or deviate off their designated script. How long this adherence would last was unknown. Rebellion was a trait embedded in human DNA, difficult to eradicate.

She smiled knowing the immense power and influence that she now wielded. A radical, unproven technology had led her to a threshold, a summit impossible to reach by other means. Neurological singularity, cognitive indoctrination, and mass-delivered social conditioning would change global engagement.

These new warriors that would be the first of many. Bloodshed was inevitable, sacrifices required, indoctrination essential. When the dust of civil war settled, aspects of the old would be forged anew.

She turned to Richards who walked tentatively beside her, looking like he'd been struck by a boxer's right cross.

"It appears that your medical procedure has terminal side effects," she said.

He rubbed his face. "Unfortunately."

"Dr. Richards, your work has exceeded my expectations. I must commend you."

"It's the culmination of my life's work." He looked around, noticing that they were the last two standing in the lab. "What do you want to do with her?"

Ji-woo handed him the conditioning profile created by the Secretary of State. "If you follow that script, valued assets get killed. I have no interest in losing my *buqu*. Those directives represent a no-win proposition for me. I suggest you follow the premise of that narrative but deviate widely at your own discretion."

Richards read through the procedures. A broad grin formed on his face. "I'm going to enjoy this immensely."

78
KEYS

Rikona Tanaka had spent ninety minutes deciding whether to break her communication silence and risk getting caught. Her directions were to avoid reaching out unless a problem arose. She wasn't sure this scenario fit those parameters.

Following the contact protocol, she accessed a designated phone located on the executive office floor, the only hardwired device on the premises that bypassed security systems. She typed in a memorized number.

After several digital rings, Debra Ford answered. "You have an update?"

Tanaka cleared her throat. "I assume you'd want to know. That FBI agent who was at ANCRI was brought here. I suspect her arrival wasn't planned."

There was a pause. "What's being done with her?"

"I followed Dr. Song to the Neurophysiology Lab."

"Are Doctors Richards and Song finished with their participants?"

"I believe so."

"Can you get into the lab?"

"Once Dr. Richards was healthy enough to carry out his duties, NeuroSteps restricted my access. I'm not allowed in the lab anymore. So I've had to piece things together. What I know is that the Chinese participants cleared treatment protocols and post-event assessments."

"Get inside. Help Morgan."

Tanaka swallowed over a knot in her throat. "I know how to secure a passkey."

"Tonight. Whatever it takes."

Tanaka owed Ford this request. The woman had negotiated her daughter's release from those who'd kidnapped her. Once freed, Ford had provided money to move her daughter to someplace safer until everything blew over. All in exchange for helping Richards rise from the dead, and for staying behind at NeuroSteps as a mole.

The time had come for Tanaka to leave, so she asked. "After I do this, I will have fulfilled my obligations. I want out. And a first-class ticket home to be with my daughter. That's what I want."

"Anything else?"

"No."

"If Richards or Ji-woo Song harms her, our deal is off. Consider that FBI agent your lifeline home. I suggest you get her out safely."

The phone went dead.

79

A DAB OF DARKNESS
TO TOUCH THE SOUL

Alone in the Neurophysiology Lab, Richards dragged the FBI agent off the gurney and loaded her into a pod. He inserted a plastic bit into her mouth to restrain screaming, and strapped in her wrists, ankles, and midsection. He lowered the headgear.

Bare scalp had been the gold standard for precise cranial alignment. He debated calling someone in to shave her hair, but wasn't concerned enough about procedural misalignment leading to inaccuracy or scrambling her brain. He skipped the ECG leads. Monitoring biometrics had no impact on rewiring her mind. He gave her no additional sedation. The FBI agent needed to experience everything, without limits.

Lowering the pod into position, he activated the neuromapping sequence and uploaded targeting modules and profiles. None of this treatment differed from the other modeling, except for the requested outcome.

The big screen exploded to life, displaying her neurological readings. A task list sequenced essential baseline templates needed for the application. While he waited for the supercomputer networks to merge with her mind, he typed in the required cues.

ARRIVE EARLY BEFORE NOON	GEORGETOWN
TANG'S MEMORIAL SERVICE	LOOK UP
KILL THOSE WHO OPPOSE YOU	PROTECT THE FOUNDERS
OBTAIN BOTTLED MESSAGE	INSIDE TUT'S BOOKCASE

After the protocols cued up, he walked to her pod.

Sedation had worn off. She started to squirm.

"Fighting it," he said, looking down at her, "will make things worse. Probably cause irrecoverable brain damage. You might end up a vegetable, wouldn't even know it—an experience I know something about. I can pass that state of existence onto you. After all of this, I probably owe that to you, Special Agent Morgan."

She froze. She tried to place his voice, figure out where she was.

Reaching inside the pod, he pressed his fingers against the right side of her chest. The panic-instilled palpitations comforted him. Her body temperature felt warm as her skin flushed with blood. She was terrified, and rightly so.

It was time to touch her soul with a dab of fresh darkness.

"Irony is the hygiene of the mind," he said, stealing a quote from Elizabeth Bibesco. "Welcome to my world, agent."

Imprisoned, Kate screamed at the tentacles penetrating her mind as the fetters restraining her thoughts evaporated like smoke drifting away from an extinguished candle. A hot darkness surrounded her, and she tried to move her limbs. Nothing cooperated.

She screamed. No sounds except those of her grunting.

Disjointed thoughts ebbed and flowed, trying to break free of a muddled mind.

It wasn't until she heard a muffled voice that she understood where she was and what was happening. She was inside a stimulation pod, a machine—connected to it, wired to it.

Kate stiffened, unsure what to do.

The voice she heard was that of Stewart Richards. "Fighting it, will make things worse. Probably cause irrecoverable brain damage. You might end up a vegetable. Wouldn't even know it. An experience I know something about. I can pass that state of existence onto you. After all of this, I probably owe that to you, Special Agent Morgan."

Kate's heart raged and almost drowned out the sound of her breathing. Her chest felt the pressure of a human touch.

"Irony is the hygiene of the mind. Welcome to my world, agent."

A portal opened in her realm of darkness. Her body lightened as if gravity had lost some of its power to bind her to earth. Restraints holding her opposed this rise, leaving her near weightless. Inside her mind, invisible forces swelled and accentuated a heightened state of awareness. She felt vibrations as snapshots and memories dotted her vision, cycling through her mind like flickering paper photographs splashed by light as everything swirled inside a dust devil. Echoing voices joined the turbulence and resonated from every corner of her mind.

Kate trembled. Breathing went ragged. In the constrained space, she strained to comprehend what was being done to her.

For a short moment, she yearned for nothing but death.

Her mind was infused with memories and thoughts that weren't hers. Fleeting glimpses pinged her mind as if she was watching the faces of playing cards during the shuffling of a deck. Images. Fast. Furious. Intense. The pictures racing through her mind in contexts she couldn't describe, bound to realities that she couldn't comprehend.

She was being indoctrinated, changed.

As long as she could, Kate clung onto something positive—a single thought, a last-ditch hope. A way to drive out the exposure to implants. Thomas Parker appeared behind the helm of a catamaran. Jib and mainsails stretched in the wind. Spray washed across the hull. An orange orb drifted above a distant sea-filled skyline. He was chasing the sunset.

To her, this moment embodied tranquility. Peace.

A jolt pulsed through her like a blinding flash of lightning, short-circuiting every thought she'd latched onto.

Thomas, I'm sorry—for everything, she said, becoming disoriented and desperate.

Kate screamed as death pierced her soul. All the energy inside her seemed to stop. Her will to resist ceased. Coldness seized her, as if she was encapsulated into a block of ice. She had an insignificant pocket of air. Enough space for a couple of breaths. Enough time to understand that she was dying, and no one in the world could save her.

Rikona Tanaka used a flat-bladed screwdriver to slip the door latch to the NeuroSteps facility safety manager's office. The door swung open. She shut it behind her.

On the wall was a gray metal cabinet.

As part of their onboarding process, every contractor and employee had to take computerized human resources and safety training sessions, arranged by the facility safety manager. Tanaka spotted the cabinet during her training. It contained generic cardkeys, access cards, and temporary identification badges.

Using the screwdriver, she snapped open the cabinet's door.

Cardkeys were arranged systematically, lowest security clearance to the highest.

Keeping the screwdriver, she snatched up the entire box of high security clearances and sprinted for the Neurophysiology Lab.

Navigating stairwells and corridors, she badged into secured spaces that she'd seen only during her first month at NeuroSteps. Encountering no opposition, she arrived at the Neurophysiology Lab, a sterile area that had a pressurization antechamber and lots of security cameras. Depending what security was doing, she estimated she had little time—a couple of minutes before someone discovered her.

At the lab, she badged into the antechamber. Doors shut behind her. She could hear and feel the pressure change. Interior doors parted open.

The large space was empty.

The forward screen bristled with neurological data.

A modeled mind was logged as Participant 31.

Automated algorithms executed applications, their results displayed in scripted text.

Tanaka's heart sank.

She'd arrived too late.

Richards entered the Virtual Reality Immersion Suite and activated the holographic console once he'd donned the silver-tipped VR gloves. He muted the virtual assistant and launched an integration routine that linked the VRI interface with the one in the Neurophysiology Lab.

The world above him exploded with neural structures matched to the last remaining participant, tagged as 31—the same number Katherine Morgan had had at his last lab. Stepping through the neon brilliance to the cosmos of her virtual mind, Richards lowered the skullcap over his head and strapped in.

Energy surged through his mind like a sudden jolt of caffeine. The algorithm designed for this AI-guided mindmeld bond followed applications used in the main lab, with one major difference. In the sheltered environment of the VRI theater, cognitive modification went one way—he was patched into Morgan's thoughts and memories, but she could not read his.

After the synchronization completed, Richards brought up a holographic control panel and accessed a new set of programs.

He could sense the terror she was feeling. Mortified, Morgan futilely resisted as memory implants took root and replicated into cognitive streams in both long-term and short-term memory. Overwhelmed by the experience, she thought of death and wanted to die. Changing tactics, she tried to block out the assault on her mind by focusing on something positive.

Richards gasped when he saw Thomas Parker standing at the helm of a boat. Wind pressed against the pluming fabric of white sails. Sprays of water crested the boat's hull as it ventured in the direction of a rippling orange ball low on the horizon.

Morgan was trying to use meditation to calm her inner storm.

Someone she loved. A sunset. A moment in time.

On the holographic control panel, Richards activated a new routine that he hadn't been able to test.

Glancing up, he saw her holographic mind blazed with tiny dots ebbing and flowing, migrations of neuro-chemical energy. Clusters of neurons fed the mix of seeds at the core memories to her mediation.

He paused the cognitive implant routines performed by supercomputers located elsewhere in the complex. Above him, most energy sparkles dotting her brain darkened and revealed only those neurons seeding her inner peace, her current thoughts and meditation.

Richards launched a new, untested program sequence.

Above, everything flashed like an explosion, white, intense.

A few seconds passed as the system recalibrated.

The moment of truth.

A small percentage of illumination powered by her inner peace disappeared.

Subtle changes in a grander tapestry of memory, lost forever.

Sailboat, water, sunset, Thomas Parker.

No longer visible.

Richards grinned. He'd touched her soul with a dab of darkness.

80
STEPS OF THE RIGHTEOUS

Ji-woo turned over her *buqu* to a dispatch team and returned to her room. After packing some last essentials, she examined her reflection in a vanity mirror. Bald. Geometric tessellations dotted her scalp. So much had changed in so few days.

Lathering up a body cleanser, she scrubbed her head to dissolve away the patterns, eradicating the outer mapping. The cleansing invigorated her like a rite of passage. After toweling off, she slid on a wig cap, which clung to her skin like pantyhose. Using a toothbrush, she applied glue and selected one of the wigs from that had been provided.

After small tweaks, she appraised her new look. Almost refreshing, except for what the wig's real human hair symbolized: oppression, dirty secrets of the global hair trade, dignity stolen from those who deserved freedom.

She steeled her eyes in the mirror's reflection. "I will become the Yellow Dragon and free those who are oppressed. I alone will be the last Founder and slay the vipers who stand in my path."

She grabbed a backup wig, stashed it into her bags and headed out with luggage in hand. Her plan was to drive to a safe house in Washington, DC, stay the night, and attend the noon memorial for the Founder who'd led her to Prosperity.

NeuroSteps' basement was utilitarian in layout and in function. Concrete block walls were painted white. Gray epoxied concrete floors stretched in all directions. Ductwork, plumbing, electrical conduits, and cable trays ran beneath open ceiling structures. Breakout rooms had been constructed to separate the Chinese participants during their post-operative evaluations.

Anything discussed was done in their native tongue, no English, no Korean.

Medical technicians recorded behaviors and mannerisms. Doctors performed physicals. Profiling psychologists conducted screening questions. Everything the participants did or said was logged, and analyzed for behavior patterns. Supercomputers located in a massive data center back-checked the human-based analysis. Barring objections, of which there were none, implantable tracking microchips were injected below the skin and between their shoulder blades. Once cleared, the mission liaisons issued field assignments along with the requisite equipment, weapons, contact protocols, safe houses, and money.

None of the participants had questioned their evolution, their new existence or new lives.

As *buqu* soldiers, they embraced serving Prosperity.

81

EXTRACTION

In the Neurophysiology Lab, Tanaka panicked when she saw the billboard-sized screen. On display were passing snapshots and imagery that had no context, as if algorithms and programs were uploading cognitive training. She saw the sails of a boat and a sunset.

An image of Thomas Parker momentarily appeared.

Then the entire tapestry of memories flashed white before fading away.

Tanaka walked past unoccupied workstations and saw the execution of automated programs, which she had no idea how to access or turn off.

From floor level, the rows of pods all looked the same. Impossible to know which, if any, were occupied. Scanning pod interiors, Tanaka made her way to the front of the lab.

Finally, she located a pod showing promise. Tiny lights illuminated the outline of a woman submerged in a tight space of gadgetry, wires, and tubing, as if the woman were buried alive inside the co-

coon-like nest. The woman's head was covered with what looked to be headgear of some kind, blocking any way to discern and identity.

Tanaka studied the box-like contraption for a master power switch, off button, any set of disconnecting terminals. She saw nothing like that.

How do I get her out?

Maybe start unhooking cables?

What if I kill her by disconnecting something I shouldn't?

Looking closer at the contraption, it was difficult to tell where the pipes and wires ended inside the tight space, and where a human body did not reside. She spotted the restraints securing the person's midsection, wrists and ankles. Dragging their head clear of the headgear looked impracticable.

Tanaka refused to take a risk among impossible choices.

Scanning the room, she spotted a workstation that probably functioned as a monitoring station, which gave her better odds than the pod. She ran to a terminal displaying an application that seemed to be running cognitive conditioning algorithms. A touchscreen provided a detailed graphical representation of a pod, tagged as Participant 31. A human form filled the pod. Biometrics reported no data readings, since no ECG leads were connected to the body.

Tanaka tapped the graphic. A new screen appeared.

A red icon was titled EMERGENCY EXTRACTION.

She tapped it.

A dialogue box appeared with three choices.

THE EMERGENCY EXTRACTION PROCESS CANNOT BE OVERRIDEN OR STOPPED. DO YOU WANT TO PROCEED? YES. NO. GO BACK.

Tanaka stabbed the selection with her finger. "Yes!"

A notification panel materialized.

INITIATING EMERGENCY EXTRACTION. ALL APPLICATIONS ARE BEING ASSESSED FOR OPTIMAL CLOSE OUT PROCESSES.

A digital clock counted down from FIVE. When it hit ONE,

room lighting flashed on, brightening the lab. The big board displayed the system status:

ALL PROCESSES ABORTED. COMMENCING DATA BACKUP.

Motors whirled. One pod in a sea of others rose vertically. She heard gases purging as cooling systems rebalanced frigid gases into manifolds.

Tanaka clutched her chest and prayed she hadn't just killed the occupant of the pod.

Kate trembled as blackness consumed her. Coldness wrapped her like a burial shroud as spike-like tentacles stabbed her mind, numbing its boundaries. Slowly, a cold, fog-laden veil lifted. Consciousness materialized, like being startled from a sound sleep or waking up after passing out. It felt like being hung over. She couldn't recall drinking, or even where she was.

The sound of her breath resonated inside a chamber. Opening heavy eyelids, she saw only darkness. She tried to move her head. It was bound in a vice of some sort.

A close, hissing noise sounded like a steam locomotive venting excess pressure.

As her awareness grew, she suppressed an increasing sense of melancholy. In the cold darkness, emptiness consumed her. She struggled to find words to describe what had vanished from her life. Muscles ached as if they'd gone to sleep. She tried to move her limbs. Nothing cooperated.

Motors whirled to life again. Vibrations shook her body. A movement felt like the upswing of a childhood teeter totter. As her body shifted, her feet felt pressure.

Her mouth was desert-parched. When she tried to speak, she realized something had been wedged between her teeth. As blood flow returned, Kate flexed her muscles and groaned.

This was the worst hangover ever.

In the Virtual Reality Theater, Richards was stunned by the lost connection. Around him, the cosmos of a human mind vanished. The spherical realm of neuromapping and brain scans disappeared. The floating holographic access panel flashed a notice:

EMERGENCY EXTRACTION. ALL PROCESSES ABORTED. COMMENCING DATA BACKUP.

Katherine Morgan's mind had been hinged open to him, allowing him to wander her thoughts and memories, tap into her deepest secrets.

And he'd just lost his nexus right when things were getting interesting.

Disappointed, he activated the room lighting and disconnected himself from the headgear. Tossing his silver-tipped gloves to the floor, he stormed out of the theater.

Tanaka scrambled over to the pod and ripped away the Velcro restraints just as the headgear lifted. Disoriented, the woman stared. Eyes blinked against harsh room lighting.

"Can you walk?" Tanaka asked, reaching into the woman's mouth to extract a plastic bit.

The FBI agent licked her lips and bobbed her head. "What?"

Tanaka grabbed the woman's face and made eye contact. "We need to get out of here. Can you walk?"

The woman scanned the room. "Where am I?"

"There's no time to explain."

"Who are you?"

"That doesn't matter. What matters is staying alive."

Tanaka seized the woman's wrist and jerked, pulling her free of the machine.

Richards badged into the antechamber and then Neurophysiology Lab. Two women came at him fast. The trailing one staggered behind the first as if she were awaking from a trance. He glanced sideways and spotted the wooden box with personal effects that had accompanied Morgan when she arrived. He popped the box's lid and snatched the semiautomatic pistol.

"Come on!" Rikona Tanaka barked.

Turning, Richards blocked the anteroom, the only entrance-exit to the lab.

Tanaka stopped. The stupefied FBI agent collided into her, nearly sending both tumbling to the floor. Tanaka latched onto her companion's wrist, pulling Morgan upright.

Richards targeted them with the weapon. "I'm not done with her."

"I saved your life. You owe me."

He shrugged. "No. You merely added days to my life, but you didn't save me."

Tanaka took a breath. "Dr. Richards, let us pass. Please."

"Return her to the pod."

Morgan finally spoke, her head turning to see where she'd come from. "What?"

Tanaka shook her head. "No. Let us go."

"Don't think I'll oblige."

Tanaka inched closer, with Morgan in tow by the wrist. "You're alive and conscious because I made it so. I could've left you for dead. I owed you nothing. Now I'd say, you owe me everything. Step aside. We're leaving—"

Richards pulled the trigger. A single retort resonated as a bullet struck Tanaka mid-torso, sending both women tumbling violently to the floor, one on top the other.

Tanaka never flinched, her eyes open in death.

Morgan shoved Tanaka's body aside and gasped. "You killed her."

"I'll do the same to you if you don't do as you're told."

Morgan's face showed revelation dawning. "These machines… you were inside my mind."

"There remain memories that you must to reveal to me. Private memories."

Morgan fixated on the bloody dime-sized hole that punctured Tanaka's clothing.

"If you don't cooperate, you'll join her."

Gripping the woman's clothing for leverage, an expressionless Morgan staggered to her knees as if was ready to comply.

The quick sweep of a foot coming his way was a blur.

Instinctively he pulled the trigger. Another shot rang out.

Morgan's arching foot caught his leg. He fell. Striking the floor, the gun slipped from his fingers. Richards rolled sideways, dodging her.

She leapt into the air.

He lunged for the weapon.

A palm smashed his face hard, banging his head violently to the floor. Another strike smashed his nose, causing his eyes to water.

Using her elbows, Morgan stretched across the floor to collect the weapon. After glancing his way, she kicked him in the face.

Moaning, he struggled to free himself from their entanglement.

A relentless barrage hit him. Whirling, she struck him mid-sternum with the weapon's grip. Air exploded from his lungs, making him gasp. The intense pain in his chest overrode the pain he felt in his face.

Straddling him, she pinned him down. Her eyes turned wild. "I remember you. You're supposed to be dead."

He punched at her midsection and arms. Her fingers found his throat. Lightheadedness overtook him and he gasped again.

Her gun hand ripped away his knitted cap, and Morgan studied the bandages taped over the scars from his cranial operations. Leaning upright, she released her grip on his throat.

She looked at the lifeless Tanaka, grunted, and screamed like a warrior. Gripping the gun in both hands, she struck down with the butt of the weapon between his eyes, and he fell limp.

Still screaming in anger, Kate rolled off of Richards and staggered to her feet. Her body yearned for energy. Oxygen was at the top of the list, so she drew heavy breaths of air into her lungs. Adrenaline surged inside like a hydrant pressuring a fire hose.

Squinting under the bright lights, she surveyed her surroundings. The lab looked vaguely familiar, but she couldn't recall anything about it. She searched for memories that weren't there. Her gaze homed in on the wooden box that Richards had found the weapon in. With its top cast back, she could see her badge and car keys.

She knelt beside the Japanese woman. Disjointed memories flashed in her mind, but none involved the woman. She sensed they'd met, but couldn't recall how. The back of Kate's head throbbed as she tried to remember.

Lifeless eyes stared back at her, telling her that the gunshot wound was fatal.

Kate closed the woman's eyes. "Thank you."

Movement caught her attention. Two security guards stormed through opening doors and started yelling at her. When they saw the woman with a hole in her chest and an unconscious old man, guns were drawn.

Instinctively, Kate somersaulted and fired consecutive shots, striking each man multiple times. The guards staggered until they collapsed to the floor. Moving on reflex, she kicked weapons from their hands and tried to decide what to do next.

She'd witnessed a murder. And shot two guards who were just doing their job.

A single thought sprang to her mind: *Run.*

She snatched up the wooden box, yanked a cardkey badge off one of the guards and fled without looking back.

Rushing down hallways, she burst into the first stairwell available. She took the stairs down, encountering no one. Breaking outside, Kate caught her breath and collected her thoughts, her sluggish mind restrained by forces she didn't understand.

It was night. Pathway lights lit up sidewalks. Crickets chirped.

Kate kept moving and followed signs to an employee parking lot. Collecting her car keys from the box, she clicked her key fob until her headlights. She climbed inside and started the car.

Run.

Don't stop whatever you do.

She slapped the gearshift into drive and whipped out onto a circular lane until she found the property's exit. Using the guard's stolen security badge, she swiped it at the outbound detector and the employee exit gate drifted open.

Driving wooded, dimly lit rural roads at night, without a map, GPS, or cell phone, it took forever to find a two-lane road marked Route 31. A choice: left or right. *Left.* She stuck to the speed limit. A couple of miles down the road, she drove past a car dealership marked "Clinton." Lots of states had towns by that name. A road sign indicated she was southbound.

Something caught her eye. Slamming on the brakes, she jerked the wheel and stopped on the road's gravel shoulder, in front of a generic office-industrial building that looked like it was closed for the day. A property sign read: NEW JERSEY WATER SUPPLY AUTHORITY. CLINTON DISTRICT OFFICE.

New Jersey?

The bureau had a field office in Newark.

Turn yourself in. Explain everything. Come clean and work out a deal.

Something inside nudged her to keep going.

Run. Don't stop. Run.

Kate hit the accelerator as tires kicked up dirt, and she returned to the road.

The pungent odor of smelling salts revived Richards. Everything hurt: head, face, chest. It took a while to clear his vision. Lifting his head, he could see others tending to security guards and Tanaka. He could tell by the conversations that resuscitation measures weren't successful. Morgan was nowhere to be seen.

A med tech knelt beside him. "Dr. Richards, let's check you out."

He shut his eyes. Tired and beaten down, he wasn't in a mood to argue.

"Dr. Song?" he asked, over a burning throat.

The med tech shook his head. "She left the facility on business. Is there someone else we can call? Family? Friends?"

He shook his head. Outside of the many staff engagements he'd encountered since arriving at NeuroSteps, it dawned on him that he knew no one particularly well. Not that it mattered, but oddly he'd known Rikona Tanaka the best. And he'd shot her.

A penlight swept across his eyes, checking his pupils for responses and dilation.

Eyes are the windows to the soul, Richards thought. He wanted to tell the tech to keep searching until he found something.

"Sir, you took quite a blow to the head. There's blood in your anterior chamber, signs of trauma, a mild grade concussion. You're going to sport quite the bruise. I'll get you some pain meds in a minute. How much do you remember?"

A security guard crouched. "Did you see who killed them?"

"No," Richards said, knowing a simple check of security footage would deliver those answers. He'd shot Tanaka. Morgan must've gunned down the guards.

The med tech felt his chest, causing him to wince.

"Easy there. I might have a broken rib." He took a shallow breath, trying not to expand his lungs too much. "There's a nurse who supported me when I arrived. I'd like to return to my room and have her complete my follow-up."

"Dr. Richards," the med tech said, "you need a hospital."

"No hospitals. That's not negotiable. Just get my nurse."

Ten minutes later in his residence, essentially under house arrest while security worked through the deaths, Richards sat on the edge of the bed. An outsider to NeuroSteps, he had no idea how he'd be treated, or if anyone in management would have the courage to turn him over to the authorities. He doubted it, but the mess he'd created might have consequences for an international corporation that hid illegal human testing with paperwork.

He held a bag of ice against his forehead while his nurse completed her examination. She listened with a stethoscope to his breathing. A wall mirror he'd passed by had showed the results of his head-on mauling. Morgan had demonstrated mercy by not killing him, a weakness he'd hope to exploit in the future. His damage was a bruised sternum, likely a fractured rib. The club mark between his eyes would last a week maybe longer. His bloodshot eye revealed no particular damage.

"This will sting," the nurse said, pressing an autoinjector syringe filled with 10 milligrams of diazepam, the generic to Valium, to his shoulder. "Let me know if you experience cramps, nausea, or

hallucinations. I'll check on you during the night. Let me know if you need anything."

He shrugged as the chemical migrated from muscle to bloodstream.

The nurse set aside his ice pack and guided him down onto a pillow.

His eyes started feeling heavy, his mind sluggish.

Before sleep overtook him, he calculated that his initial dose of diazepam would last six hours, maybe longer. What mattered now was what he did after he awoke, before his nurse could administer a second round of sedation.

As he drifted off, his last thoughts were of paying Thomas Parker a visit and finishing what he'd started with Katherine Morgan.

I-95 Highway Heading South

Kate couldn't shake the sense of being on autopilot, going through the motions, and drove like a horse headed to the barn. Her head throbbed in ways that she couldn't explain and she thought of nothing but climbing into her own bed. An invisible force, a sense of unwavering duty pushed her to stay on track and retain a singular focus: home.

Highway signs flashed past her car windows and she wanted nothing more than to leave the world of New Jersey behind.

Signs for Philadelphia, Wilmington, Baltimore came and went.

A full tank of gas had delivered her all the way to Falls Church, Virginia.

The melancholy that she'd felt earlier wormed itself deep inside her, as if detached remorse was the only emotion available to her.

Pulling into the driveway of her home, Kate parked and grabbed the wooden box with her gun and badge still inside it and trudged

up to her front porch. She unlocked her door, entered, then locked it behind her.

As the thoughts, *run, don't stop, run,* followed her inside, Kate didn't bother to turn on house lights. Tossing what she carried onto a living room couch, she wandered into her bedroom, turned on a ceiling fan to circulate air, and slid beneath her covers without changing out her clothes.

You're home now. Let go.

All Kate wanted was to forget a horrible day and sleep.

SATURDAY, DECEMBER 5th

If you live in a graveyard, you can't weep for everyone.
Aleksandr Solzenitsyn

82

PEP TALK

Parker joined the participants in the company's cafeteria. A break-fast buffet had been catered before the procedures got started. At his request, the participants wore casual clothing, loose fitting shirts. Nothing institutional. As they mingled, he noticed that conversations were solemn and appetites were small, as if this were more of a reluctant last meal than the start of a new day.

Understandable considering what lay ahead.

A great deal could go wrong.

And they might never recover.

At the closest table, he joined a mix of young men and women, college-age pioneers in their own right. They were the first humans to exchange cognitive thoughts and memories—singularity transfers. Their faces showed anxiety, a readiness to get their lives back.

A boy leaned forward on his elbows as Parker poured granola into a bowl of oatmeal. "Doc," he said with a grin, "I hear this is going to hurt like hell. I'm putting down a hundred bucks to cover

"

any and all bets. This is going to be painful. Right?"

Parker smirked. "I'd hate to take your money." He leaned toward the young woman next to him. "I'll make his treatment hurt a little, just so I can collect."

Nervous laughter rippled around the table.

He took a spoonful of oatmeal and chased it down with orange juice, then looked around at those closest to him. "There are a couple of quotes I want to share, both from Isaac Newton. The first you've heard of: 'To every action there is always an opposite reaction.' The other is, 'We build too many walls and not enough bridges.' I'm not sure how outcomes will materialize. There could be residual forces that oppose a return to clarity. Don't let those forces, no matter how they appear, destroy you or tear you down. Fight to keep hold of what matters the most. And when this is all over—and it will be—live the rest of your days learning and creating a better world rather than living someone else's dream."

Conversation resumed around him. Faces filled with a bit more energy than when he arrived. When his bowl was empty, he gathered his breakfast ware. As he stepped away, he said, "See you rocketeers in the lab."

Falls Church, Virginia

Kate buried her face in the plushness of a pillow, drowning out the sound of a siren screaming several blocks over along Arlington Boulevard. Somewhere in her head, the last remnants of a dream faded, leaving her confused as to the meaning of what was wandering inside her head. Red brick sidewalks had stretched beneath her feet, with an Old Town feel. Crowd-filled streets led to a church. People dressed in nice clothes. Somber colors. Barricades restricted traffic. DC Metropolitan Police cars were abundant, visible. Officers in their usual dark blue vested uniforms patrolled the neighborhood. K-9 teams cleared cars that hadn't been towed away before festivities began.

In her dream, Kate blended into a sober crowd. Conversations around her were quiet and reverent.

Nearby, someone whispered, "Prosperity."

She recognized the familiar streetscapes of Georgetown near the university. She often frequented the historic college town to go for weekend runs along the canal.

Ahead, Holy Trinity Catholic Church took up a full block.

As the growing throng pushed against her, she studied faces, expressions. Their lives seemed burdened, heavier.

Kate groaned and removed the pillow from her face. The dream was such a downer. Her head ached like being hungover, but she struggled to remember anything about the previous night.

The distant siren no longer wailed. Above her bed, the dark walnut blades of a ceiling fan gently spun. A glance at the bedside clock told her the time: 8:25 AM.

As a forensics investigator, she had a luxury that many federal agents didn't: a predictable Monday through Friday work schedule and few weekend obligations. Today was one of those where the week's duty had spilled into the weekend, but she wasn't on duty for another couple of hours.

Georgetown.

Field support for a dignitary's memorial service.

Kate grabbed a robe and headed downstairs to start a pot of coffee. A mug was filled. Topped off with creamer. She slipped on a pair of UGG boots and walked out on her home's back deck, which faced south to collect the sun. Overnight a storm had settled over the nation's capital and the Potomac, leaving the morning air thick and cool. Her nostrils took a deeper whiff.

Rain was coming.

Kate yanked up the collar of her bathrobe and hoped that wasn't the case. The last thing she wanted to do was work an assignment outdoors and get soaked.

After the midday memorial service was over, she yearned to stop at the hospital and check on how Jack Wright was doing. Even though they were no longer in a relationship, years over now, it'd be nice to see Jack.

Drinking her coffee, Kate saw her Saturday as just another day with a job to do.

83

ESCAPE

Stewart Richards broke free of the shackles of a drug-induced slumber. Movement in his residence caught his attention.

He opened an eyelid. His nurse had stepped into an adjoining room to have a conversation with someone he couldn't see—a man, from the voice's tone and pitch. What they discussed wasn't audible. He doubted it was positive.

By now, security would've reviewed video footage. Seen him gun down Dr. Rikona Tanaka. They might be able to overlook that single act of murder in a covert world of industrial espionage and illegal human trials, but NeuroSteps had also lost two guards, even if that wasn't by his hands. The company would be implementing damage control.

Ji-woo, her team, and the participants had transformed the theoretical to practical.

Common InSight was a reality.

Since NeuroSteps controlled the technology, they could replicate processes without further assistance.

This made him expendable, which left him with a decision to make.

If he had enough time, he'd take what he'd learned from these successful human trials and rejoin the Phoenix Consortium to resurrect his former lab, ANCRI. They'd be more than eager to pay for his newest accomplishments, what he knew, and how to go about bringing the world a very profitable technology.

Peering across the room, he spotted another pre-filled autoinjector syringe ready for administration. Another therapeutic round of heavy sedation— diazepam, no doubt. If he was going to change his predicament, he'd have to sideline his nurse.

He felt his forehead. A lump, sensitive to the touch, taught him the meaning of "pistol whipped." He would repay Morgan for the experience the next time they met.

Rolling onto his side, he faced the room and positioned his lower arm palm up. Keeping his eyelids slightly cracked, he watched the nurse return to pick up the syringe.

When she came bedside, he waited until she stood over him. Spinning, he slapped the crook of her elbow and pulled. She gasped and tried to brace herself. With her elbow locked tight, he rolled his body and leaned into her, his leverage jerking her over the bed and pinning her down, eyes sprung wide with panic. Screaming, she pushed against him with her free hand. He jammed her hand, still clutching the autoinjector, against the soft flesh of her throat—at a ninety degree angle, to maximize contact and desired placement.

The blue tip of the syringe made contact.

A needle clicked.

She tried to squirm—a mistake, since the needle made that painful.

"Breathe," Richards ordered. "Just breathe. It'll be over soon."

The wide-eyed nurse trembled, her breath ragged, almost gasping. The autoinjector was meant to be placed against fatty tissue and muscle. The needle had hit her somewhere different entirely, her carotid artery. The carotid artery was the main thoroughfare linking her heart to her brain, a blood-filled highway rarely used for the direct administration of sedation. The sedative's rapid deployment spread its effects into her bloodstream. With a final panting gasp, she fell still.

After the autoinjector clicked a second time, Richards shoved the nurse off the edge of the bed and she crumpled to the floor. He searched her scrubs for anything valuable, coming up with a small wallet. She offered no resistance.

He studied her identification badge, and an idea formed. He'd need a way out of NeuroSteps. Camouflage would help him blend in. He estimated her height. Inches shorter than optimal. She wore a practical, company-branded baggy top rather than a tailored version to fit her form.

He stripped off her top and bottom then hauled the nurse onto the bed. He pulled the covers over her, placing pillows close to her head to hide her face. Shedding his own clothes, he put on her scrubs. Tight in the shoulders. Short in the legs. Workable. He slid on his shoes and collected her stethoscope, draping it around his neck. Her identification was clipped backwards so her photo wasn't visible.

He pulled out his dresser's bottom drawer and reached into the cavity below for the bag that Ji-woo Song had provided, complete with a loaded semiautomatic, extra magazine, and Advance BioCore credentials. He took no personal belongings, but would stop at the Director's Office to collect his research notes and Parker's headgear, the latter returned to him after NeuroSteps engineers had reversed engineered the original components.

He used the nurse's badge to access the employee's locker room, careful to enter the women's side only after the coast was clear. He wasted no time tracking down her locker, taking her wallet, car keys, and cell phone. Entering the men's section, he rummaged through a soiled utility bin to come up with better-fitting scrubs. After a quick change, he found a car outside that matched his newly acquired car keys.

Driving out of the facility, he caught Route 31 south at the first opportunity. The two-lane road became a direct thoroughfare to Princeton.

84

FINAL PROTOCOLS

9:00 AM, Advance BioCore, Princeton, New Jersey

Parker was more than anxious. Medical technicians administered ECG leads and plugged the participants into their assigned pods. The last one to enter her chamber, Caroline Wang flashed him a smile. At various workstations, technicians and engineers monitored bio-readouts and telemetry. The room buzzed with activity. It reminded him of the engineers who managed flight operations in NASA's Houston Mission Control Center once spacecraft reached orbit. The Advanced BioCore team had picked up technical processes quickly for their first time out. The Wall of Knowledge blazed with data and mapping schemes.

Parker spoke into a headset. "This will take about an hour. When you wake, you're going to feel refreshed. Bright. Alive." It was a lie, but he wanted to psych them up rather than weigh them down with worries, which wouldn't help. "Welcome to a morning in the dream chamber."

"See everyone on the other side," Caroline said across the comms.

"How are we looking?" he asked to those around him. "Anomalies?"

"None," a technician called. "All systems operative. Participants are aligned with the protocols and are ready for the process. Neurological readouts and mapping are tracking as expected."

"Confirmed," a quality control tech said.

Except for his former grad student, he'd always preferred to work alone. This team concept was a foreign experience, which he'd gotten used to, even embraced, in an odd sort of way. "Let's get started. Match baselines. Initiate Protocol One."

He'd structured Protocol One as a communicative exchange, using Caroline as the receptor of content to fill in the blanks of her own collected memories. Each protocol milestone built carefully on sequences, which combined to create complete remembrance of historical events, a specific past that was not hers.

The Wall of Knowledge updated real-time images, both in motion and stills. The participants assembled a sequence of memories like group puzzle solving. Smaller pieces merged to reveal something larger. Memories. Not their own. Someone else's. Audio came to life like the tin-can resonance from old eight track tape player. Technicians added filtering refine and add clarity.

An extracted echo, a memory, a rerun of history.

Sounds of traffic swept a street.

A man glanced in his rearview mirror as he parked his car. The face belonged to Oklahoma Senator Samuel Ford. Getting out, he scanned the street before hiking up a grass incline and into a park. The color of leaves hinted at fall. Ford kept his head moving as he approached a white marble statue. Another man waited for him. The statue's footstone read SERENITY. A woman in a flowing robe sat on a small throne. Vandalism had badly damaged the stone statue, breaking off her nose and left hand.

"Sam, I didn't know if you'd come," the U.S. Secretary of State said.

Ford looked around to make sure no one else lingered nearby.

"I know about Common InSight," Ford said, getting to the point of their clandestine rendezvous. "I have evidence. Financial records. You've redirected funds to a ghost-site operation. The Advanced Neurological Cybernetics Research Institute. Overseen by the Phoenix Consortium. A technological delusion financed illegally by an assortment of agencies."

"Hardly a delusion, Sam."

"Mr. Secretary, this is beyond petty theft. It's a gross misappropriation of funds. Grand larceny. Congress appropriates funding, not the Executive Branch. You and the Vice President can't just come along and raid bank accounts at your whim. I can't turn a blind eye to this lunacy that you're championing."

A curious look came across the Secretary's face. "Your interference is a problem."

"You're a Prosperity Founder, aren't you?" A cold silence hung in the air as no answer was given. "Who are the other seven? The Vice President, perhaps? Is the President reigning supreme over this Peace on Earth initiative?"

"Not his entire administration."

"I know about Hong Kong. Assassination plots. I have emails linking you to a scheme of terrorism. You're going to start a world war on American soil, and kick it off in Georgetown."

The Secretary lowered his head. "I've spent my entire life fighting enemies of the State and getting nowhere. Now the United States of America has not only an opportunity, but the global responsibility to act."

Ford scoffed. "Do you hear yourself? Common InSight is madness. Illegal. Unethical. It's the CIA's, the Army's, and DARPA's quest for mind control programs all over again. MK-Ultra was an atrocity carried out against American citizens. Tyranny under the guise of progress and science. Criminal. The worst of us. Yet you're out to create a string of Trojan horses, super spies, assassins, soldiers, and a war."

"This technological frontier will realign geopolitical boundaries. It's a weapon. One that will be put to good use. Stop us if you dare, but this train has left the station."

"You've given me no choice. I have to try."

"And watch more innocent people in Hong Kong die at the hands of China's authoritarian invasion? Such a cancer will spread to Taiwan, Macaw, both Koreas, and eventually Japan and the Philippines. China's quest for global domination will consume the world. Acting now saves our planet from an eventual World War III, maybe even a future nuclear Armageddon. This preemptive strike saves lives."

"An ultimate weapon of war?"

"This new age in scientific discovery ends warfare as we know it. Prosperity and Peace on Earth protect our homeland, our allies. And you're worried about how funds are spent and what bank accounts the money comes from?"

"Common InSight is social conditioning on steroids. I can't turn a blind eye to that."

The Secretary shook his head. "I thought you'd say that, Sam. I wish you hadn't. We could use your influence, experience."

"Are you threatening me? I'm a U.S. Senator. Don't even think about touching me."

"You can't stop us, only die trying."

"We'll see about that, Mr. Secretary."

85

GEORGETOWN

Georgetown, Washington, DC

Debra Ford was pleased as the stir of Saturday morning in the city found a rhythm.

She'd arrived early for a dress rehearsal of sorts. The Secret Service had protection of personnel down to a science, and their involvement brought complications. Hard lessons had taught her how scouted streetscapes changed the day of an operation.

Ji-woo insisted on calling the day "*saeloun sicho*," Korean for a "new dawn." A new dawn was the day that Prosperity was born.

In order for a new dawn to be successful, the Secret Service details would need to be disrupted—outright neutralized, if it came down to that.

Barricades surrounded Holy Trinity, restricting streets to vehicle traffic. MPDC officers secured those perimeters. Public trashcans and mailboxes had been removed, unattended cars towed. Canine teams ran dogs through precursory explosive detection. Sharpshooters evaluated designated rooftop positions. An ambulance arrived early and parked, ready for a quick trip to the designated trauma center if needed.

For her part, Ford had brought several changes of clothing, sunglasses, and wigs. Three different escape vehicles had been parked within a reachable distance on foot. What the public didn't know about the Secret Service was that they often recorded "high-profile" activities as a training tool, to improve procedures and integrate lessons learned. Facial recognition cameras were mounted on poles temporarily and monitored in a Secret Service Command Center. She'd get archived in video footage, so each of her outfit presented a different persona. This morning she was a male jogger, a nerdy government lawyer wearing a matching jogging outfit, sunglasses, a mustache, and sideburns. Beneath her outer shell, a shape-altering girdle compressed her breasts and thickened her sides.

She carried a Blue Bottle Coffee disposable cup, logo facing out. She'd purchased the cup a month earlier and saved for this occasion. If the Secret Service's post-event analysis flagged the jogging suit-wearing man as a threat and tried to track him to the local coffee shop, they'd find a dead end.

Ford walked the entire block around the church, sipping water out of her Blue Bottle Coffee cup and scouting the day-of-scene. She was disappointed not to see Ji-woo or her *buqu*. To ensure success, each piece of the op had been planned and would be executed independently. If anyone was captured, they had only limited information about any of the others' plans.

Satisfied with her intelligence gathering, she wrapped up by entering the backyard of one of the row homes facing Holy Rood Cemetery. The property was undergoing extensive remodeling. A portable workshop had been erected in the backyard. Ford entered the workshop and stripped off her jogging suit and the girdle, ditched the wig, mustache and sideburns, and coffee cup. Everything went into a plastic bag. Next she layered on two outfits: a wrinkle-free suit worthy of a diplomat, and over that, baggy sweats that were a full size too large.

Ford checked her watch. She was on schedule. She was due at the Ukrainian Embassy within the hour.

86

A FINAL DISCLOSURE

Advance BioCore, Princeton, New Jersey

Caroline Wang floated on an endless expanse of black, glass-like water, gazing up at an ever-changing panorama. She was neither in control nor a simple observer, her mind ensnared by a journey she couldn't control.

Her mind stung with sensations that felt like needles, although with no pain, only pressure.

The first memory echo faded.

Guided by the data-mining AI bots, Oklahoma Senator Samuel Ford's memories transitioned to later the same day. Night. After an exhilarating romp, he lay winded and clammy, naked on the bed. A twenty-something girlfriend strutted into an adjoining bathroom and shut the door. He collected a cell phone from a nightstand and scrolled through texts that had come in during his interlude.

A noise from an open doorway caught his attention.

"Honey, you expecting someone?" Ford called to the bathroom. "Your roommate is out of the country skiing, right?"

Armed figures charged fast and furious, bursting into the bedroom and snatching him off the bed, jerking him to his feet.

"Hey! What's going on?" Ford snapped.

One of the intruders broke away from the others and entered the bathroom, startling the girlfriend and dragging her screaming and naked into the bedroom.

"Leave her alone!" Ford said as two men wrenched his arms behind his back. Rifle muzzles stabbed his sides.

"Sam, darling, I heard you've been asking about the Founders."

Ford saw a middle-aged woman holding a semiautomatic: his ex-wife, Debra. "What are you doing here?"

"The Secretary implied that you could join us. I'm so glad you refused."

"Let go of me!" yelled the coed, kicking at the man holding her.

The ex-wife turned to the girl. "We'll get around to you, just wait."

"What?" the girl snapped.

"This makes sense now," Ford said in disgust. "You're one of them. A Founder?"

"Sam, all of this is so out of your league." She pinched the coed's cheek. "How much do you know? Who's your source?"

"Go to hell, Debra."

"I won't likely get past the Pearly Gates, so yes, I'll end up in hell. But ironically, you'll be there too, Sam. I wasted good years on you. And for what?" She looked at the girlfriend again. "Really? Our daughter is older than Barbie here." She turned back. "Now look. You can refuse to answer my questions, but you, of all people, know I'll get answers. Now, let's get to the business. The Secretary sent me here on cleanup duty. Who's your informant? The name of your source? Better provide answers, or someone gets hurt."

Ford shook his head. "No."

The man holding the girlfriend hauled her over so that she and the Senator could look into each other's eyes.

Ford yelled, "She's done nothing! Let her go!"

The ex-wife snatched a pillow off the bed, stuffed her weapon into it, and fired a single shot. A retort thundered, barely muffled by the pillow. The girlfriend's eyes went wide. She screamed, only held aloft by the man behind her.

Ford screamed, too.

Stunned, the girl gasped and groaned as she bled from an off-center gunshot wound to the stomach.

"Stop, please," Ford pleaded.

The ex-wife turned around. "Names, places, details. Now, Sam."

"Stop, I beg you."

"Begging's not your style. And talking to you after all these unfaithful years is a waste of my time." Debra Ford jammed the pistol-stuffed pillow against the girl's bleeding stomach. "Dear, his list of whores like you is so long. But you're the last."

Another retort roared.

The girlfriend gasped one more time before slumping into the arms of the man holding her. The first shot wounded, warned, the second fatal. Blood oozed from the center of the girl's heart.

Debra Ford checked her watch. "Dump her in the bathtub. Cover the body with the shower curtain." She turned to Ford and slid on a pair of brass knuckles. "Bag him and carry his ass out."

"You killed her," Ford said, sobbing.

"No. You did, the moment you held your tongue."

Spinning around, she struck him with a brass-knuckled fist to the face.

Ford's memory went dark.

Floating on a waveless sea of black, Caroline shivered at the abhorrent vividness of Samuel Ford's memories. The panoramic realm above darkened to a tranquil pre-dusk light, a moment where neither day nor night existed. She could hear the adrenaline-filled throbbing of her heartbeat.

Parker noticed the horror-filled expressions on the host of scientists, technicians, and medical staff. They held their breaths not because of the awe-inspiring achievement, but because of the senseless brutality their collective work had revealed. They strained to process what they'd just seen, events never meant to be seen—secrets.

Deadly secrets.

Secrets worth killing to control.

Murder on full display for anyone who possessed the power of Common InSight.

Parker understood the witnesses' uneasiness all too well. He'd delivered exactly what the government wanted. What Debra Ford had goaded him into delivering. "When the time comes," she'd told him, "give them what they want. What the government wants. It's okay. People want to know what Senator Ford knew. Share it. If you don't, people will die."

Cognitive sampling.

Mind reading.

Cover-ups and murder.

"Memories layered in dangerous secrets," she'd said, knowing full well that those disclosures would expose her as a murderer.

Alone in a breakout room in the Security Command Center, Grayson almost started dancing. Monitors relayed the technical accomplishments that Parker and Advanced BioCore's engineers and technicians had just achieved.

With his phone on speaker mode, he dialed a number.

The answer was almost immediate. The Vice President. "Update?"

"Common InSight is real. Two memories. Both from Samuel Ford. It's like watching old-fashioned VHS tapes. Amazing. Neurological singularity will deliver you the world."

"I want a detailed briefing on everything."

"Not a problem. Everything's recorded." Grayson waited for more directions. When none came, he asked, "What do you want to do with Thomas Parker? ABI"—Advanced BioCore International— "has the data, the tech, all the coding and the neuromapping applications. We've got everything. If you want to shed excess baggage, liability, the time is now. The doc is redundant. And we no longer need the participants either."

A long pause followed. "Get rid of everyone. All non-essential personnel. I don't want to know how, who, or where the bodies are buried. Nothing comes back to this office. Just take care of it."

Grayson grinned and clicked off the phone. Exactly what he wanted to hear.

Parker knew what he must do. He transitioned the participants to the last protocol and launched a set of predictive algorithms that he termed Applied Mind, a line Richards had used in one of his research videos. Richards had said, "Without a doubt there exists a level of cognitive censorship in any applied mind therapy. Sacrifice is critical to implementing the necessary repairs that are required to make a person whole again."

Richards wasn't wrong. Parker just hoped this last protocol, built on censorship, wasn't lethal.

"Protocol Three is active. Neural engagement initiated," one of the technicians called.

Parker's anxiety grew as he watched the Wall of Knowledge focus on the mind of a single participant, a single guide leading the others down a path of no return.

"You're the last witness, Caroline," he whispered into his microphone, sending a message just to her. "Train their minds to no longer consider these memories important. Let's take them home."

Trimming cognitive awareness required bumping neurons at precise locations to change the receptive tuning of dendrites and synaptic junctions. The process was like pruning branches on a bush. An average adult brain's comprised between 80 and 100 billion neurons—10 times more than the people on earth—too many to map with a supercomputer.

As an application, Applied Mind reduced neural landscapes by ignoring neurons that didn't contribute to memory and recall, consolidating half the cognitive galaxy for engagement and evaluation. Another element of Applied Mind was tracking key neurotransmitters, the micro electro-chemical-like words used by neurons to talk to each other. As the brain stored memories in both long-term and short-term regions, neurons tuned themselves to match the properties of certain neurotransmitters. Neurons communicated to each by passing energy across synaptic cleft, a gap between membranes. Dendrites were the branches on a neuron's bush.

Bumping neurons meant altering voltage sensitivity in targeted synaptic junctions and the corresponding dendrites. In a complex form of math reduction, neuromapping the participants in advance gave the Advanced BioCore's supercomputers a fighting chance to dislocate awareness.

To disrupt select memory recall.

Enough bumping to make it difficult to relive unwanted memories.

Applied Mind eliminated repetitive memories in each participant, with the sole exception of Caroline Wang. Soon, they'd have no recollection of whatever had ever happened. That part of their past would simply evaporate, get bumped from reality.

As wetware algorithms advanced through cycles, memories were cleared like the hands on a grandfather clock, clicking and ticking off the passing of seconds. Parker had applications built to display clearing zones, using orange as "remaining," yellow as "in progress," and green as "completed."

Anxiety diminished as each green milestone appeared.

The participants lost the ability to recall their original abductions; ANCRI's madhouse of horrors; the fate of Oklahoma Senator Samuel Ford in a Georgetown townhouse; Debra Ford and her thugs; the madman himself, Stewart Richards; being taken captive by Ji-woo's science-like mercenaries; and their experience on the *Norvana*.

Neuromapping graphics showed the real-time changes inside their minds. Neurons once lit with a fiery brilliance and powered by intense memories were toned down, not significantly, but enough to reduce tuned associations to neighboring neurons.

Parker's hands grew sweaty as more milestones blinked green.

Their worlds, relationships and memories of each other had thinned.

Now one last set of memory structures remained to be purged.

87

ARRIVAL

Richards arrived at the Advanced BioCore's front gate. The badge he'd been given accessed the employee entrance. A gate arm rose. He drove onto the property and followed signs to the shipping and receiving loading dock. After parking in a loading zone, he donned an outer jacket that he'd bought at a big box retailer with the nurse's credit card, and stuffed the semiautomatic he'd been given into an inner pocket. Using his access card, he badged into a stairwell.

He needed to catch his breath.

Time froze for him.

Five minutes later a dock worker knelt beside him. "Sir, are you okay?"

Richards shook his head, unsure. He forged a surprised face. "I must've got lightheaded. Low blood sugar gets me sometimes. Nothing more than that."

"Perhaps we should have one of our on-call docs take a look at you."

He grinned. "You're right. Help me up?"

A hand was extended. Richards took it. Once on his feet, he drew his gun and fired a shot, striking the man in the head. The man crumpled to the concrete floor of the stairwell.

Pressing ahead, Richards got his bearings from what a placard told him and headed to the facility's Security Operations Center.

A guard stood watch outside the company's command center.

Richards presented his badge. "Is there a supervisor on duty? There's a security breach that I need to report. It's urgent, real urgent."

The guard escorted him into the command center.

"Wait here," the guard said, leaving him in an outer room.

He thought about tailing the guard, but decided the element of surprise worked better. Turning his shoulder, he wanted his appearance to appear natural. He slid a hand inside his jacket and gripped his weapon.

A man came out with the guard.

"William Grayson. I'm told you have information on a security breach?"

Richards turned and fired at point blank range, shooting Grayson first, then the guard. He collected the guard's semiautomatic pistol and stormed the inner areas. Screams rose. People started running. He stood firm, blocking the main entrance. Across the Command Center was an exit door with a panic bar. The first who reached it managed to escape outside, but Richards shot the second person in the back.

An intruder alarm bellowed. Lights flashed.

Richards fired both weapons, turning Advanced BioCore's Command Center into a shooting gallery. The unarmed had nowhere to flee. He kept firing until both guns were out of ammunition, their slides locked back.

Panic-filled screams and wailing fought for attention under the sounds of alarms, people hunkered under desks and dodging out of sight.

In a breakout room, monitors caught his attention.

Thomas Parker was on screen.

Richards pulled a red handle on the wall to initiate the facility's fire alarms, which competed raucously with the independent security alarms. Tossing aside the guard's weapon, he changed out magazines in the semiautomatic he carried and chambered a round.

Entering the breakout room, he studied the new batch of monitors.

Parker stood in a large room with others.

Pods filled the space.

The screen tag read: NEUROPHYSIOLOGY LAB.

88

TIME

When the intruder alert systems activated, Parker knew time had run out.

The Wall of Knowledge beamed the reduction progress in Protocol Three. All but one Applied Mind submodule had turned green. As neurons bumped and realigned, he could see neural landscapes clear. Memories of him and ANCRI no longer existed.

He considered that some people would call his use of the technology magic—the fact that he'd turned himself into a stranger.

One cognitive purge remained: Caroline Wang.

The lab's doors opened, distracting him.

A ghost from his past entered, aiming a handgun.

A retort rang out. Parker dove to the floor and ducked behind a pod.

Technicians and engineers scurried for cover.

If he didn't move, Parker knew, he was dead.

Caroline Wang couldn't explain the rising sense of urgency that she felt. Something had gone horribly wrong. As a tour guide of sorts, she scoured the minds of fourteen others, pointing AI bots to a scavenger hunt of associated memories, layers intertwined with layers. The world needed no more witnesses.

Muted alarms bellowed in the distance, warning of something ominous about to happen. Something boomed in the world beyond hers.

"It's time to let go," she told those she interfaced with. "Time to forget."

From the depths of their minds, she made sure that none remembered Parker; his graduate assistant, Becky Ward; Oklahoma Senator Samuel Ford or his murderous ex-wife; Richards; or anything connected to Common InSight or Eight Rings.

Footsteps pressed into sand were washed away by an incoming tide.

It was time for the participants to forget everything.

Richards' first shot missed its mark by mere inches, nearly decapitating its target. Parker hid behind a matrix of pods. Lab workers went to ground as well.

Ignoring the earsplitting alarms, Richards moved with purpose, taking an angle that covered both the main entrance and where he last saw Parker.

His prey leapt across a gap between pods. Richards fired several shots, striking pods and consoles. A cryogenic pipe burst, spraying a vaporous steam into the air. Richards suspected that Advanced BioCore used the compressed gases to supercool electronics and superconductors. In their liquid and vapor states, concentrations of nitrogen, helium, or hydrogen could be fatal. Anyone whose skin was touched by those vapors would receive frostbite-like burns. Anyone who inhaled those gases would have permanent lung damage, and would likely die. He would give the growing cloud a wide berth.

A figure shifted ahead. He fired. A bullet struck a different pod.

Richards stepped away from the vapors, instincts telling him Parker would do the same. He took a quick look inside a pod to assess its occupant. Headgear covering the participant's head disguised the individual's identity.

Figuring Parker hid two rows up, Richards reduced the matrix of hiding spots by shifting sideways.

He took aim at the closest pod. "Your time has come, Parker. As has mine. You'll pay for cheating me out of what I deserve. I'm here to collect on that payment. So I'll count to five. Your choice. You can save these people only with your life. What will it be?"

Parker felt trapped. Innocent people would die unless Richards got his vengeance.

Parker swung the microphone attached to his headset below his chin and broke into a sprint, taking a direct track across the lab and racing through the growing clouds of vapors.

Richards fired.

Bullets whirled behind Parker. His heart thundered in his chest. He concentrated on nothing except reaching his destination. He wrenched his eyes shut and held his breath. Protecting his face with his hands, he pierced the vaporous sprays but did not stop running. The consequences were immediate, pin-like burns stinging the back of his hands and neck.

A technician hiding behind a console saw Parker barreling at him and sprinted in a perpendicular direction.

Richards fired wildly in their direction.

Glancing to the Wall of Knowledge, Parker saw Protocol Three flash completely green. Ducking behind a console, he launched a new algorithm, one he'd never intended to use: Synaptic Touch. As he typed, the skin on his fingers tingled. Nitrogen burns, he guessed. Quickly, he isolated thirteen participants and spoke to Caroline as he uploaded enhanced access to a different string of memories.

"Enough games, Parker. I will start killing your precious participants."

Parker hit the execute command and stood, his hands extended.

The Wall of Knowledge changed to focus on a single participant.

"Caroline," he said into his microphone, "what did you do when you said goodbye to Amy Richards? Show us your last moments with her."

"Thomas, what's wrong?" Caroline asked, the concern of her voice nearly overridden by the jarring alarms.

"Don't worry about that. Just focus on Amy." Parker cringed at the pain. Drifting away from the console, he moved into the open. He called across the room to Richards. "No one else needs to get hurt. I'm right here."

Behind Parker, the Wall of Knowledge transitioned to fragmented video clips.

On screen, Caroline stripped back a sheet to expose a naked body past a bony collarbone. An emaciated woman was pale and stiff, barely recognizable. Only a grotesque outer shell remained. Her head was shaved. Alien-like deformations and sutures arced across a leathery scalp. Thin, hair-sized lines connected the dots on her scalp to larger dime-sized gray circles, the obscure tapestry forming a fragmented set of geometric patterns. Eyelids were sunken and shut, hiding what would've been the horror-filled final days of life.

"This is how we repaid you," Caroline said, her voice coming across loud speakers. Her fingers traced along Amy's scarred forehead. "I won't let your sacrifice be in vain."

The distraction had drawn Richards' attention to the image of his daughter.

From the corner of his eye, Parker saw that technicians and engineers had slipped out the lab's main doors undetected. Without abrupt movements, he walked closer to the madman, who looked like he was caught in a spell.

Richards kept his weapon trained on Parker. The lab's front screen showed a memory. He'd experienced a similar version, but as a spectator. The traitorous spy, once his second in command, was one of Parker's guinea pigs.

Caroline Wang had returned to be a test subject.

Confined to a pod, she wasn't going anywhere, wasn't a threat.

He grinned at idea of killing her once Parker was dead.

On screen, Caroline held a core biopsy needle. She kissed his daughter's forehead and thrust the needle into Amy's heart. With a biological sample in hand, she etched *AMY RICHARDS RIP* in the pale skin along the centerline of Amy's body with the tip of the needle. She capped the needle and tucked it into her coat. Next she retrieved a smart phone and tapped the device's camera feature. She returned the phone to a pocket.

After flattening a sheet over Amy's body, Caroline turned on the incinerator. A door opened. A carriage emerged from a fire box. The gurney was positioned parallel to the carriage. One arm slid beneath Amy's torso with an elbow cradling her head, the other below her buttocks. Caroline put Amy's sheet-covered body onto the carriage.

"Walk with God, in a place where no harm will come to you again. Someday, I hope you'll forgive me."

Caroline shoved the carriage into the fire box. The door closed.

Caroline flipped up a clear plastic protective cover and pressed a red button on the console. An inferno rumbled behind the incinerator's door.

Parker charged as Richards broke his stupor.

Their bodies collided violently and crashed into a pod. Parker threw the first punch, striking Richards' jaw. The man spun and wrenched his hands away to get a shot with the gun. With one hand, Parker latched onto the gun to keep it from swinging across his abdomen.

Old and shaky, Richards seemed strong enough. Coiling his legs, Parker launched himself and swung an elbow high at the man's throat.

Richards pivoted just enough to avoid contact.

Their eyes met. The older man's beaded pupils showed nothing but disdain.

Richards' gun hand swung down, discharging a round near his feet.

Parker shifted and thrust his shoulder beneath Richards' armpit. His opponent's free arm tightened around his throat, constricting his airway.

Using his legs, Parker drove Richards back against a pod. He thought he heard the odd crack of ribs. Instead of deflating, Richards bellowed into his ear and shifted his arm from his throat to clutch Parker's Adam's apple. Fingers tightened against soft tissue.

Using leverage like a wrestler, Parker dropped to his knees, flipping Richards heels overhead. Richards' gun discharged. Blood drenched both of them. Not only did ribs crack this time, ribs broke. Air erupted from lungs, spraying blood even further.

Richards lay motionless.

This time the man would not experience a second resurrection.

The cause of death was obvious: the lower third of his jaw was gone. Cheekbones shattered. Facial skin and muscle torn away to expose bone. The bullet had penetrated below the chin and exited an eye socket.

Parker coughed. The taste of blood filled his mouth. Not his blood.

Around him, alarms continued to stroke the air, strobes flashed.

Shoving Richards aside, he staggered to the closest emergency eyewash stand. Triggering a handle, he doused his face, arms, and neck with a jet stream of water. After rinsing down, he shook out his mop of wet hair and realized that he stood in a pool of water.

Those who hadn't fled rose like creatures from a whack-a-mole game, and people knew what needed to be done without him saying a word.

Parker pawed back his wet hair and closed out programs to shut everything down. The Wall of Knowledge faded to black. Pods started to rise.

He raced to Caroline's pod first, unhooking her from the contraption. Headgear automatically slid up. Her eyes locked onto him. Sluggishly, she smiled. Throwing herself into an embrace, she clutched him as if her soul needed the engagement of another human's touch, an experience essential for her life and each breath she took.

"Why'd you do it?" she asked over the blare of the alarms.

Parker let his pointing fingers be his answer. Her eyes followed them across the room until she saw the dead man on the floor. Enough of a face remained for her to know its owner.

Pulling him even closer, she whispered, "Thank you, Thomas. I won't forget this."

He leaned into her and almost laughed. "You're the only one who won't."

89

A MISSING AGENT

Directors of the Federal Bureau of Investigation rarely carried guns or led active cases. By historical precedent, Presidents more often than not plucked them from ideologically matching ranks of prosecuting attorneys or a politically-aligned lineage within the bureau or Justice Department. Most Directors were classic career bureaucrats, men who were supposed to be impartial and recuse themselves from partisan investigations.

That hadn't always been true, and this case was different. This was personal, with links to the Vice President and the Secretary of State.

On his watch, an agent had gone missing—an agent his directives had assigned to this case.

He'd wanted to send another, but that damn fool was laid up at GWU Hospital recovering from a vehicular mauling, an accident he was lucky to have survived.

Inside a Bell 407 helicopter, a pilot and copilot sat up front of the cabin packed with five passengers. Across from him sat the Assistant Director-in-Charge of the Washington Field Office. An ever-present small gold shield pinned to her suit reminded him that she was a gritty agent, comfortable with getting her hands dirty with case details. The problem, though, was that inserting two suits into a live raid was a good way to get normal stay-out-of-the-way bosses shot. Three armed agents in khakis and bullet-resistant vests filled out the cabin.

Through its Criminal Investigative and Counterintelligence Divisions, the bureau had obtained search warrants from a federal magistrate. Agents from both the Philadelphia and Newark Field offices were *en route*. As a jurisdictional courtesy, the Princeton Police Department had been officially notified at the five-minutes-out mark, not a minute earlier.

The flight to Princeton took an hour.

To retain the element of surprise, the raid on Advanced BioCore couldn't start until the Vice President had left for his scheduled memorial service in Georgetown. The aftermath of the bureau's involvement at ANCRI reinforced one belief: the more people in Washington who knew about the bureau's move in advance, the more complicated law enforcement activities got. Too many agencies and entities had skin in the game on this radical technology, and everyone wanted to exert some sort of influence over it.

The helicopter touched down on an asphalt pad, simultaneous to Philadelphia and Newark agents breaching the property's security gates.

As the Director approached the buildings, he could see flashing strobes and hear alarms. Employees fled outside, more confused about what was going on inside than outside.

Agents raided the company's main lobby without resistance, its front desk abandoned. As more agents joined them, the team split up into three groups to secure essential spaces: the company's command center, its data center, and research labs.

ANCRI's case postmortem had reinforced the importance of securing data and computer systems. ANCRI's institutional heart was its Neurophysiology Lab.

At Advanced BioCore, it was where the Director headed first.

90
DECISIONS

Parker half-expected to see Grayson and his security teams descend on them, but that never happened.

The annoying blare of alarms and flashing strobes stopped. Everyone looked to him, and he gestured for them to continue retrieving the participants. Once Caroline was clear of her telemetry tethers, he assisted other participants. She did the same.

"Dr. Parker, where's Special Agent Morgan?" a voice called.

He turned to armed FBI agents as they burst into the lab, led by a man and woman in suits. The cavalry was late.

The man introduced himself as the FBI's Director, the woman as the FBI's Washington Field Office Assistant Director-in-Charge. No further introductions offered.

"I got a message that Kate was working on that ship, the *Norvana*."

"When was the last time you saw her?" the woman asked.

"Yesterday morning. What's wrong?"

"Thomas, can I speak to you?" Caroline asked.

"Excuse me." He gestured to the lab. "I'd say make yourself at home, but you've already doing that." He started to walk away, then turned around. "There's a man named Dr. William Grayson. You'll want to talk to him."

"William Grayson?" the woman said, cupping an earpiece. She turned to the Director and whispered something. When she turned back around, she said, "Grayson is dead."

Parker pointed to where Richards lay. "He might have had something to do with that."

"Who is he?" the woman asked.

"Stewart Richards."

"Dr. Stewart Richards?" The Director looked troubled as if he'd seen a ghost.

Parker excused himself, took Caroline by the arm and led her away from the FBI.

"Caroline," he whispered, "get the participants out of here. I don't care how. Stick to our plan. Maybe in all this chaos, you guys can slip out unnoticed."

She nodded. "I think Kate will be in Georgetown."

"How do you know?"

"I don't. I mean, I'm not certain. It's something I saw. How images connected together. Samuel Ford knew something was happening in Georgetown. I saw his notes on a computer. And a date. Today's date. Noon. Today is when Prosperity launches. It makes sense that Kate will be there."

Parker shot her a stern look. "Don't say anything. Act dumb. You don't know what happened to you during these experiments. Don't know how you got here. Don't remember. Can't remember. Your mind draws a blank and you get these debilitating headaches if you try."

Caroline lowered her head, knowing they were being watched. "What are you going to do?"

"Can you identify Dr. Ji-woo Song?" the Director asked.

Parker gave Caroline a hug. Stepping in front of her, he took up all the attention. He scanned the room. The FBI didn't waste any time corralling a scared group of college students and separating them from the Advanced BioCore's staff.

He checked the time on a computer monitor: 11:22 AM. "How fast can you get us to Georgetown?"

The Director's brow furrowed. "What's in Georgetown?"

He didn't know. Caroline didn't really know. So he ran with a bluff. "Katherine Morgan, Ji-woo Song, and Debra Ford. Georgetown is where Peace on Earth and a whole lot of Prosperity are delivered."

The Director and Assistant Director-in-Charge exchanged looks that told him he'd struck gold.

Not waiting for confirmation, Parker said, "Look, we can debate this in a committee meeting or at a congressional hearing, but we really need to get to Georgetown."

Before he knew it, he was ushered out to a helicopter.

91

MAKING HASTE

Caroline wasted no time gathering the participants and guiding them out the back of the complex. The FBI agents had become preoccupied with securing the premises and herding the metaphorical cats, Advanced BioCore's staff. The simple suggestion of a group bathroom break provided the advantage they needed.

Previously, Parker had briefed her on west-side exits out of the complex.

She didn't comprehend the extent of their memory wipes, but she knew the participants had been indoctrinated to draw on essential cognitive triggers. When they saw her, they associated her with three emotions: trust, honesty, and personal safety. As they fled the complex, no one questioned her or offered resistance.

Once outside, they crossed an expanse of grass, disappeared into a tree-lined boundary and made their escape. Crossing Route 1, they walked the frontage grass until they reached the Brick House Tavern & Tap restaurant and bar. A man wearing a New Jersey

Devils ball cap and flannel shirt stood beside a passenger transit van.

The mid-thirties man looked exactly as Parker had described him.

"You Caroline?" he asked.

"You Max?" she asked.

Max handed her car keys. "I heard you're in trouble."

She shrugged. "Something like that."

Max glanced at the others. "You need help? I can drive you somewhere."

"No, Max." Parker had told her about meeting a delivery driver from Brick House Tavern & Tap when he'd ordered takeout a night earlier. They'd agreed to a profitable, no-questions-asked arrangement—funds wired directly to Max's bank account, $9,500 up front. An equal amount delivered after he provided a fifteen-person van. A third and final deposit to be made after everyone was safe. "Stick to the deal. That's how you get paid. Any deviation and you lose the rest of your bird dog fee."

He grinned. "Just offering to help."

"Thanks." She patted him on the shoulder. "We've got it from here. Come on, everyone, get in."

Caroline left Max at the restaurant and drove non-stop to Philadelphia, finally stopping at a thrift store, where everyone could purchase clothes for the trip. Cash and debit cards had been left in a satchel under the driver's seat, enough to complete the journey and help them avoid electronic and financial detection if they stuck to non-toll roads and highways.

92

THE GATHERING

Georgetown, Washington, DC

Debra Ford had prepared for the rain, slipping on a rain suit over a business suit. A light mist had settled over Georgetown. The air was cool, dense. On a bike, she rode along the campus boundary and chained the bike up in Key Memorial Park, on M Street just east of the bridge. Shedding her outerwear, she tucked everything in a small knapsack, unfurled an umbrella, and walked next door to the Ukrainian Embassy.

She'd arranged everything in advance: a quick meeting to present a donation, then a short walk to the memorial service. At the check-in desk, Ford showed a passport in the name of Sofia Bilorus, a Ukrainian businesswoman and the adopted cousin of a former Ambassador of Ukraine to the United States. While she didn't speak Ukrainian, she spoke Russian, like 30 percent of the country, a legacy from Soviet occupation. Many Ukrainians spoke both—if they were honest, they admitted the languages were very much alike.

The Ukrainian Ambassador was traveling, so the embassy's

Deputy Ambassador, Irina Reznik, greeted her. After an exchange of pleasantries, they established that both spoke fluent English, and they switched languages.

Ford had targeted Ukraine for its ease of access. As a Ukrainian citizen defined by her fake passport and a charity donor, she was permitted to skip metal detectors, instead entering through the library side of the embassy.

Ford had reviewed the layout of the Embassy buildings through photos and building permits. Part of the embassy was the Forrest-Marbury House, a historic structure that dated back to when George Washington had met with land barons to arrange the purchase of the land that would become the District of Columbia.

In a foyer, Ford slid her raingear knapsack out of sight beneath a wooden bench. She entered a sitting room where she presented a check to the Deputy Ambassador for the amount of twenty thousand dollars, seed money for a children's hospital fundraising campaign.

While they chatted about homeland politics and how hospitals needed funding for children, they drank kvass, a low-alcoholic Slavic and Baltic beverage brewed from rye bread. Ford hadn't had kvass in years; she took in a whiff of strawberries and mint, and smiled.

After some time had passed, Ford tapped a watch on her wrist. The Deputy Ambassador got the hint and grabbed her overcoat and an umbrella. They walked in the misty rain, continuing to chat. Ford was careful to ask more questions than to offer up anything about her fake life.

Deputy Ambassador Reznik was a practicing Catholic, a proud member of the Ukrainian Greek Catholic Church. Her father was an economist and professor who had worked with Ambassador Peter Tang to expand international relations between former Soviet Bloc countries and those of Asia. She was honored to attending Tang's memorial on her father's behalf.

It was valuable to have a companion at the memorial service.

Security profilers scrutinize individuals first before couples and groups of people. Ford guided her companion up 36th Street, looking for the Secret Service's sharpshooters. She saw three, on rooftops, each with an unobstructed line of sight on Holy Trinity.

Vice President Richards Mears met with Peter Tang's family in the church's rectory ahead of the memorial service. He offered condolences to the Ambassador's wife and adult children. His Secret Service detail controlled interactions and the timing of entrances and exits of others. The Secretary of State entered to extend his sympathies.

Mears shook the man's hand. "Good to see you, Mr. Secretary."

Two priests joined the pre-service gathering: the frosted-haired pastor of Holy Trinity and a Chinese bishop who had yet to surrender his thick black mane to a gray that matched his age. After another round of introductions and condolences, the priests led a family prayer.

During his years in politics, Mears had attended many high-profile memorial services. Building alliances throughout Asia, Peter Tang had certainly earned any honors bestowed upon him. As the original Founder, Tang was the person who'd recruited him as one of the eight and forged the vision of Peace on Earth and Prosperity: one democratic Asia, free of the tyrannical rule of Communist China. At the beginning such utopian notions had seemed farfetched, until a technological breakthrough emerged. When the Secretary of State joined, they'd selected remaining Founders—people who had legacy connections, financial resources, or influence. Common InSight fueled hopes for the charter of one united democratic Asia, an era that would bring peace to the entire planet.

The Vice President huddled with the Secretary. "Are you up for this?"

The Secretary smiled in a way he'd never seen, a smile predicated on anticipation or courage. "If a person wishes to move mountains tomorrow, they must start by lifting stones today."

Mears nodded. "Wisdom from a true statesman."

The Secretary shook his head. "No. Ambassador Tang was the statesman. I am honored, however, to walk in his footsteps and see the day that Prosperity arrived."

Kate Morgan shrugged off an unexplained notion of feeling trapped inside someone else's body. It was as if overnight a profound sense of duty stoked the fire to a cause greater than herself. Inside, an inner voice that didn't speak empowered her, a newly acquired energy to feed her soul and guide her.

Crowds, people dressed for a memorial service walked in the rain toward Holy Trinity. Road blocks restricted vehicle access. The streetscape matched what she'd seen in her dream. Except for the rain, it felt like she'd been there before.

Carrying an umbrella, Kate joined the movement of bodies until she arrived at the Secret Service station near a series of black SUVs. She recognized the Vice President's standard, his official coat of arms, displayed on one of the vehicles. Another displayed the flag of the U.S. Department of State.

Kate showed her badge to the Secret Service detail's site manager. "Katherine Morgan, FBI."

"I wasn't informed that the bureau was sending anyone," the Secret Service site manager said.

"Just here to help," Kate said, scanning the secured zone around the Vice President's motorcade. The entire block of O Street had been barricaded to restrict vehicle and pedestrian access.

The Secret Service agent explained the arrangement of the scene's protective zones.

"I'll walk the crowds outside and make myself useful."

"Report anything you see."

She nodded. "Got it."

Kate strolled down a red brick sidewalk and the school side of the church. Looking up, she spotted Secret Service sharpshooters on different rooftops. There'd be a third, probably, protecting the south end. She stepped into the crowd heading into the church, walking against the grain to scan faces and perceived threats.

Just people attending a memorial service.

93

THE FLIGHT

FBI Bell 407 Helicopter Flying South

Parker wanted to hit the Director with his best shot, so he asked for something to write on after they boarded the helicopter.

The FBI wanted answers. So did he.

After liftoff, the helicopter jostled before finding a cruising altitude at 7,000 feet. During his youth, his parents had dragged him off to places resembling nowhere more times than he could count. He'd been the son of a pair of wannabe gypsies who loved archaeology more than raising a family state-side. When donkey-pulled carts and old dilapidated buses couldn't reach dirt-infested archeology sites, he'd ridden in third world helicopters and single-engine airplanes that by sheer magic never fell out of the sky.

As a boy, he'd begged for rides in helicopters. Now he couldn't care less, thinking only of Kate.

His mind drifted back to their first real conversation. She'd slept in a chair across from his bed, waiting for him to wake. The night earlier, she'd tended to a gunshot wound in his side. He was hardly a grateful patient—more of a jerk—but Kate took the high road in the face of his resentment and self-pity. Good thing she'd needed him, because he doubted he'd get a second chance with her once she'd left Princeton.

"A weather front," the pilot said over comms, "has moved over the greater DC area. Rain is forecasted. The ride will get choppy as the wind picks up. Flight time is about an hour."

Parker sketched out what Kate had drawn up, linking the associations and connections. He clicked his comms. "Why would Kate disappear and not contact you?"

"We don't know," the ADIC said.

"Did Grayson work for you?" He'd heard before they left that they'd found Grayson, dead. Richards had stormed that place first and shot everyone he could, including Grayson.

"Justice," the Director said, "not the bureau."

Grayson had said as much when they met, but Parker wanted the who-works-where aspect confirmed. Grayson had mentioned his division was national security-related, which made sense.

"Why are we going to Georgetown, Doctor?" the Director asked, securing his sketches.

Parker glanced up. "What's going on there today?"

"I don't know what you're asking."

He frowned. "Look, we can play games but my involvement is based entirely on *quid pro quo*. If the FBI doesn't bring something to the table, I won't tell you what I have."

The Director and ADIC exchanged looks.

"Ambassador Peter Tang's memorial service is today," the Director said.

Since he didn't follow politics, that disclosure meant nothing to Parker except fitting the Peace on Earth part of the equation.

"Hypothetically speaking," Parker said, "if we discussed the guest list at this memorial service, I presume it would include the Vice

President, the Secretary of State, dignitaries from China and South Korea. How close am I?"

The Director wrinkled his forehead. "What's going on, Dr. Parker?"

"You might want to ask if this chopper goes any faster." Parker showed them his sketch. "Kate drew something like this up the night before last."

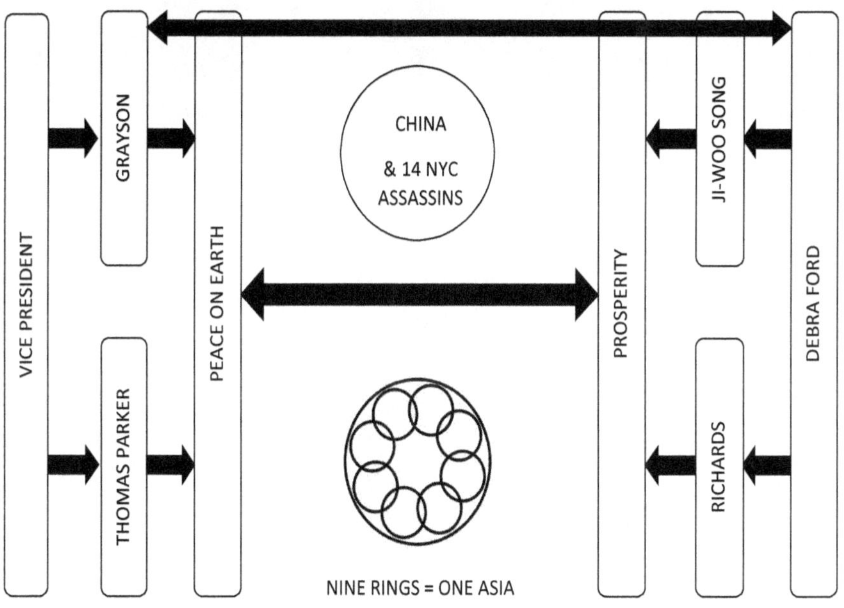

Parker left out only his research contributions and what he'd done with Caroline and the participants. He studied the shocked-as-hell faces as they connected the dots, significant elements in a grander conspiracy that the bureau hadn't figured out yet.

The Director keyed his mic. "Can we fly faster?"

"At our limit, sir."

"Put us down as close to that damn church as possible."

The Director and WFO's ADIC spent the next several minutes placing calls, dispatching agents to the church. Hostage Rescue and

Metro Police had been deployed. The last call was to the Director of the Secret Service.

"Can you identify this Dr. Song, if you saw her?" the ADIC asked.

Parker nodded, surprised that he hadn't been asked to describe his research, whether it was at ANCRI or Advanced BioCore.

94

THE MEMORIAL SERVICE

Holy Trinity Catholic Church, Georgetown, Washington, DC

Debra Ford and Deputy Ambassador Irene Reznik blended into the crowds. They presented invitations at the door, which were matched to authorized guest registry. Umbrellas were closed and personal belongings were searched at makeshift security stations. Once cleared, they headed to the balcony—for a good view. They sat in the first row, slightly off-center, with a clear view of the beautiful church.

Three stories tall, the church had been modeled after early Holy Roman structures and painted white to match the purity of the Trinity. Arched stained glass windows ran down both sides of the sanctuary. A large crucifix hung on the wall behind the altar. Wooden pews filled the nave, and the seating was almost full.

From her vantage point, Ford couldn't see the faces below, as their backs were to her. Velvet robes cordoned off a section reserved for dignitaries who had yet to arrive. A closed casket rested in the crossing, surrounded by portraits, pictures, flowers, and framed articles.

Ford continued to chat with her companion while scanning the crowd, searching for faces she'd recognize. She saw a few—ambassadors, legislators, a commissioner to Hong Kong. She resisted the urge to name-drop, fearful of exposing more than she should. The less Deputy Ambassador Reznik knew about her, the better.

Ji-woo Song slipped into the crowd entering the church. Carrying an umbrella and wearing a tailored suit with a jacket widened to accommodate her shoulder holster and 10 mm semiautomatic, she did her best to blend in. If drawn into a conversation, she hid her southern accent, sounding closer to what people expected from Korean-American stereotypes. As she walked, she looked for the others, her precious *buqu*. Three had been assigned to this dawning moment, each given a different mission objective, each with a critical role to fill as part of a successful outcome.

She identified the Secret Service agents working the crowd. At a semi-private memorial service like this, undercover agents might be mingling as well. Barricades blocked off an entire section of O Street between 35th to 34th to establish a buffer for several diplomatic SUVs.

At the church's entrance, they were checking invitations. She offered hers, and was allowed inside. After passing through a simple security check—a bag check, no metal detector—she entered the chapel and chose a seat at the end of a pew, six rows back from special guests and dignitaries. She recognized faces that most people wouldn't: ambassadors from Japan, Taiwan, the Philippines, Australia, the United Kingdom, Hong Kong, and pro-democracy Hong Kong business leaders. Officially, the People's Republic of China sent no representation since Communist China had considered Ambassador Peter Tang a threat. China's not-so-subtle dig at the memorial service of an enemy was to send instead Tung Tsang, the Commissioner of the Ministry of Foreign Affairs of the People's Republic of China in the Hong Kong Special Administrative Region.

She scrutinized security teams on the boundaries of the sanctuary: Secret Service and international security details for China, South Korea, and Taiwan. Eighteen total. A mix of men and women. All presumed armed and equipped with earpieces for communication.

Before anything could move forward, they'd need to be dealt with.

Waiting for the service to start, Ji-woo delicately fidgeted with her wig. She was completely unaccustomed to the feeling, and hadn't figured on it being itchy on her scalp. Disguise had not been part of her early plans.

Mears checked his watch. Noon. A church bell rang to signal the start of the memorial service.

It was time.

Stepping into a breezeway, Mears and the Secretary left the rectory first, followed by Ambassador Peter Tang's family. "Nimrod" by Edward Elgar played on speakers. Escorts guided them to designated seats. Tang's family sat in the first row. Mears looked around to recognize faces of diplomats and business leaders who'd come to pay their respects. He spotted an odd attendee, considering Tang's stance on Asia—China's Commissioner to Hong Kong, Tung Tsang. He nodded to acknowledge those in attendance and took his seat.

He leaned close to the Secretary. "Good attendance."

The Secretary smiled thinly. "Yes, nice crowd."

"Adagio for Strings" by Samuel Barber ended the processional music. Nervously, Mears checked his watch not knowing what would happen only that something would happen.

A lector asked people to silence their phones. A priest began the service with a prayer. Before the service turned traditional, an opening speaker spoke of Tang's accomplishments, his work for a greater Asia, how the Ambassador sought peace and independence for Taiwan, and an official end to the Korean War rather than a 1953 truce. A spiritual man filled with conviction, Tang had led the criticism of China's violent incursion into Hong Kong while standing out front the U.S. Consulate for Hong Kong and Macau. After the short moment of praise, the opening speaker turned the service over to the church.

Mears' cell phone vibrated. He glanced at an incoming text message.

ADVANCED BIOCORE RAIDED BY THE FBI.

Mears cursed beneath his breath.

Kate patrolled the crowds until she was one of the few standing outside the church. After hearing the classical music start the service, she flashed her badge at security and entered the narthex. Lingering outside the doors of the main chapel, she studied the crowd, noticing nothing out of place. The security presence was hard to miss. Secret Service and foreign security teams stood around the sanctuary and faced the crowd, paying almost no attention to the actual service itself.

In her mind, she sensed it was essential to stay vigilant, alert.

Something was about to happen, although such a notion couldn't be substantiated.

Outside, diagonally across O Street, a Chinese sniper ignored the rain and climbed up the exterior of Alumni House to the roof. Childhood gymnastics skills proved valuable later in life. He was one of thousands of children who'd been accepted into sports-centered, government-funded boarding schools. Competition for Olympics spots was fierce. Most children washed out by the time they were ten. He made it to fourteen before an injury crushed his dreams of being a Chinese Olympian. But his gymnastics and an aptitude for science caught the eye of the Chinese Communist Party, who'd recruited him into industrial espionage. Gymnastics might not have led to the Olympics, but they had given him a career as a consulate spy, then as a *buqu* soldier.

On the roof, the sniper used a dormer as shelter. From a scabbard strapped to his back, he removed a Barrett MRAD .300 magnum rifle and slid a quick-attaching suppressor over the weapon's muzzle brake. He took aim and fired, dropping the furthest of the Secret Service sharpshooters. The weapon's discharge snapped a damp echo over the street below. Without wasted movement, he pivoted and sighted his next shot. He clicked the trigger. Another dampened retort snapped out. The closest of the sharpshooters fell to the street.

Below, he could hear agents shouting out orders.

Seconds counted now.

In the distance, an oncoming rumble grew louder.

He recognized the cue. A black trash truck barreled down O Street. He sighted the vehicle to confirm that no driver sat behind the 35-ton truck's steering wheel. The battering ram was filled with 55-gallon drums of ammonium nitrate and kerosene. Diesel engines roared. The vehicle picked up speed. Thundering down the road, it stormed unimpeded at the parked motorcade outside the church's rectory.

By the time Secret Service recognized the threat, it was too late.

The truck barreled through cars and barricades.

Below, shots were fired in last-second desperation.

The Chinese sniper ducked behind a chimney stack, braced himself, and covered his ears with his hands.

The intense explosion rocked the building. His grip on the chimney slipped and he started skidding down the sloped roof. Using a carabiner as a lasso, he hooked a vent stack. The rope he held went taut just as his feet reached the edge of the roof. Even though he was a block away, heat from the swelling fireball flushed his face. He could hear secondary explosions as motorcade cars erupted.

He peered down. The entire block looked like a war zone. Where flames did not obscure his view, he could see bodies strewn about.

Seated, Mears dropped his phone and ducked just as an explosion blasted the church, so forceful that chandeliers broke away from the ceiling. Columns buckled. Shards of stained glass showered the sanctuary. Mears gasped a breath and looked at the Secretary. The man's tired face was tranquil, as if he alone stood in the quiet of the storm's eye. Screams and panic rose from the attendees. Where north windows once existed, bellowing flames and fire licked the building.

Secret Service agents sprang into action, seizing him and the Secretary, dragging them into the main aisle while pushing down others to clear a path out of the church.

Debra Ford was nearly thrown from her seat. The massive eruption outside the church consumed the sanctuary, fracturing walls and buckling columns. Fragments of stained glass sprayed everywhere. Fire and flames took hold where windows had hung. Once the explosion's brutal first wave passed, attendees were screaming in panic. Beneath the balcony, she spotted Secret Service agents and security details jumping into action.

Being relegated to the status of an observer was disconcerting, but this moment wasn't hers. Nevertheless, she struggled with her role.

Rising from a cowering crowd, a man and a woman seated in different locations sprinted to the front of the church, both firing handguns. Security teams caught between rescue and protection obligations were gunned down. The strike took out the closest security.

The Secretary of State stood and faced an assailant, a woman. She swung around and fired. A bullet struck him mid-sternum. The Secretary staggered. The female assassin fired again, and the old man finally buckled in the knees and slumped into a pew.

A hail of gunfire echoed through the church ensued as the male attacker finished off the remaining security teams, regardless of representative nation. Brutal chaos ensued. Empty magazines were discarded, new ones inserted. People caught in the firefight scurried for their lives. The male assassin pressed his attack. His aggression proved fatal when he passed an unchecked pew. A wounded security agent fought his way off the floor and shot the assassin dead as he walked past.

The remaining attacker, the female assassin, focused on the Vice President.

Kate opened her eyes. Her ears were ringing. An explosion had knocked her to the floor as she stood outside the sanctuary's doors. Stars flooded her vision as the world around her winked in and out. Secondary explosions made her cringe.

Her mind flashed over with horror-filled flashbacks.

Fire. Destruction. Death. Evil.

The sounds of gunshots interrupted the flashbacks, real-time events overriding the trauma of the past.

Gasping for breath, she fought back lightheadedness by taking in more air. Slowly, she got to her feet. Screaming people with panicked faces launched themselves into the narthex.

Kate clutched the door jamb, gathered herself, then bolted headlong into the church.

From the balcony, Debra Ford shoved the Deputy Ambassador down. "Stay out of sight," she said.

As the scene unfolded below, she noticed that the plans had deviated from original mission objectives. Having the female assassin focus on the Vice President wasn't part of the plan. He was a Founder and not to be harmed.

Only one person could have altered Prosperity's script: Ji-woo Song.

Ford now understood her role: the designated backup, the "break glass in emergency" observer, a reinforcement in case Ji-woo and her *buqu* had failed. But Ji-woo hadn't failed in her mission, she was executing a coup. The Founder must've decided to use the chaos to consolidate power and conspired to eliminate the others. Ji-woo had programmed her *buqu* to eliminate all the Founders attending the memorial service.

Ford knew she'd be on that list, too.

Retrieving a Glock that she'd smuggled into the church, Ford watched a woman storm the church, firing her pistol at the ceiling.

FBI Special Agent Katherine Morgan yelled, "Down! Now!"

People ducked out of her way. She took aim.

The female assassin standing over the Vice President readied her shot.

Morgan fired consecutive rounds. One bullet made contact, knocking the assassin off balance. Refusing to go down, the assassin swung around. The FBI agent kept charging, unwavering in her assault.

They exchanged shots. The female assassin tumbled into a pew, struck in the face.

On the same side of the sanctuary, Ji-woo Song rose, holding a gun.

Taking aim, she shouted, "Morgan, watch out!"

Both the FBI agent and Ji-woo Song looked up.

Ji-woo fired at Morgan, striking her with a bullet.

Ford fired at Ji-woo as the woman rolled away from the barrage of bullets. Ford knew her handgun's accuracy decreased as distance increased. She was more likely to kill innocent people than hit her intended target.

It was time to "break glass" and join the fray. She bolted for the closest set of stairs.

95

CHOICES FOR THE MOMENT

Outside on rooftops, the Chinese sniper ignored the fiery inferno and smoke that consumed an entire block on O Street. Smoke churned in the rain-laden air. Secret Service agents and others were down. Screams and cries for help pierced the air. People scurried into the streets.

From his scabbard, the sniper retrieved a second weapon. He threaded a long tube over a rifle-like cannon and in inserted a rope-tied collapsible grappling hook. Taking aim, he targeted the roof-mounted air conditioning units on the student apartment complex across the street. He fired. The hook streaked across a sixty-five foot expanse with a thunderous roar and buried itself into the mechanical unit. Reeling the rope taut, the assassin anchored it on a chimney stack. He clipped a self-powered wheel onto the rope. After collecting his gear, he zipped across the street while hanging below the rope.

Peripherally, he saw the smoke thicken. Cars buildings were on fire. Debris and panicked people were everywhere. The quiet college neighborhood had become a war zone.

Heat from the growing fireball washed over him as he eyed his landing.

Before the ride ended, he dropped onto the roof. Wasting no time, he stowed his weapons in his scabbard and ran along the rooftops, jumping the gaps between buildings. Sprinting to the last building on the block, he kept his speed up and leapt, using a parkour technique to clear the two-car width gap. Toes—by mere inches—found the firmness of the last roof. Using his momentum, he somersaulted forward.

Working his way to the peak of the roof, he surveyed the wet streetscape below. Chaos. Screaming. Shouting. Faces etched with terror. He swept his gaze to where he suspected the last Secret Service sharpshooter might be. Not disappointed, he found his target scoping people at the intersection of N and 36th Streets, scanning for threats. Since the man was focused on the street, he never looked up.

Using an exhaust fan for stability, the sniper removed his rifle and slid a finger over the trigger. Sights homed in on his target. A quick snap of a finger. Even silenced, his rifle snapped out an unmistakable crackle. The sharpshooter on the other roof dropped instantly.

Kate crumpled to the floor, cringing and grunting in pain, her shooting hand numb, tingling. Leaning against a pew, seconds doubled and seemed to stretch out. Her sluggish mind became a slave to time. Turning her head, she saw that a bullet had struck her shoulder. Pain shrieked through it. A patch of blood spread and her arm refused to move.

She could hear people screaming and see smoke drift into the church.

Further down the central aisle, a woman was sprawled across white marbled floors in a pool of blood. The assassin she'd killed. Blinking, Kate saw that her Glock lay just beyond working fingertips. Looking sideways down the length of a pew, she saw the Vice President crouched low. Behind him, the Secretary slumped dead in his seat. She picked on a set of panicked faces watching her, hoping she'd do something heroic.

Pain fed an increasing lightheadedness. She felt unnatural, cold.

Her mind whispered, *Look up.*

Looking past a debris-covered casket, she saw a cross on the back wall, with a sunburst at its center.

God helps those who help themselves.

Not a cliché. A reminder. Other assailants still lurked about. Survival required that she keep moving.

Fighting back the pain, she reached for her Glock with her working hand. Fingers wrapped around its grip.

✦ ✦

Ji-woo stepped into the side aisle and searched for the shot FBI agent or any other security teams who might put up resistance. Bodies were down everywhere.

The FBI agent was not in sight. Perhaps dead. Or not.

Two of her *buqu* were among the dead.

Further away, people ran out building exits. Closer to her, people hunkered down, trapped with nowhere to run. With immediate threats suppressed, she pressed ahead, passing the rows of pews and sighting down dignitaries with her semiautomatic pistol. Heads looked down in fear.

She pivoted to ensure no one snuck up behind her.

Her mission wasn't over, not yet.

Two pews up, she found her first target, the Taiwanese ambassador. The man raised his hands to protect himself. Not hesitating, she fired multiple shots. They echoed inside the already battered sanctuary.

A row up, her last target, the Chinese Commissioner for Hong Kong, lunged. Pivoting, she sidestepped his feeble assault and knocked him off balance. The Commissioner tumbled and fell against the white marble floors. In a panic, he slid up a shirtsleeve to expose a tattoo—nine unified rings.

His lips moved without sound. "One Democratic Asia."

Ji-woo responded by pulling the trigger of her weapon, killing the Founder, her competition, instantly.

Kate couldn't stand hearing gunshots resonate throughout the church. Summoning her remaining strength, she rose on trembling legs and used a pew to steady her balance. Her breath hissed between parted lips, her mind struggling to stay current with time. Raising her Glock in her non-gun hand, she knew she had little or no chance of taking down the last assassin. Nonetheless, she aligned the rear and front sights and trained her weapon on the killer.

A presence inside her spoke: *Do Not Harm.*

Overriding that lunacy, Kate pulled the trigger.

Her pistol roared.

The shot missed wildly. High, luckily, not into pews where other people sought refuge. Before the assassin could react, she fired more shots, all high and wide.

The assassin ducked behind the pews, leaving Kate to make a choice: continue the shootout, in which she'd likely die, or get the Vice President out of harm's way, abandoning innocent people to face their fates with the last assassin.

Impossible choice.

Debra Ford fought her way into the chapel, swimming upstream as people frantically escaped.

Stepping into the sanctuary, she spotted Ji-woo Song lurking behind pews, making her way to the front of the church where she could spring an ambush. In the middle of the church, a ragged and wavering Katherine Morgan aimed a pistol in Ji-woo's general direction.

Ford took long strides and aimed her semiautomatic pistol.

People herding toward the exits parted like the sea in *Exodus*, giving her a clear view.

Ford fired repeated shots.

Kate's vision started to spin. From the corner of her eye, she saw a ghost break from a storm of bodies—a woman, aiming a handgun, not at her, but elsewhere.

A shot rang out, cracking like thunder.

"Morgan, leave now!" the woman shouted as strode into the church, firing her weapon.

Movement flashed where Kate was aiming her semiautomatic. The Asian woman who'd shot her fled to a side door.

Disoriented, Kate held her fire. A miss could kill innocent people. Ignoring the fleeing assassin, she turned to her guardian angel—a stranger—the woman who'd shouted at her from the church's balcony. Vaguely, the woman looked familiar, like a diffused reflection off the surface of a pond, a mirrored image bouncing off another mirror.

That reflection was cold, without warmth, yet revealing.

What she saw was a distorted version of herself, blended into the features of the woman who'd stepped out of the noise into the tiniest sliver of clarity.

Grimacing in pain, Kate whipped around to check on the Vice President. He understood what she was thinking.

It was time to leave.

96

MINUTES OUT

Minutes North of Washington, DC

As the helicopter sped to DC, Parker listened to what chatter he was permitted to hear over his headphones. The weather had turned foul just after liftoff, as the pilot had predicted. Dark clouds hunkered down on the east coast, forcing the helicopter to drop in altitude. Rain washed aircraft windows in a sideways manner.

Something had happened.

The Director switched over to a secured line and took an incoming call. The man's solemn expression told him the news was devastating. He relayed a barrage of orders and switched over his comms.

"There's been a bombing, an attack," the Director said, turning toward the ADIC. "Secret Service is down. No word on the Vice President or the Secretary of State. MPDC is arriving now. Hostage Rescue is three minutes out."

Parker wrung his hands and looked down at his shoes, thinking of nothing but Kate. He'd made decisions that created separation, instead of welcoming her back into his life without reservation or commitment or explanation.

Everything between them—the baggage of their lives, their careers, his research and her duties—weighed heavily on him. Kate was simply doing her job, and he couldn't drive out a hunch, an instinct, that something was wrong.

Kate was in trouble. And he couldn't get to Georgetown fast enough.

97

SPLIT SECOND DECISIONS

Ji-woo dodged the hail of gunfire streaming her way. Debra Ford's skills outmatched hers, it was clear. Sprinting for the church's transept, Ji-woo cleared a door as bullets peppered walls and doorframes behind her.

The small courtyard that she found herself in was fenced to the south. To the west, a short wrought iron fence bridged a gap between buildings. A ball of orange and black churned in the low hanging clouds on the other side of the church. Without an umbrella's protection, rain pelted her face.

She hopped over the wrought iron, dropped down to the sidewalk at street level, and blended into the crowds.

Kate tried not to show the extent of the pain she felt as she led the Vice President past a debris-covered casket, past downed Secret

Service agents and other international security teams. Bodies were everywhere. Glass crunched beneath their shoes. Outside, a fiery glow illuminated the smoke consumed the church's north end, the place where she'd earlier seen the Vice President's and Secretary's motorcades. Instincts told her to avoid that direction.

Behind her Glock, she cleared a chancel door connecting the sanctuary to an attached building. Another door was marked Chapel of Saint Ignatius Loyola, one of many saints she hadn't known existed. Guardian angels frequenting the Holy Trinity seemed in short supply.

Trudging down hallways, her legs felt heavier. Her thoughts challenged her to keep going, keep the Vice President alive, get him somewhere safe.

The long parish hallway was empty.

The Vice President kept a step behind as they spotted an exit out of the building.

Debra Ford decided against pursuing Ji-woo into the courtyard, and perhaps walking into a trap. Staking out the church in advance had given her a good sense of the building's layout. Backtracking, she pushed her way into people herding in a common direction, like mindless lemmings clogging the exits.

Through the crowd, she spotted the Deputy Ambassador from Ukraine. She liked Irene Reznik, but resisted the compassionate urge to call out and provide safer escape directions.

Forcefully, Ford shuffled through the crowd and broke out into the rain. Panicked and injured people were everywhere. Debris filled the wet streets. Ford ignored the rain and ducked to her left, sprinting toward N Street with her Glock in hand.

At the intersection, Ford kept her head on a swivel and searched for targets.

If Ji-woo lingered behind, she'd be lying in wait, anxious to com plete unfinished business—eliminate the remaining two Founders in attendance.

Removing her wig and cap, Ji-woo cast both to the street and walked with the dispersing crowd. Pulling up her collar, she had changed her appearance in seconds. Rain splashing against her scalp invigo rated her. What couldn't be accomplished at Holy Trinity, would be dealt with later. After all, she possessed a *buqu* army to champion the beginning of Prosperity and eliminate any remaining Founders. There could only be one Yellow Dragon as the leader on One Asia.

In the distance, sirens wailed and lights flashed as the police arrived from the east.

Ji-woo stepped to the curb, making sure her 10 mm semiau tomatic was within easy reach beneath her jacket. Drifting to the church's south exit, she staked out a position beneath leafless maple trees.

The rain felt almost non-existent to the Chinese assassin after he'd moved to where he'd killed the last Secret Service sharpshooter. This set of rooftops gave him an unobstructed view of N Street. He'd ac tually had time to rummage through the dead agent's gear bag and collect another weapon, adding to his firepower.

Below, the street was pure chaos, people scurrying out of the church, screaming and crying. To the north, the explosion's fireball still raged, its combustible gels and kerosene mix continuing to rage unaffected by the rain, adding a glow to the thick clouds above.

From his vantage point, he tracked a Founder through his ri fle's scope—the only Founder he'd sworn an allegiance to. He was responsible for keeping her alive. She discarded a wig, flip up her jacket collar, stood by a church exit beneath a small spread of barren trees.

The attack had unfolded as expected, although he had hoped to see two *buqu* standing beside her. Something must've deviated from that plan.

That left him as the Yellow Dragon's sole protector.

Local police had begun to arrive. Inevitable. Predictable. He could hear the sirens and see multiple sets of flashing lights drawing closer. Behind this wave of first responders would be SWAT and counterterrorism teams. He glanced at his wristwatch, estimating that better armed reinforcements would arrive in minutes.

He moved his scope off of the Founder and surveyed the remaining streetscape.

A new target came into view, darting through the crowd. The woman came toward his position—armed with a handgun—a Founder he was not sworn to protect. Quite the opposite, one he had been charged with killing if the opportunity presented itself.

The fast-moving, packed together crowd blocked a clean shot. All he needed was patience. An opening would materialize when people reached the intersection and had room to spread out.

His finger on the rifle's trigger.

Kate shook her head as lightheadedness threatened to overtake her. Pain and exhaustion narrowed her reality, making it difficult to see anything outside her line of sight. The exit door to N Street was no more than twenty feet away. The Vice President held her up for a moment to look into her eyes, size her up.

In the distance, sirens wailed.

She sensed what he was thinking. "We're not splitting up, Mr. Vice President." Her throat felt dry, raspy. "We're sticking together until I hand you off."

"Agent, you have nothing else to prove. Not to me."

He slipped a shoulder under her good arm and they walked toward the exit.

Ji-woo saw police cars screech to a stop beyond the barricades. Officers started rushing down N Street, heading straight at her. She pivoted to shelter her body behind a tree trunk, readying herself to take split second action.

Debra Ford reached the intersection of N and 36th and the crowd around her thinned. The advancing sound of helicopters coming in low off the Potomac caused her to look up. FBI agents holding assault rifles sat in the door openings of three Blackhawks.

Squinting in the rain, she spotted a sniper on a rooftop, his long gun sighting her down.

Ford rolled left as a shot fired, its muted snap telling her that a suppressor had been used.

More shots followed. People started screaming and scurrying in every direction. Ford scampered to her feet and sprinted down N Street in a zigzag path, aware that an open street offered no shelter.

The sniper pulled the trigger a second late, giving his prey a slight advantage. Firing repeatedly, he knew it was only a matter of time before he hit the woman. Down below, pandemonium spread as people, unaware of where the shots were coming from, fled in every direction. He ignored the thrush of whirling blades above him, keeping his concentrating on the woman he tracked in his sights.

The helicopters drew closer, and he could almost feel the thumping chop of wet air center on him.

For a split second, he broke his gaze off his target. Above, aircraft spun sideways to show armed agents in tactical gear filling the aircraft's openings. Weapons aimed.

Rolling onto his back, he fired on the helicopters. The retaliating response left no time to consider the barrage of bullets coming his way.

The Chinese assassin felt nothing, barely even the first bullet strike.

Lifeless, he collapsed and fell still.

Ji-woo understood what the arrival of the helicopters meant.

Time was up.

With her coup exposed, the remaining Founders would fiercely oppose any additional attempts to consolidate power. But she still had an army of *buqu*, soldiers to champion future assaults against those who opposed her. As her nation's Yellow Dragon, the throne to her destiny was hers alone to seize by any means necessary.

She'd come around to the church's south-side, hoping to set a trap for the Vice President of the United States. The calculated guess locked down the most logical exit, even though the group of buildings had lesser-known ways out.

Suppressed shots sounded from a rooftop as a *buqu* sniper worked to eliminate a threat. Cocking her head, she saw Debra Ford zigzagging to avoid being gunned down in the street. Ford was coming straight at her.

The gunfire paused as helicopters arrived overhead. She couldn't identify the branch of law enforcement. It didn't matter. A swift volley of shooting left no doubt who'd prevailed. Ropes dropped out of a helicopter and counterterrorism forces rappelled onto a roof.

Ji-woo formed a new plan in her mind: wait for the first wave of police officers to pass then head to the canal and get to a rented safe house.

As she hunkered against the tree trunk, a nearby door swung open.

The FBI agent that she'd shot stepped out into the rain, helped by the Vice President.

Ji-woo acted on instinct, targeting the Vice President with her pistol.

The man before her let the agent he supported fall to the sidewalk, giving her a clean, unobstructed shot. His eyes carried a strange mixture of distain and bafflement.

A shot rang out.

Ji-woo felt a bullet puncture her side, causing her to buckle at the waist. Pain radiated through her body. She fought to remain standing and clutched the bark of the tree for a handhold with her free hand. Gritting her teeth, she pivoted to aim her semiautomatic at the approaching shooter.

In the rain, charging, Debra Ford did not waver, the barrel of her weapon locked onto its target. Ji-woo saw a muzzle flash, then heard a retort.

A searing bluntness caused each nerve in her body to boil with fire. Blood flooded into her throat, filling her mouth. Muscles lost their strength. The weapon she held fell to the ground. Slumping against the tree, Ji-woo couldn't catch a breath, even lift her chin. Crumpling onto a small patch of winter barren grass below the tree, it was all Ji-woo could do to look in a single direction. On her back, she tasted the wetness, the saltiness of blood as rain splattered her face. An adagio coldness consumed her, announcing the callous arrival of death. As cold washed through her body, Ji-woo lost all ability to feel pain.

The face of a Founder moved over her and blocked out the rain.

Debra Ford eyes projected disappointment.

People started yelling and whirl of movement surrounded her.

Ford dropped her weapon, put her hands behind her head, and knelt.

A police officer stood above Ji-woo, his weapon thrust into her face.

"Assassin," someone said. It took her a moment to recognize that the Vice President had spoken. "She was one of the killers in the church."

Her peripheral vision caught sight of movement, but no one tended to her.

Ji-woo coughed. More blood bubbled into her throat.

The childhood stories of the Yellow Dragon's glorious return, her chance at leading a new nation, began to fade in her mind. Prosperity, a chance to unify all Asian people as a new commonwealth under One Asia, would've drawn on the greatest of histories, legacies, heritage, and peoples. Now that sentiment was the dimmest star in the darkest of night skies.

Ji-woo's vision blurred and she no longer felt the chill of death.

Kate struggled to take in what was happening. The world around her was composed of blurred shapes. Obscure, fractured figures came and went. The Vice President sat beside her, his hands cradling her head.

She heard a barrage of shouts and orders, but couldn't comprehend a single word.

"Hang in there, Agent," Mears said, breaking through the muted sounds around her. "Paramedics are coming."

In the FBI chopper, Parker listened to the Director bark a string of orders.

"Don't circle! Put us down!" the Director shouted.

Looking out the rain-slicked windows, parts of Georgetown looked like a warzone. An entire city block was consumed in the aftereffects of a dying fireball. Cars and buildings were on fire. Despite the rain, thick smoke churned in the air. What seemed like hundreds of first responders had converged on the scene. Emergency lights flashed everywhere. In the rain, people were scattered around the church. Bodies lay in the streets. Attack helicopters circled.

The helicopter descended into a gated set of commons, and it took him a moment to realize that the aircraft had touched down inside the front gate of Georgetown University, two blocks west of the church.

When skids found grass, the Director was the first one out, followed by his Deputy and accompanying agents. Parker followed their lead, running in the direction of a fireball.

Barricades had been erected to hold back the increasing throng of onlookers. Parker stayed close to his escort party. They headed down a street in front of large church. Officers had secured the scene. Debris from the explosion was scattered everywhere. He could see cracks in the church's white columns. Bodies lay covered by jackets and coats. Medics tended to the wounded.

Another block up, they turned. More roadblocks. Light bars from police vehicles flashed. A gurney was being wheeled to an ambulance.

Parker saw wet, dark brown hair and his heart stopped.

An officer intercepted him.

He pointed. "I'm with them. Ask the Director."

"Let him through," the Director said, stopping beside the gurney. "How is she?"

"GSW. She needs an ER," a paramedic said.

"Take her to George Washington," the Director said.

"MedStar Georgetown is closer."

The Director wiped rain from his face and shot the paramedic a hardened look. "George Washington. Not negotiable."

Parker caught up with the gurney. "I want to go with Kate."

The Director frowned and shook his head. "Don't think so, Doc."

Someone standing nearby caught their attention—the Vice President of the United States, Richard Mears, holding an umbrella. Secret Service agents flanked him. The man's jacket was drenched in a mixture of blood and water. A few feet away lay a body covered by a sheet.

Mears nodded solemnly.

"Okay, Doc, go ahead," the Director said.

Parker wasted no time climbing into the ambulance. Doors shut behind him. The paramedics, one at her head and one at her feet, threw him unreceptive glares.

Parker offered a thin smile, his focus solely on unconscious Kate who was oblivious to his presence.

The ambulance lurched forward. Sirens chirped and screamed as the vehicle sped away.

He touched Kate's leg and gave paramedics space to tend to their patient, as much as a crowded ambulance permitted. He soaked up as much of her medical details as possible. Single gunshot wound. Right shoulder. Vitals were stable. Leads were pasted to her chest. Nasal cannula touched the bottom of her nose. A blood-soaked compress bandaged her right shoulder. No other injuries were visible.

Parker studied the stillness of her face. Her normal skin hues had faded. Not unusual for what she'd gone through. The road ahead for her would be a long one. Gunshots were violent piercing wounds. She'd have muscle, bone damage, blood clots. Months of rehab, barring infection, setbacks, or complications. At least she hadn't taken the bullet inches over, mid-sternum, which would have dramatically complicated things and might have been fatal.

If there was any luck in getting shot in the torso, Kate had cashed in on that.

Mears waited for the Director to turn away from the ambulance after it cleared the perimeter. The man was an agent's Director, less bureaucrat and more beat cop, investigator, a leader who cared about the people who worked beneath him.

Mears pointed to the sheet-covered body on the ground. The Director and ADIC knelt. The sheet was reeled back to expose a face: Ji-woo Song.

Mears passed off his umbrella to the ADIC and reentered the church, two Secret Service Agents right beside him. His wet shoes clicked on the tiled floors. Behind him he heard the Director follow.

98

HOSPITAL BOUND

In the ambulance, Parker studied Kate's readings on the vital signs monitor.

Squawks and chirps and the full out blaring of sirens accompanied the jostling ride and took him back to med school, when he'd done a rotation with paramedics in Denver while he finished up his residency at the University of Colorado.

He continued to hold Kate's foot since no hand was available. Her expressionless face and wrapped shoulder revealed the frailty of the human form, a biological machine with no purpose other than to carry the mind. History had proven that a human's stream of consciousness was the most dangerous substance on the planet, capable of executing the grandest of atrocities without exhibiting the slightest bit remorse or sorrow.

He thought of the mind's metaphysical dualism: two irreconcilable realities, good and evil. In absolute terms, Richards' ambitions had few boundaries. Parker recognized that his own presence had emboldened Richards to take extreme actions. He himself had bartered ideals and the lives of others to achieve his own victories—becoming a paler darkness contrasting Richards. Months ago, he should've told Kate no and refused to help the FBI and NSA. If he'd done that, the neurological singularity wouldn't exist, and Kate wouldn't have ever been shot.

When the ambulance stopped, doors swung open to reveal waiting ER staff.

The gurney was pulled out and sped into GW's Level 1 Trauma Center. He walked with her into the hospital, his hand not leaving her foot.

A staff member held him up. "Sir, you're going to have to wait in the lobby."

"I'm a doctor," he said, more as reflex than anything else.

"Are you family?"

He didn't know what he was: lover, friend, occasional partner?

"We're colleagues, close friends," Parker said as ER doors closed. Through windows, doctors and nurses jumped into action. He'd been through similar exercises, albeit on the other side during medical school and residency rotations.

Helpless, his eyes teared up. They lifted her from the gurney and placed her on a table. He knew by reputation that GW's staff was some of the best at what they did. He wiped his eyes and sniffled.

"As a physician, you know we need to do our jobs. Come on, come with me." The ER tech guided him past a pair of doors and into a family waiting, separate from the ER's lobby. "Is there anyone we should call for her?"

Another question that he didn't know the answer to. Kate's parents had passed like his. No siblings. No close relatives. He thought of Jack Wright, her old flame, who might be in that category.

"No." Parker collapsed into a seat in the empty waiting room.

"Let us know if we can get you anything. I'll have a doctor provide an update when possible." The ER tech badged back into the trauma center, then held up at the door. "What kind of doctor?"

"Neurologist." He took a long breath. "From Princeton."

A nod was given before the tech left. "Someone will be out in a little while."

99

THE CHAPEL

Holy Trinity Catholic Church, Georgetown, Washington, DC

In the Chapel of Saint Ignatius, Debra Ford sat handcuffed to a chair, hands and ankles cuffed independently. The FBI had gone to great lengths to secure her in such a manner as to make escape impossible. The rectangular chapel had three rows of chairs on each long end facing a lectern and communion table with a pair of tall candles. An area rug covered the center of the floor. The room's only windows were behind her. Two FBI officers in tactical gear and holding semiautomatic rifles stood at the doors.

Everything she'd possessed, found through a body search, filled a wicker tithe basket, including her semiautomatic, shoes, fake Ukrainian passport, and the skin patch on her side that hid a polycarbonate handcuff key.

The Vice President of the United States and the Director of the FBI entered. The Director asked the two agents guarding her to step outside. The men kept their distance, staying on their side of the room.

Mears grinned. "This is an unusual look for you, Debra."

She let the Founder have his jab. "Is she alive?"

Mears nodded. "We don't have any updates yet." He exhaled noisily. "It's hard for me to say this. You saved our lives."

"I guess you're not entirely a dick, Dick." She laughed, anticipating how an off-the-record conversation might go. "I didn't want Morgan to die. You were... a consolation prize."

The Director crossed his arms. "Sounds like you're getting sentimental."

Ford laughed again. "Don't spread rumors. I would've let Ji-woo Song kill Dick, just not her." She winked. "Of course, we're coming up on an election year. Maybe the voters will do what Song couldn't."

"Ouch, Mr. Vice President," the Director said. "That might have hurt more than getting shot."

Mears smiled thinly. "Oh, Princess, what to do with you?"

"You know I hate that nickname?"

Mears smile broadened. "Yes, I do."

Silence hung in the air for a long moment.

"Truce?" Ford finally asked, knowing that the Vice President couldn't risk having the FBI bring her to trial for her husband's murder, his girlfriend's, and the former Deputy Director of the FBI. A Founder of the Ring of Eight and a former State Department spy had a lot of secrets that needed to remain secret. And Richard Mears was no killer, rather a politician. What Mears contemplated was how to get rid of her, silently, permanently, without evidence or blowback. It served her little purpose not to find equitable middle ground.

The two men exchanged looks.

The Vice President spoke. "I don't know how that would work in our current state of affairs."

The Director took a seat opposite her across the room. "These soldiers or spies or whatever Dr. Ji-woo Song called them—without a leader, who will they follow?"

She ignored the question and asked her own. "Where's Stewart Richards?"

The Director shook his head. "Dead."

"Survivable dead, or just dead?"

"Dead, dead."

Ford frowned. "That's unfortunate."

"How many are there?" the Director asked.

Ford shrugged. "How many were killed today?"

"Three plus Song."

"Eighteen total, including Song. Four adopted, Korean-born Americans. Fourteen Chinese nationals."

The Director wrung his hands together. "What's their mission?"

"Don't know. That was outside my purview. But I bet there's one person who can figure that out. Where's Thomas Parker?"

"He went with Morgan to the hospital."

She looked at Mears. "In the church, I tried to warn her, but I'm not sure she recognized me."

Mears understood the significance of that statement even when the Director didn't. The two men huddled and whispered a brief exchange.

The Director shot her a glare. "Did you hurt or injure any of our people today?"

"Not one."

From the wicker basket, the Director retrieved her skin patch, which concealed an embedded handcuff key. Separating its latex layers, he pulled out the key and unlocked the handcuffs on one wrist. He set the key on her lap, put her shoes on the floor, and collected the wicker basket.

"A Deputy Ambassador to Ukraine sat beside me during the service," she said.

The Director nodded thoughtfully. "We'll talk to her."

Ford understood that to mean that the FBI would intimidate the woman to make sure she talked with no one, nor became the source of any news leaks.

Mears nodded his thanks and left the chapel.

The Director checked his wristwatch. "We're changing out a rotation. You get one minute. Go down the hall. Exit the Parish Center. East side. You already know this, but don't return to your Maryland residence. Perhaps winter someplace warm where you can work on your tan."

The Director took the wicker basket with the remainder of her belongings and left.

Ford had her three remaining handcuffs off in thirty seconds. She grabbed her shoes and headed out of the chapel barefoot, leaving through a door opposite to the one her companions had used. Assuming no shoot-to-kill order had been given, she took the Director's cues literally. The Parish Center was the church office. An east-side door provided a way out of the building.

She put on her shoes in a courtyard and walked out to O Street. Rain fell from a cloud-laden sky, soaking her instantly. The throng of first responders filling the street was impressive. Lights flashed from police cars and fire trucks. Barricades cordoned off the public. Helicopters still circled above.

East was not one of her planned escape routes, but the hall pass was acceptable. After a block, Ford turned north to reach Reservoir Road, which offered a straight shot to the hiking trails of the heavily wooded Glover-Archbold Park. The escape route through the national park had no surveillance cameras, no law enforcement, with the exception of a few symbolic park rangers who were meant to keep honest people honest.

During her stroll in the rain, without an umbrella, she kept her head down. Elongating her strides, Debra Ford, the rainy day walker, focused on putting distance between her and Georgetown. She disappeared on a beaten-down trail and headed north, knowing a change of clothes awaited her in an escape vehicle in Battery Kemble Park.

100
WAITING FOR NEWS

George Washington University Hospital, Washington, DC

Parker moved waiting rooms when Kate went into surgery. The initial diagnosis from the trauma center's surgeon on-call was positive, but he wouldn't know more until the surgery finished. News had spread that Kate was an FBI Agent, and the staff treated her like patient royalty. Sitting alone, he read a year-old version of *Consumer Reports* with a story that promised "The Best Mattress for You." He didn't know how families did it, sitting around waiting for news on their loved ones and reading outdated magazines.

"So you're Thomas Parker?" a man said from an open doorway.

Parker glanced up. He did his best not to appraise the man. Wheelchair. Hospital gown. Socks, no shoes. Handsome in a rugged way, with a suave layer of weekly stubble.

"You must be Jack," he said, putting on his best smile. The last time he'd seen Jack was at Princeton, where the man had taken point-blank gunshots to the chest. Nonsurvivable wounds. Jack had lost weight, probably from an extended string of liquid diets. Parker remembered asking Kate if she loved Jack. Her answer of "no" was hardly convincing.

"You like her?"

Parker nodded. "Yeah, I do."

Jack wheeled over and they shook hands. "She wouldn't leave me alone after the total beatdown I took. Felt responsible for what happened to me. She wasn't. Not by a mile. In a way, she was my surrogate angel, helping me get through rough days in the ICU and through follow-up surgeries."

During their vacation, Kate had avoided talking about Jack, and allowed only tiny glimpses of their time together when asked. If she wasn't offering to pour out her heart, Parker didn't ask. That left him knowing very little about this man.

He sensed Jack was trying to be the better man, break the ice of an awkward moment. He found himself wishing that Jack hadn't come.

Jack kept talking. "Man, it was hard but I did get Kate to talk about you. A couple of times. She loved sailing. The best time of her life. Ever." He flashed a movie star smile and shifted his wheelchair back and forth. "Lighten up, man. The docs around here are good. I'm a walking testimonial for the work done around here. She'll be okay."

Parker offered a polite smile. "I know."

"So when you're not some kind of super doctor—"

"I doubt that's what Kate said about me."

Jack chuckled. "Don't get defensive, Thomas. Let me run with this, okay? I think I need some pointers." The man held out his hand as if he was projecting an image. "You have this captain of the open seas thing going and a rented yacht—"

"Sailboat."

"Whatever, Thomas. I saw the pictures of beaches and sunsets and that boat. What I want to know is, does this sailor gig really work on the gals? After listening to Kate jabber on, maybe I should trade in my golf clubs for a boat."

Parker couldn't help himself. "Stick to dry land, Jack. That way you won't get all wet."

Jack laughed. "Just wanted to see if I could get you riled up. I think she loves you. Won't say it, of course. But she's smitten. Keep taking her out on those yachts, and you'll be okay with her." His expression turned serious. "Some advice from a guy who knows a thing or two about messing up relationships. When that terrorist attacked DC, he really messed her up. Kate's going to need space to catch her breath. Or come to think of it, maybe another trip to open seas would do the trick."

The surgeon came into the waiting room.

Parker stood, wringing his hands.

Jack wheeled around to face the newcomer. They shook hands, obviously already acquainted.

"You're looking good, Jack," the surgeon said. "When's your discharge?"

"Next week. The docs around here keep running non-stop tests. It's like everyone loves me so much, no one wants to discharge me."

"I can inquire about moving up your date."

"Nah. I can tolerate a few more days. Hey, when I'm back in shape, I think spring will be a great time for golf… that is, if I'm not sailing. You still up for a round?"

"Absolutely. I can get us on at either Washington or Belle Haven." The surgeon jumped into business. "Well, Kate came through her procedures. She had a lot of damage. I brought in our best orthopedic trauma surgeon to assist. She faces months of recovery, but Kate should be okay."

Parker let out a long exhale, not realizing he had been holding his breath. "Thanks."

The surgeon shook hands with him. "Jack, I rarely pass up a round of golf, so I look forward to it. Dr. Parker, it was good to meet you. We'll sedate her until tomorrow morning. Want to take it slow

with her. So, I suggest you get some rest for the night."

Parker headed to the elevator and punched a button. Doors to an ascending elevator opened. The Vice President Richard Mears stepped out, escorted by Secret Service agents.

"Dr. Parker," Mears said, nodding. "I hear you've done some extraordinary work on behalf of the United States government. So much so that we've lost some people."

"I have no idea what you're talking about," Parker said.

Mears excused himself from his government entourage and gestured for Parker to walk with him down a hallway. "Where are they?"

"Are you still looking for them?"

"Not if I think I know what happened. As I understand it, they have no recollection of what happened to them. I received a briefing on what you did at Advanced BioCore, or what we think you did there. After Grayson's untimely death, we're picking up the pieces, as it were."

"I want the other fourteen participants."

Mears chuckled quietly. "You're in no position to bargain."

Parker shrugged. "Perhaps."

Mears handed him sketch that he'd done for the FBI based on Kate's notes. The last time he saw the paper, the FBI Director possessed it.

"This doesn't mean anything to me." Parker crumpled up the paper and discarded it into a recycle bin. "I'd like to keep it that way."

"I'm not sure Prosperity can allow that to happen."

Parker didn't take offense. He'd have been disappointed if they hadn't threatened him. "If you'll excuse me, Mr. Vice President, I've had a long day."

He walked past the Secret Service agents and hit the down button to the elevator. Doors opened with a ding.

From the corridor, Mears stared him down. "If there was a secret so secret that it could destroy the world, what would you do to prevent an impending disaster? If you could save lives, would you?"

Parker smirked and hit the down button inside the elevator. "I already have."

The doors closed.

In the lobby, Parker realized he didn't have the foggiest notion of where he was going, figuratively or literally. He looked around the hospital entrance and realized that part of him yearned to return to medicine and leave research altogether. At least in medicine, he didn't end with getting shot at the end of a shift, an occurrence happening all too often lately.

Night had fallen. The rain had let up.

He'd flown to DC on the FBI chopper without a change of clothes, a cellphone, a wallet or money, a car, or any plans for lodging.

Across 23rd Street, a horn beeped and headlights flashed.

He laughed and did what he wasn't supposed to do—walk toward the light. Again.

Windows to a BMW sedan lowered. Debra Ford smiled at him. "Need a lift?"

"Are you for real?" he asked, ducking down to make sure she wasn't pointing a gun at him with a hand that he couldn't see.

She sheepishly shrugged. "When I need to be."

The doors' electronic locks disengaged. She cocked her head. "I promise to play nice," she said. "For a little while."

What the hell. If she wanted me dead, she'd done so a long time ago.

101

THE SURPRISES KEPT COMING

Parker got into the BMW and Ford started the car. Speeding down the street, she chirped tires just because she could. Grabbing the outer lane of Washington Circle, she picked up New Hampshire Avenue.

"You need money?" she asked.

He raised an eyebrow. "I don't think I should be taking anything from you, including advice."

She pointed. "Glovebox. Take what you need."

He opened the glovebox and found an envelope. Opening it, it was stuffed with crisp $20 and $100 bills. He returned the envelope to where he found it.

"Thank you. But I don't think so."

"Suit yourself."

She dodged traffic and kept her speed up where she could.

"Did you save them?" she asked, keeping a focus on the road.

"Yeah."

"Dr. Wang too?"

"Yeah, Caroline too."

Ford glanced at him briefly then turned back to the road. "So you accomplished what you wanted."

"You could say that." He eyed the woman behind the wheel, realizing that he'd never seen Ford this close before. Middle-aged, but well-aged. Probably had a few cosmetic enhancements. Attractive. Clever. Dangerous. Lethal with a gun no doubt. He asked what she hadn't. "You haven't asked about Kate."

"Don't need to." She winked at him. "I'm a donor to the hospital's Women's Board. I placed a call and got a personalized update on Katherine."

"So much for patient confidentiality."

Ford made a pair of left turns and stopped at the curb on O Street.

They got out.

She retrieved a travel bag behind the driver's seat then tossed him the car's key fob.

"Where are we?" he asked, looking around the residential street.

"The Mansion," she said, pointing. "Follow the lions. They use code words here, a way to let staff know that you're closely associated with a particular guest, party, or activity. The Mansion is discreet. Inside tell them you're part of 'Applied Mind.' A special guest."

Applied Mind? Her code word was one of his neuromapping applications. The coincidence was troubling on many levels. And she seemed to indicate she wasn't accompanying him into the hotel. Lost, he scratched his head and struggled to find the right words. "I thought you were—I don't know—you were—"

"Hitting on you?" She stepped around the car to put her palms on the front of his shirt. She caressed his chest then straightened his collar. "What happens at the Mansion stays at the Mansion. I'd love to, Thomas, really. Perhaps next time. When you're not in a relationship."

"Whew, I thought I'd have to tell you no."

"Yeah, me too." She gave him a flirty bob of her head and walked backwards. "Dear, give 'em the keys. They'll park the car." She pointed to the lions again. "The Monterey Suite. Paid for in advance. Stay as long as you want. If you need something, ask. They'll take care of you."

He watched Ford walk down the street to the next intersection. The driver of a black car got out and opened a door. Before getting in, she blew Parker a kiss. The door shut behind her. Car taillights came on before it rounded the corner and disappeared.

After locking the car, Parker walked across the street and stopped at a pair of lions, which vaguely reminded him of the bronze and gold versions on the Princeton University campus. An unpretentious sign signaled his destination. He took the stairs down, entered the Mansion on O Street, and walked to the front desk.

The eclectic, almost magical interior furnishings were intriguing. A cordial staff greeted him.

"I was told I had a room," Parker said looking around, trying to find words to describe the hotel's ambiance. Unique came to mind first. "Can I have someone take care of my car outside?"

He held out the car's key fob.

"Of course." The clerk took the key. "Do you have a name for the reservation?"

He thought about using Debra Ford's name then decided differently. "Applied Mind."

No eyebrows were raised. No questions came his way. Inputs were made into a computer.

"Yes, Dr. Parker. We've been expecting you. Are you traveling with any luggage?"

He shook his head.

"Well, then, I'll show you to your suite." The clerk escorted Parker down winding hallways, past signs that read:

THIS IS NOT A SECRET DOOR.

"First time staying at the Mansion?"

"Yes."

"Well, let us know if there is anything you require."

An elevator took them to another level. A series of hallways later, he entered the Monterey Suite, a southwestern-themed room. His escort handed him room keys and left.

He perused the spacious accommodations. A large kitchen seemed fit for a chef. On a counter entering the kitchen stood a three-foot angel with gold wings. An acoustic guitar sat perched on a stand. Outside was a private deck with a grill. From the furnishings, Parker guessed that Ford had spent a little money on the apartment-style suite.

He passed a Happy Hour sign and a wetbar stocked with a mixed variety of leftover spirits from prior occupants. In the bedroom was a Victorian bed with matching ornate chairs and end tables. A grand piano filled a windowed alcove.

Returning to the living room, he spotted something on a glass coffee table: a leather folder with his name on it. A symbol adorned the folder's jacket. An image he'd seen before. Prosperity.

Inside, Parker discovered papers—legal documents. Carrying the papers with him, he returned to the bar and poured himself a neat double of Crown Royal XO, obviously compliments of Debra Ford, who seemed to know his tastes as well as everything else about him.

The papers were patent and trademark applications.

Everything was in his name.

What the hell did Debra Ford do?

George Washington University Hospital, Washington, DC

The FBI Director entered the private patient room on an upper floor of the hospital. In case of reprisals, MPDC officers had been placed outside the room. None were expected, but the Director wasn't about to take chances.

When he took this position, the Director promised to meet with each and every agent or consultant for the bureau who was injured on the job, as well as attend every damn funeral.

After checking with doctors, he walked bedside.

Heavy sedation had knocked her out. Special Agent Katherine Morgan looked better than he figured she should look, although in many ways she'd seen and experienced far worse in recent months, her recent gunshot notwithstanding. Like most Directors, he took pride in getting to know his people. Heroes, each and every one of them, regardless of whether their cases or investigations ever made the news.

A man of faith, he said a brief prayer, then placed a small teddy bear in the notch of her bandaged arm. He gave her hand a quick squeeze. It was the same gesture he'd shared with all agents, regardless of rank or years served.

Morgan, whether she realized it or not, had become the focal point of overlapping cases and conspiracies, and her engagement with the bureau mattered more now than ever. He hoped Kate was up for the roads that lay ahead.

He nodded his thanks, even though she couldn't see the gesture, and left.

SUNDAY, DECEMBER 6th

We may with advantage at times forget what we know.
Publilius Syrus, a former slave and Latin writer

102
MORNING

George Washington University Hospital, Washington, DC

Parker rose early and dressed in cleaned, laundered clothes that he'd given to the hotel staff to wash overnight. He skipped breakfast and drove straight to the hospital, arriving at the start of visiting hours.

After surgery, Kate had been moved to a private suite on the upper floors.

He'd checked in at the nurse's station. They'd been expecting him.

He entered her room and pulled a chair bedside. Someone had combed her hair and washed her up. A small teddy bear sat in the bend of her injured arm, which was secured to her side. An IV drip line ran to the crook of her good elbow. He took her good hand in his, careful not to knock off the pulse ox monitor clip on her finger.

Slowly, Kate's eyelids fluttered open. For a long moment, she stared at him and tried to focus harder.

"Do I know you?" she asked flatly.

The piercing sting of her words was impossible to shake and Parker's heart sank lower in his chest.

"I feel like we've met," she continued, "but I'm not sure. Have we?"

He squeezed her hand tighter until she pulled it away.

"Who are you?" she asked, her eyes narrowing.

Parker swallowed over the knot swelling in his throat. "A friend. Thomas."

"Thomas. Well, that's a nice name."

He took a breath, unsure what was going on with her. "Kate," he finally asked, "do you like sailing?"

She shook her head, as much as the discomfort of being shot would allow. "I've been on motorboats on the Great Lakes but I've never sailed. Why do you ask?"

He looked away. "Just needed to know, that's all."

Someone else entered the room, and Kate immediately perked up. "Jack!"

"Kate!" Jack Wright spun his wheelchair into the room, "I heard you've been dancing with the devil again. Going full-out commando on us. Morning, Thomas."

"You know each other?" she asked.

"Met last night," Jack said, rolling to the other side of her bed.

Kate swung her pulse ox-monitored hand across the bed and Jack took it.

"How are you doing?"

She shrugged. "How does it look? I'm glad you came to see me, Jack."

"It wasn't too hard," he said. "I'm roomed just down the hall."

Parker sensed the attraction between them. He was a third wheel, the odd man out. Taking his cue, he moved his chair back to where he found it.

"Get better, Kate," Parker said, choking back what he really wanted to say, the things he yearned to tell her. He noticed that she was transfixed on Jack, his presence. He cleared his throat until Jack looked up. "Take care of her."

"Hey, man," Jack said, "tell Kate about those sunsets you're itching to chase."

"Sailing?" Kate asked. "Guys, what's this sudden obsession with sailing? I'm not that crazy about boats. I grew up near Chicago. Baseball games, those I get. Boats, not so much."

The perfect cue had been delivered.

Parker nodded to Jack and left. Kate didn't even acknowledge his departure.

By the time Parker reached the elevators and hit the down button, his chest had tightened, constricted so tight that he was struggling to breathe. Kate had changed. He couldn't explain it, only theorize. Her amnesia made no sense—unless Richards had given it to her.

Thankfully, the bastard was dead.

Kate had seemed to revert back to her life with Jack.

Perhaps that was the best for all involved.

Not a notion that he wanted to foster, but one that might be better for Kate and her career as a federal agent. This was Kate's time to shed her kryptonite.

He took the elevator down, left the hospital, and climbed into Debra Ford's BMW. A quick glance at the gas gauge showed a full tank. He started the car, pulled out of the parking lot, and took 23rd Street out of the nation's capital.

Using the cash that Ford had left in the glove box, he drove until driving was no longer an option.

103
TWO DAYS LATER

Marathon, Florida Keys. Florida

Parker struggled to break the self-pity chains of jealousy, resentment. The long drive south hadn't helped. After an overnight stop because of exhaustion, he drove the rest of the way to a plantation-style estate in the Florida Keys.

He rang the bell at the property gate. Someone answered and allowed him to drive into the protected compound. He found the van as expected.

Wearing a long, flowing white dress, Caroline Wang waited for him alone under the sheltered drive of the waterfront mansion.

"I didn't think you were coming," she said as Parker got out of the car.

He smiled. "Neither did I."

"You didn't call."

He shrugged. "Didn't want to risk it." He took a breath. "How is everyone?"

She smiled and extended the crook of her elbow for him to take. "Come and see."

They entered the beautiful multi-level house. Arching hardwood stairs split in two directions. A welcoming marble floor spread from the foyer and into the house. Windows with a view to die for faced the ocean. A large sitting room brought in ample daylight. Balconies ran along each side of the elongated entry.

"Wow," he said. "I didn't know I was paying for all of this. It's impressive."

Caroline rubbed her bald head. "The kids love it. They ask lots of questions. But they still love it."

They passed a well-stocked bar with tall bar stools. He made a mental note to circle back. Caroline led him outside, where decorative pools filled with fish and waterfalls offered a paradise oasis with palm trees overhead. Caribbean music played. He heard noise from nearby sport courts. The participants, freed from captivity, enjoyed themselves in the MTV-like playground. Those not playing tennis or volleyball sat in beach chairs on a small stretch of sand and soaked up the sun.

Somewhere in the back of his mind, he recalled the property's list price. Twelve million. A daily rental rate of five thousand dollars. He wasn't sure how long the participants could shelter this far out of sight, away from the watchful eyes of the government, but right now every day of their lives mattered, regardless of the costs. After getting over the extravagance and the awe of what money could buy, he asked the question that mattered most.

"Caroline, how much do they remember?"

She took his hand and led him out to the beach. "Almost nothing. They're content. Understand that they need to be patient before returning home. They trust us, you and me."

Parker felt Caroline's fingers tighten around his. He thought of Kate and her new life with Jack. He let go of that memory, choosing to stay in the present, what could be felt and shared. He squeezed Caroline's fingers back and followed her out to a stretch of white sand where the sun dropped low over a western horizon.

- 525 -

THE END

THIRTEEN MARKERS

A new novel coming in 2021.

Chapter 1

Dan Grant

FBI Special Agent Kate Morgan returns to Washington, DC, and struggles to pick up the pieces to her life. Memories, lost and forgotten, are not the only troubles plaguing her. What Kate thinks she knows of her life and past again are tested as she faces a race against time to find thirteen markers.

After healing up physically, her quest starts with a murder and ends only after she clears a gauntlet of challenges.

Learn more by visiting www.DanGrantBooks.com.

MindScape Press, Inc.
www.MindScapePress.com

CHAPTER 1
THE FACE IN THE CROWD
EARLY JUNE

National Mall, Washington, DC

Memories.

A lot like rehab. Some days easier than others.

Kate Morgan hated that she couldn't recall certain events, people, or even discussions from her past. Her mind, a lot like her injured right shoulder, proved a work in progress.

With precious little to go on, she'd been given a face. A black and white photo revealed a weathered face, salt-and-pepper beard, and mangy mop of hair. A man whom she'd met before. Supposedly. Although, she had no idea who the man was or why he was important as an informant.

Already late, Kate moved quickly into the throng of people on the National Mall, shouldering aside men and women gathered for the civil rights march. Shouts and chants and raised voices made focusing hard. Homemade signs carried above heads and shoulders blocked out part of the historic landscape. People as far as she could see. A global pandemic and faces covered with masks and bandanas didn't help her search. What she attempted seemed impossible. Find a man, seen from a photo, in a mass of thousands.

The needle, the only phrase given to her.

Kate moderated her pace and rode the crowd's momentum rather than apply blunt force. She comprehended that the migration of bodies from the U.S. Capitol had a united destination, the Lincoln Memorial. And along the way was the needle and an informant.

Kate took advantage of gaps in the crowd as people slowed to cross 14th and 15th Streets. The white marble obelisk became her focus, the needle. The Washington Monument, the tallest structure in the Nation's Capital, towered above the masses. The crowds had ignored the corded off grass and marched up the shallow knoll. She could see the ring of American flags fluttering in a mild breeze. DC Metropolitan Police officers and U.S. Park Rangers surrounded the monument, guarding it from vandalism.

"Didn't think you'd make it," a voice said, thick with nervous irritation, just as she stepped onto the monument's circular gray stoned base.

Kate turned to find a man as ragged and weary as the photograph had shown. His unkempt beard looked as if it carried crumbs from his morning breakfast. He wore a black face mask, a t-shirt a size too large for his torso, and baggy cargo shorts. His stern gaze projected a disproportionate anger relative to his appearance.

The march of people, chanting and yelling, parted around them.

The man stepped closer.

Kate searched her mind for any notion that she'd known the man or met him before. Nothing. Her pulse quickened and she finally asked, "Your name? Who are you?"

Voices rose in the crowd as someone started a rallying cry for justice.

"Pierre Landry," the man said as he shrank his stature, making himself smaller, less visible in the crowd. "You don't remember?"

"No." She tried to remember. The man's first name seemed French, but his voice carried no accent. "What do you have for me?"

"If you don't remember, then we have nothing to discuss," he said bluntly, his eyes narrowing. "I made a mistake thinking I could trust you."

Landry flashed a gun, holding it low at his side.

Kate cursed silently and reached to her hip, then realized she'd decided against carrying her Glock into a crowd of protestors while she was off duty. Boxed in by bodies, she comprehended the trap.

There was nowhere to run or hide, no way to fight.

"No, you didn't make a mistake," she said, stalling, scanning the crowd for the closest law enforcement. "We came to meet, right?"

Landry's gun hand rose and cold crept down her spine.

She'd endured a year of case assignments from hell, leaving her with considerable battle scars, and this was how she was going to die—at gunpoint—shot dead by a stranger.

She steeled a breath and stared down Landry. "Trust works both ways. Okay? Tell me what you know. I'll do the same."

Something flicked in Landry's eyes, which wasn't good.

A retort rang out, startling Kate.

People around them screamed and scampered away in every direction. Kate clutched her chest before realizing that she hadn't been hit.

In shock, Landry crumpled onto the gray granite circle surrounding the monument. He struggled for a moment, crawling toward her. Blood gushed from his nose and mouth, pooling on the hard surface beneath him.

Kate wrestled the pistol from his grip and aimed the weapon in the likely direction of the killer. All she saw was a world of chaos and people running.

She glanced down and Landry rested his chin on the granite

walk. She could see the bullet penetration mottled in the man's hair. An off-center shot to the back of his skull.

"What did you want to tell me?" She knelt and touched his shoulder.

"Markers," Landry said, his voice strained and garbled with blood. After a gasp, he slid his non-shooting hand forward. "Thirteen."

He let out a faint groan, like he'd been troubled during sleep, and lay still.

Kate peeled back his fingers to expose the coin-like medallion on a thin silver chain that he'd clutched. The images and characters stamped into the metal's round face didn't make sense to her. Nothing about her supposed meeting made sense.

Behind her, voices started barking. Their directions being shouted at her grew louder. She snatched up the medallion and raised both hands in the air.

"Federal Bureau of Investigation," Kate called out, making sure she could be heard. "Special Agent Katherine Morgan. Washington Field Office. I have identification. It's in my pants' pocket."

Police surrounded her, their weapons aimed on a single target.

ACKNOWLEDGEMENTS

A global story world beyond *The Singularity Witness* was fostered by a simple suggestion, a challenge to think beyond the limits of a single story. And of course, Stewart Richards, and the cold-hearted villain that he grew into proved to be an effective resurrection of his old self and a mirrored shadow to Thomas Parker. Thanks Steve for the suggestion.

Thanks to the staff at the Mansion on O Street for information and input. I believe a return in the works.

During research for *The Singularity Witness* and *Thirteen Across*, I asked several questions from the Federal Bureau of Investigation. Many of those answers translated into this story as well. I want to thank the agents for their time, insight, and input on how certain aspects of the bureau operate. Any narrative discrepancies that don't match actual FBI procedural or operational parameters were done either deliberately or for the consolidation of characters and time. Any inaccuracies or misrepresentations are mine.

Thanks to my editor Ellen Clair Lamb for her contribution, skill, insight, and help in making *The Singularity Transfer* better; and to Rob for his eleventh hour reads.

And, finally, my wife Leslie is always my first reader and sounding board. She asks questions and quizzes me on characters and concepts. I'm grateful for her input, patience, and encouragement. She's given me the support and freedom to tell stories and take chances.

BACKGROUND

The Singularity Witness featured two parallel main characters: Thomas Parker and Kate Morgan. In that tale, both characters are co-heroes with their own quests; the story required a contribution from each of them and it made sense to bring the two back together again. While *The Singularity Transfer* cannot move forward without Parker, it was important that he partially shared a common path with Kate. Will they return together again? We shall see.

The Singularity series are research-based, cross-genre science-fiction/science-medical suspense thriller style stories. As a writer, part of the storytelling challenge is how to weave aspects of science, medicine, and technology together as a backdrop and tapestry that the story and characters are painted onto.

Most research never makes it into the story. With few exceptions, most locations are real. Where possible I visit each location and walk in the footsteps of my characters, taking in the sights and sounds to create an authentic story stop. If there are factual inaccuracies in the real research presented or in the locations, it was done for narrative convenience. Any misrepresentation is my fault alone.

To learn more about *The Singularity Transfer* visit
https://DanGrantBooks.com/Singularity-Transfer

ABOUT THE AUTHOR

Dan is the bestselling author of *The Singularity Witness* and *Thirteen Across*. He loves intriguing tales that weave science, medicine, technology, or history into the fabric of the story. Stories are about characters forced into extraodinary situations.

He's a licensed professional engineer with degrees from Northern Arizona University: a bachelor's in electrical engineering and two masters' (college education and English with an emphasis in creative writing). His engineering projects have provided opportunities to get exposed to a variety of medical and technological applications, and get behind the scenes of several military facilities. These project experiences add depth to "what if" scenarios and allow him to ask questions to a variety of deeper storylines.

An example of a past project that fostered story development is: years ago Dan worked on a state-of-the-art neurological operating suite for a cancer institute in New York state. During the survey on the existing OR that was to be upgraded, he asked the neurosurgeon about his work and how the new medical application would be put into practice. The doctor's response was magical. The way he saw the application of modern technology made him a better doctor and dramatically improved the lives of his patients. This informal interview proved to be a character sketch for Thomas Parker and the basis for Parker's research.

Dan lives in Colorado with his wife, two boys, and two dogs. He's still practicing engineering while writing stories. His next thriller is a Kate Morgan continuation called *Thirteen Markers*.

To find out more, read author notes, and learn about background material, go to **www.DanGrantBooks.com**.

www.ingramcontent.com/pod-product-compliance
Lightning Source LLC
Chambersburg PA
CBHW071422190726
48292CB00001B/78